Herman
Had
Two Daughters

Novels by Zelda Popkin

Herman
Had
Two Daughters

ZELDA POPKIN

J. B. Lippincott Company

PHILADELPHIA & NEW YORK

The characters and plot episodes in this novel are fictitious: the background of certain twentieth-century events and attitudes is, unfortunately, all too true.

To Tay

Herman
Had
Two Daughters

One

Herman Weiss had two daughters. Neither was a beauty, a genius, or a front-page delinquent. Nor did either one donate a hospital, a playground, or a museum to the city of her birth. Yet of all the girls who grew up in Grady's Mills before the First World War, only Herman's daughters, Celia and Jessie, are remembered nowadays. Should I chance to stroll along First Street this very afternoon, most of those who'll stop to say "hello" are bound to add, "And what's doing with the Weiss girls, Sam?" They'll have forgotten that both are where I can't keep up with them; they'll have remembered only that Sam Rosenbaum was the one who kept in touch after the girls left town.

Normally, Grady's Mills is possessive, holding fast, forever, to those who have diplomas from its schools, nourishing its civic ego on their modest triumphs far beyond its hills. A business promotion in Arkansas or South Dakota, a combat medal to a G.I. whose dog tags bear a California home address, can be local-boy-makes-good, provided that his high school graduation photo is in the *News-Record*'s morgue. If so, he'll rate a single-column cut and a paragraph in "Folk You Know," though he may have been just a transient whose father had a job here while the kid was in his teens.

The Weiss girls, however, are its own, born and brought up in the town, and their parents lie, side by side, permanently bedded in its Sons of Judea Cemetery. Moreover, they had attained their unique distinction before they left for good and all: both of them went to college out of town.

Those days female higher education was a seldom thing for girls in Grady's Mills. A clergyman's daughter might enroll at State Normal to be taught to teach; a bluestocking escape to Mt. Holyoke or Bryn Mawr from a millowner's mansion on fashionable

Grady Avenue. But the Jewish families who lived up the Hill did not send even sons away to college. Not that they denigrated higher education. On the contrary, it was the dream, the aspiration, the fairest promise of the promised land. But, plain and simple, they could not afford it. They were an immigrant generation, driven by pogrom and poverty out of Eastern Europe, briefly to toil in New York sweatshops and suffocate in slums, then come wandering in the hit-or-miss hegira of their Westward Ho! across the Allegheny foothills, to settle for no patent reason in the drab textile-factory town called Grady's Mills. Here they'd made a ghetto, on Fifth and Sixth and Seventh Streets, up the steep slopes of Center and Market, in wooden dwellings, huddled close, as if for protection from the winter winds and shikkorim from the Flats: sixty-odd families, stemming from an original handful, the cousins, landsleit, fetched straight from Ellis Island, apprenticed to the baker, the fishmonger, the butcher or equipped with oilcloth-covered baskets to go afoot, peddling needles, pins, thread, thimbles, shoelaces, matches, lampwicks and spectacles to the farmers' wives, until they'd saved enough to buy a customer-peddler's horse and buggy or to open a little store, then send ship's tickets for their families and rent a house on the Hill.

When the Weiss girls and I were growing up, the families around us were tradesmen, mainly, selling bread, meat, fish, fruits, vegetables and groceries to each other on the Hill or downtown on First Street, retailing yard goods, cheap ready-made apparel, shoes, watches and wedding rings to millworkers' families. Sol Katz's hole in the wall on First Street carried bolts of silk, as well as gingham, and a sign lettered "Bon Ton Dry Goods Store."

Several were junkmen, collecting, sorting, dealing in discarded metal, bottles, old clothes and textile mill ends. Abe Finkel, who'd started out with mill ends, had amassed sufficient capital to invest in real estate and lend money at interest. My father was a tailor, one of the few who worked with their own hands. The generation that would be professionals—doctors, dentists, lawyers, teachers and accountants—was in knee pants in the first decade of this century.

Two families of Jewish origin, the Hartmans and the Meyers, lived over on Grady Avenue. Their forebears had come, like ours, across the ocean and the hills, but they'd come from Bavaria while this countryside was wild and virginal and acreage could be acquired for a demijohn of whisky and a handful of greenbacks. Their descendants enjoyed the rents of blocks of commercial buildings on First and Center Streets. Their men had Teddy Roosevelt mustaches, their sons Buster Brown haircuts and collars, their daughters gold wire on their teeth, and their women, shopping at Fletcher's Market, which was trefe, invariably wore hats. No woman of my mother's generation on the Hill owned a hat. They wore shawls and kerchiefs and wigs on shaven heads.

The Hartman and the Meyer children attended a private elementary school at the end of Grady Avenue, and where they worshiped, if they did, I do not know, since they never turned up at our shuls. We had two shuls, built of yellow brick in the semi-Oriental, semi-Slavic architecture of the European ghettos; two congregations, one Russian-Polish-Litvak, one Hungarian-Galacian, usually at loggerheads, carrying on the feuds of eighteenth-century theologians. For instance, in the Hungarian-Galacian shul, on a Simcath Torah eve, you might see registered Republicans of Grady's Mills, U. S., writhing, chanting, clapping hands in Chassidic ecstasy, while in the Litvak shul, the velvet-covered Scrolls were carried in a dignified procession, only little children prancing, shouting alongside. The Galitzianer rejoiced in the Law; the Litvaks respected and feared it. One Law, however, and one God. Two arms of a single body, clinging tenaciously and equally.

There was a mikvah in the basement of each shul, a bathing place, off limits to men and boys, whose function never was explained to me. I knew my mother, every thirty days, went to the mikvah, which struck me as unnecessary, since we had a zinc tub in our house and a copper boiler in the kitchen to warm the water up.

The Hill had two rabbis, bearded, learned, shabby; two cantors so poorly paid one eked out his family's subsistence by selling matzohs, sacramental wine and brandy, the other by drilling boys for Bar Mitzvah with a singsong falsetto and a stinging cane; two starveling sextons to open, close, sweep out the synagogues and supervise the burials, as well as one shochet to slit the jugulars of fowl and calf that we might have kosher meat. For circumcisions,

11

a mohel was transported from Philadelphia or New York, which made the advent of a son and kaddish not only joyous but expensive.

On Friday mornings, racing to school, I heard the rhythmic chop-chop-chop of iron blades in wooden bowls all along Fifth, Sixth and Seventh Streets, yellow pike, whitefish, carp and buffle minced in every kitchen on the Hill. Friday afternoons, walking home, I smelled the gefüllte fish and the chicken broth simmering, the Sabbath chalah and the küchel baking. The aroma was heavenly. On Saturdays no stove was fired, no lampwick ignited, no coin or handkerchief publicly carried. All shops on the Hill were closed, although not everybody spent the day in shul. My father, exhausted by a whole week's labor with a heavy pressing iron, often slept around the clock, while I lay, snug on my belly on my bed, reading library books. What's wrong in that? God ordained it as a day of rest, did He not?

On the Holy Days, however, everybody sat in shul all day, the girls sweltering in their new winter dresses, peering over the rail of the women's balcony, giggling at the boys who were sweltering in *their* new winter suits. The shofar whooeed, the cadence of Hebrew prayer rose and ebbed in the autumn-tinted, maple-shaded streets. On Rosh Hashanah afternoons, the grownups in their festive garments paraded to the brook at the edge of town, a turgid streamlet grayed by offal of the mills, and into it they shook a whole year's sins. We might have been in Marc Chagall's Vitebsk.

It is no simple matter for later generations to comprehend our Hill: a severed limb of Eastern Europe, preserving the mores and the superstitions of a complex and exotic culture, sprung from a religion of such magnificent simplicity that ten brief paragraphs encompass it: a straightforward affirmation of one all-powerful God and a code of ethics, this overlaid by rules and regulations prescribed for nomadic Middle Eastern tribes, interpreted, reinterpreted, updated by savants of many lands and centuries; an alien-people island, set down in the middle of another culture that was barely out of swaddling clothes, reaching toward that newer culture with as much distrust as avidity.

The Hartmans (possibly the Meyers, too), a personal experience led me to believe, were distressed by our ways.

When I was eleven or thereabouts, one autumn afternoon as I was mounting my bike at the curb before the Public Library on the courthouse square, a lady approached me. I say "lady" advisedly. "Woman," "female," will not do. To the unsophisticated, clothing makes the lady, as it does the gentleman. This lady's suit was stylish, nipped in at the waist, hem an inch above the sidewalk. (I was a tailor's son, as aware of fashion plates as a doctor's child of stethoscopes.) The lady wore a hat of shimmering green-black feathers bound with a dotted veil, speckling her cheeks and nose, and yellow chamois gloves.

"Aren't you Samuel Rosenbaum from the Hill?" Her voice was genteel-Gentile. "Miss Ehling, the librarian, tells me you're a great reader."

Flattered, although puzzled, I admitted being Samuel, the great reader.

"Trying to improve your mind. That is admirable." A gloved hand stroked my forearm. "Well, now, I do believe you're just the boy to help me start my project. I am Mrs. Hartman. I should like to help the poor Jewish children on the Hill." Gloved fingers gripped my handlebars, detaining me, since my feet were on the pedals, prepared to wheel away. "I have been thinking of organizing a little club. We might, in the beginning, meet in my house, enjoy some light refreshments. . . ."

My eyes must have begun to sparkle; any mention of refreshments lifts the spirits of a growing boy.

"You'd like that, I see. Then"—the chamois fingers closed on mine—"we could have discussions. I should like to teach these children to be good Americans."

I was stunned. I managed to reply that all of us, in chapel assembly every morning, placed our right hands on our hearts and pledged allegiance to the flag.

"Aha! But this is not what I mean. There are certain foreign customs, quite outlandish ones. . . ."

" 'Scuse me, I have to hurry," I mumbled. "My mama's waiting for me to bring my father's supper to his shop." I believe I did remember to tip my cap to her.

13

Pedaling up the Hill, I was short of breath with fury. *She's* going to teach us to be good Americans! Who does *she* think she is? We're Americans, just as good as she. Why, I was born right here in town. Most kids I know were born here, too. We go to school; we study civics, history. And Papa votes Republican. For Roosevelt, for Taft who is a friend to Jews. Taft told the Russian government, straight out, the United States won't do business with a country which is mean to Jews. And Mama, though she doesn't vote, is more strong Republican than Papa is. Republicans, she says, are unshtandig—honorable, refined, high-class—while Democrats are prost—a spit word, uncouth, cheap. "Where do you find the Democrats?" This is Mama asking. "In the beer saloons in the Flats."

Was Mrs. Hartman hinting we were prost? "Certain foreign customs, quite outlandish." What's outlandish about us? How we live? Orthodox? Kosher? Aha! That's it! "Enjoy some light refreshments." "Will you step into my parlor?" said the spider to the fly. Yop, she wants to get the kids into her parlor to trick them into eating trefe.

Unquestionably, trefe was another reason, an overriding one, why not even young males from the Hill were sent to college out of town, where they'd be offered pork, ham, bacon as well as other meats not slaughtered ritually, fish without fins and gills, fried foods and baked goods made with lard. For girls, there were additional perils, from white slavers, Jack the Rippers, or dashing rogues who sweet-talked them out of chastity. Moreover, a bookish girl, as every Jewish mother knew, sooner or later had to wear eyeglasses. Who marries girls with glasses?

Herman Weiss, it was generally agreed, was of outstanding piety. While my parents went to shul (the Litvak one) only on the Holy Days, Herman wore his tallith there morning and evening and all day Saturday. His right hand lacked an index finger. He had submitted to its amputation to avoid service in the armies of the Czar, where Jewish lads, like other conscripts, were expected to eat pig. This alone made his liberalism in the matter of his daughters' education astonishing.

That pious man, between prayers, ran a grocery on Sixth Street, in a two-story, gray-shingled building with a porch. The family

14

lived above the store, private entrance at the right, a narrow door to a steep, uncarpeted staircase. The sign above the store entrance read "Herman's Grocery," not "Weiss's Grocery." The sign was frivolous since everyone, including Ida, Herman's wife, referred to him as "Mr. Weiss." He was a man of formidable dignity, rather tall, sturdily built, with a short chestnut beard meticulously combed, a handlebar mustache, gray eyes, steady behind gold-rimmed spectacles, and wearing, even in July and August, a vest spanned by a heavy gold-filled watch chain that ended in a dollar Ingersoll. The fringes of his ritual undergarment sometimes showed beneath his vest.

The store was stocked primarily with foods and condiments for the cuisine of the Hill: coarse salt for dredging every drop of blood from fresh meat, sour salt, molasses "fish-cake" for sweet and sour fish and stuffed cabbage, stick cinnamon, herrings (shmaltz and matjes, in pungent, slimy barrels), dried prunes and apricots, split peas, green and yellow, dried lima beans, groats, sunflower seeds, almonds in the shell, all in open sacks, Wisotsky's tea, farmer cheese and sweet butter, kept firm in a scabrous ice chest, as well as Hecker's flour, Fleischman's yeast, sugar, lump and granulated, and Kirkman's soap, whose coupons provided decorative glassware for our Seder tables.

The porch of Herman's Grocery was the news center of the Hill. Here Mrs. Katz reported she had tangled with the rabbi over a blood speck she'd discovered in the egg in the womb of a freshly slaughtered chicken. The fowl is trefe, discard it, the rabbi had admonished her. But who can afford to throw out a springer? And where find a goy to buy it at half price? Here, Mrs. Finkel mentioned she, too, was having trouble with that rabbi: a few drops of boiling milk, so tiny you could hardly notice, had spattered on the outside of a meat pot on her stove, but she intended to defy his ukase to throw the pot away. The women debated, taking sides, for and against the rabbi: yes, he was correct; no, he was old-fashioned, too strict. In America, such strictness is unreasonable. Yet in America, strictness is more necessary than in Shnipishok. The temptation to neglect, forget, is great. Defection in domestic trivia is the first step toward apostasy. The Holy One, blessed be

His name, will pour fire and brimstone on those who break the Law.

They gossiped about who had recently gone shopping in Philadelphia or New York, what new garments had been purchased, how much they had cost, and were the styles too fancy-shmansy for the Hill? Who had consummated a good business deal, how much profit had been made (exaggerated, naturally), who had suffered a financial loss and was facing bankruptcy (exaggerated, too). They tsked over the fact that the Litvak rebbitzin again was pregnant, already four, like steps. And, endlessly, they held medical consultations on Herman's porch, clucking over every case of quinsy sore throat, constipation, or rheumatism and agreeing that, no matter what, chicken soup was the perfect medicine. Tea with raspberries was useful, too, and, in extremity, licorice powder or a dose of castor oil.

Ida Weiss was the supreme authority in every field, being educated. She spoke and read three languages, more or less—Yiddish, Russian and English. She could follow the reading of Hebrew prayers, though I doubt she knew the meanings of the words, and on the Holy Days the women crowded around her in the balcony of the shul, since she could let them know when to say Yiskor, the memorial prayer for their dead. Ida also read Russian novels and serialized romances in the Yiddish newspapers. To whom it might concern—and whom it might not—she let it be known she was descended from famous rabbis and scholars and had brought Herman a substantial dowry because he was a Talmudist.

Herman's learning we took on faith, since he never bragged. In fact, he seldom talked at all. When I was a youngster, I was sent often to his store, but I can't recall him saying anything to me except how much my purchase cost. The only times I heard his voice raised were when he read from the Scrolls at the Bema in the shul. Then his voice seemed hoarse, as if rusty from disuse. And he had a noticeable lisp.

Ida talked for two. She was an enormous woman, slow-moving because of overweight and with vestiges of prettiness. Her nose was small and shapely, her skin without flaw or wrinkle, her hair, mahogany in color, healthy, sleek, worn in a high-rising pompadour whose bone hairpins were forever slipping out. That aggressive pompadour, in a way, symbolized her character: a less self-assured woman, married to a pious Jew, would have meekly shaved her head and donned a wig. With years and too much starch and shmaltz, her girth became elephantine, her bright, dark eyes sank into bulbous cheeks, her upper lip sprouted a mustache. Yet she tossed her head coquettishly, imagining herself a beauty still.

Directly after sunrise and in winter frequently before, Herman unlocked the grocery, carried in the cake of ice, left on a piece of burlap at the curb, dropped it into the ice chest, swathed it in pages of the *News-Record,* opened a canvas bag, shook out brown-paper-wrapped rolls of quarters, nickels, dimes and pennies, spilled them into their respective grooves in the wooden cash drawer, pulled up the door shade, and sprinkled sawdust on the floor. Herman's Grocery was ready for business. Ida came down to mind the store while he went off to shul for morning prayers. After he'd returned, taken his breakfast of the oatmeal and coffee Ida had left simmering at the back of the coal stove upstairs, she went up, presumably for housekeeping, though all morning she was up and down to gossip on the porch. Noontimes, she stood behind the counter while Herman went up to eat and nap. At dusk when Herman went to shul again, Celia and Jessie tended the store after they'd helped in the house. At night the girls did homework in the kitchen while Papa and Mama stood behind the counter side by side, she towering by half a head because of the pompadour, a Grady's Mills Gothic out of the Lithuanian province of Vilna. When trade was slack, as it usually was after supper, Herman studied Talmud behind the counter.

I used to watch the Weiss girls running home from school on winter afternoons, slithering along the rutted, icy road, swinging their school books by the straps, two pudgy girls in navy-blue wool pea jackets, too big or too tight, never the proper size, legs thickened by heavy underwear inside ribbed black stockings, bulging above high button shoes, tight brown braids tied with plaid ribbons under black plush sailor hats. The hats had a comical pretentiousness. In winter, all the other kids—girls as well as boys—wore knitted stocking caps.

They seemed like twins, being dressed alike and of one height, though Celia was the elder by two years. Running, always running, together yet separate. Never did I see them speak or laugh together or even bicker while they ran and, though I cannot tell you why, it struck me Jessie was deliberately setting the distance between them.

In the store, each sat on a box behind the counter, Jessie poring over a library book—the *Green* or *Blue Fairy Tales* or one of the *Little Colonel* series—Celia embroidering cross-stitch or French knots on a blue-stenciled cloth held taut in a wooden hoop. It was Celia who cut the customer's wedge of sweet butter, sliced the farmer cheese, scooped prunes or split peas from the sacks, weighed and neatly wrapped the purchases. Jessie made the change. Jessie was lightning fast and accurate at making change, being E (for Excellent) in arithmetic.

Jessie Weiss was also E in spelling, grammar, composition, reading, geography and civics, although only F (for Fair) in penmanship in the sixth grade at public school, when Miss Clarkson, the principal, decided to skip her into the eighth grade. This was the year when Celia's marks in eighth had been P (for Poor) with E only in penmanship, and the same Miss Clarkson decided that Celia was to be left back. So there they were, two years apart in age, in the same classroom, where Jessie, without effort, collected E's, and Celia, mortified and fumbling, bit her nails.

One evening Mrs. Weiss waddled over to our house up the street and offered me twenty-five cents a night to help Celia with her homework so she'd be sure to graduate the same year Jessie did. I was a junior in high school (average E-minus); my father's tailor shop was not exactly a gold mine; two bits a night was a windfall. So there we sat, evening after evening, under the Welsbach mantel at the round oak table in the Weisses' kitchen-dining room, doing eighth-grade homework, me drilling Celia in compound fractions, showing her how to parse and wishing she would concentrate. Jessie worked alone and with such speed that, long before Celia and I finished Celia's lessons, Jessie's nose would be buried in a library book, although now and then, when I happened to glance up, I'd find Jessie watching with a desperately worried look, as if she somehow blamed herself for Celia's predicament. Her eyes—large, gray and expressive, her most striking feature—seemed to be begging me: please, please, help Celia pass, please make sure she doesn't fail. Once, while Celia was at the kitchen window testing a pan of cooling fudge, I asked Jessie why she didn't help her sister herself. She answered, low and furtively, "She'd kill me if I tried."

One warm evening when the girls had their middy blouse sleeves rolled up I noticed a purple bruise on Jessie's upper arm. "Hey, how'd you hurt yourself?" I asked.

"A fresh kid pinched me," Jessie said.

Celia thrust a plate of penuche at Jessie. "Here, take a piece."

Jessie bowed her head above her book, pretending she hadn't heard, rolled down her middy sleeves, and after a moment or so went off with her book to the room where the girls slept together in a brass double bed. Next night, she waited at the bottom of the stairs for me and, with a glance over her shoulder, whispered savagely, "Sammy, make sure she passes. You hear me? If she fails she'll kick me black and blue. Want to see what she did?" She raised her skirt. I turned away, too bashful to examine Jessie's thighs. It had been careless of Celia to pinch her sister where it showed.

Celia passed with F (for Fair) and everyone was relieved, including me, since I'd been made uncomfortably aware that Ida Weiss had additional plans for me, namely son-in-law, and was prodding Celia to court me. This can be a nightmare to a youth of seventeen. Even had the girl been a beauty, which she decidedly was not, Sam Rosenbaum wasn't in the market for child brides. Maybe in the old country it was all right for girls to be betrothed at fourteen. In Grady's Mills, robbing the cradle was held to be uncouth.

The attempt at my entrapment had begun with fudge, penuche and cupcakes, which I enjoyed till I sensed the snare behind the sweets. I told Celia I had to make a confession: eating her goodies had been a sin for me. We always had meat for supper. Not till six hours later was I allowed to eat cake or candy made with butter and milk. She must have reported this to Mama since, after that, Ida kept trundling up the steps with prunes, almonds and sunflower seeds that even the strictly orthodox could nibble on directly after meat.

Ida tried broad hints and confidential conversations next, hovering at the bottom of the staircase to catch me, coming or departing. "My Celia is no dumbbell, eh, Sammy? She had a little trouble; that teacher was an anti-Semitt, she kept picking on my Celia, made her nervous in the class. That principal, that Miss Clarkson, that old maid, is a rishes-ponem, too. Maybe I'll report the both of them."

Or: "Too bad you wouldn't eat Celia's baking. I didn't think your family was so strict. Maybe you'll carry home in a bag a couple cakes, your mother would enjoy. My Celia takes to baking, cooking, like she's married a dozen years. Such a wife she'll make! And her embroidering, you should see. Golden hands. Jessie, that Jessie, can't put an elastic in her bloomers even, you should excuse me. . . ."

Or, archly, one hand on her bosom: "A tutor in the house! Like Chekhov, like Tolstoy. If you knew to read Russian, Sammy, I would give you a beautiful story. The tutor and the daughter of the house"—a nudge to my ribs—"they fell crazy mad in love."

Or about my personal plans and prospects: "A boy with such a head like yours, you could be a druggist, even. A wife with a little money—Herman's Grocery is a nice piece of bread. And for who are we slaving? The children. What else? You want to be a journalist? Feh, Sammy! That is no profession for a Jewish boy. For bummers, for shikkorim. Where do you find them, the journalisten, here? Downtown, in the beer saloons. Now, in Europe, a journalist is something elegant. You heard maybe from Herzl? Herzl the Zionist? *This* was a journalist, a refined gentleman."

Only once, aside from the remark about the bloomers, did she mention Jessie. "Mr. Weiss was very disappointed, the second one a girl. He asked for a boy."

She wasn't. Jessie Weiss was all female. Certain teen-age hoodlums discovered this before she was aware of it herself.

One evening, while I was waiting for Celia to get finished primping in the bedroom—she was forever changing her hair ribbon or blouse—I passed the parlor door and noticed Jessie sitting in the dark. When she answered my hello her voice was thickened with tears. "Hey," I whispered. "She pinch you again?"

"Hay's for horses." Jessie's breath sucked in, readying to explode. "Dirty, rotten, stinking pigs! I was by the brook, picking violets. They came around. They hollered"—her voice dropped: maybe she was blushing; perhaps she thought I would—" 'Show us your cunt, sheeny kid.' "

I blushed. That four-letter word wasn't said aloud, even by decent boys.

"They tried to drag me behind the bushes." She snuffled a noseful of tears. "It's not the first time, Sammy. I'm ashamed."

"Tell your mother, tell your father, why don't you?"

"Tell them! They'd holler at me, kill me. They'd say, Whose fault is it? What business do I have going by myself to pick violets by the brook? Stay with Celia. No one bothers her."

That was true. The boys ignored Celia. Some girls have the yeast, some not. It's intrinsic, like the color of their eyes. And Jessie Weiss had more sexiness, as well as more intelligence, than any girl I knew, assets that might carry a woman far. What she lacked was beauty, conventional beauty, the shapeliness, the aura of good looks. Nevertheless, as she grew up, short and stocky, with dark hair straight as a stick, men found her desirable. Even I, intermittently.

For the graduation party, her mother, with Celia's help, had run up white dotted-Swiss graduation dresses for both girls on the Singer sewing machine. Jessie's fitted like a flour sack and, with outsize pink taffeta ribbon bows atop each of her braids, she looked the fat, homely kid she was, the baby in the crowd. Celia's dress fitted perfectly and her braids were pinned up, like the other eighth graders and first-year highs who were practicing young ladyhood.

The mama had decreed the graduation party, a social debut for her daughters, and the parlor, with its heavy mission chairs and settee, its garish Axminster rug, coarse lace curtains, phonograph, gilt-framed, tinted enlargements of pictures of Ida's and Herman's parents, had been freshened and adorned. All day Jessie had swept and dusted, washed windows and scrubbed sills; Celia had strung pink and green crepe paper streamers in a lattice below the ceiling, baked cakes and brewed lemonade. The girls soaked in the zinc tub before they buttoned one another into dotted Swiss; Celia tied on Jessie's ribbons and pinned a sachet to her own camisole. Ida dressed up, too, in the black silk, twinkling with jet beads, years

21

out of style, pulled at the seams and redolent of sweat and camphor, that she wore to shul on Holy Days. Into her ear lobes she screwed litle diamond buttons, on her bosom pinned a glittering brooch, before she stationed herself at the top of the staircase to greet the arriving guests. After they were distributed on the mission furniture and the oak dining chairs carried from the kitchen to round out a circle, Ida went down to stand beside Herman and impress late customers.

My mother, stopping by for two cakes of Kirkman's soap and a pound of yellow split peas, was informed, "Mrs. Rosenbaum, you should take a look what's going on upstairs. Like a cated affair. My Celia made it all herself. Such a girl. A diamond."

Being cued, my mother remarked on the earrings and the brooch.

"The pin Mr. Weiss gave me for engagement, the earrings for the wedding. Do I need diamonds to stand in a grocery? No. The first one my girls gets married I give her. . . ." A pregnant pause. "Ah, my Celia!" Then, with studied casualness, though my mother didn't miss the trick: "You have a fine child, too. Your Sammy, a head like a professor."

My mother changed the subject, saying, "I'll take a matjes herring, also, Mrs. Weiss."

All the Litvak teen-agers were in the parlor, which didn't make it many. Mixed parties—inter-faith or inter-shul—weren't held in Grady's Mills, all social mingling having been ordained by prejudice, inherited and idiotic. There were Pearl, Nettie and Hymie Rogoff, whose father had a fruit and vegetable store on lower Market Street; Aaron Leiberman, the cantor's son, a quiet but singularly handsome lad (resembling Francis X. Bushman, the girls maintained: the profile, the wavy hair); Bella and Isie Katz, offspring of Sol of the Bon Ton Dry Goods; Sadie Finkel, black-haired, bold-eyed, whom my mother called a "hoor" because she dabbed rice powder on her nose, daughter of Abe, who was doing well in real estate and loans; and Joey Slomowitz, eldest child and only son of Max, who collected metal scrap. Joey had the worst pimples in the crowd, which some of us said was because he masturbated, some because he did not. At this date—so much Freud having run under the bridge—I'm not certain whether it was too much sex or total abstinence we blamed adolescent pimples on. The boys all wore blue serge, though the night was hot. They kept mopping brows and necks. The girls, in cool-looking china silk, dotted Swiss and organdy, seemed uncomfortable, too. We sat in a circle, I the oldest there, Jessie the youngest, twiddling thumbs, not knowing how to start a party till Mama Weiss came puffing up the stairs. "Why you sitting quiet, young ladies and gentlemens? Celia dolling, play some music for the company. We got Caruso, Yossele Rosenblatt. Enjoy."

Jessie cranked the phonograph. Celia put on the discs, carefully adjusting the needle to its groove, while we sat mute and respect-ful, the boys lightly scuffing shoes, the girls tugging skirts down over their crossed knees, listening to grand opera and Hebrew liturgy until nine o'clock when Mama Weiss again appeared. "Celia dolling, maybe the company would enjoy the refreshments you made."

Celia stopped the music. She and Jessie scooted to the kitchen. Celia carried in two layer cakes, blanketed with whipped cream, topped with shredded cocoanut, dappled with maraschino cherries. Jessie brought in plates, glasses and forks. Celia went back for pitchers of lemonade, rattling chips of ice, floating maraschino cherries. Evidently a banner day for the maraschino bottlers.

Mama Weiss fixed me with a rebuking eye. "Maybe tonight you could be not so frum, taste a little Celia's baking. A cater, that girl could be, in the finest places." She departed for downstairs. Celia started slicing. She handed us our generous portions, pushing her flat chest forward so we'd catch a whiff of her sachet. Lily of the valley, she announced, when Sadie Finkel asked what that dee-light-ful aroma was.

The cake was delicious. The boys had second helpings, and none of us was crude enough to mention how recently he'd eaten meat. Bella Katz, a nice kid, got up to help clear away. "Don't bother," Celia said grandly. "I did the preparing. Jessie washes the dishes." She pulled a straight-backed chair next to Aaron Leiber-man and sat, smiling nervously, her hands with their ragged nails clasped on her lap, expecting I know not what. Nothing happened. Girls always buzzed around Aaron, he having those good looks, but he was pleasant indiscriminately and never more than that. He stared at his knuckles, Celia stared at hers, till Sadie Finkel, on the other side of Aaron, asked, "Why don't we play some games?" Hymie Rogoff snickered. "Yeh. Post office."

That evoked some giggling and blushes here and there, but Bella Katz, that nice kid, strode briskly to the kitchen door and called to Jessie, who was banging plates, "Come out. We have to use the kitchen for the post office." Bella doused the kitchen gaslight.

In the parlor, Hymie Rogoff, Isie Katz and Joey Slomowitz were in a huddle, whispering with sly expressions on their pimply faces. I suspected something not kosher was in the wind. Isie announced he'd be postmaster, no one else seemed eager for the honor, and Hymie volunteered to deliver the first letter. He went into the kitchen. Isie buzz-buzzed with him at the door. The girls sat, pink-cheeked, jiggling.

"Letter for Miss Sadie Finkel," Isie announced. Sadie, glancing coyly over her shoulder, entered the kitchen. We heard a smack that might have been a loud fake kiss or an authentic slap. Hymie came out, looking noncommittal. "Letter for Mr. Aaron Leiberman," Isie announced, predictably.

Aaron blushed but, being a good sport, went behind the kitchen door. After a suitable interval Sadie emerged, looking smug, letting us infer that Aaron had kissed her. Celia inched forward, nibbling her fingernails. Isie buzz-buzzed with Aaron at the door. Then, to everyone's amazement, Isie yelled, "Letter for Joe Slomowitz!" Something was up. I didn't like the smell of it. When Aaron came out of the kitchen, too quickly, his expression gave no hint of what had happened or what would.

"Letter for Miss Jessie Weiss!" Isie shouted, louder than he needed to.

Jessie stood rooted, turning scarlet.

"Go on, Jessie, give the boy a thrill." Hymie Rogoff smirked.

"Go ahead, Jessie." Pearl Rogoff gave her a shove. "It's only just a game."

Celia let her fingernails alone and began to bite her lips.

Jessie hesitated one more moment before she pushed Isie from the doorway. She marched into the darkened kitchen, slammed the door. We heard voices, Joe's and Jessie's, loud but indistinguishable behind the wooden barrier, then Jessie's screech, enough to wake the dead, a yelp from Joe and, after that, shoes thundering on the stairs.

Hymie mumbled, "Bet he tried to stick his finger up," while I rushed to get the gas lighted before Herman and Ida reached the top of the stairs.

Herman stood in the kitchen doorway, his mustache bristling, his eyeglasses glittering, though, as always, inarticulate. Behind him, Ida bellowed, "Who hollered? Who was hurt?"

Obviously, Joe. Blood was oozing down one cheek where Jessie's fingernails had raked it. He was blubbering and she was white and trembling and her graduation dress was ripped. "Papa," Jessie whimpered. "Papa. Papa. Papa." She rushed to him, hugging him around the middle, hard, so hard that when he pushed her off the print of his watch chain on her cheek was like a whiplash, like a punishment.

"You touched her!" Mama Weiss's index finger stabbed at Joe. "Bummer!"

"No, I swear. We were only playing a game."

"Some game!" Ida sniffed. "Go put cold water on the face, your mama shouldn't say wild Indians was in mine house."

We played no more Post office, or any other game, just sat twiddling our thumbs, the Rogoff girls trying to calm Jessie, Sadie Finkel looking disgusted, Celia vaguely unhappy; the boys, some sneering at Joey, some glowering at Jessie. It is hard, in the early teens, to assume a correct attitude when a crude sexual advance has been treated like a rape. I broke up the party. Being the oldest, I had the privilege. They rose meekly when I said, "Time to quit." Bella Katz and the Rogoff girls thanked Celia for a "chawming" evening.

Ida Weiss trapped me at the bottom of the stairs. "Mr. Journalist, practice. Put a write-up in the paper, please. Make a nice write-up."

"*Mr. and Mrs. Herman Weiss entertained at their residence at 103 Sixth Street last night*," I wrote, "*in honor of the grammar school graduation of their daughters, the Misses Celia and Jessie. Nine classmates and friends of the Misses Weiss heard a phonograph concert and played games. The parlor was attractively*

decorated with pink and green crepe paper streamers. A colla-
tion, prepared by Miss Celia Weiss, was served. Those present
were. . . ." I listed the names and spelled them right. The *News-*
Record ran it in "Folk You Know." It seems fitting that my first
journalistic effort should have been about the Weiss girls. Much
of my life I've been giving them write-ups. What else am I doing
here and now?

*   *   *

After the girls entered high school I saw them seldom. They
were freshmen, I a senior, and these are worlds, as much as years,
apart. Occasionally, I'd see Celia or Jessie scooting through the
halls, Celia with her best friend, Sadie Finkel; Jessie with her
favorite companion, Jessie Weiss. Celia had grown tall and slender;
Jessie had remained the chubby child. The girls looked well, I
thought. They'd both inherited their mother's dainty nose and her
fine complexion, nice coloring, no pimples.

How Celia was progressing I didn't know. In any case, I had no
time for tutoring. The higher education bug had bitten me, and I
was cramming to take College Entrance Boards. Columbia University had established a School of Journalism. If they'd admit me, I'd
make any—every—sacrifice to go. My father couldn't afford to
send me, but we worked out a fiscal plan. He'd take a loan from
Abe Finkel for my first year's tuition; I'd need to earn the money
after that by vacation jobs in Grady's Mills and part-time employ-
ment in New York. My mother had a distant cousin in the Bronx.
She agreed to bed me down on her dining room sofa, give me
kosher meals and laundry for five dollars a week. Papa would
advance me this until I found a part-time job. Before the First
World War, poor boys went to college with holes in their shoes
and didn't mind too much.

I graduated salutatorian of my class. The School of Journalism
accepted me. On the strength of my eagerness and promise, the
News-Record gave me a summer job. I was the staff gopher. "Sam,
go for a can of beer." . . . "Go for a pack of Fatimas." . . . "Go for
two baloney sandwiches on white. Don't forget the mustard." Between errands, I roamed the streets to garner "Folk You Know"
items. One afternoon when three fires broke out simultaneously in

different sections of the town (we were having a hot, rainless summer and most of our houses were wooden), I was sent to cover one. During that torrid summer I got acquainted with the firemen, the police, the courthouse hangers-on, two whorehouse madams and several downtown saloonkeepers. And Ida Weiss had been correct: my colleagues were Goyim and boozers, but this Jew-boy never met a finer bunch of men. They were witty, bawdy, inventive in profanity. They were sharp penny-ante players and, in conversation, connoisseurs of broads, though their own marriages were models of respectability. They voted Democratic—nose-thumbing at our upper-crust Republicans—but I decline to tag them with Mama's epithet of "prost." Though they pretended to be cynical, any seedy bum who straggled down the pike could cadge a meal from them—there but for the grace of a steady job go I. The steady job paid fifteen dollars for a work week of six ten-hour days (with Christmas off and July Fourth), yet they preferred to borrow from the business office rather than demand the twenty-two that union printers' devils got, for they'd been mesmerized by the "romance" of the trade: chase the hook-and-ladder, the paddy wagon, ambulance; circulate, with spectator status, among robbers, rapists, murderers; smoke cigars with politicians and second-guess their strategy; receive the unexpected, the improbable, without as much as a "Gee whiz!" Someday each of them was going to write a book.

While a war was festering in remote Europe, I left the *News-Record*, vowing, like MacArthur later at Corregidor, "I shall return." I didn't, for a while. College bored me for two years, but New York pleased me very much. I found a job as gopher on the lobster shift of the *Evening World*. Theater passes circulated in the shop. Now and then a pair dropped into my lap. Broadway became my secret passion. It remains that to this day.

When I returned to Grady's Mills it was to say goodbye. "We won't be back till it's over, over there." Selective Service had thumbed Aaron Leiberman and me. Sadie Finkel got the boys and girls together at her house to give us a sendoff. The Finkels, getting richer year by year, had moved uphill to Eighth Street, where the houses were large, spaced apart, and set back by lawns.

The girls came bearing gifts: handkerchiefs, pocket combs, nail

27

clippers and limp leather books, like *Paradise Lost*, light reading for dull days in the trenches. Celia had knitted sweaters for Aaron and me and pinned identical notes to each: "*To keep you warm with this reminder that a devoted friend prays for you night and day. (Miss) Celia Weiss.*" The penmanship was beautiful.

While Celia, with a wistful smile, was handing me her present, I heard Jessie, behind me. "Sam, I tried, but I can't knit a stitch. All I have for you is my best wishes."

I slued around. "Thank you very much. Just what I can use."

"Who'll tickle the ivories?" Sadie, the hostess, cried.

The Finkels had acquired a piano. Out of the camaraderie of our ghetto they'd invited any kid whose parents could afford to pay for lessons to practice in the Finkel parlor. Pearl Rogoff, Joe Slomowitz and Sadie had learned on that upright. Pearl twirled the stool up and spread sheet music on the rack. We clustered around and sang: "Swannee River," "Old Black Joe," "Redwing," "Juanita," then, inevitably, "Over There" and, after that, to the tune of "Men of Harlech" our high school song:

> "*Glorious High of Grady's Mill,*
> *To thee staunch and loyal still*
> *Master always of our will.*"

Celia's voice rang true and sweet; Jessie's voice was loud and stubbornly off-pitch. "A vocal solo, Celia," Sadie demanded. Blushing, simpering, Celia riffled the music sheets. She drew out "In the Gloaming" and propped it on the rack. Joe said he knew the piece. He lowered the piano stool and sat down to accompany her. Celia sang it well, I thought, and when we clapped she looked so happy she was almost pretty. Her cheeks were pink, her eyes sparkling. What that girl needed, all she needed, to make a mensch of her was a triumph now and then. Like everybody, now and then. She was growing up passably, her figure neat, though flat, her mouse-brown hair done stylishly, in a bun filled out with a "rat," her nose and brow and chin discreetly powdered, and a lily-of-the-valley fragrance hovering. Ladylike. Period.

"Who wants to dance?" Sadie cried again.

The young ladies chorused, "Everybody." The young gentlemen hung back.

28

Pearl Rogoff counted the house with a quick glance. There was a slight shortage of young males. "Let Joe dance," she volunteered. "I'll play."

"Roll up the carpet, boys," Sadie ordered.

Pearl began a waltz. Aaron Leiberman touched Celia's arm. "May I have this dance?" Her face lit up like the electric bulb in the Finkel kitchen as he glided with her to the middle of the room. She danced as nicely as she sang. The hostess looked at me expectantly. I shook my head. I wasn't in a dancing mood, I said. Joe's arm circled Sadie's waist; Hymie paired off with Bella Katz, Isie with Nettie Rogoff. That left Jessie and me; no one had asked Jessie whether she was in the mood. We stood together watching. They switched partners for a two-step—this time Sadie got Aaron. Jessie yawned, edging toward the door. I edged with her. Watching bored me, too. We gravitated toward what Sadie called "my father's den," an alcove crowded with a roll-top desk, a swivel chair, a sectional bookcase jammed with pristine "sets," a mission table with a garish lamp, and a decrepit Morris chair. I bowed Jessie toward the Morris.

"After you, my dear Alphonse," she said.

"After you, my dear Gaston," I said.

"Age before beauty," she said.

"Crazy kid," I said and took the cushioned seat.

She perched on the arm. Looking back, I realize that thus, by a casual arrangement, the design for our permanent relationship was set, Jessie higher than and looking down on me.

"Why don't you dance?" I asked.

"Why don't you?" she answered.

"I asked you first," I said.

"I have two left feet," she said. She swung them out. She was wearing patent-leather Mary Janes, kid's shoes. The older girls were dancing in buckled, high-heeled pumps.

"How about in school?" I nagged. "The dances in the gym?"

"It's polite to wait until you're asked. And I'm short and fat and homely and younger than, so the boys don't ask. Oh, once in a while a chaperone makes a poor kid ask. And the boy complains I try to lead. Or he has to drag me."

"Behind the bushes?" I asked.

"Trying to make me blush?" She shook her head. "Those days are gone and past." Spoken with sang-froid, remarkable, if not put on, in one as young as she. "Doesn't Celia dance well?" she went on to ask. "In aesthetic dancing, she's best in the class."

"And in what else?"

"Well, in glee club, chorus. And domestic science."

"How about Latin and algebra?"

"Don't ask," she said.

"And you?"

"Jessie Weiss is excellent in algebra and geometry." She sounded as impersonal as a report card. "She's also good in Latin, though Caesar bores her stiff. Who cares about those wars? Cicero should be more fun. He was an orator, you know. I'll get pointers from him. I'm on the debating team."

I nodded, approving. "Debating's best?"

"Oh, no, Shakespeare is." Her eyes began to shine. "Sammy!" No longer impersonal. "I'm in love with Shakespeare. Such words!" She clasped her hands and hugged them to her chest. "I never dreamed the English language was so beautiful. It's like music. His words keep running, running, in my head. Sammy, do you read Shakespeare?"

"We had *Macbeth* in English—remember?—and *Midsummer Night's Dream.*"

She nodded. "*Macbeth* was wonderful. I was crazy about it. I begged Mr. Proctor—he's the elocution teacher, he's new, he wasn't here in your time—to let us put it on. I thought maybe he'd let me try out for Lady Macbeth."

I had to smile. That pudgy child Lady Macbeth! Then I thought, By gosh, she's it, she's perfect for the part, that voice, the dark intensity in her.

"But he decided," she went on, "to do Midsummer's Night instead. More parts for girls. Celia got a part, a fairy part. She danced it like a dream. She wanted Queen Titania but she couldn't do the speaking parts. There's a lot of memorizing. She isn't good at that." She was speaking matter-of-factly, presenting data and without hostility. "Sammy, have you read *Hamlet?*"

I said I'd seen it on the stage, in New York.

"Have you really?"

30

Her eyes opened so wide and with such awe, I had to quote, "'And did you once see Shelley plain? And did he speak to you again?'"

"Browning, isn't it? I like him, too." She rootched on the chair arm, easing her buttocks. I started to get up to offer the cushion. She pushed me down, talking all the while. "Oh, it must be so wonderful in New York! Theaters, museums, everything. Darn shame you have to leave New York, and college, too, just to go to war." She caught herself, went silent, to find a less portentous conversational gambit, came up with, "I would love to go to college."

"Why don't you?"

"Oh, they'd never let me." They, I gathered, meant the parents. "You see, Celia could never make it even if we had the money, so they would never let me." There was no resentment in her voice, not even indignation, though her eyes were eloquent.

This I knew for truth and let it pass, asking merely, "Well, then, Jessie, if not college, what else would you want?"

Her hands gripped tightly. She stared at the table lamp. "If a fairy godmother would turn up this very minute, to rub that fancy-shmansy lamp and say, 'Jessie, I'll give you three wishes, only three, whatever you want most. . . .'" I caught a kind of detached gleefulness, an imagination vocalizing. "First, I'd wish to be beautiful, blonde and blue-eyed, tall and willowy—gosh how I hate fat women!—and curly haired, with big deep dimples in my cheeks. . . ."

"Do you have to be?"

"It would help. You know it would." She gave my shoulder a poke. "Second, I'd wish I could sing. Oh, not just as good as Celia. Much, much better. Galli-Curci. . . ."

My eyebrows shot up.

"Now, Sammy," she said, dead serious. "That's as wonderful as being blonde and beautiful. Do you know—can you guess?—how cheap I feel when the singing teacher says, in front of the whole class, 'Jessie Weiss, please do not try to sing. I don't know why it is but you're the only one one who never gets the pitch.' That, when your insides are busting with songs you want to sing?"

"Stupid! Do it anyway. Go off somewhere. . . ."

"By the brook?" With a more roguish expression than any I

had ever seen on her face. "No siree-bob! Can't you see me singing away while the boys yell dirty words?"

I could. I smiled. "What's the third wish?"

"I wish I could do handsprings."

I exploded, roared.

"Don't laugh." She squeezed my shoulder. "It isn't funny. It's natural as can be. When something wonderful happens, like reading *Hamlet* for the first time, and it makes me very, very happy, what I'd like to do is turn handsprings. Anybody would."

"For the love of Pete, handsprings are a cinch. Practice in the gym."

"Never." She shook her head stoutly. "I'm a clumsy ox, always been, will always be." Then she bent to drape her arms around my neck. "Sammy! Sammy! Be sure you come back. You're the only person on the Hill who knows *Hamlet* isn't something Jews are not allowed to eat. I can talk to you about anything and you don't make fun of me."

Myron, Sadie Finkel's kid brother, chose that moment, when Jessie Weiss was all but strangling me, to stick his long nose in. "Hey! Don't you two want to eat? Sadie's serving the refreshments. Yummee, yum, the punch is spiked."

Sadie asked me and, as my farewell gesture toward the Hill, I wrote up the social function at the residence of Mr. and Mrs. Abraham Finkel at 249 Eighth Street. Mallory, my erstwhile city editor, a persnickety sort, read the item through and jabbed his copy pencil at one line. "*Miss Celia Weiss rendered a vocal solo.*" "Samuel," he said sternly, "I do not know what they did or did not teach you at that so-called journalism factory in New York, but on this paper *fat* is rendered. Vocal solos are *sung*. This editorial admonition may not be useful where you're heading presently, but kindly tuck it in your memory for after you come back to us."

He bought me a beer, told me a job would be waiting and they'd stay in touch. He kept his word. Bundles of the *News-Record* wandered around Europe and eventually caught up with me in France. From the home-town paper I learned that Hymie Rogoff was a sailor on the bounding main and that Aaron Leiberman had

32

died in battle not twenty kilometers from where I was safe and damp and cold and miserably lonesome.

I tried to think of Aaron dead and found that wasn't difficult because I had few memories of him alive. Beyond the good looks all the girls admired was what? A pretty boy infant who wore long golden curls until he reached the age of five; a beautiful child whom a doting mother protected, not letting him go coasting on the Hill or ride a bike lest he hurt himself; a courteous youngster, pulling a red wagon to deliver wine and matzohs for his father; an average student, E in deportment. I was a junior when Aaron entered high school. Of his scholastic career, all I remembered was that he was often picked for leading roles in plays and dropped after two weeks of frustrating rehearsals. No talent. What, then, was his potential? What sort of person had been lost? A docile husband for an adoring wife whose family owned a business that could use a son-in-law? A conscientious father and a loyal son, who'd always try to help his parents out? An observant Jew, a respectable citizen? What more can you ask? Well, a spark, a something-out-of-the-ordinary to add poignancy to sacrifice, a few words, a pungent, cogent phrase, to be repeated when old friends got together, embellished, transmuted into legend. "Hello." "Goodbye." "Here is your change, Mrs. Rosenbaum. Thank you." "May I have this dance?" Can drama grow from commonplace?

My mother, a faithful correspondent whom I myself had tutored up to the point where she'd convinced herself she'd mastered the English language, wrote that Mrs. Leiberman had started to behave queerly. She stopped cleaning her house, didn't feed the younger children, drank a bottle of iodine. "*They decided it was better she should be in a sanditorium,*" Mama wrote. "*I will be worse meshuga, Semmele, if something bad happens with you.*"

Celia Weiss wrote me two letters in her excellent penmanship, each praying I'd come marching home soon and safe and sound. "*We cannot spare you, dear Samuel. You are very dear to us.*" She also mailed me a home-knitted pair of gloves and a box of cookies that arrived all crumbs. There wasn't even a card from Jessie Weiss. I was not surprised. W. Shakespeare was the man she loved. However, I did see Jessie's face on page three of the *News-Record*, big eyes above plump cheeks, illustrating the announcement that

33

she was valedictorian of the class of 1918. The list of graduates was printed. Celia's name was bottom of the list. Under the leaden winter skies of France, I ruminated over this. Alphabet, I told myself: Watts, Victor; Weaver, Mary Beatrice; come ahead of Weiss, Celia. However, whatever, Celia'd made the list. It would have been hell for Jessie if Celia had been left back this time.

I was at Chaumont sorting Pershing's mail, some months after the world had been made safe for democracy, when I came upon a "Folk You Know" in a delayed batch of *News-Records: "The Misses Celia and Jessie Weiss, daughters of Mr. and Mrs. Herman Weiss of 103 Sixth Street, will leave this week to attend college. Miss Celia Weiss is enrolled in State Normal School at Beaver Valley and Miss Jessie Weiss in the Emerson College of Oratory at Boston. A farewell party will be tendered them tonight at their parents' residence."*

And Celia will sing a solo. And the boys and girls will dance. No, there won't be dancing, unless they import ringers from the Hungarian-Galician shul. Extreme measure, but what can you do? Drastic shortage of Litvak males. Aaron's gone for good; I'm over here; Hymie's on a ship who knows where. That leaves Isie Katz and Joey Slomowitz. Bad eyes? Flat feet? Weak bladders? Who knows why the draft passed them up? Who cares? I was far more curious about the fact that both of Herman's daughters were going to college out of town, and I wrote my mother for details. By the time her answer came, I'd forgotten that I'd asked. *"Mr. Proctor, the elocution teacher in the high school (What is elocution, Semmy? Like president election, maybe? I don't understand), he started the whole thing. He said Jessie was born for elocution teaching so she must learn it in the college where he learned. Mrs. Weiss said no, Jessie can't go if Celia can't go. Mr. Weiss said no, the both can't go, they will must eat trefe. So what can I tell you, Semmy dolling? Was fights, arguings, every night in Weiss's house. You know how Ida hollers, Jessie hollers even more. Every word everybody hears. It was a scandal. Ida don't give in. If Jessie goes to college, Celia has to go. So takke, where? Her marks, I don't need to tell you, Semmy, F minus is the best, and every summer, summer school. Then they find out the State Normal will take Celia to learn to be a cooking-sewing teacher.*

Domestics science is the fancy name. For this you don't need algebra. A thimble maybe and a kochleffel. Schoen gut. So what about the trefe? Well, Herman Weiss remembers he has a landsman in Boston, a Hebrew teacher, a poor man. He writes a letter. The man is happy to earn a few dollars from a kosher boarder in the house. So already settled with Jessie. And Celia makes a promise she will eat hard-boil eggs and can salmon and sardines (she shouldn't leave the can stand open in the room, it could be poison) and celery and tomatoes and fruit, a glass milk, nothing cooked, only what the mama sends. And Ida every week brings in the post office a nice package, chalah, strudel, cookies and sponge cake. . . . Your papa sewed beautiful tailor suits, fits like a glove, for the college girls. Two days Ida made them walk on Sixth Street, up and down, showing off. . . ."

It made a diversion for my final weeks in France to try to calculate how many cans of salmon and sardines would be required to see Celia through two years at State Normal. What I found harder to figure out was how the Weisses had swung it financially. "Herman's Grocery is a nice piece of bread," Ida had assured me. Undoubtedly, they had plenty stashed away. "For who are we slaving? The children." Sacrifice? Nope, foresight. Both girls were going off to train for salaried careers.

I came home in December and went straight back to the *News-Record*, no longer a gopher but a full-fledged reporter, covering everything and too busy to socialize. Christmas week Celia came home for vacation. Jessie didn't come, the trip from Boston being long and costly. Celia mailed me a note on perfumed linen paper, inviting me to supper, no party, just two couples, Sadie Finkel, Joe Slomowitz, me and herself. And R.S.V.P., if you please. Who for whom in this coupling? Speaking for myself, neither of these girls. Overseas, I'd met an army nurse, a blonde. She was in New York. I had visiting privileges.

Sadie welcomed me at the kitchen door and flung her arms around my neck. She was wearing spit curls and a prickly, musky, Chinese incenselike perfume. "Our hero!" she cried.

"Cut that out," I growled.

"Hinky, dinky, parley voo." This was Joey in a natty suit. His pimples had faded, though his cheeks were pitted by the acne scars; his hair was slick and smooth with scented grease. The shining Reo in the road, I knew, belonged to him. Lacking natural charm, he'd need such accessories.

"Parlez-vous yourself," I answered him.

"Your French, no doubt, has improved," Sadie said.

"Nothing for mixed company," I said.

Celia emerged from her bedroom—that last-minute primping. Her right arm curved to me. "God has spared you, Samuel dear. I am so grateful."

"Sardines agree with you," I said.

My wit baffled her. "Let us adjourn to the parlor," she said.

In my absence in the combat zone, the Weisses had wallpapered the parlor a durable brown and had wired it for electricity. A bulb glowed cozily within a fringed chandelier of green and red and yellow glass. There was a sofa, with a carved wood frame, upholstery of olive plush, and hand-embroidered pillows braced in corners; two green armchairs; a dark brown rug; ecru curtains, overhung with green plush draperies. The ancestral photographs had disappeared; a mahogany-cased Victrola replaced the antique phonograph. A mahogany table beneath the chandelier held a cut-glass vase with artificial flowers and a green limp-leather volume of Shakespeare's tragedies. Hideous, more so than the tragedies.

My friends stood hushed, surrounding me, awaiting praise. A statuette saved me. A dainty thing of bronze, it stood, a-tiptoe, arms outflung, on the Victrola lid. "Pretty," I remarked.

"My Good Fairy," Celia purred. "I am delighted that it pleases you. Our tastes seem to correspond."

"It's common," Sadie said. "Every Tom, Dick and Harry buys it."

Celia bit her lip.

Sadie linked her arm into mine. She drew me down to the sofa, plumped a cushion behind me, snuggling close. "I was so surprised when I heard you came back to Grady's Mills. I was sure you would remain in New York."

"Missed my mama's tsimmis. Nobody in New York makes it like she does."

She ignored the statement of fact. "I just adore New York. I was down last week, to shop. . . ."

"For your hope chest." Celia's tone surprised me; she'd never been a cat. Oh, I get it, girls, she belittled your Good Fairy; tit for tat. . . .

"You've been sewing your hope chest for years," Sadie retorted.

I hoped I wasn't Celia's hope. Or Sadie's. The boy who drove the Reo had my permission to take first and second prize.

"Tell us all about the war." Celia seated herself the other side of me. Three on the sofa crowded it.

Joey took a stance, facing Sadie. "War is hell," he informed me.

"War is dull," I informed him. "And dirty. Mud and monotony."

He leered. "How about the Madamesel from Armentears?"

"There are ladies present," I warned him.

The ladies tossed their heads archly. Silence followed. I twirled my thumbs, wondering whether we'd play Post office or Cantor Rosenblatt. Then, Sadie pressed her hand against her breast. "Poor Aaron," she sighed.

Celia groped up her sleeve for a handkerchief, so lugubrious I'd have guessed she'd cast herself as Aaron's widow. "May he rest in peace," she said.

"Amen," Joey said.

Sadie brightened. "Did they tell you his name will be on the Victory Statue in the courthouse square? With a gold star. A Jewish boy, a hero, that laid down his life for Wilson's Fourteen Points. He proved Jews aren't cowards."

That fatuous remark, plus the recollection of my dreary thoughts when I'd learned of Aaron's death, roiled me up. "Bullets do not ask who's circumcised," I said.

The girls tsked, looking shocked.

I was a Jew, I thought I needed to explain, who didn't look upon himself as brave or cowardly. I had a duty to my country and I did it. If live ammunition had come my way, I also might have been a casualty. As it turned out, I'd not been shot at nor had I fired one shot. An army clerk behind the lines serves his country, too, though out of target range.

"They also serve who only stand and wait," Joey hurried to assure me.

37

"Joe and his father bought a thousand dollars' worth of Liberty Bonds," Celia said.

I bowed to him. "Merci beaucoup."

"The Mayor gave them a certificate," Sadie said. "Suitable for framing."

Joe fumbled in an inside pocket as if to produce the document.

"Stick it up," I said. I'd never liked that boy; something told me I wasn't going to like the man he would become.

Celia gasped.

"You've changed," Sadie chided me. "You used to be refined."

"It's time to serve," Celia said. "I'm sure you must be famishing."

She spread an embroidered cloth upon the parlor table, carried in new china plates, new Rogers silverware, and hand-embroidered napkins. She served veal cutlets and mashed potatoes, Waldorf salad (the mayonnaise homemade, she bragged), and there was a paper lace doily beneath the sponge cake, all of which showed me how much Celia had been learning at State Normal. Both girls ate pinkies up. Sadie said the meal was superb. Joey said, "Not bad for an amachoor." Sadie said, slyly, "I'll bet you missed your girl friend's cooking."

I said I knew it was not polite to eat and run but Mallory, my boss, had at the last minute handed me an evening assignment, some shindig at the Elks. Business before pleasure; I was sure they'd understand. I shook hands all around and squirmed into my overcoat. "Do not be a stranger, Samuel," Celia said. "The welcome mat is out."

Ida Weiss was waiting for me at the bottom of the stairs. "You noticed how Celia is improved? A college girl is not an ordinary person. Something exceptional. A young man like you can appreciate."

"Ah, Mrs. Weiss," I said. "I bet you tell that to all the boys."

She pinched my cheek. "Only to you, boychick; I had my eye on you since you were a pisherel."

To find out what Jessie Weiss had been learning up in Boston, I had to wait till June, and then I learned that, despite the dietary supervision of the Hebrew teacher's family, Jessie had sampled broiled lobster and steamed clams, had found them succulent and, in a voice that clanged through every open window on the block, proclaimed that the whole kosher business was nonsense; God—if there is a God—is too busy to worry about menus. Also, she had bobbed her hair, marched in a suffrage parade, and employed her debating talent on behalf of a pair of Anarchists accused of the murder of a Braintree paymaster. Why Herman did not disown her then and there, I couldn't understand. It took many years before I realized he had always been inordinately proud of her.

Two

"The engagement of Miss Jessie Weiss of
Grady's Mills to Mr. Horace Simon of New York was announced
today. Miss Weiss is the daughter of Mr. and Mrs. Herman Weiss
of 103 Sixth Street. She is a graduate of Grady's Mills High School
and for the last three years has been a student at the Emerson College of Oratory in Boston, Mass. Mr. Simon, the son of Mr. and
Mrs. Adolph Simon of New York, is a scene designer, associated
with theaters in Provincetown, Mass., and Greenwich Village in
New York. Marriage plans will be announced shortly."

I didn't compose this social item. It's not the News-Record's
style. We lead off such announcements with the fiancée's parents'
names and end with the date of the nuptials. This was scribbled on
a lined sheet torn from a loose-leaf college notebook and handed
to me in the newsroom by the bride herself. "This will clinch it,"
she assured me. "It will end the argument."

There had been finality, not argument, in the way she introduced the groom: "My husband, Horace Simon."

In reflex, I glanced at her left hand before I glanced at him.
Jessie wore no ring, and what she'd picked for herself I wouldn't
have, for her. Delicate was the word for Horace. (My mother
cried "consumptive" the minute she laid eyes on him.) He was
slight, with freckled, milk-white skin, ginger hair, toothbrush
mustache, prominent front teeth and feverish blue eyes, Goyish-
looking except for a gallows-humor expression in which, along
with, usually there is a dash of superciliousness.

I said, "Congratulations."

He said, "Thanks. You're the first who's offered it."

They perched on my desk. He brought out cigarettes. Jessie and
I took. He held a light to hers, a courtesy not often seen in 1921

in Grady's Mills, where women smoked, when and if, behind locked bathroom doors.

"Papa'd kill me if he saw," Jessie said.

"Still afraid of Papa?" I asked.

"Nacherly. The right-hand man of God."

"You're a married woman, are you not?" I asked.

"I'm his child, am I not?" she asked.

I reread her announcement. "Betrothed or wed?"

"Both," Jessie said. "Depending where I go to bed."

"Jingle," Horace said.

Then, alternating gravity with jest, they filled me in on what had gone before.

They had arrived yesterday. Jessie'd been expected, this being the semester's end, but she'd neglected to warn the family she was bringing company.

Ida, hot and disheveled, was frying blintzes on a wood fire in the stove. The kitchen was hazy with charred butter smoke. Flypaper spiraled above the table where the dough discs cooled. The flies, numerous and intrepid, swooped low, ignoring it.

"Who is there? Aha, Jessie! You came on the five o'clock? Celia comes on the six-fifteen." Celia, teaching domestic science at Hartzville, twenty miles west of here, commuted on the interurban electrified trolley line.

"Mama, this is Horace Simon."

Mama slued around. Her chins went slack. "Good afternoon, good evening, gentleman." She wiped her hands on her apron and touched his outstretched fingertips. "How do you do? From where? . . . From New York? You come for vacation in Grady's Mills? A nice place. Fresh air. Not like New York." She was burbling, out of nervousness. "So, Jessie, why don't you mail a postcard you are bringing company from New York?"

"We figured we'd get here before the card," Jessie said.

"Excuse me. My blintzes." Ida flipped the film of batter in the pan and mopped her neck with a dish towel. "You like to stay for supper, Mr. . . . Mr. Simons? A plain family supper. Cold schav and blintzes with pot cheese and sour cream. Hot weather, who eats more?"

"Thank you," Horace said. "I'll try anything."

Her glance was suddenly distrustful. "You a Gentile?"

"Hardly," Horace said.

Ida swung her pan over to the table, flopped a dough disc out and dipped her ladle into batter.

"Horace, put the valises there." Jessie pointed to her old bedroom.

The batter spoon clanged on the floor. "In Celia's room! You crazy? He's gonna sleep in Celia's room?"

"In my room," Jessie said.

Blood rushed to Ida's face. Her eyes began to bug. "What are you? A hoor?"

"We're married," Jessie said. "A week ago. By a Justice of the Peace."

Ida's sharp eyes darted toward Jessie's waist.

"I'm not pregnant," Jessie said.

(Horace on my newsroom desk was listening to Jessie's verbatim account with rapt attentiveness and a crooked smile, as, no doubt, he'd listened to the kitchen dialogue. "I was fascinated," he put in, "by the pompadour and the general type." "Mama is no type," Jessie retorted. "She is an original. Nothing like it anywhere. And thank God for those small kindnesses.")

The original was turning purple; they were afraid she'd have a stroke. "I forbid it," Ida sputtered. "Celia gets married first."

"She missed the boat," Jessie said.

"Boat? What boat? Where is the ring?"

Jessie took a gold hoop from her purse.

"So! You're ashamed to wear it. He must be a Goy."

"My parents are Jewish, German Jews," Horace said.

Ida spat. "Fui. Worse. Reformers, no?"

Horace smiled indulgently.

"Justice Peace to a Reformer is no marriage." Ida clasped her cheeks and rocked her head. "Oi, wait till Mr. Weiss and Celia hear this monkey business!"

"Come into the parlor, Horace," Jessie said. "Let Mama fry and stew."

When Celia heard the news shortly after six, she blanched, said "Oh!" and then "I'm not hungry, it's too hot, I'll go down, relieve Papa, let him enjoy his supper with Jessie's company."

("An excuse," Jessie told me. "To get away, be by herself, not let me see her busting out in tears because I'd found a husband first.")

"Jessie's here, she can set the table," Celia added. "And kindly do not use my drawn-work tablecloth."

Herman, they went on to tell me, took the matter with more aplomb than anyone'd expected. He merely asked Horace, "You're a Jew?"

Ida got the answer in before Horace had a chance. "A Reformer, worse even than a Goy."

"My parents belong to Emanuel, the Temple," Horace said. "They consider themselves good Jews. They contribute to the Federation. My father is a banker."

Ida snatched that up. "He will support you?"

"I doubt it," Horace said. "They don't like this any more than you."

"What's not to like?" Ida flared, defending her own. "A college girl. From a educated Jewish family." She eyed Jessie. "Aha, you want my diamonds. You need my diamonds to show off for his family."

"It never crossed my mind," Jessie said.

"You don't get." Ida banged the table with her fist.

"Did I ask you, Mama? Keep them. Wear them in good health."

"And imagine, Sam," Jessie interpolated for me, "my mother knowing me so little, I should care about her diamonds—me! Let her choke on them!"

Horace stroked his mustache. "My mother-in-law is crass, I fear."

"Not Papa," Jessie said. "He was dignified, if not altogether sensible. 'Our child will be married by the rabbi, under the chupa, in this house.' That was what he said. 'Our daughter stays here, in our house, till we decide how to arrange. The young man cannot sleep here; it is forbidden.'"

"And so," Jessie went on, "Horace slept at the hotel last night and I slept back to back with sister Celia; not a word between us. To keep me chaste—not virginal, chaste—till the folks decide when to let us marry orthodox. It's stupid! Idiotic! So we decided to bring things to a head by announcing it this way. When the

43

Hill starts asking, 'Nu?' and 'When?' they'll have to get busy. Otherwise"—she shrugged—"we'll pack and hop the train. I hate, I really do, to hurt my old man but Horace has to get to work. He has this summer job at Provincetown. . . ."

"Provincetown!" I'd noticed the name in the paragraph; I'd been trying to associate. "Eugene O'Neill!"

"Uh huh," Jessie said.

I showed excitement. "Have you met him? Do you know him?"

Jessie laughed. " 'Did you once see Shelley plain?' Yes, sir, we know Gene." She looked at Horace rather hard. "He drinks too much," she said, whether meaning Simon or O'Neill, I could not decide.

"He writes good plays," Horace said.

"The theater's our life," Jessie said.

"I envy you," I said.

As soon as our paper hit the porches on the Hill, phones began to ring—Should we congratulate Herman and Ida or commiserate with them? One call, from another part of town, to Herman's Grocery, just before the closing hour of nine, settled all the arguments. Ida took the receiver off the hook. "Hah-lo, Herman's Grocery."

"I'd like to speak with Mrs. Weiss."

"She is speaking. Who is calling?"

"This is Mildred Hartman."

"Mildred Hartman? From where? . . . From Grady Avenue!"

"Mrs. Weiss, I saw the announcement of your daughter's engagement in this evening's paper. I called my friend, Mrs. Adolph Simon, at once, long distance, in New York. . . ."

"Your friend! Long distant! New York!" Ida was impressed.

"Blanche Simon was shocked. She and Adolph—Mr. Simon—are frantic. Horace is their only child. They begged me to do anything, everything, to stop this insanity."

"What's the matter? The young man is crazy in the head?" Ida privately had thought as much.

"The young man is crazy to throw away a fortune. He will not have a penny, not one cent; Blanche authorized me to tell you people this. He will be a pauper if he marries your daughter."

44

"And what is missing with my daughter? A college girl from a educated family."

"She's simply not their kind," Mrs. Hartman said.

Ida, when she told my mother and her other cronies afterwards, said she was certain she would plotz, then and there, standing at the wall telephone. She clung to the box and summoned her pride. "Our kind is Jewish scholars, rabbis, not big-money people. And we also are not happy our daughter wants to marry with some-body who is not *our* kind. But we are modren people. We under-stand the world is different in America from in the old country. My own father found for me the husband, a Talmudist, a gentle-man of highest quality. And I am proud to be his wife. In America, the children are the boss. There is not respect for parents. So they decide to get married, so we do not stop and we make the wedding unshtandig. Saturday night, next, eight o'clock in the parlor from our house. Sooner we would make it, only Mr. Weiss and myself are every day and evenings in the store, earning an honest living. Saturday, our Shabbos, we are closed, we rest. So the nighttime we have strength to make the wedding. So, please, Mrs. Mildred Hartman, you will be so kind, make one more long-distant call. Tell Mr. and Mrs. Simon from Mrs. Herman Weiss, they are in-vited to the wedding in our house."

When I learned about the conversation, I was pleased. The genteel busybody, Mrs. Hartman, had been taken down a peg.

Ida phoned me at the paper the next afternoon. "Sammy, I want to make an appointment with you. Business."

"I'm no longer tutoring, Mrs. Weiss."

"Don't make jokes. It is important, Sammy, please. Only your mama shouldn't know, Mr. Weiss shouldn't know."

I agreed I'd stop in at the grocery on my way to work, while Herman was at morning prayers.

"Sammy, something you must do for me. I want you should buy a box expensive letter-writing paper—I will pay for it. On this you should typewrite for me a letter to Mr. and Mrs. Adolph Simon in New York, invite them in polite words Saturday to come to their son's wedding in mine house."

"Nothing doing. Leave me out of this."

Her plump fingers squeezed my arm. "Sammy, I feel for her, his

45

mother. A mother's hearts is all the same, broken in little pieces when the children is making a terrible mistake." She paused to change her mood and tone. "A bargain Jessie catched! Skinny like a herring! White like a consumptive! Poor like a captzin!" Another pause, to shift the mood again. "Her, the Mrs. Simon, me the Mrs. Weiss, the two of us could cry out our hearts together, our children is making a terrible mistake."

Mildly, I said, "If there's to be inviting, Horace has to do it. Phone them, write them, bring them here, that's up to their son," though I suspected it would be far worse if they came. The herring barrels, Ida's pompadour, the brown and green plush parlor would convince them that their son had fallen among primitives.

When I relayed Ida's request, Horace smiled. "The ceremony is just to humor Jessie's dad," he said, adding, to enlighten me, that marriage was a personal affair, a compact between adults and no one's business but their own; all the rites and rituals, laws and customs, were superstitious crap. This, I gathered, was what is meant by being bohemian, which I presumed they believed they were.

There was one more battle, brief and loud and nasty. Sixth Street heard it through the open windows and Sixth Street was appalled, Jessie shouting, "Let's have no more talk. I will bathe in *this* bathtub and nowhere else. I will not have those alte bobbes poking at my tits."

My mother went white. "Not go to the mikvah! A big sin." She shook her head ominously. "From this they have bad trouble, sure and positive."

It was a small wedding. I was there because Jessie had requested the honor of my presence; my parents were asked because I was. The rabbi brought his wife; she had to bring along five little ones (like steps). Cantor Leiberman, sad-faced, shrunken, came with his teen-age daughter. The shamas and his son (just past Bar Mitzvah) were included, so that they, with my father and myself, might hold up the four sticks of the red velvet bridal canopy, a function traditionally performed by male kinsmen of the bride. The rabbi's consent to give his blessing to a bride who had rejected the ritual bath was, undoubtedly, a deference to the respected Herman Weiss, a special kindness, not to lay a further burden on an outraged heart. Now that I think back, I'm sure there was no minyan. Under the circumstances, no one made an issue out of this.

The night was too warm for Ida to wear her Yom Tov black silk, even had she felt festive. The bride, scorning convention, wore a sack of red batik, though, perversely, she'd hung a wisp of veiling on her face. The groom wore a borrowed yarmulka, tilted rakishly on his ginger hair.

Horace was the most nonchalant bridegroom I have ever seen, acting like a bemused spectator rather than a participant, repeating the vows and prayers after the rabbi with an intonation that was insulting mimicry. And Jessie, for once, kept her voice to a whisper and grinned wickedly when Horace put the gold hoop on her fourth finger. It was as if both of them had set out to make a farce of this. Her parents stood side by side, the Grady's Mills Gothic, stern and more than a little sad. The rabbi's children had to be shushed constantly.

After the groom had stamped and smashed a wine glass, as instructed, and raised the veil to peck Jessie's cheek, there were bleats of "Mazel Tov" from the rabbi's wife, my parents and the shamas. I kissed the bride's cheek. "Thank you," Jessie said. "I'm glad someone did." My mother bustled, passing squares of sponge cake and glasses of sweet Passover wine. The carpet and the green upholstery were sprinkled with yellow crumbs. One of the rabbi's children jogged an elbow and a wine glass spilled. The son of the shamas, believing now he was a man, guzzled too much wine and threw up in the kitchen sink. The rabbi's children became pests underfoot. Their mother shepherded them home to bed. Jessie disappeared into the bedroom to gather up her things, and the rest of us stood around, wondering how soon we ought to leave. Ida, red-eyed, red-faced, kept slicing cake and decanting wine, saying, "Take a piece. Take another glass. We got plenty."

I saw Herman touch his son-in-law's arm, lead him to his bedroom, shut the door. Then, for the first time in that hypocritical evening, I became aware of Celia. She crouched in a green armchair, cradling something in her lap. Tears were coursing down her cheeks. I touched her arm. She glanced up with streaming eyes. "My Good Fairy," she sobbed. She took her hands away from what was in her lap and I saw shards of plaster, tinted bronze.

"My Good Fairy was smashed," Celia wailed. "At my sister's wedding."

Now, surely, this was none of Jessie's doing, intentionally or otherwise—one of those rambunctious kids, no doubt—but just as surely Jessie would be blamed for it. I'm reasonably certain, too, that Jessie never knew about the accident, nor about the debate that started on the morning after. My mother, bless her heart, was responsible for this.

"I am the witness, and the One Above should give me strength," my mother told the women on the porch of Herman's Grocery, her fist beating her chest for emphasis. "To me Ida said the first one married gets the diamonds."

"Mrs. Rosenbaum, dolling." Mrs. Katz confused the issue. "First one means first-borned, married or no married."

"First *married*," my mother insisted.

"Ask her," Mrs. Rogoff suggested, pointing to the stairs and meaning Ida.

"Who could ask?" Mrs. Katz shrugged her hands. "To her, better not to talk. The mother's heart is broke. Jessie grabs from who knows where a boychick. Leaves the sister sitting, an old maid. Diamonds, yet, the mother should give?"

"I was by the wedding." By this advantage my mother had become the unimpeachable authority. "A wedding! I would be ashame such a wedding in mine house. Sponge cake. Pesach wine. Not even a küchel and chop herring. Did Ida wear the silk dress? No. A shmate she was wearing, like for standing in the grocery. Did Ida wear the earrings and the pin? No. So Jessie must got. No?"

Phones rang again in all the dwellings on the Hill, which divided into factions that argued heatedly. Did Jessie get her mother's diamonds? Should Jessie have received the diamonds? If Jessie didn't get the diamonds, was it fair to punish her for marrying before Celia did?

As far as I know, Jessie left with only her clothes and books when she and Horace boarded the midnight for New York. I did inquire about the gems, obliquely, in October, when I called on the newlyweds in New York. Ida'd found their address for me, scrawled on a penny postcard: "Jessie Weiss and Horace Simon at home at—"

Home was the basement of a Greenwich Village red-brick. I inhaled must, mildew, mice droppings and the leakage of bad plumbing as soon as Jessie let me in, and from the looks of the front room this couple was living mainly on literature, cigarettes and love. There was a wall of book-filled shelves ("Horace built the shelves," Jessie informed me); two day beds, right-angled to each other ("Second-hand," Jessie said); two low tables, one bright blue, one bright red ("Horace made them"), both holding crude clay ash trays, heaped with butts; a chest of drawers, bright yellow ("Bought from Salvation Army—Grand Rapids oak—Horace scraped and painted it"); a fireplace, choked with wood ashes, paper bags and stubs of cigarettes; bare floor; iron bars outside the windows, cracked green shades within.

As an old friend, I could be frank. "Why didn't you hock the diamonds and buy yourselves some chairs?"

"Who has diamonds?" Jessie asked.

"Let it pass," I said. "Your love nest is, let us say, different, and you're looking fine. Married life agrees with you."

I heard a gurgle, a gush, a door slammed. The bridegroom entered, buttoning his fly. "Oops! Didn't know we had company. Hey, the wedding guest!" He came, unsteadily, to shake my hand. I smelled wine on his breath. He plopped on a day bed, fumbling with his buttons. "What brings you?"

"John Barrymore and *The Emperor Jones*," I said. "And curiosity."

"How're my parents?" Jessie asked.

"Don't you hear from them?"

"Not even a shonatava. My fault, I presume. Everything is. Make like a reporter, Sam."

"I saw them in shul Yom Kippur, fasting, looking hale and hearty."

Horace made a strangled sound, a chortle or a hiccup. "My pious father-in-law," he said.

"What else is new?" Jessie asked.

"We're about to get a Y," I said.

"We had a Y," she said.

49

"We had a C.A. We get H.A., Hebrew Association. Hymie Rogoff got the inspiration from a Jewish chaplain in the war. Mrs. Hartman—*the* Mrs. Hartman—heads the Board. I interviewed her. It's been her lifelong ambition, she wanted me to know, to help the poor Jewish children from the Hill."

"Fascinating," Jessie said. "I heard how she tried to help this poor Jewish child."

Horace scowled at her.

"Enough of Folk You Know," she said. "How about some vino? Our Italian neighbors manufacture it. Safe for babes and nursing mothers." She started toward the rear. I followed, being curious about the domestic arrangements of *la vie bohême*.

A big room with peeling paint, bare floor, barred windows and conspicuous pipes and heating ducts abutted on a yard that had an ailanthus tree. In a bricked recess where a coal stove had been was a rickety, greasy gas range. I saw an ancient icebox, an iron sink piled with dirty dishes, and a battered kitchen table, supporting a fairly new Underwood typewriter. The place had the frowsiness of poverty plus indifference to housekeeping. "The going's not so good," I said.

"On the contrary. We're not precisely plutocrats but we both have jobs." Horace, Jessie went on to tell me, was working for the Provincetown Playhouse on MacDougal Street, designing sets, though since the theater was not commercial his pay was sporadic and picayune. "He's making a name; he'll be famous, just you wait and see." She herself was doing piecework, reading for the eastern office of a Hollywood motion picture company. "Such garbage! I could do better with both hands tied behind my back."

"Why don't you?" I asked.

"I will. I've started a play."

"Good luck!"

"You can count on it," she said.

"Get any help from Horace's family?"

"We're on our own," she said. "And at the risk of sounding repetitious, may I add we're doing fine."

We watched a large cockroach scoot out into the sink—I with horror, Jessie with indifference—when she took a Mason jar of red ink from the drainboard. She lifted three cloudy glasses from a dusty shelf, gave me the glasses while she carried in the jar. Horace had sprawled on the bed, his trousers not adjusted properly. "She been complaining?" Horace asked.

"She's been bragging," I said.

"She'd better not complain. Her papa laid down the rules."

Silent and unsmiling, Jessie poured the wine. Horace sat up to wave his glass toward both of us. "The home-town kids! The blessed hicks!"

"Proud of it," Jessie said.

"That's my girl," I said.

"Mine," Horace said.

"Don't fight over me, for gosh sakes," Jessie said. That startled me. I liked the girl all right, though never had I contemplated ownership.

We drank. The wine was vinegary. Horace flexed his skinny arms above his head. "Got a great story for you, Sam. Saving it, hoping you'd turn up. What Jessie's old man told me on that wedding night."

"Oh, Horace, no!" By the panic in Jessie's voice, I gathered the story hadn't been saved for me, but told too frequently.

"Nah, nah." Horace wagged a bony finger. "Sam has got to hear it. He'll appreciate it. Who else do we know knows your old man?" He set his glass on the floor and arranged himself, pulling his shirt-sleeves down, straightening his trouser belt, getting all of him in order, as if dressing to play a part. "The whole experience was one I couldn't have imagined in a million years. Coming into that smoky kitchen with that enormous woman with the monstrous pompadour, frying those pancakes. Believe me, Sam, so stunned was I by her proportions I missed a lot of detail. All my eye caught was the flypaper swinging from the ceiling over that dough on the table and a pair of tall brass candlesticks on a shelf. But that parlor, that wedding scene, I got every bit. It was like a setting for *The Dybbuk*, the red canopy, the snickering kid who helped you hold it up, the beards, the rabbi's wife, with wig, the squalling, squabbling babies underfoot, and the reluctant bride. . . ."

"Horace, quit!"

He paid no attention. "Sam, were you aware of the moment

51

after the mumbo jumbo beneath the velvet tent, when Herman seized the bridegroom's arm and led him from the cakes and wine into his bedchamber? Did you wonder what happened there?"

I shook my head. Actually, I hadn't given it any thought. Celia's mourning for her Good Fairy had distracted me. Actually, too, I didn't wish to know—even a reporter respects certain kinds of privacy.

"I shall tell, and you shall know, all of it, complete. . . . . Herman waved me to a chair. 'Sit, sit, I don't keep you long.' Though he kept pacing, up and down, around. 'Young man, my new son, your fader did not come, so I must speak vid you.' " He'd caught Herman's voice, the hoarseness and the sibilance, due, I'd suspected, to badly fitted dental plates. "I wondered was he going to explain the birds and bees, and if so, Horace, concentrate; this will be priceless. 'Young man, my new son, your bringing-up vas different from Jessie's. I do not know vas you Bar Mitzvah.' (My comment, 'No, sir.') You did not know to say vun Hebrew void. I vould be happy if you vould study our religion. It is your religion also. I do not expect my daughter keep a kosher house.' " He paused to toss an amused glance at Jessie and tap the floor in a kind of gleeful, childish jiggle. " 'I ask only duh bod of you respect duh Jewish God and raise your children up vid Jewishness.' " Again the gleeful jiggle. "Then he held his right hand up and pointed with the other hand to where an index finger was missing. 'Dis vas my own sacrifice,' he said, 'to duh Laws of duh Jewish religion. Abraham, our forefader, he vas prepared to sacrifice his son, Isaac, at duh command of God. So from dere comes duh Law of duh Bris Millah. My finger I gave to keep duh Law of duh Kashruth.' Now, there, Sam Rosenbaum, is one for Dr. Freud. Little Isaac's penis-tip and Herman Weiss's finger. Sliced off. Sacrified. The symbolism's perfect. And incredible."

Incredible to me, for sure. In those early nineteen twenties, the urban intelligentsia in the United States had rushed to study and embrace the theories of the Viennese doctor. We in the hinterlands had heard only leering tidbits about sex symbols and dreams. It scared the bejesus out of us.

The disgust on Jessie's face was so painful I wanted to slap the whippersnapper's face. Herman's hand, to us in Grady's Mills, had been a symbol, too, though of another kind. It was an awesome mark of his integrity. Maybe, maybe, Horace did have some respect behind his shallow glibness, for his pale, freckled face fleetingly achieved sobriety. "That impressed me when I thought about it on the train," he went on to say. "Lots of boys made weird excuses to get out of military service, but as for mutilating your own hand!"

"I was in, were you?" I asked.

"Skip it," Jessie said quickly. "How about more wine?"

I put my hand over my glass. She refilled her own and Horace's.

" 'Let me tell to you vot is a vife is,' " Horace began again in that too-accurate imitation of Herman Weiss. " 'A vife is a helper. A Jewish vife lives for duh family, never for duhself. Mine Ida is to me a helper. Voiks vid me like a slave in duh store. Keeps duh house and raises up duh children, vorrying dey shall study, be somebodies, educated. . . .' "

Secondhand, I was getting, I realized, the longest speech—possibly the only speech—Herman had ever made.

" 'Ve have vorked, ve have sacrificed for duh children. Ve have lost vun child from duh house. Soon, God villing, duh odder also goes. Ve be two old people, all alone. Bring us naches, my new son. Jessie is a brilliant mind. She is an honest girl. She vill be a help for you.' Then he stood up, placed both hands on my head and said some Hebrew words. And that was all of it."

He eyed me, awaiting comment. I couldn't speak. I'd been touched and I'd been hurt. This callow lad had been mocking a good man and he'd been mocking us, the people who respected Herman Weiss, mocking principles that were also ours. How often he'd recited this, I could only guess; frequently, no doubt, a favorite parlor trick, he had it down so pat. Possibly hearing him tell it to strangers had not hurt Jessie as much as hearing it told to me. She was puffing like a chimney, the cigarette smoke across her eyes more concealing than her bridal veil had been. I tried a light jab at Horace. "*Your* father doesn't have an accent, I presume?"

He winked. "Oh, doesn't he! Hoch der Kaiser."

"Surprise, surprise," Jessie murmured. "I can't wait to hear it."

"You know, come to think of it"—he ignored her comment—"there's a touch of Lear in Jessie's old man." He leaned to the cater-cornered day bed to poke Jessie's knee. "Will you be Cordelia, love?"

"No, Lady Macbeth," I said.

She pressed her cigarette into a bowl of butts, tamping it down hard. "Papa won't be Lear." She stirred the ashes with her index finger. "There's no earthly kingdom he can lose. His is the kingdom of God. Eternal, everlasting." Brushing off her fingertips, she rose. "Let's go out and eat."

"I married the wrong Weiss girl," Horace said. "This one can't boil an egg." It was the first time Celia had been remembered by either one of us.

They led me up a dusty staircase on Sixth Avenue, rapped on a door, said "Good evening, Luigi" to an eye at a peephole, and we were admitted to a steamy room, redolent of oregano and garlic, where we feasted on antipasto, minestrone, squab, spaghetti, fruit and cheese and emptied two water pitchers of red wine. The dinner was on me. I was firm; they didn't fight me for the check. After all, Luigi sold that banquet plus the booze for one buck apiece, and I could go home and boast I had had entree to a speakeasy in New York. Of such triumphs was status made in places like Grady's Mills.

*   *   *

In April of the following year, I made my semiannual junket to New York and rang the bell of the Greenwich Village basement. Jessie, wearing a blue smock, horn-rimmed spectacles and a distracted air, opened the door. "Oh, Sam! Why didn't you telephone?"

"Never occurred to me you had a phone," I half apologized. "Glad to see me? Yes or no? No, I'll turn around and leave in a huff."

"The subway's quicker. Okay, okay, come in." She yanked my sleeve. "It's just I get cranky when I'm interrupted in the middle of a scene."

"That play?"

"That play. It's hell, a torment, but how I love the goddam thing. Come in, come in, don't stand in the doorway." She nudged me into the hall. "My bitchy landlady listens at the mouse holes.

She'll be sure I'm playing matinees." She slammed the door. "And where in the name of Jesus did you get that coat?"

I bristled at the profanity as much as at the insult to my balmacaan.

"This coat," I said, whirling to show it front and back, "was made by my father's golden hands, out of tweed loomed in Grady's Mills. By Leeds."

Her forehead crinkled, questioning.

"You've been long away, my child. We have a woolen mill. Set up by the family Leeds. Jacob Leeds, né Levy, out of Lodz, Poland. Brief sojourn in the British Isles. Levy emerges Leeds, tweed manufacturer. Abe Finkel has a tract for sale, Jake Leeds buys and builds, son Walter manages the factory. Fifty Goyim are employed."

"Gee whillikins!" She ran the cloth between her inky fingers. "Good goods. But hideous. I wouldn't wear it to a Polish funeral."

"Son Walter, aged twenty-five, getting bald," I said, "is marrying Sylvia."

"And who is Sylvia?"

"Abe Finkel's black-eyed Sadie."

She laughed. I laughed. We laughed together, doubling over, couldn't stop. "Aren't Jews ridiculous?" she gasped. "Chameleons. Change their names, their colorations, quick, quick, quick."

"Easy, kid," I said. "Did Ida and Herman think up Jessie?"

"Hush your mouth. Are you a Gentile spy? When's the wedding?"

"June. Hiram Grady Hotel ballroom. Philadelphia caterer."

"Pish-pish! Fancy-shmansy! If she sends me an invitation I'll ignore it. I despise the bitch. Celia's buddy-buddy. At school, she treated me like dirt."

"Your sister tried for Walter, too," I said. "Not a chance. Sylvia had the bosom. Her old man had the moola."

"My old man hasn't? Or are they keeping secrets?" She braced her spine against the passageway wall. "Christ! There were other guys in town. Rogoff. Katz. And the creep Slomowitz. What are they up to?"

"Hymie's polishing apples in Papa's fruit market. Isie's measuring yard goods in the Bon Ton. Joey's his father's right hand in the junkyard and man about town, with a car."

"Well?" Meaning, Why can't Celia grab one of those?

"No class," I said. "Your sister, be so kind as to remember, is a college girl."

"Pish," she said. "Who's she to be choosey?"

"Also, it's polite to wait until you're asked. Moreover, your mama still has hopes of me."

Her eyebrows rose above the spectacles. "You run like hell, you hear me, Sam?"

The passion made me smile. "Don't worry, kid," I said. "I hate Waldorf salad. And how about asking me to take off the coat, come in and sit?" It occurred to me she had kept the conversation going out here in the hall as a hint to make my visit brief, but having come this far I had no intention of running, and so I hung my coat on a peg and walked ahead of her into the front room. It looked frowsier than before.

"No wine," Jessie said. "How about a so-called beer?"

"Anything," I said. "And thank you politely." When she fetched a bottle and two milky tumblers, she was without the smock and cheaters. She had thinned, which was to the good, though her cheeks looked hollow. I pried off the bottle cap and poured. "Where's the master of the house?" I asked, handing her her glass. "When's Horace coming home?"

"Never, if my luck holds. Easy come, easy go."

I whistled. "Divorced?" There was no ring on her hand.

She caught my glance; her eyes rarely missed a trick. "Ten bucks at the pawnshop," she said. Then, unexpectedly, her naked fingers wove and writhed on her lap, before her head came up, spirited and arrogant. "I told him let his father buy us a divorce. The bastard never gave us a wedding gift; let him pay for the divorce. But darling Horace will not let me off the hook. My fatal charm. My intellect and what's between my thighs."

"Refinement, please." Like all men discomfited by a woman's forwardness, I reached for a cigarette.

"Don't be a miser. Give me one," she said.

Holding the match for her, I said, "I picked Horace for a lemon

56

the minute I laid eyes on him, Jessie. Why in hell did you marry him?"

Her eyes met mine, as always, candidly. "To get away from home. And—this I won't tell another soul—because I was afraid no one else would ask. Jessie, the too-smart kid who never had a date. Dragged behind the bushes, yes. Who wants that slop? Ask her for a dance? Ninny-on-your-tintype, Bub. Class valedictorian. Now, isn't that just great! My luck it was wartime; let's cut out the senior prom. No humiliation over the no bid." She dropped silent, puffing furiously, before, "Sam, all of life is either/or, and what was my alternative? Finish Emerson, go back to Grady's Mills, find an elocution teaching job in some one-horse town. And" —her mouth corners curled—"compete with Celia for Joey Slomowitz."

"How'd you get so smart so young?" I asked.

The question amused her. "Of course"—a trace of coyness— "there was you. But I never took *that* prospect seriously. Older brother. Bachelor uncle. It's practically incestuous."

"Have another cigarette," I said. "Your fingers are burning."

"And your face," she said. "Yes, thank you, sir, I will have another cigarette; I happen to have just run out." She lit it from the stub. "You won't believe this," she went on. "Actually, I felt flattered when Horace announced he'd like to marry me. Said he, too, couldn't live with his goddammed family, those Fifth Avenue Philistines. So there we were, orphans of the storm, waifs, rejects, and of a single mind, we thought." She shook ash from the cigarette with excessive vehemence. "You live and learn."

"Cliché," I said.

"Solid truth," she said. "And New York is a place for learning— that a cooperative dame is worth her weight in groceries." She paused, eyeing me, wondering whether I'd grasped what she was saying. I thought I had. I decided on no comment. "Sam, truly, I'm delighted you barged in. I was sitting, typing, famished, wondering where my dinner would come from."

I was readying an apology, since I had a date with Mabel Armbruster, the nurse I'd met in France, and on the phone Mabel had mentioned what a grand meal they served you for a dollar at Lorber's on Broadway: the olives were so crisp and fat, they alone were worth the price, and it was just across the street from the Metropolitan Opera, a hint that gave me the wild idea that maybe my *News-Record* credentials could get us in on passes. Mabel said that would be absolutely heavenly; she adored singing. However, something about Jessie made me hesitate. The girl did look hungry. "It'll be my pleasure," I replied.

She squeezed my arm. "I know a better place than Luigi's. They have Scotch."

"I'll have to use your phone," I said.

She caught on. "Postpone, don't call off your date." Then sighed, a long, deep sigh. "Restful. No gymnastics on the day bed after. Exercise, you know damn well, is dangerous on full stomachs."

We didn't talk much during dinner, she being occupied with gobbling and I with the upsetting thought that it was a shame that Herman Weiss's daughter had to hustle for her grub. As we left the speakeasy, I pressed a folded bill into her hand.

"What's that for?"

"Groceries," I said.

By the street lamp's foamy light, I could see her jawline hardening. She raised her arm as if to fling the bill away. I caught her fist and held it closed. "Idiot! Go on, be dramatic! Throw it in the gutter. Then, we'll grovel in the muck, the two of us, to hunt for it. I can't afford to throw away ten bucks. Sure as hell, you can't. So behave, be sensible. Say thank you, Sammy-buddy-pal, when I have I'll pay you back."

She eyed me stonily, growling, "Urrgh." I let go her fist. She opened her flaccid handbag and dropped the money in. No "thank-you, Sammy-buddy-pal."

While we walked to the basement flat, I talked to her Dutch Uncle. "Get a job, any kind of job: salesgirl, washing dishes, typing, minding kids. Quit writing plays till you have a knippel saved."

"How you run on, honey chile," she jeered.

"And listen to me, stupid." I pushed her chin up with my thumb. "When you're short, don't be proud. Or promiscuous. Prostitution is against the law. Cops haul you in for it. And if you do it for a dinner, just, the whore's union will get after you. Five bucks is the going rate. You're broke, you write a letter, hear? Or call me up collect—"

She muttered, "You should live so long."

"—and I'll send enough to keep you fed." I got the sentence finished.

"Good night, Mr. Rosenbaum," she said. "Preserve that coat. It's a museum piece."

Well, maybe she would turn out to be a playwright. She was a whiz at dialogue.

She didn't write or phone collect, and I told myself, Hell with the slut, if that's how she wants it, that's how she can have it, with my compliments. You make your bed, you lie in it, with the Seventh Regiment.

I came to New York again, went to Lorber's and to shows with Mabel, who was blonde and cuddlesome though on the dullish side. I didn't ring Jessie's doorbell or call her on the phone, and a year went by before I wrote a certain "Folk You Know": *"Among those present at the opening performance this week of Broadway's newest hit, 'The Awakening' by Jessica White, were Mr. and Mrs. Herman Weiss, parents of the playwright, and her sister, Miss Celia Weiss. The metropolitan critics were unanimous in their praise of the opus by this local girl and have predicted a long run for it."* Our paper ran it with a single-column halftone of the valedictorian's photograph. Herman's Grocery was closed while the kinfolk were in New York.

I stopped by to ask Ida how she had enjoyed the play. "What can I tell you, Sammy? Mr. Weiss and me, most of it we didn't understand. A poor Jewish family, living in a poor New York neighborhood. What do we know from such a life? We are country people, living in the mountains with fresh air. And such a family! Everybody mean to everybody, not a real Jewish family, loving one anudder, sacrificing. . . ."

"I know what you mean," I said.

"The skinny-herring husband I didn't see. What happened with them, Sammy? Maybe she told you? No? So I'll tell you what I think. Those kind of people, theater people, don't understand from family life. I read in the Yiddish paper cases just like this."

"What did the Yiddish paper say about the play?"

She shrugged. "They licked the fingers, I can't understand. So maybe she'll make a lots of money. So maybe she'll buy herself a decent dress. Like a slob she looked, the hair not even combed. Celia was so neat, so up to date. We went after in a kosher restaurant to have a glass tea and cake. A fine young man in the place, he couldn't take his eyes off her."

"Bye-bye," I said. "I have to run to work."

Celia Weiss's spinsterhood had become my cross. More than one of our mutual acquaintances had pointed out, at Ida's prompting, what an ideal match we'd make; she'd had two years of college, I'd had two. We were educated, Americanized Litvaks, our families were friends, and mine as anxious as Celia's to see me wed. I being an only son on whom my father counted to perpetuate the unique name of Rosenbaum. My mother fretted I'd be snared by a shiksa. She suspected, though she wasn't sure since I elected not to tell, a Mabel Armbruster in my life.

Sylvia Leeds, née Sadie Finkel, arranged intimate little evenings in her elaborately furnished house two doors from her mother's up on Eighth Street, where she tried out recipes from the *Settlement Cook Book*, with Celia functioning as critic, Walter and me as tasters. The purpose of the supper parties was so obvious I begged my mother to start a whispering campaign that overseas I had contracted an unmentionable, incurable disease. She declined to cooperate. "So what is so terrible with Celia?" she asked and chortled wickedly. "A diamond with golden hands!"

I sent a congratulations wire to Jessie's old address in the Village. Western Union notified me they could not deliver it. I readdressed it to the theater. After a fortnight, a typed penny postcard came. "Thanks for the congrats. Well deserved. When next you get to town, I'll have two on the aisle down front for you and Madam X. Call me this number. . . ." Signed "Jessica."

The show had been running a good half year before I scooped up two-on-the-aisle-down-front at the box office and on the phone arranged to meet the playwright after the performance.

Mabel assured me she *loved* the play, lying gamely since she'd used Act Three for catching up on sleep. I liked the play moderately. It had vitality, dramatic drive and crackling dialogue. Not Shakespeare, nor Eugene O'Neill, remotely; even several steps down from Elmer Rice. (By what right was I a critic? Every right. I came in on a pass, didn't I?) *The Awakening* was clearly autobiographical, though its setting was a New York slum and its sibling rivals boys, sons of immigrants: the younger a sensitive adolescent, shrinking from dogmatic parents, humiliated by their crudities, escaping through poetry into a fantasy world; the older complacent, conforming, preferred, and raising hell with the poet's sensibilities. The elders were grotesque, to my mind unfairly so. The basic theme—the clash between the generations—and the proletarian realism of the background was in the geist of the period. The acting was adequate. The cast took five curtain calls.

Jessie was waiting at the head of the aisle, wearing a ruby velvet suit, her bobbed hair shining, kempt. "Well?" She held out her hand.

"Beyond my hopes and expectations. Mabel Armbruster, Jessica White."

"Miss White! I am so thrilled to meet the author." Mabel's soprano quavered. "I was so moved by your lovely play, I almost cried. It was so true, so—so. . . ."

"Don't strain," Jessie answered. "Come home and have a cup of coffee."

"I'd be thrilled, just thrilled. You're sure it isn't too much trouble!"

"Let's hop a cab," Jessie said.

She had moved; that was why my telegram hadn't been delivered. She was living, as befitted a successful playwright, in a brownstone in the East Forties. The parlor ceiling was lofty, the parquet floor dotted with Oriental rugs. There was a white marble fireplace whose polished tools were bright as Ida's candlesticks, tasteful furniture and shelves of books. Jessie pressed two fingers to her lips, pointing to closed white folding doors. "Quiet. Horace may be sleeping."

My eyebrows twitched. "He's back?" I glanced at her hand. Still no wedding ring.

"Fetched him from the hospital," she said.

Mabel said, "I'm a nurse. Can I do anything?"

"Nothing. His mother's with him, giving tender, loving care. Make yourselves at home. I mentioned coffee. In a public place it doesn't pay to advertise, but there's Scotch and wine on the premises."

Mabel said she'd settle for the coffee. To impress her with my character, I said I didn't wish to flout the prohibition law. "But do you know how to make coffee?" I asked the playwright.

"Show me how," she said.

Mabel decided to be tactful. "I'm sure Sam will be all the help you'll need. Let me relax in this charming room."

The Underwood stood on a porcelain-topped table in a spic-and-span kitchen. Jessie caught my querying glance. "I've always written in a kitchen. Has success changed Jessie Weiss? Not so you could notice it."

"Horace?" I replied. "You patched it up?"

"Think I'm nuts? He flopped on a sidewalk, drunk, and split his skull. Wonder—yes, a pity—that he didn't die; don't look at me that way, I am no hypocrite. They carted him to Bellevue. Only name and address on his person was yours truly. A cop rang my bell. And what was I to say? Don't know the bum, don't want him, go away, don't bother me? So off I went to Bellevue. And there he lay, the poor slob, coming back from hell and yonder, clutching both my hands. 'Jessie, you are all I've got.' Which is crap. Mother, father, uncles, aunts, cousins whom he reckons by the dozens—" Tears glazed her eyes, canceling out the flippancy. "Yes, I brought him here. Yes, I telephoned his parents. They had a right to know and a goddamned duty to look after him. And in that stinking ward they met the screwball from the sticks who'd stolen their dear darling. And, Sam, what happened? Come on, guess! They bowed down low . . . to Jessica White, the celebrity. Out of my way, I'm going to vomit."

"Not on the clean linoleum," I said. "And watch out for the dress."

She didn't vomit. The gorge dropped faster than it had risen. "Tell me, smart guy, tell me, what else was I to do? He's a human being. I'm a human being, and legally I'm still his wife; I had to bring him home, didn't I? Damned good thing there were twin beds. Someone has to be right there, on call, at night, when he needs the pan. . . . Oh, dear mother helps. She does the seven P.M.

to midnight shift and two matinees. And a maid comes in every day. I trust you noticed that this kitchen is immaculate."

She took a jar of coffee from a cupboard, set it on the range preliminary to coffee-making, though not yet ready to put the percolator on. "It was nauseating. It *is* nauseating. The bitch goddess waves her wand. The kid from the Hill becomes a queen." She leaned against the kitchen wall, simmering down. "Shtunks," she muttered. "All the world's a shtunk. All but thee and me. And sometimes I think. . . ." She paused, looking mischievous.

"I dare, I double-dare," I said.

"You are my rock, my fundament." Her tone was sassy, mocking. "My true and honorable knight, Sir Shmulke Galahad. . . ."

"Continue," I said.

"And in the lonely hours between two and four A.M., I think of you with awe and disbelief. . . ." She broke off. "Excuse, pliz. Make the coffee; I have to get something."

She whisked from the kitchen. I measured coffee and water into the percolator, lit the gas. She returned to press a bit of paper into my hand. "Don't do this to me again," she said.

The paper was a ten-dollar bill. "Thanks," I said. "Any time."

"There will not be an any time." She sat down before the typewriter and beat a tattoo on its keys. "Never poor no more. Jessie's done her tour of duty with the proletariat. She knows the stink of poverty. She will have none of it." She bit her lower lip, waiting, then looked up at me with a kind of somber anger. "Sam, for once and for all, let's quit kidding; I have something important to say to you." Her eyes met mine, implacable and slightly menacing. "Nothing, nothing in all this world, is more despicable, more degrading, than a small handout to a friend in need. Particularly when a lecture comes along with it." She sucked her breath in sharply, the way she used to as a kid when she was readying to explode. "Those shtunks who bought me dinner and took it out in trade were better men than you. They let me also give. And may I add, in modesty—which isn't quite the word—they got value received. But you, Sir Shmulke Galahad, you offered only charity. And charity, in my book, is an extremely dirty word. It degrades him who receives and also him who gives. Because, in his heart, he knows he is a lousy hypocrite. He's giving money, only money, to grab something for himself. The feeling-good, the feeling-big. You're a nothing. I'm a king. Giving money is a greed, my friend, not a generosity. Now"—briefly, a pause for breath—"if you had said, 'Tough going, kid, but I have faith in you. Let me help you over a hump, share what little I possess with an equal, with a friend.' But no, you offered me advice instead. Get a job. Stop screwing. Grady's Mills morality! Ten lousy dollars gave you the boon and privilege. . . ."

I stood flabbergasted, reddening to the ears, unaware that in this kitchen where the percolator burped I was receiving wisdom. Of all the words Herman's daughter Jessie, a high, wide and handsome talker, was to say to me through all our years, none would be more pertinent to my own existence, none closer to the bull's eye of truth. However, now I couldn't let her get away with it. I needed to hit back. All I could think of was, "How'd you get so smart so young?"

She sneered, "Buy a new line. May I recommend the Bayonne Cliché Company," and banged the typewriter keys with her open palm. We stayed silent, seething, both of us, while she untangled the keys. Then, she rose and smiled—"Forgive me, Sam. I had to get that off my chest. It's been heavy there"—and wound her arms around my neck, cooing into my ear, "I love you, Sir Shmulke Galahad," before she hauled off and slapped my face, not hard enough to tingle, just hard enough to let me know exactly where I stood, after which she went to a cupboard and took cups and saucers from a shelf, talking while she did. "All that is academic, now. Fini. I *am* going to be rich. You watch, Sam, look out for my dust."

I found my voice. "With Horace hanging on?"

"No siree-bob. The very second he is on his feet, out the poor slob goes. *Out. Out. Out.* And I give up this place. It's a sublet; nothing here is mine except the Underwood. Then off I go to Paris, to sit on Montparnasse, to write. And to get me a divorce. . . . That coffee smells done." She lined up four willow-patterned cups and saucers on a lacquered tray. "Dear mother may deign to have a cup before the chauffeur calls." She popped the refrigerator open. "Dammit, no cream. We'll have to borrow milk from Mr. Simon. He has changed his beverage." She let me carry in the tray, marching grandly, head up, in front of me.

A petite, nervous-seeming woman with corrugated iron-gray hair was chatting with Mabel in the living room. "Jessica, darling!" The woman rose, politely deferential. "He's really better. Why, tonight he asked me to play the radio."

"This is Sam Rosenbaum from Grady's Mills," Jessie answered her. "A Yid from up the Hill. He was at our wedding. Far and away, the best man."

Mrs. Simon gulped, said "Oh!" and flushed and twittered. "Wouldn't you like to go in, say hello?"

I glanced at Jessie, not trusting to my judgment, murmuring, "It's late."

"It's later than you think," she said.

After the oratory in the kitchen, I could take a petty satisfaction from knowing Jessie wasn't always brilliant. When she ran low on original dialogue, she shopped at the Bayonne Cliché Company, too.

Three

Steve Durgin, a cop I'd met in the practice of my trade, dropped into the newsroom one afternoon in the fall of 1926. He tapped me on the arm. "Talk to you, Bub."

I took a quick look around. Mallory, the city editor, was away from his desk, probably in the stereo room knocking off a penny-ante game between press runs. My colleagues were lolling at their desks, ostentatiously pretending not to be inquisitive. "Here or privately?" I asked.

"Private," Durgin said.

I led him to the toilet, where I latched the door. Let any bastard in a hurry bang, not barge in on us.

"You live up the Hill?" Durgin began. "You know all them folks?"

"Man, woman, child."

"A family named . . . Shlumpowitch?"

"Slomowitz? Max?"

"That's the one." He scratched his jowls. "Not Max. Joe, Joe Shlumpowitch."

"The son," I said. "He been stealing brass?"

"Not stealing," Durgin said.

Mine not to probe, his to enlighten. I waited. He obliged.

"This morning Ed McCarthy come in the station house. You know Ed? Works in Babcock's Mill. Handyman. Boozer. Hauled him in a couple a Sattidy nights ago. Disturbin' the peace. Beatin' his old woman. . . . Nah, you didn't read it on the blotter. Didn't book 'im. What's the point in it? Let him sleep it off in a cell. Turned him out to early Mass. So he figures I'm his friend. Well, today Ed comes in with Dolores, his kid. Wants a warrant, chargin' rape. Girl is in the family way. So you could notice, no mistake. Seventeen, he says."

"Statutory," I said.

"That it is. Ten years in the pen if Shlumpowitch don't marry her."

"I knew that Reo'd get him into trouble," I said.

He looked confused. "Reo? That what you Hebes call a prick?"

I didn't smile. "An auto. Reo make. Since the old man made a pile, Joey's been joyriding. All the mill girls in the county. . . ."

Durgin's jaw jutted. "Sex maniac. Maybe we better run him in. You know how us Irish feel about the chastity."

I'd heard the line. I also knew the ethnic backgrounds of bastardy in our county; hence, all I said was, "Joe's folks are decent people, good citizens. Remember the Liberty Bonds the old man bought? The Mayor gave him a certificate. You wouldn't want to shame them, would you?"

"That's why I come to talk to you," he said.

I rattled coins in my pants pocket, he watching me, waiting for the crucial words. Eppes, the old Jewish instinct, fifty per cent reliable, prompted me. "How much?" I asked.

His glance pretended to rebuke me; how could one equate virtue with cash? "Ed trusts me," he said. "There's the expenses—" He dropped his mask. "Sam, what's it worth to get them off the hook?"

I shrugged. "Haven't any notion what the traffic's going to bear."

"They got dough. All you Hebes. . . ."

"Take it easy, Steve. In my family, five bucks is big dough."

"Exceptin' present company," he conceded. "And my apologies." He stepped up to the urinal, opened his fly, not to waste an opportunity. "Sam, I come to you knowing you're acquainted with the other party," he continued over the hiss of his stream. "I come to ask you talk to them, tell them the conditions that prevail. Me, I can talk to Ed and he'll settle how I say. Just me asking where Dolores got the shiner. A peach. That Ed's wild when he's boozin'." He closed his pants, looked toward the wash basin. Apparently, he knew the niceties, though he wasn't wasting time with them. "Now, if we brung both sides together, you and me." The gleam in his eyes, no words required, told me he'd be in on the take. "You talk to old Shlumpowitch, then you call me on the telephone first thing tomorrer mornin'. You say somethin' like, 'Durgin, I just seen the organ grinder's monkey walkin' up the street.' I ask you 'Where?' You gimme the time, the address where we meet."

The knob was rattled. There was peremptory pounding on the door. I raised the latch. Mallory strode in. He is an old soldier—Spanish-American War. He exudes military discipline. He eyed us frigidly. "Welcome to our urinal," he said to Durgin. "The *News-Record* is not inhospitable, though I have not heard your station house is lacking these facilities. Get the hell out, both of you."

We slunk. He'd be asking questions. My answers needed to be good. Mallory despised corruption. It was his business to.

Slomowitz went ashen when I told him. He snarled, "The bummer! The outcast!" He moaned. "My wife is a sick woman. She will take convulsions." He pounded his desk. "The girl is a no-good, a tramp. What can she prove? I betcha she's been laying around with every shikker in the Flats. She finds out Joey's family has a couple dollars, so it's a blackmail, a holdup."

"Or ten years in the pen; she's only seventeen," I said. "Listen, Max, her father came in for a warrant. My contact talked him out. For the time being." Gratuitously, I added, "It's no skin off my back. I only got into this to protect the good name of the Jews."

"How much?" Slomowitz asked.

"We didn't talk turkey," I said. "But you can take it easy. Guys like McCarthy don't think big."

Max rocked his head between his palms. "All my life I slaved, I struggled, I worked like a dog. So I made a couple dollars. Now that bummer, Joey. . . ."

"Get him out of town," I said. "And married fast. To a nice Jewish girl." Then, a brainwave struck me. I was dazzled by a vision of freedom from pursuit and I was mean enough to seize the opportunity. "I know just the girl: Herman Weiss's daughter, Celia. She could make a man of Joe."

Next morning I phoned the station house and told Durgin the organ grinder's pet could be nabbed at eight o'clock that night in the shack in Slomowitz's junkyard.

"You be there, too," he said. "I don't trust those monkeys."

68

Tough luck. Being witness made me an accessory to blackmail, which, in our statute books, is criminal. I went to the junkyard early, to make sure Max was calm, prepared to negotiate, without shouting, threats or blows.

The night was nippy. A pumpkin-colored moon was rising, gilding the rusting iron pipes and corroded copper boilers out of which Max Slomowitz was coining gold. The shanty's shades were drawn. Threads of light showed around the edges and between the cracks. The door was unlocked.

Max sat hunched above a ledger at his roll-top desk, small and shrunken, old and weary-looking in the wan light of the hanging oil lamp. Above the desk, in a gilt frame, was the Liberty Bond testimonial. A fire was going in a potbellied stove, salvaged from somewhere. There was a ragged wicker rocker, a kitchen chair with busted seat—a junk collector's gleanings—and a square of dirty, torn linoleum on the floor.

Max closed the ledger, carried it to a mouldy safe, put it carefully away and twirled the knob. I took the rocking chair. He went back to his desk swivel. "Nu?" He shrugged his hands. "Where's the other party?"

"Where's Joe?"

"We are opening an office in New York," he said.

Max was smarter than I'd realized. He'd removed the culprit.

"Sammy, how much do they want?"

"Don't offer. See what's on their minds." I'd been wondering, too, having had no previous experience in this area. "A man like Ed McCarthy," I ventured, "might think a couple hundred is a fortune. The cop is the one to keep in mind. He'll take from McCarthy. But also he'll expect from you. So you will put one hundred dollars in a plain envelope and I will deliver it." This they never taught me in the School of Journalism in New York. Eppes had dictated Durgin's price.

Max looked shocked. Apparently, his business operations had been honest; he'd had no experience bribing cops. Any bootlegger in our county could have put him wise. Before he had a chance to voice his shock, we heard the adversary's footsteps. I got up. Max, watching me, did likewise, backing against his desk.

Ed McCarthy, a hulk, entered first, shouldering the open door as if he meant to shatter it, after him a wisp of girl, shivering in a sleazy coat, bunched across the middle where it emphasized a bulge, and, trailing them, Steve Durgin, in mufti. Max threw a furtive glance toward the girl.

"Mr. Slomowitz, meet Mr. Durgin," I said. Durgin grunted. Max nodded. No hand was extended. I didn't present McCarthy and Dolores. They were strangers to me, too.

"Give the girl a chair. She's in a delicate condition," Durgin said.

I moved away from the rocker. Dolores sank into it and fixed her attention on the cracked linoleum. Her father took his stance beside the chair, towering over it. Sniffing belligerently, he inspected the shanty. His roving gaze halted at the iron safe. Durgin straddled the kitchen chair. I leaned against the door, in neutral ground, between belligerents. Max sat on his swivel, the castors rasping as he wheeled to face the cop, his eyes avoiding McCarthy and Dolores. We stayed silent, looking grim and hostile, all of us except Dolores, who looked pitiful. Her snub nose was blue with cold; her pallid cheek had a purple bruise beneath the right eye. Her dull blonde hair was frizzed unbecomingly; coarse cotton stockings drooped on her pipestem legs. Perhaps she had had sweetness, charm. In the shanty in the junkyard all I saw was misery, shame and advanced pregnancy.

Durgin commenced. "You see the girl's condition, Shlumpowitch?"

Dolores caressed her middle, saying nothing.

Max hawked, saying nothing.

"You know who is responsible?" Durgin asked.

Max found his voice. "I don't believe."

"Tell him." McCarthy's ham hand crushed his daughter's shoulder.

"Joe forced me," the girl faltered, not looking up.

"Did he promise to marry you?" Durgin asked.

Her mouth opened to speak but it was her father's voice we heard, loud and harsh and venomous. "We wouldn't have the sheeny for a gift." Crimson flooded Max's face. His fingers closed and opened spasmodically. Hitherto, I'd never thought of Max as prototype, yet thus I saw him now. With hooked nose and black

70

pointed beard, he was the cringing Jew of every libelous carica-
ture. Now, both men were fathers whose offspring had sinned,
and fornication is impossible except by two, yet only Joey's father
trembled, as if his child, and his alone, was guilty, and Joey's
father, only he, merited the punishment. And watching those two
fathers, I felt another thing, the inherited hostilities, profound and
permanent: in one, hatred of a people blamed for Calvary, in the
other, tribal memories of the Inquisition and pogroms.

"Seventeen," Durgin said ominously.

Dolores raised her head, again to speak. Her father pushed it
down. "Rape," McCarthy said.

"Ten years," Durgin said. "Him"—he jerked thumb toward me—
"he begged me hold off the warrant, not disgrace the Jewish
people here."

McCarthy pursed his mouth. His spittle sizzled on the hot stove
lid.

I cleared my throat. "I assured Mr. Durgin you'd do the right
thing," I told Max, "because you were an honorable man." My
hand wave, my head nod, directed their attention toward the
framed certificate above the desk. No one looked at it.

"How much?" McCarthy growled.

The dickering began and it was brief. My pre-judgment had
been accurate. Ed McCarthy sold his daughter's virtue at a bargain
basement price, three hundred dollars cash, taken from Max's
iron safe, counted out upon his desk. McCarthy stuffed the wad of
paper into a jacket pocket. Durgin winked at me. The unborn
babe fared better. For it, by oral agreement witnessed by Durgin
and myself, ten dollars would be mailed to Dolores McCarthy
every month until the child reached the working-papers age of
sixteen.

"Thank you very much," Dolores said.

"I wish you luck," Max mumbled through his beard and gritted
teeth.

The girl raised her arm as if to offer him her hand. Her father
yanked her from the chair and, fist prodding her spine, pushed her
toward the door. It occurred to me he might have been gentler,
since her delinquency was paying off.

71

"You wouldn't have a shnapps, a bottle of wine, around?" Durgin asked.

Max did not reply. I saw them to the door. "Four o'clock in the men's room," I told Steve.

"Knew you were reliable." He seemed extremely pleased with how the meeting had gone, only one insult and a minimum of dickering.

Max handed me an envelope with ten ten-dollar bills. He locked the safe and shanty. We walked together up the Hill. The harvest moon was full overhead, the temperature dropping. We were chilled and not feeling talkative. At my corner, leaving him, I said, "Stop worrying, there won't be more trouble."

"God willing," he told his beard.

"The girl's not mean," I said. "Her old man put her up to it."

"The bastard!" He caught the double edge of the word. "It's hard to be a father in America." He sighed. "Too much money, no respect."

"Get Joe married," I said. "That'll settle him."

Mallory gave me a hard time. Why in hell was that cop hanging around with me in the toilet? By God, if we were perverts, or if we were conniving on some crooked deal, he'd run both of us out of town. "Durgin's having trouble with his wife," I said. "Wants a shoulder to cry on."

"And what advice could *you* give him? Send him to his priest."

I never told Mallory or anyone else about the transaction in Slomowitz's shack. As far as I know, neither Durgin nor Max Slomowitz, each for obvious reasons, ever mentioned it, Max not even to his wife. It was one secret sedulously kept from the gossips on the Hill. Maybe Ed McCarthy, flashing greenbacks in speak-easies in the Flats, blabbed a bit about squeezing an old Jew, though I doubt he went further than the obscene cursing of all Jews which was standard practice in his set. And Dolores wasn't a troublemaker, close-mouthed even in childbirth.

She died after a delivery which was prolonged and agonizing, she being narrow-hipped, rachitic, malnourished. Caesarian section might have saved her, but the midwife chose to send for a priest rather than an obstetrician. She did have a glimpse of her black-haired boy and managed to whisper "Jody," an acronym of Joe and D that became his name. She made a good Contrition, Durgin came to tell me, though what she told the priest remained between him and her and God. The *News-Record* listed her in its obituary column, stating cause of death as "complications," which was true enough and customary, since the local undertakers, who notified the paper whenever they were summoned to a corpse, ascribed to "complications" most deaths without visible abrasions or shattered bones. Some of Max's down payment provided a silk-lined casket and a Mass, and Dolores's mother undertook to raise the child. Max mailed the ten a month conscientiously to Ed McCarthy, though I began to hear mutterings in saloons in the Flats about rotten, stingy Jews. Grady's Mills never had had overt anti-Semitism. However, in the months after Dolores's death, a miasma was perceptible.

One night the lock on Max's shanty was forced, the safe moved to the middle of the room, though not broken open. Max complained to the police. Steve Durgin was assigned to investigate. He did a Sherlock Holmes imitation, pretended to look for finger- and footprints, and assured Max it was just a bunch of kids, show-ing off they were strong, they could shove around a heavy safe, nothing pinched, no harm done. To me, Steve said he had given Ed McCarthy what for; another stunt like that, he'd lock him up for breaking and entering. Ed must have been cockeyed to try it.

Now and then, when a fire or an arrest took me to the Flats, I'd catch a glimpse of the grandson of Ed McCarthy and Max Slomo-witz, a pretty child, black-haired like his father, blue-eyed like his mother—Irish and Jewish genes combine agreeably—but usually filthy dirty and with a running nose, sitting by himself on the doorstep of his grandparents' shanty, playing with a stick or empty can, never with toys or other kids.

When the depression hit Grady's Mills, the factories shut down and McCarthy was out of work. With time on his hands, he drank rotgut and beat his wife. One night she fell—or was pushed—down the steps within the house. Her neck was broken. There was a loose board, the police found; it could have been an accident. The next-door neighbors had heard only Jody screaming. Before the wake, McCarthy vanished. Since there was no money in the house, the county buried Jody's grandmother. Neighbors looked

73

after the boy for a week, then dispatched him to St. Michael's orphanage. I doubt St. Michael's was informed that little Jody might bring them ten dollars every month to pay for his porridge. Two of those who knew were dead, one a fugitive from justice. And my surmise is that Max, informed of the accident and its aftermath, decided to let discretion take the place of generosity, for by that time Mr. and Mrs. Joseph Sloan were personages of social consequence. As for Durgin, he'd become ambitious for promotion. If the Fathers at St. Michael's, tipped off, had chosen to investigate, the revelation of the facts behind the financing might have proved embarrassing to Steve as well as to the Sloans.

Joe had changed his name informally to Sloan before Jody was born to Dolores and, legally, before Ilene was born to him and his wife, Celia.

Max Slomowitz had acted on my second suggestion with alacrity, just as he'd responded to the first. Since tell-a-woman was how news spread on the Hill, most people knew the details of the courting of Celia Weiss.

The marriage was arranged, old-country style, with the groom invisible and the bride uninformed during the preliminaries. The rabbi called on Herman and Ida to sound them out. Herman remained silent while the rabbi hemmed and hawed, trying to praise Joey Slomowitz, but Ida, hard put to suppress her glee, cried, "So let the parents come and talk. Who needs shadchens on the Hill?"

Max and his wife, Lena, made a formal call on Herman and Ida, at night, after the grocery was closed. Celia, who'd been given hints of what was in the wind, had tactfully taken herself off to Sylvia's. The Slomowitzes were offered tea, homemade cherry preserves and sponge cake, after which the men sat, milking beards, while Ida delivered an oration about her family tree. Did they know—she was never one to boast—that she was blood cousin to the celebrated Vilna Gaon, of blessed memory? Yiches of the highest order. Whoever climbed a branch of that tree became attached to nobility. Joe's father kept his head down, aware that Joe, that bummer, that outcast, was damaged goods, snatched by timely, secret intervention from ten years in the penitentiary. Herman, being of two minds about the shidduch, said nothing.

Ida, basking in her yiches and sensing, though she didn't know the specifics, that there was urgency behind this matchmaking, took an upper hand and drove a hard bargain: there must be a diamond engagement ring and a solid gold watch for Celia; the Slomowitz family was to pay half the wedding costs, buy a set of Rogers' silverware, and furnish the couple's home with up-to-date furniture, no junk (a slur at Max's occupation), everything as high class as Sylvia Leeds's.

"And what do you give?" Lena Slomowitz, also not knowing the specifics, demanded.

Ida's two chins rose. "A college girl, a teacher, a balaboosta, first class."

"Tachles," cried Mrs. Slomowitz, meaning, Come down to earth.

"You should ask? A girl, a diamond, with golden hands. Come, I show you, napkins, tablecloths, hemstitch, embroidered, cutwork, drawn work. Like for a queen. Everything the best."

Max made his own requests and rationalized them adroitly. The marriage must take place right away; Joe is lonesome in New York, no home, he has to eat in restaurants, and busy, busy, setting up the branch office; a wonderful business head that boy has; his wife will never need to put her hands in cold water. The nuptials must be celebrated in New York, he added, explaining that his relations and his wife's, none of whom had ever made a trip to Grady's Mills, lived in Manhattan, Brooklyn and the Bronx. An only son gets married, the family should be invited, so if everybody had to travel out to Grady's Mills, where would they sleep? Moreover, in New York, the best hotels arranged kosher catered affairs and—he asked no favors—he would personally pay whatever it might cost. The Weisses and whichever local friends they chose to ask could ride to New York on the train at his expense, only not too many, please. Ida, who'd had visions of a wedding at the Hiram Grady as elegant as the Finkel-Leeds nuptials, capitulated to the glamour of a catered affair in New York. She began to enumerate kinfolk, hers and Herman's, who all these years had been nameless and invisible, who positively must be asked, and to anticipate the presents they would give. Not cupidity, understand, just exuberance.

When Celia was officially informed, she threw herself into the situation with what can best be described as an air of excessive triumph. What her down-deep emotions were at learning she'd be yoked to Joe in perpetuity, I would not dare to guess. For sure, he'd never been this college girl's ideal. But Aaron Leiberman was dead, Isie Katz as good as engaged (all but the ring) to the younger Rogoff girl, Nettie; Hymie Rogoff indifferent, Sam Rosenbaum recalcitrant, and only Slomowitz available. A professional marriage broker might, in time, have produced a candidate, provided a sufficient dowry was posted. A groom in hand is worth ten in remote possibility. She had been sought, bribed with regal gifts, and a sumptuous New York wedding suited her just fine. Of her local acquaintances, the only ones she was eager to invite were Sylvia and Walter Leeds and their respective parents, whose lavish presents could be counted on, and me, no doubt to torture me with envy of the lucky groom.

Sensing she had an upper hand, she added two requests: for a honeymoon in Paris, "Where my sister Jessie is," and that Joe change his name to something more American. Her future father-in-law agreed but balanced it with new stipulations of his own: there must be no write-up in the paper until after the wedding, no publicity on the betrothal or the wedding arrangements. When a shadow of disappointment crossed Celia's face, Max stammered till he came up with a valid explanation: once the engagement was announced, the entire Hill would expect invitations; you could spend a fortune transporting everybody to New York, and even if they paid their railroad fares, a catered wedding dinner at so much a couple—Celia was a practical young lady, would she not rather have the money for a Paris honeymoon? After they were hitched Sam could make a nice write-up.

That she was Joe's life sentence for the rape of Dolores, Celia could not have guessed, since those who knew weren't of a mind to blab. Yet had she known I don't believe it would have changed her mind, she having no alternative save arid spinsterhood. And to my knowledge, the fact Joe's parents had done the courting did not trouble her too much. She'd known Joe all her life. Between them there had never been the remotest prospect of romantic love.

It's hard to explain the male indifference to Celia Weiss. She was not repulsive. Her figure was trim, though her bosom was flat. She could sing and she could dance; she could bake a cherry pie and sew a pretty seam. Yet she couldn't rouse the beast in men.

During Christmas week when her school was closed, she and Ida traveled to New York for a rendezvous with the prospective groom. I can't record a rush into each other's arms, since I wasn't there and Ida and Celia were mum about it after they returned, but I do know Celia brought back a solitaire diamond, set in platinum, and a platinum wrist watch. The ring and watch had set Max back far more than the virtue of Dolores.

Celia rang me on the phone to tell me what I already knew, in intimate detail, that she was engaged to Joe. Was I surprised? Not entirely, I forced myself to say, and in my opinion Joe was a lucky man.

"It is kind of you to say so. You're such a good sport, Samuel, to take it so nicely. I shall never forget how sweet you've been to me. And I trust we shall remain good friends."

She asked me not to write the engagement up for "Folk You Know." Father Slomowitz didn't want the entire Hill clamoring for invitations. "Of course, Samuel, you are an exception. We want you." She added Joe wished me to be his best man—he'd have written to ask me but he was busy as a beaver, getting everything all set before they sailed for Paris.

"Will I need a tux?"

"Certainly. Rent it. Charge it to Father Slomowitz. He's paying for everything."

Washington's Birthday was the date. She would be teaching to the end of the semester; you can't resign in the middle of a term, it's not fair to *them*. Up to then she'd be too, too busy, running to New York to select furniture and have fittings; her bridal gown, her trousseau were being made by a New York modiste. Doubtless, on those weekend trips she also said hello to the exiled lover.

My mother was miffed that she'd not been invited. "So Celia catched a feller. A matzeah. Prost. Ida is ashamed, must be, she don't ask nobody from her friends. She sends the daughter two years in the college, so they make a shidduch with the junkman's son. From high school, not even he didn't grajiate."

With Slomowitz relations and Weiss kin there was a sizable gathering in the Hotel Astor ballroom. Celia was an eyes-swollen bride, though svelte in white satin with a long veil and train. Joe, in tails and silk hat, was a nervous groom, who kept glancing over his shoulder, as if expecting to see cops at the ballroom door. Sylvia Leeds, in turquoise velvet, attended the bride. Sylvia's four-year-old Carol Frances and Lena Slomowitz's five-year-old Bessie, in white organdy, scattered rose petals before Celia's satin-slippered toes. I, in rented tuxedo, walked beside the groom, prepared, on cue, to hand him the diamond-encrusted platinum wedding band. Ida, in gray taffeta, was obese but dignified; Lena Slomowitz, tiny, bird-beaked, was in navy blue. Both mothers wore mammoth purple orchids on their left shoulders. Neither one wore gold or diamonds, a decision tactfully arrived at, I concluded, to assure parity. Max and Herman looked absurd in rented silk hats and tuxedos. Minnie and Goldie, the older Slomowitz daughters, were sulking because they'd not been asked to be bridesmaids. There were enough male cousins of the bride to support the velvet canopy. A New York rabbi and a cantor with a smooth-as-syrup tenor officiated. Walter Leeds, standing behind me during the long ceremony, snickered into my ear, "Nobody has to teach Joe about the birds and bees, heh, heh."

Waiters heaped our plates with chopped liver, stuffed derma, sour pickles, sour tomatoes, olives, celery, salted almonds, chicken noodle soup with mandelen, roast chicken, potatoes, carrots and green peas, and melting water ices. After we were stuffed like the derma, and while the waiters were circulating, offering toothpicks to cadge gratuities, Walter, flushed and tipsy, rose to read the telegrams. Although the wedding date and location had not been published, everyone on the Hill knew when and where. Most of them had spent two bits on ten-word telegrams.

Walter struck his water goblet with a fork, noise to beget silence. "I have a very important telegram to read." He harrumphed portentously, looked down at a strip of yellow paper in his hand, pretending to read. "Mr. and Mrs. Joseph Slomowitz, Hotel Astor, New York, New York. Health, wealth, happiness and joy. And in a year a baby boy." A few young girls tittered; a few older people clapped. Walter harrumphed again and raised his voice dramatically. "This is signed, Calvin Coolidge. From the White House, Washington, D. C."

The applause was wild. Celia covered her face with white-gloved hands. Slomowitz cousins, below the head table, nudged each other. "You hear! The President knows Maxie's boy." I began to laugh; it was the funniest thing I'd heard in years. I laughed until I choked. Walter whacked my spine before he hit his goblet, grinning inanely. "Folks, that's only the beginning. This important wedding has been taken notice of not only in Washington, D. C., but also in foreign parts. I hold in my hand a cable from Paris, France. Part of this cable is in the French language, which is not mamaloschen to you or me, so if I make a mistake, you'll excuse me, please. 'Mr. and Mrs. Joe Slomowitz, Astor Hotel, New York. Regards to all,'" he read. "'Meet you at Le Havre. *Bum chance.*' It is signed Jessie."

There was a general gasp. Celia flushed purple. I snatched the cable out of Walter's hand and stumbled to my feet. I wasn't going to let Walter's bibulous wit chalk a black mark against Jessie. "*Bon chance,*" I half shouted. "*Bon!* That means good in French. Good luck. Jessie wishes them good luck."

With all the excited buzzing, the scraping of shoes and chairs, I doubt that anybody heard me. In any case, a cabled insult is far more titivating than conventional good wishes. I sat down and drank morosely. The orchestra struck up a waltz. The groom led his bride out to the waxed floor. Celia, as usual, danced gracefully. Little kids slid and chased each other between the dancing couples. Around midnight, the older folks joined hands and stomped in a kasatzke. Weighted down with food and bootleg whisky, I sat watching, wondering where Ida Weiss had found the energy to dance. From joy, I guess. Celia was off her hands.

Rice was thrown, the bride and groom departed, both mothers wept. On the train, Sylvia Leeds gave me accurate descriptions of the bridal party's gowns and suggested Celia would be pleased if I spelled her name Cecilia and changed Joe's surname to Sloan. Hence, in my write-up of these nuptials, the name of Joseph Sloan first appeared in print. I mention this for the benefit of future historians.

The newlyweds were on the rough high seas when Jody McCarthy was born and Dolores died. No one cabled them that news. And they were in Paris when Ida Weiss died suddenly. This cable I sent personally, aware that the girls could not get back for the shiva week, let alone the funeral. One of them might, however, I pipe-dreamed, arrange for a kaddish to be said for Ida in the synagogue on the Rue de la Victoire.

On a Friday morning, at nine o'clock, a busy hour in Herman's Grocery, Ida had a heart attack and, just about as fast as I can write these words, was dead. She had been weighing sugar and regaling a group of customers with an enumeration of the presents Celia had received. In the middle of a sentence, she began to heave and pant and her eyes opened wide as if astonished by what was taking place in her. She managed to gasp "Don't feel good" before her eyes rolled back to sightless whites. She swayed toward the counter, her breasts striking the scales, spilling sugar, before she crumpled and slid to the floor. The pompadour broke from the bone pins; the long hair streamed. She lay wedged between the counter and the shelves while the women scattered, frightened hens, cackling, "Water!" "Ammonia!" "Call a doctor!" Herman, who had been at the ice chest cutting a pound of butter for Mrs. Katz, took one long look at his stricken wife, went gray as ashes and began to shake. Tears sprang to his eyes and rolled down his cheeks, dampening his vest.

Someone—I'm not sure who since each bystander claimed the credit—took the phone receiver off the hook, cranked the box, and screamed at the operator to send a doctor, quick, to Herman's Grocery. A doctor came. There was nothing he could do except write out a death certificate. The butter melted on a strip of paper on the dairy scale while congregation members, summoned by the shamas, panting, puffing, carried Ida up the stairs and stretched her on the bedroom floor. Two poor, pious crones who, between ministrations to the infrequent dead, sorted for a ragpicker, sponged Ida's abundant flesh, closed her eyes and swathed her in a linen shroud.

There was a bustle and a rush, since the Orthodox must be consigned to the grave within twenty-four hours after death but never on the Sabbath. And so, at half past three, before Friday's pale March sun was gone, we were burying Ida Weiss. Herman stumbled after the pine box, numbed with shock, all but sightless in his grief.

We who had been Ida's friends and neighbors clustered at the open grave, the men summoned from their businesses, the women from their cooking pots. We tamped the last of winter's snow to slush and shivered in the knife-sharp wind. We listened, tears unrestrained and unabashed, while Cantor Leiberman sang the "El Mole Rachamim," the deeply moving prayer-chant which is no dirge but an affirmation of the wisdom of God. With aching hearts, we marked that Cantor Leiberman looked beyond Ida's yawning grave toward a snow-covered mound with a granite slab that bore the name and life-span dates of Aaron Leiberman, a small mound, a small stone, for a life too brief to have attained significance.

The heavy, raw-pine box was lowered inch by inch, on ropes. A few of us stepped forward to drop clods of frozen earth upon the lid, the dust to dust. My mother gripped my arm so tightly that I sensed her fear: Will I be next? Hold me fast, keep me, do not let me die. Then Herman disengaged himself from arms that supported him, fearing he would fall, and standing alone, straight-spined, commenced his own prayer for the repose of his departed wife. His voice, quavering at first, swelled, resonant and rich. Few of us understood the Hebrew words, yet all of us were awed and touched, feeling that the man communed with worlds far beyond Grady's Mills. When the prayer was done, he began to speak rapidly and earnestly, in Yiddish, to the box in the ground. "Ida, my dear and faithful wife, if God gives me strength, what you wished, I will do. I give my word before witnesses." His coat lapel was slashed, the symbolic rending of garments, before we turned and trooped back to break bread in the flat above Herman's Grocery. Mrs. Slomowitz and her eldest daughter, Minnie, had set out the traditional foods, the hard-boiled eggs and bagel which are the symbols of eternal life, the herring, küchel and sponge cake that generations in the Eastern European ghettos have supped on after burials, and the shnapps and wine with which to sanctify the Sabbath and bless the Lord of Hosts. Lena Slomowitz had lighted candles in Ida's brass candlesticks and had sheeted all the mirrors.

Ten of us males stood together, praying, then washed our hands at the kitchen sink. Mrs. Slomowitz held a pitcher, pouring, and handed us the towels, embroidered by Celia's golden hands, before

81

we drew chairs to the round kitchen table. I couldn't help remembering—my head was full of memories—the other evenings when I'd sat at this table, with one or both of Herman's daughters, Ida bustling in and out and Herman a pervasive presence, though invisible. Now there was only Herman, surrounded by strangers—devoted strangers, true, yet none of his flesh.

We spoke about the girls that night, as we would speak of them on subsequent evenings. How soon would they return? Would either of them, could either of them, remain here with Herman? Would either of them insist that he leave Grady's Mills and live with her? Meanwhile, who would stay behind the counter while he went for prayers? This was more essential than before, since he had a duty toward his dead, to say the daily kaddish for twelve months. And who—this was a problem to be solved immediately— would look after Herman during the shiva week?

My mother, bless her, solved the last problem. She proposed, and Herman was too numb or too courteous to object, that she and my father move over to his flat and sleep in the girls' double bed, she to cook his food, receive his visitors, and provide unobtrusive companionship while he sat, shoeless, on a wooden box, immobilized, in the procedure of mourning. Much as I hesitate to question the motives of a parent, my mother's, I suspect, were not entirely altruistic. In that week she visibly enjoyed herself, not only with the sense of being important and considered noble but with the pleasure of rummaging through Ida's bureau drawers, examining the wedding finery, folding the gray taffeta dress into tissue paper, washing, ironing, stacking Ida's nightgowns, petticoats, bloomers, corset covers, aprons, and calculating which poor woman on the Hill could make use of what.

The store stayed closed all week. A few housewives were unhappy because they had to shop in the trefe market. Then, after the shiva, Herman unlocked his store, carried in the cake of ice, dumped the coins into their grooves, and waited on the customers. The second son of the shamas, a quiet, honest lad, too young to get working papers but in desperate need of pocket money, relieved Herman when he went to shul for mincha and maariv. A Polish woman came in once a week to clean the flat and wash and iron Herman's shirts. Neighbors took turns bringing him cooked food.

Looking after a mourning widower is a mitzvah. A celestial bookkeeper adds up mitzvahs. The score determines the disposition of
your case when Judgment Day arrives. So I have been told.

We wondered when the girls would come. Mrs. Slomowitz let
it be known she had heard from Celia, who was so overwhelmed
with grief she lacked the strength to cross the stormy seas. As
soon as she was able, she would fly on wings. No one heard from
Jessie.

*　　　*　　　*

Crab grass had sprouted on Ida's grave before the girls returned.
While I was walking home from work, I saw the depot taxicab
pull up before Herman's Grocery and Miss Jessica White and
Mrs. Joseph Sloan emerge from it. Jessie saw me, Jessie waved, a
casual, come-hither gesture as if she'd seen me only yesterday.
Celia didn't notice, being busy paying off the cab. I crossed the
road while the driver was lifting two valises to the curb.

"Sammy! Johnny-on-the-spot!" Jessie pinched my arm and gave
me a smile, broad and friendly, quite as if she'd never slapped my
face. Celia extended a black-kid-gloved hand. "How do you do,
Samuel." I caught a strong whiff of French perfume. "We expected to be met at the station," Celia said.

I stooped for the valises. "I'll carry them upstairs."

"We'll stop in the store and see Papa first," Jessie said.

"He won't be there," I said. "Shul. Maariv. Kaddish."

"Mama's kaddish." Celia's eyes began to fill. "My poor, darling
mama." She whipped out a fresh black-bordered handkerchief and
shook it open to receive her tears.

"Let's get the hell upstairs," Jessie said. "Weeping in the street
is vulgar."

Celia dabbed her eyes and managed a wintry smile. "Samuel,
will you be an angel and bring my bag to Mother Slomowitz's
house. I'll be staying there. Tell her I've arrived. Joseph was supposed to telegraph we'd be on the five o'clock."

I trailed them up the staircase, carrying the valises, which were
light—evidently neither girl had packed for a long visit. They came
into the kitchen, Ida's kitchen, reeking of her years of cooking
chicken soup, stuffed cabbage and gefüllte fish, Ida's kitchen with

her candlesticks on the shelf, her copper kettle on the stove, her dish towels alongside the sink, her worn, stained oilcloth cover on the round table, all as though she'd just left to step down to the grocery. For an instant the girls stood staring. Then Jessie stuffed her fist into her mouth, a plug damming tears, and Celia sobbed aloud. At that moment I believed it was Ida whom they mourned. Thinking about it later, I was not as sure. More than likely it was loss of childhood they grieved for. Neither one, as I knew well, had been happy in this house, yet in retrospect, when the disappointments and the pains of adulthood pile up, those early years become the time of idyllic happiness.

Weeping uglies women. I wished Celia would stop. She gulped, "Have to go lie down," and bolted from the kitchen. I watched her entering her parents' room. Celia has graduated again, I thought, no more brass double bed.

"Celia's pregnant," Jessie informed me. She yanked off the felt coal scuttle that covered her bobbed hair and flung it on the table, atop the crumbs of Herman's breakfast roll. "Sit down, Sam, sit. Talk to me." She tossed her coat across a chair. Beneath it she was wearing the velvet suit I'd seen on her in New York, and the elbows were bald. Jessica White, the playwright, apparently, had not got rich enough to purchase Paris clothes.

I took a chair beside her, picked up the hat, began to spin it on my fist, wondering what else about her had not changed. The gray eyes were lively as before, the old cockiness was in the way she held her head, chin up.

"We confer in kitchens, you and I," she began.

"Shall we adjourn to the parlor?"

"God forbid!" She shuddered. "How's Papa?"

"Bowing to the will of God."

"What will we do with him?"

"*We?* He's no infant. He is managing."

She stayed quiet, absorbing that, and—it struck me—with relief. "I suppose the Hill is calling me a louse, not rushing back."

"There has been talk," I said.

"I wanted to, believe me, Sam. I wanted to grab the next boat. She wouldn't let me. Celia. It was most peculiar. She was pregnant, staying in bed at the Lutetia—" Her expression changed, a flicker

of impudent humor. "It was a riot, Sam, the way Celia proclaimed
the joyful tidings. I'd suspected it, she'd been so picky with her
food, in the best restaurants in Paris, I can tell you. Her sniffing,
her sending back to the kitchen, offended *more* chefs and maître
d's! That morning, we were having coffee at the Dome. All at
once she stood up and shrieked, 'Don't you two realize I'm pregnant!' Then a whoops, a geyser, before she passed out cold,
knocked the table over, smashed crockery, on her way down to
the floor. Oh the French, they are extraordinaire, so sympa-
thetique—"

"I know," I murmured. "I know the French."

Her swift glance held a hint of sneer, of how-would-you-know?
before, "Ah, yes, the A.E.F. How time does fly! The proprietor,
the waiters," she went on, "they pounded Joey black and blue,
congratulating him. A gendarme kissed him on both cheeks after
he'd flagged a taxicab for us. And the driver, when we mentioned
Madame was enceinte, crawled to the Lutetia, honking all the way.
I tell you it was magnifique." She paused. "Can I bum a cigarette?"

"Not in Papa's house," I said, though I laid my pack on the
table. She didn't reach for it.

"If I stay, I'll have to sneak smokes in the bathroom," she said.

"Staying?" I inquired.

A shadow of unsureness crossed her face. "I don't know. Believe
me, my heart goes out to Papa, I love my old man." She snatched
the felt helmet from my hand, twirled it on her fist, dropped it,
spread her hands. "Sam, what shall I do? Could I stand my father?
Could he bear with me? Why, I'd bruise him every time I turned
around. I smoke, I drink, I swear, I like to screw, as you were long
ago informed. Why, the women on the Hill would make hack-
fleisch of me." She reached to my cigarettes, drew her hand back,
snapped "The hell with it" and took a cigarette. I held a match for
her and rose to find a saucer she could drop the ashes in. Her voice
came at me, after me. "This. This miserable, unimportant cigarette.
This is precisely what I mean. Here, I'm scared to be myself. Papa
would disapprove, people would gossip. Away from here, any
place but here, in Paris, in New York, I'm free and independent,
I'm myself. Here I'm only Herman Weiss's daughter. Sure, sure,

they know about my play. They pretend they're proud of me."
She shook her head. "Tain't so. They deplore me. She got married,
didn't she? So why don't she wear a ring?" She laid the smouldering cigarette on the cracked saucer and stared at her naked hands.
"No, Sam, I must go back."

"To France?"

"To New York. There's where Broadway is." She took a short
puff before she stubbed out the cigarette and pushed the saucer
over in front of me.

"You have your divorce?"

She shook her head. "Who needs it? If I were planning to marry
again, which I am not. Never, positively not." The heel of her
hand scraped together crumbs of Herman's roll. She picked the
crumbs up, one by one, and jounced them on her palm. She was
nervous as a witch. "Marriage!" She grimaced. "*You* should talk.
Why haven't you got hitched?"

"Because you're not available." It was a wisecrack, nothing
more.

Her eyebrows arched. "Are you sure? Have you tried?"

"Don't raise false hopes," I said, kidding still.

"You could have had me for ten bucks, you know," she said.

"Let's not bring that up," I said. "He who got slapped."

"Oh, that!" she said. "A grudge-bearer."

"I like clear-cut relationships," I said. "Yes or no. Not maybe,
now and then."

"Mon ami, you are most unreasonable," she said. "You ditched
the blonde Miss What's-her-name?"

"Vice versa," I said. "For an M.D. Same age, same religion. Perfect match."

She spilled the crumbs on the oilcloth; her stubby forefinger
traced a circle with them. "Doctors are nice," she said, thoughtfully. "The father image."

"Don't fool with that. It's loaded," I snapped.

I got the look again, the withering how-would-you-know? and
at that moment I detested Jessie Weiss. Sam's a dope, Jessie's smart.
Only Jessie's smart.

She seemed to read my mind, for she changed the subject instantly. "I have a new play in rehearsal," she said.

I reached to my pocket to get copy paper to make a note for "Folk You Know." She held my arm. "Not yet. Give you details in due course." And as if no chitchat had intervened, she was again discussing family. "No, Sam, if they hadn't written me to meet them at Le Havre—and by the by, Celia mentioned the faux pas at the wedding banquet; no Freudian slip, believe me, that was malice pure and simple—I'd have been here before Mama died. And we might have gotten a few things squared away, she and I." Her fingers fluttered, a gesture of dismissal or impatience. "We have unfinished business, Mama and me, to settle in the other world. Can't you see us at God's footstool, yelling, arguing about why Celia was the darling and I the cross she had to bear?" Her gaze veered toward the sink, as if expecting to see Ida's backside there. "Maybe she despised me because I was like herself. A know-it-all. Only one allowed per family. Maybe she felt Celia needed her protection, Celia was so weak. Jessie? She was iron. She could manage. Sink or swim. And good riddance to bad rubbish if she sank." The stopper fist pounded her mouth. "Celia weak! My ass! That one makes a strength of weakness. 'You can't leave me here with strangers, I am sick. You can't go before I can. You have to wait for me.' Was she afraid I'd rush to Grady's Mills and Papa'd think I loved him more than she?"

"You are naïve," I said, pleased that, for once, I was smarter than she was, for all at once I'd realized why Celia had dashed into her mother's room: to rummage in Ida's bureau drawers. There was no chance to say it. We heard Herman's tread upon the stairs. Jessie pushed back her chair. She stood an instant, waiting for him to become aware of her, before she flew to him, crying "Papa, Papa, Papa!" hugging him around the middle so exactly like the twelve-year-old I'd seen do that in this very room that I wondered would his watch chain mark her cheek. This time he didn't thrust her from him. Eyes brimming, he bent and kissed the crown of her head, murmuring, "Mamenu."

I rapped on the bedroom door. "Celia, your father's home."

"Oh! In a minute." I heard the shutting of a drawer.

I said, "I'll bring the valise to the Slomowitzes" and departed, leaving Herman's daughters with their father. What went on that evening, I know only secondhand. Joe's family went over, taking pots of food, after I'd dropped off the suitcase and told them Celia was in town. Sylvia and Walter Leeds stopped by. My mother, naturally, had to see the girls and what they wore. The Finkels and the Rogoff young folk dropped in. Of what was spoken when Herman and the girls were alone, I have just one detail, and this my mother, who in the shiva week had become Herman's confidante as much as anyone could be, passed on to me. It seems Celia made a proposition to her father. "I'll take Mama's pin, Jessie can have the earrings; I don't wish to pierce my ears." Herman said he didn't answer Celia, he couldn't, his heart at that moment was too full. My mother wished he had. She was burning with curiosity about Ida's diamonds, since she, too, had scoured the bureau drawers and hadn't found the gems. She was certain Jessie had them, squirreled away in New York.

My mother disliked Jessie; she made that plain in the relish with which she passed on a bit of gossip contributed by Celia's mother-in-law. It was Jessie's fault and only Jessie's that the girls had not come sooner. Celia, a loving heart, wished to fly on wings but Jessie—"Semmy, you know how that one hollers—day and night she hollered to Celia, 'So suppose you hurry up, could you help poor Mama? You're here in Perris, France. Who knows when you could come again? So see Perris.' What's to see, Semmy? Styles? Naked hoors? 'Enjoy Perris.' Who was enjoying? Who could enjoy? Joey, that Joey, I betcha a hundred dollars he was enjoying naked hoors while Celia with her broken heart was laying sick in bed. You hear she is pregnant, Semmy? Just beginning. Lena Slomowitz told me. Don't put it in the paper, don't advertise the news, people is afraid you tell too soon you give a kenenhorah. That Jessie, married how many years? Not even a miscarriage. What kind of wife? This is a girl without a heart, I tell you, Semmy. An intrigante. Always she would cheat Celia. Even from the father's love."

Jessie, having checked with her producers, dropped into the newsroom to give me a go-ahead, and I wrote for "Folk You Know": *"Mrs. Joseph Sloan and Mrs. Horace Simon are visiting their bereaved father, Herman Weiss of this city. Both ladies were in Paris, France, at the time of their mother's sudden death and have just returned to the United States. Mrs. Simon, under the pen name of Jessica White, was the author of 'The Awakening,' a Broadway success of several seasons back. Her latest brain child, written abroad, is 'The Fatal Innocence,' a drama presently in rehearsal and due to open shortly on Broadway."* To give the girls equivalent publicity, I might have added that Mrs. Sloan also was with child, but tell-a-woman had taken care of that.

Jessie left town the day the item appeared, saying her presence was demanded by the director, not saying when or whether she'd return. "Should you chance to visit the big city," she told me in farewell, "kindly look me up. I am not always bestiale. Sometimes I enjoy a cup of tea."

Celia stayed the week. The Slomowitzes pampered her, letting her sleep late, took rolls and coffee to her bedside, waited on her hand and foot. Sylvia Leeds entertained for her, a quiet afternoon tea, since Mrs. Sloan was in mourning. She, too, departed without a commitment to return. The girls, it was apparent, had concluded Herman Weiss could manage by himself in Grady's Mills.

In the first week of September, "Folk You Know" announced, *"Word was received here today of the birth of a daughter to Mr. and Mrs. Joseph Sloan, formerly of this city and now of New York. The baby girl was born last night at Lenox Hill Hospital, New York, weighing eight pounds, two ounces. The infant will be named Ilene in memory of her maternal grandmother, the late Mrs. Ida Weiss.*

"Mrs. Sloan is the daughter of Mr. Herman Weiss and the late Mrs. Weiss. Mr. Sloan is the son of Mr. and Mrs. Max Slomowitz, all of Grady's Mills. Mr. Weiss and the Slomowitz family plan to spend the Labor Day weekend in New York getting acquainted with the new member of the family."

The gossips on the Hill counted on their fingers and badgered Lena Slomowitz. "A seven month," Lena told them firmly.

"A seven month, eight pounds!" they clucked. "That Joe! That Celia! Such a love, they couldn't wait. That's why Ida didn't invite to the wedding. Ashamed. The kalah was pregnant."

Goldie Slomowitz ran into me on the street and told me, with nose-crinkled disgust, that Herman had hung Celia's room at Lenox Hill with strips of paper bearing Hebrew prayers, to keep evil spirits from the mother and the babe. "We were ashamed for the nurses. Someone should tell Herman Weiss this is not year one, it's nineteen twenty-seven."

She told me, too, that Celia had had a hard time, so difficult Ilene probably would be an only child. "A darling baby. Like a doll. My mama says she resembles our family."

She also had inspected the Sloan apartment on West End Avenue. "A palace! I'll say this for Celia, she has wonderful taste. Of course, they can afford the best. My brother's making a fortune. Celia will have two in help, a nurse for Ilene and a full-time servant girl. She'll never have to stick her hands in cold water."

As before, Jessie was distant when the clan was gathering. She was in Hollywood. *The Fatal Innocence* had received fair notices, though it hadn't lasted long enough for me to see it. I was sorry about that since this dealt with a Weiss-Simon-type modern marriage, and one critic had highly praised a scene in a hospital ward as "so realistic it is hard to believe the playwright had not spent long, harrowing hours in Bellevue." A famous motion picture star decided the play's heroine was a perfect part for her. Her Hollywood employers had bought it and had given Jessie a contract to work on the screen treatment.

That female lead, I gathered from reviews, was a bitchy, proud, misunderstood woman with inordinate zest and a heart of gold. Miss White, it was evident, continued to find inspiration in the life and self-love of Jessie Weiss.

Four

A box on page one of our paper said the first three days of July, 1937, had set an all-time heat record. The Fourth dawned, no exception, eighty-eight at 6 A.M., no relief in sight.

I'd expected to spend this Fourth at Grady's Lake, a restricted Eden on the mountainside. Sylvia and Walter Leeds invited me. They owned a cottage there, the first Jewish family permitted to buy lake-front property, a circumstance which can lead to strain as well as self-congratulations. Jews let in where other Jews are barred are on the spot in more ways than one. They have to prove their presence won't devaluate the neighbors' property.

I'd seen the Lake a couple of times, on assignment to a Knights of Columbus picnic, an outing of the Epworth League. It was pretty, though not spectacular: grayish water ringed with silver birch, pines and gingerbready cottages, a muddy shoreline littered with discarded beer bottles and condoms. The frontage at Walter and Sylvia's place—I could give you written guarantees—wouldn't have as much as a waterlogged Crackerjack box. They'd win the neatness prize.

I'd never cottoned to Sylvia. She had a gift for sniffing out and flaunting the fashions, phrases and postures destined for vulgarity. But for Walter I'd acquired respect. He lost his hair and gained a paunch while he ripened into a leading citizen, vice-chairman of our Red Feather drive, a big man in Kiwanis and the Masons, and a macher in the Jewish community. Right after the war, he swung the deal that acquired the old Elks Club building at the corner of Grady and East Market for a Y.M.H.A. and currently he heads the committee that's raising funds to build the Brookfield Heights Temple. The foundation has been dug, the rabbi hired, a clean-shaven type who's undecided, like his congregation, whether to be

91

reform-traditional or liberal-orthodox. On this year's Holy Days the congregation will pray in the former Elks Club building, in the Aaron Leiberman Memorial Auditorium, the men and women side by side, men without hats, women with, and Kol Nidre will be sung by a choir that's mainly Welsh Presbyterian. My mother's scandalized, but Walter's pleased and proud. It's been my impression that he's trying to lead his people from the wilderness, gently, with refinement, to confound the anti-Semites by showing them that Jews are merely members of a house of worship that convenes on Saturday.

"Sam, dear," Sylvia told me on the phone, "Walter just called to my attention you have off on the Fourth, so how's about spending it with us up at the Lake? Swimming. Rowing. Fishing. Roasting wienies. How's it appeal to you?"

I smelled ulterior motives, she'd never invited me before, but at the peak of a heat wave I'd have been crazy to refuse.

"Good! I'm delighted!" Sylvia said. "No crowd. They're funny-peculiar at the Lake, look cross-eyed if we bring a mob on holidays. Just Walter, me, our kids—my folks are at the shore—and my cousin, Ruthie Posner, she's spending her vacation here with us. You'll meet her at the Lake."

Aha! That's where the dog lies buried. Why must married women keep baiting traps for bachelors?

"You'll like Ruthie," Sylvia promised. "She's your type. Vivacious. Intellectual."

"My type is any blonde who spreads her legs."

"Try not to be crude, Sam. It's later than you think."

"Now, seriously, Sylvia, why should intellectual, vivacious girls want me? What's the big matzeah? Rosenbaum, the reporter, four-eyes, receding hairline, small biceps, salary fifty-two fifty."

"You could better yourself. All you need is the incentive. Just come on up to the Lake. . . . Walter, I have Sam on the wire. . . . Hold it, Walter wants a word with you."

Walter got on the extension; Sylvia clicked off. "Listen, shmo, nobody means you harm. Is it poison if you meet a nice Jewish girl? Say 'Hello, how are you? Please pass me the mustard.' Then what'll be will be; let nature take its course. Moreover, I have something to discuss with you and it is not a shidduch. You and me, we'll take a couple of rods, we'll row out in the middle of the Lake and talk. . . ."

He said they'd pick me up at ten the morning of the Fourth. At quarter of, Walter phoned to say he'd just gone to the garage to get his Buick and found both the rear tires flat. Nails. Couldn't imagine where he picked them up. He'd phone around, see if a service station was open that could come and get the tires. He had just a single spare.

At eleven he rang back. The only open service station was on the highway, ten miles out; the one attendant on duty couldn't leave his pumps to drive in for the tires. And none of the neighbors was around, not a soul to help him out. "Looks like we're stuck," he said.

Sylvia picked up the extension. "Sam, dear, I can imagine how you're disappointed. But what can we do? Walter has been going crazy on the phone trying to get help. So look, Sam, you planned to be with us, so come anyway. This house is comfortable. Thank God Papa made us insulate. I have a couple of big fans. The back porch is screened, and I'll turn on the sprinkler in the yard, so bring your bathing suit. I have plenty ice cubes—thank God for Frigidaires—beer, soft drinks, anything your heart desires. We'll have the wienies and hamburgers I bought for the Lake, make our picnic here. . . . Come on, be a sport. Have you anything—"

"Better to do?" I finished her sentence. "No." Whatever, Sylvia's porch was sure to be cooler than the Rosenbaum's front stoop.

It was brutal walking over to Brookfield Heights. "Heights" exaggerates the slight rise and roll of the terrain beyond the brook that Abe Finkel had acquired at sheriff's sale during the depression. Abe had let the acreage lie fallow until his son, Myron, finished a college course in business administration and came back with a scheme for creating an upper-middle-class housing development, hopefully nonsectarian.

The Goyim didn't bite. Partly, blame Barry Neale, the *News-Record*'s current city editor. Barry dubbed the project "Abie's Acres" and spread his wisecrack with a smirk and snicker until Brookfield Heights became our second ghetto—gilded, to be sure.

The dwellings, American Colonial, were spacious, the landscaping admirable, shrubs and flowers according to the calendar: tulips, daffodils in March; azaleas, April; rhododendrons, May; roses and gladioli, June and July; petunias, August; cannas, September; mums and salvia until the killing frosts. The street lights were replicas of the lantern Paul Revere carried on that ride; the winding shaded macadam roads were named for deceased presidents. Sylvia and Walter lived on McKinley Road; Myron Finkel and Evelyn, his bride, on Theodore Roosevelt Boulevard; Irwin Katz, who grew up as Isie, on Cleveland Road around the bend from Garfield Drive where Sol Katz, Isie's father, owner of the Bon Ton Department Store, had added Grecian columns to his red-brick Colonial. No one lived on Harding Place. It was a short connecting lane, dead end.

Sylvia had ignored the prospectus. She'd built a split-level modern. Her house held a mammoth Frigidaire, an oil burner, a console radio, a grand piano, Persian rugs, sterling silver tableware and a brace of etchings. Walter had been (this is no mean distinction) the first resident of Brookfield Heights to purchase, on his own initiative and following his own taste, original works of art.

A by-the-hour Italian gardener kept their lawns emerald and smooth, their weeping willows, dwarf cypresses and Japanese maples manicured. A sleep-in maid, local Slovak, and a part-time laundress, Irish, did the housework. Sylvia did the cooking, American-Jewish, which meant she bought her chickens from the kosher butcher and broiled them with butter. She lighted candles Friday nights and Walter donned a yarmulka to say a Hebrew brocha over shrimp cocktails. The candles, yarmulka and prayer were so the children would remember they were Jews.

The children were two, Carol Frances and Harold, both plump and rosy-cheeked and with braces on their teeth. There also was Rags, a wire-haired terrier.

Our Jews with money had left the Hill, all but the Rogoff family, who were planning to as soon as they found a buyer for their house. The Slomowitzes had been the first to go. The year after Joe's marriage, Max began to complain of sharp pains in his chest. Angina pectoris, the doctor called it, not dangerous in itself, a warning; take it easy, keep this vial of pills in your vest pocket, take one when you feel a twinge; you can live with this for twenty years. Max had acquired beach-front property in Miami during Florida's bust following its boom. With a heart condition, an ailing wife, three daughters afflicted with delusions of social grandeur by a catered affair at the Hotel Astor, Joe running the scrap-metal business from an office in New York, and the winters harsh in Grady's Mills, why remain on the Hill?

The business—Victory Steel, M. Sloan, President; J. Sloan, Chairman of the Board—had been phenomenally successful. A scavenger's trade, it had soared during the depression, ready cash in the iron safe handy for snatching bargains, a bankrupt rail line, a moribund iron foundry. Joey—what's true is not to be denied—was a business genius. He'd flunked in geometry, but at multiply and add he was a whiz. We heard he traveled widely, making deals, though he hadn't set foot in our region for close on to eleven years.

Max retired to Miami, built a mansion on his beach-front lots, lolled on the sand, dipped into the surf and bought a bag of golf clubs. Then, Lena Slomowitz died of the cancer that had been gnawing her for years. After Max had planted a hundred trees in Palestine in memory of his wife, he shaved his beard and went prospecting among the divorcees and widows who came down to the sea with bankbooks pinned to their brassieres and selected Mitzi, a henna-haired divorcee twenty years younger than himself. Some people questioned Max's sanity. Others said, so crazy I should get the chance to be! He should live and be well and enjoy to a hundred years!

Those who'd remained on the Hill were the unambitious, the unsuccessful, the set-in-their-ways and the strict Orthodox who had to be in walking distance to a shul, like the Rosenbaums, unambitious, and Herman Weiss, strict Orthodox as well as set-in-his-ways.

Herman's building had become ramshackle: the porch floor boards were loose and dangerous, the side shingles flapped, paint peeled from the window frames. His stock was meager, his customers dwindling. A poor piece of bread, Ida would have said. Yet, morning after morning Herman carried in the cake of ice, dropped it into the old-fashioned chest, locked the door and, stooping slightly, plodded off to shul, came back, tied on his canvas apron, weighed sweet butter and granulated sugar on the iron scales, wrapped herrings in the *News-Record,* and made change for his customers.

He was aging, though so gradually that when you saw him every day the change was not perceptible. I realized how he had aged when, during a long Yom Kippur afternoon, I chanced to look in his direction and was startled by the grayness of his beard and mustache, the purple, wrinkled hollows underneath his eyes.

The women worried about him. They knew he barely made a living, having competition. Perlzweig's Jewish-American Delicatessen-Restaurant, midway between the downtown business district and the Hill, carried most of the special culinary items Herman's Grocery did, and the Brookfield Heights crowd, understandably, shopped there, across spic-and-span counters and from a sparkling Frigidaire. Herman didn't seem to mind. How much does an old man need? For whom must he provide? As a matter of fact, he himself, now and then, dropped in at Perlzweig's for cold borsht or blintzes and Mrs. Perlzweig clucked over him affectionately, like the women on the Hill. Everybody fretted about his solitary state and, with diligence and cunning, the women schemed to get him married off. Mrs. Rogoff brought a spinster sister from New Jersey for a long visit, during which the sister did the family marketing at Herman's Grocery; the Litvak rabbi produced a childless widowed cousin, a younger woman, good-looking and religious; a New York marriage broker, alerted by Mrs. Katz, turned up, deplored the rundown condition of the grocery, said the widow he had in mind possessed ten thousand dollars (her late husband's life insurance) that she was prepared to invest in a business, maybe she didn't mean exactly a grocery, but if this one could be brought up to date—

My mother had him to our house for Yom Tov meals and talked to him from the heart. "You could live yet, Mr. Weiss, like a mensch. Ida, she should rest in peace, she would be the first one to say, 'Mr. Weiss, I want you should get married, a partner to help you in the store, a wife to cook for you tasty meals and wash and press the shirts, a friend for you in the house.' Mr. Weiss, you are a person, not a stone. So if you get sick, who will come, take the fever, bring the aspirins, make the hot tea, chicken soup? God forbid you should need to on-come to the children. A mother, a father, for ten children they have room. Ten children, for one father, do they have a place?"

Herman had two children. As far as we could see, neither one had offered him a place. Solitary he remained and—the evidence was visible—tormented by loneliness. A single light bulb burned upstairs all hours, and occasionally Herman fell asleep in shul. Obviously he wasn't sleeping soundly, alone in his double bed.

We missed Ida, too. Something vivid and exciting had left the Hill. "Our kochleffel is gone," my mother cried. True, Ida had been the mixing spoon, the fomenter, the arguer, the voice of authority. No one could replace her. No one tried.

The new people who had moved into Katz's house, Slomowitz's, and Finkel's, were Jews, yet alien to us. They were out of Germany, offensively ingratiating but arrogant and enjoying luxuries of which most of us had never dreamed. A former Berlin manufacturer for whom Abe Finkel had signed the affidavit that delivered him from Hitler's Germany had moved a Bechstein piano into a dwelling on the Hill. Abe's family were invited to see but not to touch the instrument. A pallid, black-bearded scholar from Frankfurt, where his family had lived four hundred years, was trying to support himself by teaching Hebrew to our kids. He constantly complained of their manners and ignorance. A physician from Munich had a Cherman-only-speaking wife who wore a Persian lamb coat and dined off Rosenthal china. The doctor planned to practice here after he passed our State Boards. Meanwhile, he antagonized the staff at St. Luke's by lecturing them on the superiority of German medicine and downgrading ours.

I'd interviewed each refugee after he moved in but learned very little, since all of them had kinfolk still in Germany and they feared reprisals. "We did not believe it could happen to us," the doctor told me. "We were Cherman." He had an Iron Cross from World War One. "The Ostjuden, ya, the Polish Chews. Not us."

Nevertheless, they lived—welcomed, sheltered, shielded by Ostjuden: Litvaks, Poles, Galicians—on the Hill, where they stuck out like sore thumbs and by their very foreignness threatened the precarious balance of tolerance in the rest of Grady's Mills. The German Jews on Grady Avenue, ironically, ignored them.

*   *   *

Not a leaf was stirring when I plodded up McKinley Road, not a bird chirping. One fat sparrow, one alone, alighted on a telephone wire, seared its toes, winged off to the shade of a maple tree. Stars and Stripes hung limp on all the flagpoles on the lawns. Behind Walter's house I heard a sprinkler hissing and children whooping discreetly.

I started around back. Sylvia, opening the front door, intercepted me. "Welcome, welcome, stranger! Long, long time no see."

Time and motherhood had padded Sylvia with more of what she'd started with. The halter she was wearing showed me what I hadn't seen since I was weaned. I backed up and bumped the cousin. She'd sneaked in, behind. I was trapped between.

Cousin Ruthie was a dog—buck teeth, thick lips, thick eyeglasses, extensive buttocks—and she was wearing shorts, a frank obscenity.

"Ruthie, this is my dear, dear friend, Samuel Rosenbaum," Sylvia said. "I know you two are going to get along just great."

Ruthie offered me a paw. "My pleasure." Add to her liabilities, adenoids that needed shrinking.

"I just know you two will have so much in common," Sylvia said. She led me through the house, Ruthie trailing, breathing on my neck.

Walter, in bathing trunks, more hair on his chest than scalp, was sprawled on a chaise on the screened back porch, a tall glass, rattling ice cubes, in his hand. "Aha! The chinless wonder!" he greeted me.

"Bring your bathing suit?" Sylvia asked, though she could have seen my hands were empty and my pockets flat. Lawn sprinklers don't entice me. "Somebody will be disappointed. Somebody who was waiting till you came to show off her new suit."

"Let her show it to the kids," Walter growled. "Sam and I have things. . . ."

The kids, soaking wet and faintly bluish at the gills, dashed across the lawn to eye me through the screen. "Aw!" young Harold growled. "Eek!" Carol Frances squealed. Scorn! Had they been promised Tarzan, or Adonis?

Cousin Ruthie shifted from foot to foot, making up her mind. "Awright, kiddies, I will be a sport. I'll come out and play with you," she bleated through the screen.

My hostess clutched my sweaty hand. "Sam, dear, we have missed you, honest, true we have. We used to be such friends. You remember"—her hip nudged my thigh—"those darling little supper parties we used to have when I was just a bride? You and Walter were so brave, eating my experiments."

"I've been on milk toast ever since," I said.

Her elbow jabbed my ribs. "Same old Sam, the perfect louse. I was so sure you and Ceil—little did I dream she was stringing you along till Joe got ready to propose."

Walter hoisted himself from the chaise. "Come out to the garage. Want to show you what some bastard did."

The nailheads in his tires were approximately half an inch across. It was hard to imagine Walter, a careful driver, not seeing such spikes in the road. "Tires were okay when I drove in last night. Matter of fact, I had air put in when I stopped for gas and oil to be ready for today." He kicked one flat, disgusted. "The way I figure is somebody wanted that lake Judenrein today." He scowled. "But who could have done it? My gardener? My neighbor's handyman? Some lousy shikker from the Flats? Sneaking around your garage while you're fast asleep. Scares hell out of you, don't it?" He kicked the other tire. "Hate to think we have to keep garages locked in Brookfield Heights. Maybe the News-Record should look into it."

"I'll mention it to Neale."

"That momser!" Walter said.

We strolled back looking worried, both of us.

Sylvia had two big fans going on the porch. They stirred a modest breeze. I took off my tie, opened my collar and stretched out on a chaise. The dog was yipping, the kids whooping, Cousin Ruthie cackling inanely in the yard. Now and then, intentionally, I do believe, a thin spray from the hose filtered through the screen.

99

"Watch it, kids! I'll break your necks!" Walter barked before he pushed his chaise parallel and close to mine.

"What will you drink?" Sylvia asked. "Sassparilla, cokes, cream soda, beer? Iced tea? Walter's sticking to iced tea."

I said I'd have the beer; it hits the spot for me in hot weather.

"Take off your shirt," Walter urged. "We don't have to be bashful for the Goyim here." I yanked off the shirt.

Sylvia staggered out with a heavy tray. She'd brought two bottles of beer, a pitcher of iced tea, sarsaparilla, and extra glasses, in case the shpritzers craved refreshment, too. I rolled a chilled bottle between my palms, held it to my wrists, cooling my pulse while Sylvia poured tea for Walter and herself. She handed Walter a glass, me a bottle opener, before she pushed my feet aside to crouch on the footrest of my chaise, ever one for intimacy. "I saw an old friend of yours," she began between sips. "In New York. I went up to buy my Easter—my spring outfit. Ceil. We shopped together. She had entree to wholesale houses. Ceil is stunning, so—so distingée . . ."

"Your family was never good in French." I lifted off a bottle cap, studied the foam rising in my glass.

Walter wrinkled his elongated forehead, wondering what I was referring to. "Aha! I remember. Sam rushed to defend somebody's honor." He punched my knee. "She deserved it. That one is no mensch."

"Et tu, Walter? Joined the knockers of Jessie Weiss?"

"That one's nothing to me nor I to her," Walter said. "I hardly know the bitch. Gave me a back-hand howjado when she was here with Celia, that time, to see the father, after the mother died."

"To know her is to despise," Sylvia said promptly and with decision. "She is conceited and as selfish as they come. How two such different girls could grow up in one family I will never understand. Ceil has the most beautiful apartment. Like a palace. Over on Park Avenue. Nobody lives on the West Side any more, she says, except German refugees. Ceil has to go over there to shop for Pesach: matzohs, horseradish, fish. The markets in her neighborhood don't carry Jewish items. She has twenty–twenty-five for Seder every year. And guess who conducts it? Herman Weiss!"

I'd surmised something like this. Each Passover week Herman

locked his store and disappeared. Being uncommunicative ordinarily, he didn't tell his neighbors where he went. If to Celia, fine, a sound relationship. Yet again, as when Jessie's name had come up, I was only mildly interested. You lose interest when old acquaintances are long away from town. I drained my glass, waiting till Walter found a chance to speak of what he wished to speak to me about. "Ceil had a couple of Goyim last year for the Seder," Sylvia burbled. "Business friends of Joe's. They were *so* impressed with Herman. 'Your dad looks like an Old Testament prophet,' Ceil said they said to her."

I mumbled, "Where'd they ever see one?"

She rebuked me with a glance. "Must you always be a smart aleck? Ceil wants her father to come live with them. They have the room and she keeps kosher, four sets of dishes, even two for Passover. She hates the idea of him selling herrings on the Hill."

"He likes it."

She ignored me. "Ceil begs him to retire. She was hoping he'd move to Miami when Joe's folks settled there. But then Max went nuts and married that redhead. Minnie and Goldie phoned Joe long distance to come down, do something, buy the floozie off. Joe wouldn't stir off his backside in New York. Ceil is *so* humiliated. She refused to meet Mitzi. When Max and Mitzi come to New York—on business—they stay at a hotel. And run around to night clubs. Imagine! Max Slomowitz with his weak heart. He could drop dead dancing."

"I understand Joe went to meet the bride." Walter slipped a few words in. "Came back drooling at the mouth."

"Figures," I muttered.

Walter winked at me. We'd seen eye to eye previously on Joey Slomowitz.

I raised another bottle cap, poured more foaming brew. It wasn't too bad on this porch. I was getting comfortable. Also a certain type of gossip amuses me. "Anybody hear from Jessie Weiss?" I asked.

"Don't you?" Sylvia asked, answering.

"All I know is what I read in the papers." Which was little enough. As far as I knew Jessie had remained in California, writing for the films, and Hollywood, as everybody knows, is a morass into which writers sink, weighted down with gold. Infrequently, I'd seen Horace Simon's name among the credits in a theatrical review: "Settings by Horace Simon." He was East and she was West, a perfect marital arrangement for two no longer of a single mind.

"A disgrace." Sylvia kept babbling while I mused. "The way she's cut herself off. Wants nobody, needs nobody. Oh, now and then she sends Ilene some trinket, a bracelet or a string of beads. In awful taste, Ceil says. That Ilene is dressed like a model. A very lovely child and well-behaved. Ceil brings her up just so. I wish I could make my brats—the language Harold uses. . . . Let's not go into that. What was I talking about before? Jessie. Yes. At Chanukah, Jessie mails Herman a check. Ceil got her father to tell her that much; he's close-mouthed, as you know. Just a check, not even—this is the God's honest truth—a letter, a few words, a How are you? How do you feel? How is business, Papa? Love and kisses from your daughter." She took a sip to oil her vocal chords. "Why, Ceil and Joe had a tenth anniversary and did Jessie so much as wire flowers from the Coast? Not even a cheap, cut-rate, night-letter telegram."

Walter's eyes met mine. "Bum chance," we said together.

"You boys know the score on her," Sylvia approved.

"True and enough already." Walter stirred and stretched. "Syl, don't you need to peel potatoes or something?"

"You boys want to talk dirty, eh?" She rose, taking the hint and her empty glass.

"I love my wife." Walter sighed profoundly. "But when she starts yakking about her dear friend, Ceil. . . ."

"Me, out of sight, out of mind, for both Weiss girls," I said. "So, now what's your big news?"

"Hold your horses." He sat up to find his pipe and pouch and I had, perforce, to wait while he filled the pipe bowl, tamped tobacco, worked a cleaner up and down the stem, struck match after match, drew in, retamped, recleaned. I'd smoked half a Camel before he had the pipe drawing. "Okay." He leaned back, his bald skull wreathed in sweat and pungent smoke. "Sam, what would you think if I bought WGMX?"

I whistled. WGMX was our local radio station.

"Knocks you over, eh?" He chortled. "Under your hat, understand? Not for publication, yet. But in the works, on the fire."

I rested my cigarette. "Gimme, gimme, tell."

He parked his pipe beside my Camel. "The present owners may lose the franchise. Certain textile unions have been complaining to the F.C.C. Station too one-sided, broadcasting too much anti-labor stuff."

"True, true, and not the half of it," I said.

His upraised palm silenced me. "Certain Protestant ministers have been griping, too. GMX is an outlet for Father Coughlin, that rabble-rouser priest. And ain't it wonderful for our side"—he grinned—"when Christians get roused up? Would anybody listen, pay attention, if only Jews complained?"

"No argument. Tell more."

"Well, sir, if they lose the license, the syndicate I've lined up is putting in a bid. It'll take a lot of cash. My dad and Sylvia's will put up some, and Joe Sloan—say what you want about the guy and all of it is true: he's prost, a loudmouth, nut, but he understands what's happening in the world—he thinks he can swing a substantial loan for us in New York."

"Congratulations, great." I offered my hand.

He shook it, dropped it, hunted for a penknife, found it, began to scrape his pipe, saying, "If we get the station, I want you in with us."

Excitement flooded me. My hand trembled when I took a cigarette from my pack.

"You're an experienced journalist." Walter spoke my thoughts. "Crapping on a lousy paper, getting no place fast. A bright boy with no future, passed over for a crummy Goy."

There are few secrets in Grady's Mills; most people know what's going on, even though it's not in "Folk You Know." When Mallory retired last year to go tarpon fishing in Florida, I had hopes of promotion to the city desk. Other people guessed I did. Sol Katz, for one. He bumped into me on First Street one afternoon and said, "Sam, I hear Mallory is getting out. Want me to put in a word for you? Could be they would pay attention. The Bon Ton advertising."

It was tempting but I said, "Better no, let nature take its course."

Nevertheless, I have reason to believe Sol tried, because just before Barry Neale got the nod, a steno in the business office told me they'd been getting calls, mentioning how bright and competent Rosenbaum was. To be fair, Barry rated the promotion. For one thing, he was older, pushing fifty, and with city desk experience. During the depression he had drifted out our way, from Philadelphia, where newspapers, like other businesses, were laying off. For another, he had chutzpah, the ability to push guys around, which is one of several qualities I lack. And, finally—this I admit reluctantly—Grady's Mills was not yet ready to promote a Yid to so conspicuous a spot.

Barry didn't like me. It was mutual. Much of this was bigotry. Barry coined the "Abie's Acres" crack. He repeated it in every bar in town and he threatened to put it into my copy whenever I handed him a social item about a resident of Brookfield Heights—just kidding, understand, but such jokes I can do without. About our refugees, he'd growled, "Come here to steal the jobs from good Americans," and one recent day, when a couple of us were sitting around, discussing the U.P. service copy out of Europe, young Dick Adams, a good kid, asked wasn't it time F.D.R. did something to put the skids under Hitler. Barry turned from him to look me in the eye. "I have a son," he said. "He is a senior in high school. If I can help it, and by God I'll try my best, my boy is not going to war to save the goddam kikes." And this spring, after certain happenings. . . .

In April, a fire in the Hungarian-Galician shul. By the time the minyan arrived for morning prayers, flames were licking the basement ceiling, directly underneath the Ark. Short circuit, the fire chief concluded. Okay, accept it. Do you have a choice? But, sure as shooting, no broken copper wire desecrated Aaron's grave in the Sons of Judea Cemetery. That little mound and headstone is pretty much ignored these days. Aaron's family has moved away; it's almost twenty years since he was buried there. And alive, except among the girls, he'd cut no ice, a courteous, dull, pretty boy. Nevertheless, there was considerable enthusiasm when Hymie Rogoff proposed we name the Y auditorium in memory of Aaron. The Legion also remembers him. Each Decoration Day, they stick a flag into a metal tube before the granite slab. When they arrived on this year's Decoration Day to place the flag, they found the headstone uprooted and a crimson swastika painted on its back. Aaron had, at last, attained significance. Shock raced through the Hill, through Brookfield Heights. We expected it would rock all of Grady's Mills. I wrote it up, for once discarding journalistic objectivity. Barry read my piece and scowled. "Nothing doing, Bud. We blow this up, we give other hooligans ideas." He passed my copy over to Gus Stengel, who, being of German ancestry, might also have had a nonobjective view. "Fifty words," Barry said, though to mollify me he offered to talk to Steve Durgin, our chief of police, see if Durgin had any clues. No use my talking to Durgin. In my excited state, I'd just antagonize the chief. He added he wanted a column on the bidding on the county sewer contracts; he suspected something really shady there, and he had the gall to hint that if I paid stricter attention to the courthouse, my regular beat, I'd be more valuable to the *News-Record*.

The paper didn't print even fifty words when in June, during Shevuoth services, a stone was flung through a window of the Litvak shul, grazing the skull of Bobby, Hymie Rogoff's little son.

Some anti-Semitism Grady's Mills has always had—the amount that's considered normal in American small cities: ignorant kids yelling "sheeny" and "Christ-killer" at us in the streets; social segregation after school, we going to our parties, they to theirs, no interracial dating openly. The Hilldale Country Club barred Jews, even as members' guests; Grady's Lake restricted property ownership. However, we were welcome in the public schools and public library, in Rotary, Kiwanis and the Masons, and most of the Jewish boys had learned to swim in the Y.M.C.A. pool. When necessary or desirable, certain Jewish citizens relieved themselves with shiksa whores, they being the only variety locally available.

What we'd known up to now was petty irritation. This spring we'd begun to know fear.

"With WGMX"—Walter's mind, apparently, was traveling the same route as mine—"maybe we can help ourselves. Goddamit, I never thought would come the day when I'd feel scared in Grady's Mills. This was a nice town, I always thought; we behave, they behave. Brother, it has changed. Sam, those spikes in my tires were no accident. They were a warning: Jew, stay away from the Lake;

don't contaminate our water. Well, sir, I for one do not intend to take this lying down. No siree. Aaron's grave. The shuls. My car. I tell you we have Nazis here in town. Maybe in the Flats. Maybe in the better neighborhoods. Maybe even in the City Hall. Maybe it was the refugees moving in that stirred it up; a little rishes here we always had. Did I tell you the third degree they put me through before they let me buy that cottage on the Lake? 'How many of you people will be coming here on Sundays?' 'What language will they speak?' Even, believe me, 'Does your wife use garlic when she cooks?' Aaah, who needed it? To please Sylvia, I made nice, nice. Well, all I know is, Sam, we are in trouble. And we have to take some steps. You follow me?"

I did. I would have said so had he given me a chance.

"Now, mind you, Sam, with the radio station, we would have a voice, speak up, speak out, let all the people know exactly what the bastard Hitler is, what he's out to do, yes, what Fascism is, what Father Coughlin is, a tool, a stooge for Fascism. . . . Sam, you sit there like a dummy, like a sphinx; maybe you don't think my idea is so hot, Jews taking over, running a radio station in a town like this; how will it look to the Goyim? Next thing they'll try to take over City Hall, the government. Might make matters worse." He picked up his cold pipe, sucked the stem, put it down. "Listen, Sam, a damn fool altogether I am not. We will watch our step. We'll have Gentiles in our corporation, hire a Gentile manager, our own Christian front." He leaned to me. "There's another side, the cold business side. This isn't charity, by any means, I'm no bighearted shmo. WGMX has been a nice piece of bread and these Goyim could have kept it for a million years, except they let their bias show. For my part, I'm delighted it was the labor people and the ministers got on their tail. Now our station"—he was talking as though he had the franchise in his pocket "—will play fair and square. Equal treatment for labor, for the businessman. Say there's a little trouble over wages in the mills, we give both sides a chance to tell their side. But on Nazism, Fascism, one side. Against."

"Communism?" I did get in a word.

"Against," Walter said, flatly. "*American. Capitalist. Democracy*. Good enough for F.D.R. Good enough for me."

"And me," I said. "With you all the way. When do I start taking elocution lessons?"

He raised his hand. "Take it easy, there's no rush. Maybe we won't even use you to read news. Maybe you'll be one who makes it. For example, how would you like to do an exposé of a prime son-of-a-bitch, a chief of police who wouldn't lift one little finger to find out who painted a swastika on a Jewish hero's grave?"

I went hot and cold. Something ugly crawled from underneath a slimy stone. Because I'd wanted to forget it, I told myself I had forgotten it. I managed to mumble, "That's dangerous ground."

Walter glowered at me. "Lost your nerve, before we even start. Sam, do you realize that's exactly how it came to pass in Germany?"

Cousin Ruthie pushed the screen door open. I could have kissed her for barging in. "Brrr, I'm freezing. Ee-magine freezing a hot day like this!" Rags, the terrier, slithered in behind her, shaking water off his pelt onto my white pants. "Serves you right," Ruthie said, "for being a poor sport."

Walter rolled off his chaise. "I'm going under the sprinkler. Too bad you didn't bring your suit." He wagged a forefinger at me. "Come on in, the water's fine. Take the plunge, show guts."

"When you're all set, whistle," I told him.

We had hot dogs, hamburgers and potato salad on the porch. Ruthie dressed in something pink, with ruffles, and left her glasses off, but her case remained hopeless.

While Ruthie and the youngsters were twirling sparklers on the dampened grass, Sylvia pleaded, "Take her out just once, Sammy, I'll appreciate it. To the Bijou for a movie. How much can it cost? For a walk, a soda. Anything. Give the kid a whirl."

"You're not obligated to marry her," Walter added, "unless pregnancy results."

I buttoned my shirt, tucked my tie into my pocket. "You make fine potato salad," I told Sylvia. "I'll tell Mama to call you for the recipe."

Walter walked me to the road. "I'll let you know developments. And if you hear anything—somebody at your office might just drop a word—give me a buzz."

I walked home slowly, mulling. Sure, I'd love to try radio newscasting. Sure, I wasn't happy slaving for Barry Neale. Five more years, I'd be another middle-aged newspaper hack, worried about bright kids gunning for my job. Sam, it's later than you think.

But how real is the menace here? Is Walter making too much out of the malicious mischief of a couple of hooligans? Walter's a European, out of Poland, where they have pogroms. I'm a local boy. Anti-Semitism never has touched me, never done me harm. So why was I steamed up about Aaron's grave? Racial memories? Racial solidarity? Look, see here, you were with Walter all the way; you thought his plan was great. Only to a point, to the point where he suggested you stick out your neck. Investigate Steve Durgin. Uncover a long, dirty trail that leads back to me. To me and to Max Slomowitz. And Joe. And that pathetic little chick, Dolores McCarthy. She's dead; the boy is who knows where. But I am here, I who made the deal and bribed the officer. Let him who is without sin. . . . Who the hell is?

Walter is, I think. Walter can take risks. His hands are clean. But I? One shady deal, one buried scandal. Must it make a coward of me for the remainder of my days?

The Hill was half abed, most of the houses darkened, though here and there through the open windows of unlighted rooms I could hear the radios. Above the dry, dusty maples, Roman candles showered stars of blue and red, green and gold. A car slithered along the road, spattering tarry gravel. It stopped at a curb, unloading weary picnickers. There were no nighttime strollers. The heat was like a heavy woolen blanket.

Mama and Papa were on our stoop, on the swing behind the morning glory's screen, trying to keep cool with tumblers of iced water and palm leaf fans. I squatted on the top step, panting, inhaling the heated tar, poured yesterday to lay the dust in the road.

The swing creaked, Mama bending forward. "You want a cold drink? We got in the icebox a bottle cream soda."

"And a bottle beer," Papa said. "Sam likes better beer."

"We got plums in the icebox. I get for you." The swing squeaked as Mama made to rise.

"Sit," I said. "I'm not hungry."

"By who did you have supper?" Mama asked.

"Sylvia Leeds."

"So-o-o. She made a nice supper? What was served?"

"Hot dogs, hamburgers."

Her tongue clicked against her palate. "Rich people! By us, plain people, would be a shame to give a guest hot dogs. For this she invited you?"

"Walter invited me. We had something to talk over."

"Temple business?" Mama scoffed. "Temple-shmemple business?"

I lit a cigarette.

"You smoke too much," Papa said.

"What did you two do today?" I asked.

"What could we do?" Mama answered, asking. "A heat like I never saw in mine whole life. Sophie Rogoff came with the car. They bought big car, a Hudson. She invited we should take a little spin. Believe me, in the car was more hot than the house."

I pressed my cigarette out beneath a step, flung the butt away.

"Take care!" Papa cried. "Could start a fire."

"Who had appetite for supper?" Mama said. "Cold schav we had. After, Papa walked downtown and bought a pint ice cream. Stromberry. The German doctor, he came over and we treated him."

"He was looking to talk to you, Sammy," Papa said. "September, he takes the tests. He asked maybe you know somebody. . . ."

"No." I spoke sharply. "If he can pass, he'll pass."

"Shah!" Mama halted her swinging-fanning. "From such trouble like he had, we should never know. A whole life building up a doctor practice, a beautiful house with expensive furniture. Then comes anti-Semitin, chase him out. Comes here a poor man, saves his neshoma, nothing else."

"With what did I come?" Papa grumbled. "With two hands."

"Come to bed, Papa," Mama said. "You talk already foolish; you compare yourself with an educated German doctor."

I sat on the top step, smoking another cigarette. Sixth Street had finally retired; every house was dark. Even Herman's, up the street, had doused its upstairs bulb. A gray cat without a collar nosed my shoes. An old Ford rattled past, spraying tarry pebbles. The car was jammed with youngsters, popping cap pistols. They yelled "Ikey-Kikey." Or maybe I imagined it. The courthouse clock struck ten. I pulled myself up, climbed the stairs in the oven of our house, stripped and took a cold shower. Drying, I caught a glimpse of myself in the medicine cabinet's flaking mirror, a narrow face, dark nearsighted eyes that held a trace of melancholy, a bristly jaw, not more, not less than average. "Chinless wonder"? What gives Walter the right to insult me? A bank account, a house in Brookfield Heights, a job to offer. Come off it, Sam, don't start getting hypersensitive. That's the Jew disease.

I turned on my fan, crawled naked into bed, expecting, hoping I could quickly fall asleep. Seven o'clock I had to be at work. Barry would be snottier than usual if I came in late the morning after a holiday. The room was a sweatbox. Our attic wasn't insulated; all day the sun had baked the roof. My fan made a racket, needed oiling, or a screw was loose. I got up, switched it off, went back to bed.

I smelled smoke. Where there's smoke, usually there's fire. I rolled off the mattress, opened the door just a tiny crack not to stir a draft. I sniffed the upper hall. Nothing was burning on our premises. I crawled back to bed and tossed. I counted eleven strokes of the courthouse clock. I heard Roman candles hissing, cannon crackers sputtering, cap pistols' rat-tat-tat. Down to the wire, Grady's Mills was celebrating Independence Day. And enough, already, please. Any moment, any second, it will be the fifth. And any minute, any second, the temperature will drop. It must. The main thing is to stop thinking. Tell me how. You can't switch off a brain the way you do a fan. What Walter and I had talked about kept my brain spinning. It could change my life—and none too soon. It might even change the world. And in this year of 1937, change was overdue. For the better, I mean. Walter's plan made sense. It might lead to bigger things. A pebble tossed into a pond sends its ripples far.

Perspiration glued my body to the sheet. And I kept smelling smoke. I got up again to sniff the hall. Must be the tar I'm smelling. Or the firecrackers. I switched the fan on. Once more, the grinding racket bothered me, and that smell of smoke.

The third time I climbed out of bed I caught an orange glow, reflected on my propped-up window pane, and when I leaned across the sill I saw flames up the street. I ran downstairs to the phone, shouted to the operator: "Fire. Weiss's building. One-oh-three Sixth Street," leaped upstairs, yanked on my pajama bottoms. The alarm siren was wailing while I ran, without glasses, barefoot, tar sticking to my soles, up the street toward the grocery. At an upstairs window, I saw a white shadow, maybe Herman, maybe myopic distortion. Then gray smoke billowed past the window and all I saw was smoke and tongues of bright red flame licking the parched side walls and the porch of Herman's Grocery.

A hook-and-ladder, a chemical engine, clanged and chugged up the hill. At the hydrant on the corner, firemen sweated, swore, connecting the hose. The pressure was low; just a trickle ran. "Hurry, Crissake, hurry!" I begged. "A man's trapped in there."

Jack Jones, the fire chief, a brave man, dashed across the burning porch and drove his axe into the staircase door, splintering it open. Dense smoke, rolling down, forced him back. But I'd seen Herman at the head of the steps, alive and on his feet. A tongue of flame leaped from the stairwell wall, catching his beard, catching something in his left hand. "Jump, Herman, jump!" Reckless, I stood yelling, "Roll down! Jump! I'll catch you." Smoke swirled around me, choking me, the fire crawling near.

He came down, inching, blinded by the smoke, flame like a bright beard around his jaw, the nightshirt smouldering on his back, the something in his hand blazing like a torch. Jack Jones and I grabbed him, carried him to the grass and rolled him in a blanket to smother the flames. He moaned but did not cry out.

The roof crashed, showering sparks and embers. Had there been any breeze at all, Sixth Street would have seen a holocaust.

Herman was unconscious and stark naked—the nightshirt had fallen away in black shreds—when the ambulance arrived. I rode to St. Luke's beside him. There, pale nuns hovered, soft-voiced, murmuring prayers for him, cool-fingered nurses brought unguents, and an intern fretted about smoke damage to his lungs. I left him in Emergency, walked home, blackened, barefoot, to pick up our phone, ask long-distance information to look up the number and ring Joseph Sloan of Park Avenue, New York. Joe woke Celia, brought her, sounding drowsy, to the phone. I told her Herman was alive though in critical condition and I thought she should get here at once. She said she'd come as soon as possible and would I keep an eye on everything till she arrived; especially I was to make certain nobody removed anything whatsoever from the building. So peremptory was her tone, I neglected to tell her there was no longer any building.

I pulled on shirt, pants, shoes, hooked on my spectacles, and ran back to the fire. The water flow was still inadequate and the firemen, judiciously, had chosen to spread what there was around, not on, to keep the fire from spreading. Up and down Sixth Street, families were lugging out valises, just in case, and lining the curb to watch, coughing, fanning away drifting smoke. I saw my mother in kimono, wringing her hands, weeping, and I went to her. She clutched my wrists. "Herman! Will he live?" She paused, sighing. "What's he got to live for?"

"Good question, Mama. I'll think about it when I get a chance."

Until daybreak, I stood watching the firemen play thin streams upon seared grass and glowing embers, then went back to St. Luke's to check on Herman Weiss. He was still in Emergency, still in shock, but breathing. I went home, showered, scrubbed my feet, shaved, changed to clean clothing and before seven o'clock was in the newsroom, typing. The lead on my story was: *"Herman Weiss, a long-time resident of Grady's Mills, is in St. Luke's Hospital, fighting for his life, after sustaining severe burns in a fire of mysterious origin which shortly before midnight destroyed his business building and residence."*

Five

A Cadillac pulled up before the smouldering ruin of 103 Sixth Street. A liveried chauffeur opened a rear door; a golden-haired duchess stepped across the curb. Kids who'd been tentatively poking rubble goggled and ran yelping, "Look! Come! See! A Caddy!" It took me several seconds to recognize Mrs. Joseph Sloan, née Celia Weiss.

She extended a white-gloved hand. "I expected to find you here, Samuel." She was toothpick thin and haggard-looking. Midday sun is merciless.

"Your father is alive," I said.

"We left at six A.M.," she answered, "to avoid traffic."

"Come over to our house. Mama will make coffee."

"We stopped for breakfast." She moved toward the ruin. "Why, there's nothing left!" she cried.

We stood together in smoke-hazy sunshine, staring at the broken beams and crumpled window sashes, the blackened chimney, upright, with timbers jumbled at its base, the zinc bath tub, the toilet bowl, the web of tangled bedsprings. Our eyes were dripping, mine from acrid smoke, Celia's, I had little doubt, from grief.

"At least he was saved," I said.

"We'll have to rake the ashes," she replied.

"Shall we go to him now?" I asked.

"Who's guarding this?" she answered.

"He's in St. Luke's," I said. "They're doing everything."

"Maybe we can find them. We will try," she said.

I gripped her skinny shoulders. "Don't you hear me, Celia?"

She exhaled with the kind of tired patience one uses on a stupid child. "Samuel, I know my father has been rescued. This you told me on the phone. And I came to him as quickly as I could. I haven't slept a wink. However, I am not a doctor or a nurse. Therefore, I must take for granted St. Luke's knows how to treat his burns. My problem—this, apparently, hasn't occurred to you—is to make certain there's no looting. There are valuables in here."

I held my temper. "That mess is still too hot to touch," I managed to say. "Let's get on over to the hospital."

The chauffeur drove us there. We talked little on the way. She asked, "He's expected to recover, isn't he?" I answered, "Ask the doctors." She asked, "Did you phone my sister, too?" I answered, "No, did you?" "It wasn't necessary," Celia said.

Sharp in tone and manner as in hip and collarbones, brittle, taut, straining in a vise of nervousness, and imperious, yet practical in small ways, she had the chauffeur stop at a florist's, where she bought a dozen spicy pink and white carnations, and at Rogoff's Market, where she purchased a basket of fruit. "The nurses will enjoy it, if he can't," she said. "They expect these treats."

He was semiconscious, a mummy in reeking bandages, with slits for nostrils, mouth and eyes. She bent over, cooing, "Papa, Celia's here. She'll take care of everything," walked away and crisply ordered a private room and special nurses, then, in clipped exasperation, turned on me. "Now, Samuel, will you kindly do what I requested when you phoned. Arrange for guarding those premises. I am shocked that you neglected it."

"I'll see to it, stop worrying," I said.

First, however, I had to get back to the *News-Record*. Barry Neale had changed one word in my lead paragraph, substituting "undetermined" for "mysterious," and I could not complain. A happening is not mysterious until its cause has been sought and has not been found. One of the other guys had collected the names of the fire laddies who responded and performed. I rewrote my story for our last edition, adding those names, the latest word on Herman's physical condition, and the fact that his daughter, Mrs. Joseph Sloan, had arrived from New York and was at her father's bedside. Then I hiked over to Police Headquarters to ask a favor from the chief.

Steve Durgin, portly and pompous, shirt-sleeves rolled high on his freckled, hairy arms, defunct cigar between his ecru teeth, waved me to a desk-side chair where the standing fan drove its lukewarm gust directly at my nape. "Long time no see. Hear Barry has you on the courthouse beat. How come you're chasin' fire engines, Sam?"

"Good thing I did last night."

A big hand roweled his desk, groping for matches, while he frowned mildly. "How come last night?" The tone of the question struck me as, You looking for trouble, Bud?

I pushed my paranoia back. "Dumb luck. If I hadn't had insomnia, the old man might have roasted alive."

He found his cache of kitchen matches but kept me waiting while he struck one on the sole of a shoe, bit, spat out the moist end of his cigar and got the tobacco ignited. "Barry called me. Barry said you writ the fire was mysterious. Now will you kindly tell me why you writ it so."

Unquestionably, what had been discussed at Walter's in the afternoon had made me choose that word. "You know, chief, as well as I do," I attempted to explain. "Mysterious things have been happening lately on the Hill. That fire in the synagogue. . . ."

"Short circuit in the basement." He rested the cigar on an ash tray's lip. "Weiss had electricity, didn't he?"

No denying it, Weiss did.

Durgin nodded, Q.E.D. "Same thing here. Yes? No?" He picked the cigar up for a reflective puff. "Or candles. You Hebes light candles, do you not?"

On Friday nights, Holy Days and Yahrzeits, I informed him, not on July Fourth.

"Matches? The old man could of lit a match, dropped it?"

"He didn't smoke; he rarely cooked," I said.

Durgin shrugged. "Pokin' around, huntin' for somethin'." He cackled disagreeably. "Maybe countin' up his miser's gold."

No percentage in arguing with nastiness. I mentioned I'd been sitting on our porch steps till after ten o'clock and had seen no light in Herman's building, up or down; the old man surely was in bed, asleep.

"Could of been a spark. Fireworks. Those old shanties, dry as bones. Fire hazards, every one. Ought to pull 'em down, clean the district out." He parked his cigar and scraped his chair to the desk. Then, his gaze fixed on me, and in a tone unlike any I had, in a long acquaintance, ever heard from him, he asked, "Sam, how much fire insurance did the old guy carry, would you know?"

I began to sweat. "Look, he damn near died. Would he have risked. . . ."

"His business was on the skids, I hear. Now, you Hebes. . . ."

"Speaking to me or about me?"

"Hold your piss, Sammy-boy, you and me always understood each other good."

I rose. "Chief, all I stopped by for was to ask would you assign a couple of men to guard those premises. Make sure there is no looting. A couple of honest men."

"That goes for the entire force, man and man," he said.

"The lady will appreciate it." I turned to leave.

"What lady?"

"The daughter, Mrs. Sloan."

He was slow on the uptake. The name stumped him for an instant. Came the dawn, possibly out of wedding and birth announcements that Rosenbaum had written for the *News-Record*'s "Folk You Know." "Shlumpowitch! The guy that beat the rap!" His belly shook. "Shlumpowitch-Sloan!" he roared. "What do you know!"

I had pulled a boner.

"Shlumpowitz here, too?" His amusement was abating; his expression changing to downright ugliness.

"She came alone. To look after her father."

"Awful quick. Who sent for her?"

I backed away from that one, too. "One of the old neighbors must have gotten in touch."

He grunted, not believing me. "Where's Shlumpowitches living nowadays?" A sneaky shift of glance from me to his desk inkstand made his intention clear: record a certain address for hanky-panky at some future date.

"I haven't got the least idea," I said.

"In a pig's eye," he said.

I moved toward the door.

"Wonder what happened to the kid. Must be a big boy now." His eyes narrowed, his tone became deceptively tender. "Poor little orphin kid. Be a kindness if somebody was to let him know he had a living papa. Rich. You wouldn't know where the kid's at, would you, Sam?"

Now, surely Durgin had heard about St. Michael's taking little Jody in; he had enough contacts in the Flats to keep him well informed. Was he trying to drag me back into that mess to do for him what he, in his position, didn't dare to do direct? Straight-faced, I answered that I didn't know and didn't want to know about the kid. Let sleeping dogs lie, I said.

His wagging index finger chided me. "We let 'em off the hook too cheap. Rich kikes. Immoral. You want to know why people hate the Jewish people? There's your answer: Shlumpowitch."

I walked over to the courthouse, thinking, Walter knows the score: start with Durgin, s.o.b. Grade A; thinking, Durgin wouldn't dare; thinking, you bet Durgin would. Rosenbaum, keep your nose clean. If possible.

*　　*　　*

The sun was no longer blazing directly overhead and the damp rubble had stopped smoking when Celia and the Cadillac again appeared on Sixth Street. The chauffeur removed his jacket, rolled his shirt-sleeves up and carried a new rake and shovel from the car. Two cops and a gaggle of urchins watched him yank away springs, iron scales, the head of the old brass bed, iron barrel hoops, dented pipes, scorched metal bins, and commence to rake ashes. Before darkness made the chauffeur stop, he had found—and laid in front of Celia's patent leather pumps—Herman's upper dentures, one brass candlestick, several small tin chests of Wisotsky's tea, and a few blackened coins. The kids pressed forward, scenting treasure trove. A policeman drove them back.

Celia rubbed her swollen eyes. "We'll start earlier tomorrow. It has to be in there."

"Celia, what's so urgent?"

"Are you stupid? Don't you realize? Mama's diamonds." She climbed into the car. "I tried to ask Papa. They have him all doped up. I don't know if he heard one word I asked." She gave the chauffeur Sylvia's address and suggested that I join her there after supper. "Sylvia has kindly offered me her hospitality," she said.

After the car had rolled away, I wigwagged the cops, gave each of them a five-dollar bill and said I knew they'd guard these ruins well. "What the old Jew have in there?" one asked. "Gold pieces? Diamond joolery?"

Mama had cold borsht and canned salmon salad waiting. "You ate today, Semmy? I betcha not. Catch a dremmel first, your eyes is red like fire." She told me everybody had been phoning everybody, saying Herman had a fortune stashed away in the building, and she said it with such certainty I half believed it, too. She also said Sophie Rogoff told her Hymie said sure and positive I'd get a Carnegie's medal for saving Herman Weiss.

I didn't feel heroic when I left for Sylvia's. I felt beat. Necessity, however, primes the pump. I owed Celia the facts preceding the fire; I owed Walter the follow-up to the conference he and I had had. I looked forward to a tête-à-tête on the cool back porch. I found a crowded living room. The Katzes and the Rogoffs—young and old—were there to see Celia and to offer sympathy and, in addition, the Brookfield Heights rabbi and his wife and the refugee doctor, without wife. Two fans were spinning, making little headway against the stultifying heat.

Celia, in a blue chiffon negligee, drooped in a chintz-covered chair. Sylvia was pouring iced tea, cousin Ruthie passing cookies, Carol Frances and Harold, in pajamas, were watching from a doorway, and Walter, in the grand piano's curve, was holding forth. He frowned at me; my entrance had derailed his speech. Several people nodded brusquely. Only Cousin Ruthie looked enthusiastic. I leaned against the wall near the door and hugged Carol Frances to my hip. "Ugh, you smell smoky," she muttered and jerked away from me.

The refugee doctor edged toward me. "I was yesterday to your parents' house. I wished to speak with you." I crossed my lips with two fingers because Walter was scowling.

"Please, Sam!" He clapped his hands for silence and attention. "Now, as I was saying, we need to consider this not as an isolated incident but as one more atrocity. First, the fire in the Hungarian shul—"

Sol Katz, a sober citizen, broke in. "The insurance underwriters said short circuit."

Walter raised his palm. "Okay, we accepted that verdict. What choice did we have? But about Aaron's grave there couldn't be. . . ."

Celia's golden head jerked up. "What about Aaron's grave?"

"A swastika was painted on the stone," Walter told her.

The refugee doctor panted asthmatically. "Chust like Chermany."

"Aaron was the sweetest boy," Sylvia explained to the rabbi's wife. "Handsome as a movie star. And waltzed like a dream. He and I, you know—" She sighed, nostalgically. "That was before Walter's family moved to town. . . ."

"Mama's grave," Celia interrupted tartly. "Is that one okay?" And added with surprising coolness, "I'd best make sure the plot next to it is available."

Mrs. Rogoff gaped. "Herman's gonna live."

"And be well to a hundred years," Mrs. Katz added.

"American doctors," the refugee said. "Who can expect—"

"Who would on purpose burn up an old man?" Mrs. Rogoff demanded. "To who did he do harm?"

Cousin Ruthie squirmed to my side. "May I have the privilege of serving you iced tea?"

Walter clapped again. "As I have been trying to explain to Celia, we have had these several incidents. The stone in the Litvak shul was certainly no accident."

"My grandson, Bobby, he should live and be well!" Mrs. Rogoff cried.

"Like Chermany!" the doctor wheezed.

"Max Slomowitz." Mrs. Katz spoke up. "His place of business was broke in. That gave him the heart trouble."

"Father Sloan retired," Celia said wearily. "He wished to relax in his later years."

"Don't fool yourself." Mrs. Katz fought back. "Lena Slomowitz, she should rest in peace, she herself told me Max was scared, they made him sick to get a heart attack."

"Who's *they?*" Irwin Katz put in. "There weren't any Nazis, not even in Germany, the year Max retired."

Walter cleared his throat peremptorily and spread his upraised arms, begging for silence. "You were not invited here tonight to decide why Max moved to Miami. Celia knows why, I am sure.

She's had enough heartaches today without us upsetting her with this. What we're here for is to try and find an answer to *our* problem. What to do and how we get started. Now, I do have some plans. A couple of people in this room know what they are and I hope and trust they will keep mum because premature publicity could spoil the proposition. And, anyway, what I had in mind is a long-range proposition. What we're concerned with is tonight, tomorrow, the day after. Who knows whose home, whose car, whose store, whose life." His voice—enunciation, use of dramatic pauses—was excellent. Frustrated actor is as good as any reason for wanting to own a radio station. "What we've got in Grady's Mills is Germany in miniachoor. A nest of anti-Semite Nazi rats, and God alone knows in which sewers they are hiding, and getting bolder every day. One day they paint a swastika on a Jewish hero's grave; next day they throw a stone into a shul. And in the middle of the night, a night sacred to independence, to freedom and democracy, they set fire to a Jewish home and business place. What is next? Who is next? What are we waiting for? Pogroms?" He stopped. The murmur of fear swept the room. The rabbi cleared his throat and stepped toward the grand piano's curve, to seize a chance to speak. Walter ignored him. His arm swung in my direction. "Sam, what steps do we take? Come on, give us your advice. Don't hold back, you're with your own. How about, for instance, a stinging editorial in the *News-Record?*"

It wouldn't be easy for me to persuade Barry Neale to publish one, I told them. I was just a working stiff. A big advertiser like Katz or Rogoff might impress him more. Or better yet, a Goy, some prominent Rotary or Kiwanis member. Walter, Sol, would know the proper individual. In any case, the type of hoodlums who perpetrated acts of vandalism like these wouldn't give a hoot for editorials; probably they couldn't even read. Yet since my advice had been asked, I felt I ought to warn them that it was rash to conclude that the fire was arson. Unfounded accusations often boomerang. Then, being overtired, I let myself, for the second time that day, be indiscreet. I indicated what I meant by boomerang: Chief Durgin had hinted Herman Weiss might have set the fire himself to collect insurance.

The room exploded; everybody screamed. "Oi veh, a police chief!" "The lousy anti-Semite!" "The momser!"

"Sam!" Walter's voice soared above the shouts and mutters. "Get that man fired at once."

I glanced at the diamonds on Celia's left hand. "It's not advisable," I said.

They converged on me, they pressed me to the wall, they yanked my sleeves, my tie, they pounded on my chest. Cousin Ruthie lost her head and spilled the plate of cookies on my shoes. "Coward! Traitor!" Irwin Katz shook his fist at me. The doctor squeezed his suet cheeks between his palms and moaned, "Like Chermany. Our leaders said keep quiet."

What am I, folks, hero or yellow-belly? Make up your minds. If not for me Herman might have burned up with his grocery. And, also, friends and neighbors, if not for me, Joe Slomowitz might be crawling from the penitentiary today, not living on plush on Park Avenue, New York, N.Y. True, that s.o.b. at headquarters is dangerous, but not how you all think.

I heard Celia's dulcet voice. "I wish Joseph could be here. He'd show you an example of a Jew who's not afraid." (My jaw sagged.) "Joseph is on a committee with the most important Jewish leaders in New York. They have engaged Madison Square Garden, the largest auditorium in New York, to hold a mass meeting. To demand our government do something against the anti-Semitism in Germany. In September, right after Labor Day, when people are back from vacation."

And how many fresh atrocities between July and when people get back from vacation? Don't be cynical. A Garden-ful of people, hearing speeches, might accomplish more than one Sam Rosenbaum bucking one Barry Neale and one Steve Durgin in Grady's Mills.

The room was hushed, all attention on the slender figure in chiffon who personified the valor of New York's important Jewish leadership. There will be a mass meeting in the Garden. Raise your heads, your hopes, Yiddin.

"Though I shall be busy preparing for Yom Tov"—at last the rabbi had his chance to speak—"I should like to attend that meeting. Perhaps the Brookfield Heights congregation would send me as its delegate. I could bring them a report on our local problems and obtain the best advice of the New York leadership."

Walter frowned. He had no intention of letting this one get away from him. "We'll appoint a delegation," he decided. "I'll take my car; we'll drive together. Rabbi? Okay. Sol Katz? Okay." He looked in my direction. "And Sam? If he's not afraid to ask his boss to give him one day off. It'll do him good to meet some Jews with guts."

I wanted to protest the attack on my character but I was too exhausted and too disgusted with myself. Through force of circumstance and an unguarded tongue, I'd muffed a chance to leave the *News-Record*. Walter now despised me. However, since I had already said too much, I nodded sure, okay, at Walter and stepped over to Celia's chair to ask what she planned to do about Herman, assuming he'd survive. "Why, I'll remain with him this week. Fortunately, Ilene is at camp. Then, as soon as he is able to be moved, I'll take him home, to me. I'm quite certain he won't wish to live here after this."

Mrs. Katz and Mrs. Rogoff exchanged humpfs. "Why not?" Mrs. Rogoff wished to know. "Here is all his friends."

"What about Jessie?" I ventured.

"I presume I shall have to let her know . . . if Papa passes on."

"God forbid!" Mrs. Katz and Mrs. Rogoff cried.

*　　*　　*

The Rogoffs, living on the Hill, offered to drive me home in the new Hudson. I was grateful for the lift. "Well, we made a start, we accomplished something," Hymie said. "We organized a committee. Next step is to start raising funds."

"What for?" I asked.

He paused. I must have made him wonder what for, too. "Why, for expenses," he said finally. "That's how it's done, isn't it?"

*　　*　　*

Celia sent her car and chauffeur to New York—Joe had said he needed the car—and settled in at Sylvia's. Walter loaned her a porter from the work force in his mill. The man, catching the sporting nature of a treasure hunt, worked uncomplainingly in the hot sun, raking debris, and, using old screen doors, he sifted ashes painstakingly. Each evening one of Walter's trucks carted the accumulated junk over to Walter's garage in Brookfield Heights. Durgin's honest cops shooed the kids away.

Mornings, Celia stood beside the ruin, supervising. Afternoons, she sat near Herman's bed, digging in another way, since the conscientious raking-sifting had turned up eight dollars and twenty-six cents in coins, Ida's other candlestick, her blackened knives, forks and spoons, Herman's watch chain and his watch, crystal missing, but no diamond jewelry.

"Papa remembers nothing," she complained to me. "Not even where's his fire insurance policy, his bank books and the deed for the cemetery."

"Paper," I reminded her, "burns first and fast."

"Diamonds don't. I keep asking Papa where he put them; they may be in a vault somewhere while I go crazy hunting in that mess. All I get from him is a mumble. I can't make out one word. Of course, without his teeth. . . . We did find his upper; the lower must be there someplace. . . . Poor Papa! I do hope his brain is not affected. That would make things very, very difficult for us."

Abruptly, she decided to return to New York. She phoned me at home in the evening to say she had a Pullman reservation on tomorrow's 10 A.M. express; she had just spoken with Joseph long distance; he'd reminded her she did have responsibilities in New York. So sorry she wouldn't have another chance to see me; tonight she had to pack—she was taking Mama's candlesticks along to get them refinished; let Papa decide, when he was able, what to do with the stuff in Walter's garage. She'd spoken to Dr. McGrath, the medical superintendent, told him she felt there was no point in her sitting like a dummy next to Papa's bed. She had the fullest confidence in his doctors and nurses, angels of mercy, every one. And the nuns! She'd never dreamed nuns could be so sweet; she'd always been afraid of them; sort of spooky, she had felt they were. She'd explained to McGrath that if there was any change in Papa's condition—for the worse, she meant—he was to notify her friend Mrs. Walter Leeds, who would contact her immediately. She'd left her personal check for the room and special nurses for this week. And bought candy for the nurses. Did I think Whitman's Sampler was nice enough? And would the nuns expect some, too? What was the protocol? Oh, dear, it all had been so frustrating, so heartbreaking, she could hardly think straight any more.

She talked so fast, so hysterically, I had no chance to ask whether the raking-sifting-guarding was to continue.

Sylvia drove her to the depot and dropped in at the newsroom afterwards. "Ceil was so upset last night she forgot to tell you she appreciated all you've done. But she wanted me to tell you she hopes you'll come down in September with Walter's delegation, and if you do, she wants you for dinner at their place. Specially to meet Ilene. She knows you will adore the child; everybody does. What a heartache Ceil's poor mother, may she rest in peace, never knew Ilene. But, Sam, such worries Celia has! If her father's brain has been affected by this accident, will it be safe to have him live with them? Safe for Ilene, she means. That child is her whole life. Joe, I'm sure you realize, was never Ceil's intellectual equal. He's—well, to put it mildly, crude. You can't make a silk purse—"

"Out of a horse's ass," I said.

"Shush! I wouldn't exactly call a man who's made a million dollars a horse's ass," she said.

Barry Neale was glaring, outraged because our conversation was too low-toned for him to eavesdrop on, so I walked Sylvia out to the hall, where she reminded me that Ruthie would be around another week and I was not to take to heart Walter's sarcasm the other night; he was overwrought, carried away, he's good as gold at heart, as by now I ought to know, he'd give me his last shirt, and I was always more than welcome in their home; Ruthie thought I was simply wonderful the way I'd been completely honest with that crowd, and modest too, admitting I wasn't important enough to get Chief Durgin fired. . . .

"Or free Tom Mooney," I managed to put in.

She gave me a look—"Don't you worry about Goyim. Take care of your own"—glanced over her shoulder at the ogre behind the city desk and faked a slight shudder.

I asked whether Celia had left any message about continuing the treasure hunt.

"She said forget it. She realized she'd just been making a fool of herself; no doubt Jessie's had the jewelry all the time. And anyway, all she accomplished was raking up old bitterness. But it wasn't the monetary value, it was the principle. It was her right and privilege to protect her inheritance. She is the oldest, isn't she?"

That evening at supper my mother asked me did I have any idea of what Police Chief Durgin had talked to Celia about yesterday. From our stoop, Mama had watched the chief's car pull up, Durgin lean out and summon Celia from the sidewalk to his running board. Naturally, Mama couldn't hear what was being said, but she noticed Celia got red in the face and acted very nervous.

He wouldn't dare, I thought. Oh, wouldn't he? The bastards are in the saddle, riding high. And we're running circles, scared.

At the end of the week, Herman was wheeled into a ward and the special nurses taken off the case. The women on the Hill cooked chicken soup, took turns carrying it to St. Luke's and trying to cheer Herman up. He still wasn't talking, they reported, not even with his God.

A couple of junkmen from the Flats started to scavenge in the ruins, carting away pipes and plumbing fixtures that might bring a buck or so. This, when you came to think of it, was how the Slomowitz fortune had begun. Curious how the wheel turns, isn't it?

* * *

Late one afternoon, several days after Celia left town, I received a phone call in the newsroom. "Sam? This is Jessie Weiss."

"Oh, hello! When did you arrive?"

"Just now. And a goddam shlep! The Super-Chief was late. Missed connections in Chicago. Century wouldn't wait. Missed connections in New York." She sounded hoarse and tired. "Why in hell didn't you wire me about Papa?"

"Did I have your address?"

"Call yourself a newspaperman? You could have found out where I was. I presume that takes initiative and a little brains."

Here we go again. Haven't seen her in a decade. She re-enters swinging from the lip.

"Listen, Jessie Weiss, you do have a sister. . . ."

125

"Who took her good-natured time sending me a telegram. Night letter, twenty-five words for two bits, fifteen bawling the kid sister out for lack of filial devotion. Had to phone transcontinental to find out what was up."

"Takes a catastrophe to bring you here."

"Cut that out. You make me sound like a buzzard."

"Nope, she beat you to it."

"What in hell are you batting about?"

"Skip it. Where are you now?"

"The Hiram Grady. Room six-twenty-one. A slum. Listen, I'm going to use the john, wash my face, grab a taxi to St. Luke's. Would it be too much to ask—I hate to impose on an important journalist, but my local friends are few and far between—for you to meet me here, in the bar at nine P.M.?"

The jury in a vehicle homicide case dawdled over dinner, their last free feed at county expense. It was eight before they brought their verdict in, nine before my story was typed up, ten past when I reached the Grady.

That barroom is a cavern, dim, dank and beery-smelling. It was practically deserted; the important drinking here is done daytimes by downtown businessmen. A pair of traveling salesmen were trading wisecracks at the bar with the waiter and the bartender, who raised his eyebrows, seeing me. *News-Record* reporters seldom patronized the place, it being overpriced for us. In a booth at the far end, under a whirring ceiling fan, Jessie sat, an empty shot glass, an overflowing ash tray on the table before her, dark head and horn-rimmed spectacles bowed above a scratch pad on which she was scribbling. I slid onto the leatherette seat opposite. She did not look up. Her face muscles were sagging; her complexion was ghastly. She looked so beat I almost pitied her. I reached across and laid my hand on hers that held the fountain pen. "Turned any handsprings lately?"

Her lashes fluttered. "Oh, hello! Give me another second, will you? I have to put down everything."

I dumped a cigarette from my pack, smoking while she scribbled, gnawing at her lower lip, until with "That is it," she capped the fountain pen.

"Local color?" My tone wasn't pleasant.

126

"Louse." She removed her spectacles, folded them inside a leather case, dropped case, pen and pad into an alligator handbag and clicked it shut, decisively. "A list," she informed me. "Things to check up on. Did Papa have fire insurance? Life insurance? With which companies? Bank accounts? Where? How much? Deed for the property. Is there a mortgage? Are the taxes up to date? Deed for the cemetery plot. When was he born? Where? When naturalized? All kinds of documents need personal data. Do you realize every scrap of paper was burned up? Even"—she forced a smile—"my magnificent report cards." She thrust the handbag from her and braced her spine against the seat back. "What's your beverage?"

"Beer," I said.

She tapped the shot glass—"Make it Scotch. Don't be stingy with my money"—craned her neck and snapped her fingers. The bartender disengaged the waiter from the drummers at the bar. She ordered Scotch, double, for herself, no ice, water chaser. I still preferred the beer. "And bring me the check," she told the waiter firmly. He gave me a funny look. Women don't buy drinks for men in Grady's Mills. "Don't argue," she told me. "I'm too bushed to fight." And sighed. "Such a vast United States! Three days, three nights, on wheels."

"How'd you find your father?"

"Groggy, weak, depressed. Cheered up, I think, when he realized daughter Jessie had arrived. I believe the old man likes me, Sam. And why's he in that noisome ward?"

"He had a private room while Celia was in town."

"Why didn't she leave him there? Christ! My darling sister's husband has two dollars more than God."

The waiter brought our drinks. He dropped the check precisely in the center of the table. I reached for my wallet. Jessie gripped my wrist. "I pay for my guests." She scrawled her name and room number on the tab, tossed a dollar from her alligator satchel on the tray. The waiter beamed. Grady's Mills tippers were strictly ten per cent.

She flung the whisky down her throat, not wincing at its bite, and wiped her mouth with the back of her hand, muttering, "Lebensmittel." This it must have been for her; her eyes began

127

to come alive. "Dr. McGrath made noises about skin grafts," she went on to say. "I said daughter Jessie would provide. Flesh of his flesh."

"Could your father talk to you?"

She shook her head. "He tried. He mumbles so. No teeth. Bandages. And weak. He's badly burned, you know. Lies there, silent, thinking. And who's smart enough to fathom an old man's thoughts." She sipped the chaser, unfathomable, too.

"How old is he, do you know?" I asked.

She set down the tumbler. "Fifty, sixty, seventy, who knows?" She raised her head and forced a smile. "Well, Sam, Lear's earthly kingdom's gone. What do we do now?"

Not my problem, not my show. "Play Cordelia," I said.

"Not this bitch." Her headshake was sharp, final. "She hasn't even got a home to bring him to. Moves from sublet to sublet. . . . Okay, suppose I try to set up a home for him. What would Papa do in Hollywood? Can you picture Herman Weiss in Schwab's?"

I wanted very much to ask her how one lived, what one did out there, pick up a few crumbs of inside information, but she was galloping ahead, preoccupied with misgivings, observations. "I don't know my father; he does not know me. Which child knows a parent? For that matter, who knows anybody?" She groped for my cigarette pack. I lighted one for her. She took a long, hard pull, then held it between her fingers, waving smoke. "Sam, all the way across the continent, I kept thinking about my father: who is he, what is he? I need to know so I can help him best. Don't look so skeptical. I love my old man even if I haven't sucked around the grocery. Well, we rode across New Mexico. I thought, This is Papa, stark, craggy, lonely, aged, ageless. Old tribe. Like the Indians. Scratching a bare living out of hostile soil. Well, we went through Colorado. Grandeur. By God, that is Papa, too. Then Iowa. . . ." She smiled. "Iowa is soft and lush and very, very beautiful. No kidding, Sam, it is. And Iowa reminded me of Mama's great big bosom. Honestly, I am not crazy. Yet Iowa was Papa, too. The richness in the soil. So what does it produce? Corn and hogs. Sister Celia and myself. Guess which is which." A sassy grin alighted on her mouth. It flew away. Somberly, she said,

"What lonely hell it must have been for him, deserted by his womenfolk."

"Did you have to?" I drained the lees of my beer.

"Little birdies leave the nest." Lifted eyelids, gray eyes probing, for the first time this evening seeming altogether aware of me, as me. "And why haven't you?"

"I like the nest," I said.

The impish smile brightened her tired face again. "You wouldn't lie to me? Want another beer? . . . Do I want another Scotch?" Her voice was almost gone. A woman is not made of iron; three days, three nights on wheels. "Nope. Enough's enough. Just tell me something, one thing. The rumor is, I half caught it from my sister's stingy narrative, you were a sort of hero. True or false?"

"Half true," I said. "I turned in the alarm; the fire chief smashed the door."

Her hand stretched across the table, covering mine. "Thanks, Sir Shmulke Galahad." The touch, the name, the recollection, made me wary. I drew my hand away. She didn't seem to notice. Her forehead wrinkled. "Tell me something else. This afternoon Papa said something I couldn't quite make out. Sounded like 'tickets burn,' and he tried to point to his left hand. Tickets for where, for what? Do you figure he was trying to go away, possibly to me? Was there something in his hand?"

"When he came down the steps his hand was like a torch."

She turned slightly more pale, more tense. Her shoulders drew together. "No more tonight. Details can wait. I'm bushed. All I wanted was to share a drink with somebody who gives a damn. It's horrible to feel an alien, an outlaw, in your own home town. Sam, that's what happens to me here." She hung the alligator satchel on her arm. "Could you meet me here same time tomorrow? I'll be occupied all day."

"If it's raking ashes, you're too late. The ghouls have cleaned the premises."

Her heavy eyebrows arched, questioning. "No, looking after Papa and my list." Hands' heels on the table, she pulled herself erect.

So many years had gone by since I'd last seen Jessie Weiss I had forgotten she was short. The way she talked, tough and authoritative, gave one the impression of tallness. She slid out from behind the table and tilted up her face. "Sam, do one thing more for me," she said with a quiet urgency. "Put your arms around me, hold me for a second very tight. And if you do not mind too much, kiss me, will you, kid?"

I held her and I kissed her, blushing hot, and that was not because the bartender was leering but because kissing her had not occurred to me. A man takes the initiative; a shlemiel waits to be asked.

Her mouth was warm and sweet, her small, plump body inviting.

"Thanks, pal," she said huskily. "Thank you very much."

We walked out together and in the lobby stood a moment, surrounded by the cracked, black leather chairs, the dusty potted palms and brass spittoons, tongue-tied, both of us, yet keenly aware of what we wanted, each of us, and what, having known each other all our lives, we wouldn't get. She mumbled, "G'night." I said, "Try to get some sleep." That was it. That was all of it.

I went out into the empty downtown street. We have 9 P.M. curfew for age sixteen and under; we pull in the sidewalks at half past. I climbed Market Street wondering why I didn't try to go to bed with Jessie Weiss. She was in the mood, not passionate but with another sort of need, for the comfort of a man's embrace. And this was a woman who might be great in bed. She had warmth and wit as well as sensuality. Strange, I cannot treat her like a woman. Wisecrack only, kid around, before she makes a nothing out of me.

That's it. She frightens me. Her bark and bite, her brashness, she wears it like a sandwich board. And why? To cover up a loneliness? To deny an ache for love so painful she's ashamed of it? Well, one thing is for sure, she's selling herself short. She could be lovable if she half tried. The mouth is soft, the body yields. Be honest, Sam, could you love Jessie Weiss? Be honest, Sam, you do. In your fashion, you have, since she was twelve years old. But she? She needs, she takes. Then cuts me down to size.

Tomorrow is another night. What will be will be. For God sakes, Sam, don't be afraid. Jessie Weiss is Herman's daughter, Ida's daughter, a kid from the Hill, she's not Mrs. Jesus Christ.

She was waiting for me in the barroom. Her lipstick was on, her eyes clear and bright. She greeted me with a brusque nod, no pathos, weariness, or even personal interest. We both ordered beer. While we waited for the beer, she told me she had had her father moved to a corner room where, propped, he could glimpse trees and petunia beds, and she'd engaged private nurses, one of them a buxom, cheerful young woman who'd been in her class at high school. Between them, they'd coaxed Herman to sip chicken broth through a straw. "A Mrs. Rosenbaum brought it, Sister Veronica said. Your mother's home brew, no?"

The waiter set the foaming schooners down. She let me pay. She drank, not speaking till the register had rung my money up. "Okay, Sam, now give me all of it. Before, during, afterwards."

She let me talk, no interruptions whatsoever, and she listened with a concentration, as though memorizing every word, while I told her about the other fire, the tombstone desecration, the stoning, the spikes in Walter's tires, the conversation he and I had had on Independence Day, and how Durgin had acted when I came to ask him for the guards. Obviously, I had to tell her why I'd made that request, and when she heard how Celia'd rummaged in the ashes, she muttered, "Buzzard, get you," and wrinkled her brow— "But doesn't Celia have the diamonds? Vaguely, I remember she mentioned them to Papa when we were here, after Mama died"— shrugged, then waved me to go ahead to describe the indignation meeting in Walter's living room.

"Seriously, Sam, not off the top of your head, do you honestly believe that fire was arson, deliberate incendiarism?"

I hedged. "Might be. Suspicion isn't proof."

"But why? What's to gain for whom by burning a run-down Jewish grocery store? By trying to kill an old Jew who never harmed a living soul?"

"Jessie, anti-Semitism has no rhyme or reason, you know that. It's a disease, in the blood stream, in the bones. A senseless hate that started way, way back. Maybe when Abraham smashed the idols. Maybe when a certain Jew was nailed to a cross." I leaned across the table, lowering my voice. "Jessie, there are cesspools in this town, as in most small towns; there have always been—you know this, too—kids who learned it with their Catechism, ignorant

131

people, snobbish people, who hated Jews before Hitler gave them the green light. Durgin will not dig them out because they're his people. And do not ask me how I know."

Her expression did not alter, and it occurred to me she might have stopped listening. All she said was "I think I'll hang around" with a peculiar glitter in her eyes, and I got the queerest feeling that Jessie was no longer across a table from me in the Grady bar but had wandered off into a private world.

I waited, not speaking, for her to return. I prompted, saying, "Well, I'll say good night."

"Good night." She didn't rise or tip her face for a kiss or indicate anything except that she had nothing more to say or hear. I plodded up the hill, alone, nonplussed.

She remained in Grady's Mills a month. What she did I got in bits and pieces from individuals she went to see and, sporadically, from her by phone and accidental meeting. We had no further trysts in the Hotel Grady bar.

She dropped in at each of the local banks, introduced herself to the manager, said since all her father's papers had been consumed in a fire, she needed to discover where he had accounts and how much were the balances. He had a savings account, consisting entirely of deposits of the Chanukah gift checks she had sent, and a business checking account with a miniscule balance from which he paid his wholesalers. She called on the insurance agencies, found one with a record of a five-thousand-dollar straight-life policy, paid up, of which she and Celia were equal beneficiaries. The policy provided for disability payments which might cover part of his hospital expenses. She also learned he had had fire insurance until the policy lapsed a year ago because he hadn't paid the premiums. She was businesslike and thorough. She obtained photostats of everything.

She carried the photostat of the cancelled fire insurance policy when she called on Fire Chief Jones and Police Chief Durgin. Jack was flattered by her visit—he called me up to tell me so—since she'd begun with graciousness, thanking him for what he'd done to save Herman. He protested, as was seemly, that a man expects no thanks for doing what's his duty, but he became uneasy when she commenced to quiz him on whether he'd smelled kerosene around the premises, or found suspicious footprints near the building, or noticed any other circumstances that might hint at arson. "You see," Jessie explained, "I have to do the investigator's job, since no insurance company is involved. Unfortunately, Dad let his policy lapse." She brought out the photostat. "Getting old, maybe absent-minded, forgot to pay the premium."

"Absent-minded, eh? Maybe he forgot he left a candle burning. You folks light them for religion, don't you?"

"On certain occasions. July Fourth is not one." Then, pretending casualness, she added, "It is a bit mysterious, no? Like that fire in the synagogue."

"That was short circuit, ma'am," Jack said and clammed up. "Glad we saved your father," was all he said after that.

Durgin got a similar routine. "Chief, I'm Jessie Weiss of Hollywood. Came all the way from California to look after my dad. Thought I should stop by and thank you for those officers who guarded my father's property. Too bad there was nothing left to guard. A total loss." On his desk, too, she dropped the photostat. He glanced at it and Jessie said (I hope she told the truth) he blushed while he scowled. The scowl may well have been because, uninvited, she'd pre-empted the chair beside his desk. "I'm sure you're making a careful investigation," she purred. "You'd not be in your present high position if you weren't a conscientious law-and-order man. Some people do suspect there may have been a robbery, before, and the fire set to cover it up. And others have been hinting that it might have been arson, malicious vandalism. Now that's very serious, I'm sure you will agree. It would be important, wouldn't it, to discover whether the town had a gang of dangerous criminals? There have been other incidents, I've been told."

"By whom?" Durgin growled.

"Why it's an open secret, Chief. For instance, when a hero's grave is desecrated, just because he is a Jew. . . ."

She had him where the hair was short. Therefore, he turned bellicose. "Miss, don't go fishing for trouble, don't go stirring dirty water up. You look for trouble, you find trouble, more'n you expect."

"Like what, Chief?"

"Excuse me, miss, I'm a busy man," Durgin said.

He phoned me. His call was a warning. "You tell that dame lay off, mind her own business. She goes too far, she'll be sorry, Sam."

I got her version of these visits on the courthouse steps when we met by chance, she coming out, I going in. While we sat broiling in the noonday sun, facing the Victory monument, the bronze doughboy, lunging with his bayonet, atop a granite pedestal that bore a tablet that had the names of Aaron Leiberman, Hyman Rogoff and Samuel Rosenbaum, Jessie told me, "Both monkeys were so cagey. Hear no evil, see no evil, speak no evil, when the evil stinks to high heaven."

"What in hell are you up to?"

"Research. And believe me it is like pulling teeth. The town is run by idiots. Take a f'rinstance. I have just spent two hours and twenty minutes in this building, merely trying to get copies of the deed, mortgage and tax record of my father's piece of property—God help the ignorant and timid who come seeking information here! Well, there's no mortgage, the lot is free and clear, taxes up to date. Papa was a conscientious citizen. Lot might be worth a couple hundred after the debris is cleared. If we cash in the life insurance, sell the lot, Papa will have something to start over with." She paused, staring at the monument in silence, before she said, low and thoughtfully, "If he wants to, if he can. Not an easy thing." She rose, dusting her skirt with her hands. "Aaron has a gold star," she murmured, irrelevantly. "You just went along for the ride, didn't you?"

"Go to hell," I said.

"Not today," she said. "I have an appointment at St. Luke's."

She went horizontal there that afternoon. Her epidermis was flensed and strips transferred to Herman's back. I heard about the skin graft from Dick Adams of our staff, who had St. Luke's on his beat. "No visitors" was on her door, he said. I stopped at a florist's, before I went to crash the barrier, and had a hard time deciding what to buy for her. There is a language of flowers. We boys memorized it when we began to take girls to the high school dances: red for passion, white for purity, yellow for friendship, pink for sweet sixteen and women in childbed. Mabel Armbruster, of dim memory, had made it easy; she adored tea roses. What do you bring a Jessie Weiss? Thistles or cactus? When the clerk began to show impatience, I said, "Okay, carnations, white ones with red stripes."

"Perfect for a hospital," the florist said. "The refreshing whiff of spice."

Through a closed door, I heard laughter and Jessie's husky voice. Diffidently, I opened the door. The patient lay propped on her side, a covey of nuns and nurses clustered around her bed, giggling, while she parceled out tidbits about the private lives of Mary Pickford, Douglas Fairbanks, Gloria Swanson, Shirley Temple and Rin-Tin-Tin. I stood listening, interested, too, until a nurse spotted me and began to shoo me out. "Oh, hello." Jessie waved from the bed. "Fancy meeting you." Reluctantly, with swishings of starched frocks, rustlings of habits, the audience fled. A nurse snatched my bouquet for watering.

"How's our heroine?" I asked the patient.

"Anyone I know?"

"It was big of you, doing this for your father."

She reached back to her upraised buttock. "Plenty more where that came from."

"What made you do it?"

"Foolish question."

"How do you feel?"

"Healthy." Her gray eyes focused on my face, intent and disconcerting.

I labored to make small talk, about Herman's physical condition, the continuing heat wave, the surprising, charming gayety of the nuns. She answered with monosyllabic grunts and the intense stare.

"Would you rather I didn't stay?"

"Up to you."

"Just stopped by for a minute, have to get back to the office."

"See you in church."

"I brought you flowers."

"A friendly gesture," Jessie said.

I didn't return to St. Luke's. The rest of what she did in town I know chiefly secondhand.

Dr. McGrath, the medical superintendent, was quite taken with her. He brought his wife around to meet her. They invited her to dinner at their house, a landmark event, since no Jew, male or female, had, to my knowledge, been a guest of the McGraths. The social ice having been broken, Mrs. Roger Burton Harper, president of Sorosis, our ladies' literary society, decided to give a tea for her at the Hilldale Country Club. That, truly, was a crashing of the barriers. I wanted to cover the party but Barry sent our society reporter, and it was from "Folk You Know" I learned that Miss Jessica White, formerly of this city, now a Hollywood screenwriter, had given a delightful talk about personalities in the motion picture colony, after which cheese and olive and minced ham sandwiches, Lady Baltimore cake and iced coffee had been served, and that "Miss White, who is petite, dark-haired and gray-eyed, was becomingly gowned in a summer suit of oyster-white raw silk, with exotic garnet jewelry."

When I stopped in at the library that evening to exchange my books, Miss Ehling, our librarian, said wistfully, "I wish it wasn't summer and so hot in the building. I'd love to have a reception here for Miss White. It isn't often Grady's Mills entertains a real celebrity."

After she read the paper, Sylvia Leeds phoned Jessie at the Grady and said she'd like to give her a small dinner party to meet some of our prominent Jewish people. She also asked would Jessie care to spend a few days convalescing at their cottage at the Lake. Jessie said—rudely, I have no doubt—her social calendar was filled. However, she did have lunch with Walter in the Grady dining room, where they discussed Adolf Hitler, the grave of Aaron Leiberman, and the menace of anti-Semitism here and overseas. She also asked Walter if he'd be good enough to make inquiries, through his parents and in-laws, for a modest kosher boarding house in the Catskills where Herman might recuperate. She'd phoned to suggest the meeting. Walter was delighted to oblige, though he was annoyed when she said, no, she'd rather he didn't bring Sylvia along. He told me he'd found her well-informed, intelligent, though stuck on herself, talking a blue streak, so that he couldn't get a word in edgewise about radio broadcasting. Having attended the Emerson College of Oratory and worked in Hollywood, she might have had a few ideas for his radio station. She brushed him off, too, when he asked what she wanted done

with the junk piled in his garage. "I didn't put it in; I don't propose to take it out," she said.

My mother wanted her for supper—so far, she hadn't visited the
Hill, not even to see the ruins of the family property. I phoned the
invitation. "Thank you, no. When I left the Hill, I left for good."

"What's the matter, we ain't stylish enough?" Mama grumbled,
adding, with a belligerence worthy of Ida Weiss, "A Jewish anti-
Semitt, that's the worst."

Done with the Hill and, from her silence and indifference, done
also with Samuel Rosenbaum.

On a Sunday morning, near the end of August, I heard the
celebrity's imperious voice over the telephone. "Sam, I'm checking
Papa out tomorrow. Taking him to the Catskills. I've bought him
everything he needs: shirts and socks and BVDs, a suit, a sweater,
shoes. False teeth. Temporaries. But where in God's name do I go
to buy a tallith and tfillim?" She chuckled, amused in advance by
what she was about to say. "It never occurred to me people shop
for these. Somehow, I felt Jews acquired them, like halos, by acts
of piety."

I hadn't the slightest notion either of where to buy a tallith, and
come to think of it I never had been curious. The narrow satin
prayer scarf I wore on Holy Days had been bought for my Bar
Mitzvah; all my years I'd worn no other one. Yet I was sure I
knew where Herman's tallith was and so I said, "I'm surprised
Herman doesn't remember."

"Poor dear, he doesn't remember much," Jessie said. "I can't pull
words out of him."

"I'll bring it to the Grady," I told her.

After dinner, I walked over to the Litvak shul, to the queer,
cozy, tiny building of yellow brick, dingied by time and factory
soot, styled after memories of Lithuania, Poland, the Ukraine, an
outside stone staircase leading to the wide oak doors, round eyes
of colored glass, one blue, one red, above the door, a bronze Star
of David on the roof. I mounted the stairs. The front doors were
locked. I went around the sides and rear, trying knobs. One
yielded to my turning. It let me into the Beth Hamedrash, the
study hall, the long, bare room where sponge cake crumbs from
yesterday's Shabbos Sudah dappled a wine-stained cloth on the

137

trestle table. Books, bindings tattered, lay helter-skelter in a dusty sectional bookcase, out of Abe Finkel's erstwhile den. I climbed upstairs, my shoe steps echoing in emptiness.

I came into the big room. The descending sun had struck the colored windows, draining shafts of red and blue from them, lighting the yellow varnished benches, playing on the fringes of the Bema's purple velvet cover, skipping along the wooden doors that concealed the Scrolls, red-velvet-wrapped and silver-tipped; skirting the steady, small Eternal Flame. Dust motes shimmered in the shafts of light. There was a touching beauty in the silent room. Silent, yet clamorous with hoarded sounds: the cadence of the ancient prayers, the whooo of the ram's horn, the children's squeals and shouts in the procession Simcath Torah night, and Herman's hoarse voice, reading from the Scrolls. Then, suddenly, the place was peopled with my friends: Isie Katz and Hymie Rogoff, Joey Slomowitz and Aaron Leiberman, jostling me on varnished benches. I was again a boy. The boy was part of this. It was awesome to stand alone here with my childhood.

The prayer shawls hung on a chromium rack just inside the door, shawls of soft, creamy cloth—is it linen? is it wool?—black-banded, fringed, and narrow satin scarves striped with blue or gray and tinsel-trimmed. Herman's—this I remembered well, since I had seen it often—was a white with black, the shroud-imitating tallith. But which? Oho! it's a cinch. On the shelf above the rod from which the prayer shawls hung, were the small sacks of phylacteries, a neat straight row, each sack in its designated place, above the owner's tallith. I saw a purple velvet sack, with Hebrew letters sewed in silver, Herman's initials, exquisitely embroidered, by Celia's golden hands, no doubt. The tallith directly underneath would be Herman's. I took it down, folded it, draped it over my arm and tucked the velvet sack into my pocket.

I turned to leave, turned back, and took my sweat-stained, sleazy satin tallith from the rod. I knew, not knowing why I was so sure, that I, too, was finished with the Litvak shul in the ghetto on the Hill.

In the dismal hotel lobby of the dusty potted palms, cracked black leather chairs and brass spittoons, I handed over Herman's tallith and tfillim. "Curious yet most fitting," Jessie said. "This is all my father has got left." Then she said, "Excuse me, Sam, no time for a farewell drink. Packing, phone calls, stuff. We're leaving early. I've hired a car and driver."

"Isn't Herman going to say goodbye to his old friends?" I asked.

She frowned, perplexed. "That's another screwy thing. He doesn't want to see a soul. Maybe I'm a witch, but eppes tells me he's ashamed to face his friends. But why? Because his beard's burned off?" She rose on tiptoe to brush my cheek with a kiss. "Thanks for everything," she said. "See you in church."

As before, I didn't try to hold her, claim her, and, as previously, she neglected to leave a forwarding address.

Six

I fell in love with Ilene Sloan. She was ten, which is the best age for little girls. It's the interval of grace and quiet between childhood and teens, a period unnoticed generally because it makes so little fuss. Besides, this ten-year-old was exquisite. She had Ida Weiss's tiny nose and porcelain complexion, Herman's large gray eyes and chestnut hair, and Celia's slenderness, plus a sweetness all her own. No trace of Joey Slomowitz.

I saw her big eyes peering around a doorway's arch into the apartment foyer where a Negro butler took my hat, before I was ushered into the Palace of Versailles: rosewood, brocade, velvet, marble tabletops on gilded legs, Aubusson carpet, tapestry, gilded picture frames for Cupid's messengers, crystal chandelier prisms, gold satin draperies, rose quartz and cloisonné tsatskes. I'd seen nothing like it since I was a doughboy, sightseeing in France.

Celia, in a gold cloth hostess gown, sat beneath a life-size portrait of herself, hair honey-blonde, throat like a swan. A pretty penny must have oiled the artist's brush. The masterpiece was lighted from above. The subject, under it, looked bleak. She extended a limp-wrist hand but did not rise. "How nice to see you, Samuel! It was good of you to come."

The child stood watching with bright, anticipatory eyes. "Ilene, dear, this is our friend, Samuel Rosenbaum."

Ilene made a pretty knix.

"Hi, sweetheart," I said.

"Samuel was the best man at Mommy and Daddy's wedding. That makes him a sort of uncle, doesn't it?"

I heard the chime of silver bells, Ilene's delicious giggle. "Then he's Uncle Sam."

"Sorry, I forgot the stovepipe hat and swallowtail," I said. Once more the bells chimed.

"Do sit down, Samuel," Celia said. "Joseph has been detained."

I sat. The child sat, too, demurely, alongside her mother. I inquired after Celia's health, received an evasive answer and a perfunctory question about mine. A dull start, unpromising. Ilene whispered to her mother's ear. "Yes, of course, dear," Celia said. "You may show Samuel your room. If he is interested."

I rose. Ilene tucked her fingers into mine.

"Gone goose," I told Celia. "Your daughter is a dream. Had I but known, I'd have flown on wings."

Instead, I'd come in Walter's Buick with the delegation from Grady's Mills to the mass meeting at the Garden. Walter had written Joe that four of us were coming and please reserve good seats. Only I had been invited to dine at Sloan's before the public gathering. Celia's perfumed note in the E-for-Excellent penmanship said, "Joseph and I would like to have you as our guest for dinner in appreciation of what you did for Dad." And about time. After Celia had left town on the 10 A.M. express there'd been no written word to indicate she was aware of what I'd done. Jessie's noncommunication I expected; Celia's irked, particularly because money was involved. I hope I am not petty, yet it rankled that my wealthy New York friend hadn't asked whether I had had to tip the cops, if so, how much? let us reimburse and thanks for your cooperation, Sam. Carnegie medals I will shenk you. Just return my out-of-pocket cash.

Walter seemed put out when I mentioned I was dining with the Sloans; I'd join the delegation later at the Garden. His behavior toward me on the drive to New York had been ambivalent: not entirely hostile, disillusioned rather, and sarcastic intermittently. Sam, the local shnook, had balked, had publicly declined to stick out his neck. We demote him though we can't dispense with him just yet.

"Please come in. This is my room," Ilene said. "I hope you will like it."

I said I did yet I was disappointed. It was pink-walled, excessively ruffled, and more like a toyshop than a room in which to grow and dream; a big doll house, a stupefying assortment of dolls and woolly, furry animals. Too babyish.

She removed a life-sized doll from a rocking chair. "Won't you

sit down?" She laid the doll gently on the bed and drew an otto-
man over to my chair, fluffed her skirt out carefully before she
seated herself. We smiled at one another. I wondered what we'd
talk about. My conversational experience with ten-year-old girls
had been limited.

"I hope you didn't mind my saying *Uncle* Sam," she began.
"You see, I never had an uncle."

The pleasure was mine, I answered, and the deal was perfect,
because I'd never had a niece. We smiled again. I remarked about
the abundance of the dolls and beasts. "Oh, they're my dear, dear
friends," she said. "I call them my family. I'm an only child, you
know."

"Me, too," I said.

Her look commiserated; we had a bond. She inched the otto-
man closer. "Did you mind it very much?"

"Not particularly," I said.

"I do. I try not to but I do." Thumb in chin, she pondered the
difference between our attitudes. "Prob'ly your mother didn't
have appointments," she decided, coming right up to the truth.
"My mother does, from the minute she wakes up. Her fittings, her
hairdresser, her dentist and her doctors. And her Hadassah and
her Temple Sisterhood. And all the teas and lunches where she
simply has to go. She's hardly ever home. Do you know what I
wish the most?" Her expression was poignantly wistful. "Some
day when I come home from school, I'll find Mommy here, waiting just for me."

My mind's eye saw two little girls with absurd plush sailor hats,
skittering along an icy street, hurrying home from school, to Ida,
obese and overbearing but *awaiting;* to Herman, stern, withdrawn,
but *there;* sisters alien in temperaments yet side by side, doing
homework at the kitchen table, sharing a double bed, scrubbing
floors and window sills above the grocery, sitting behind the
counter in the store, siblings, bruising one another, jealous, quarrelsome, but *together there.* Better by far and much a quarrel
than the echo of a solitary voice in emptiness.

"Most girls have grandmothers," Ilene was saying. "They come
to keep them company when their mothers aren't home. Both my
grandmas have passed on. Mitzi—she's Grandpa Sloan's wife—she

isn't my real grandma; 'sides, she's in Miami; she never comes to visit us. And Mommy looks mad when I ask why she doesn't visit us, so I just don't ask. And my aunts are in Miami, too, except my aunt Jessie. She's Mommy's sister. She's in California. I've never seen her in my life. Did you know my aunt Jessie before she moved to California?"

"Quite well," I said.

"I wish I did," she said. "She must be very different from Mommy and Mommy's friends."

"She is," I said.

"I thought so from her presents. Let me show you what." She bobbed up to open a dressing table drawer. She brought out three little packages, removed their tissue paper, held up a string of crude-cut turquoise beads, two silver bangle bracelets, and a pair of tiny Chinese brocade slippers. "Mommy won't let me wear this jewelry," she said with her grownup gravity. "She says it isn't suitable for me. And the slippers! I love them but whose feet can they fit?"

"Cinderella's," I said. That pleased her but she shook her head. "I'm not going to the ball. And there isn't any prince. And I don't have hateful sisters." She wrapped the trinkets neatly, and with reluctance. I felt she really wanted to like Jessie's gifts. She squirreled them away and came back to the footstool.

"I guess Aunt Jessie doesn't know children very well. Just the same I would like her to come to visit." She sighed. "I wish anybody of my family would."

"You should have let me know you needed me. Sent up smoke signals."

She giggled as I'd hoped she would. It was immoral for a pretty ten-year-old to be as serious as she.

"Mommy said she'd forgotten all about you till Grandpa Weiss's house burned down and she had to go look after him. And she met you and she remembered how you used to help her with her lessons and you came to all the parties in her house. Did you have lots of fun?"

"Lots of cake," I said. "Your mother's a wonderful baker."

"You must be mistaken. Mommy never bakes. The cook does that. Our new one, I mean. Mommy had to let Anna go. She was

143

a sleep-in. We had to have her room because Grandpa Weiss is coming here to live. Did you know that?"

I didn't know but I was not surprised, I said.

"He's been very sick," the child informed me, again with grownup gravity. "He's in the country getting strong. Daddy's going to send the car to bring him here to us." A frown creased her forehead. "But he sort of frightens me. You see, he used to come to us for Passover and Mommy used to take a room for him in a hotel and he'd take the bus over here for Seder. And I'd watch him sitting high up on the cushions, reading the Haggadah and looking, looking like—" Her hands spread, baffled trying to describe Herman.

"Like an Old Testament prophet?"

"How did you guess? That's what Daddy's friends said last year. So it must be so. Only he made me nervous when it was my turn to ask the four questions—I learned them in Temple Sunday School. But just in English, and I thought he'd feel bad if I didn't say them in Hebrew. But he never said a word, just went on reading like before. He never talked to me at all."

I was sorry about that, I said. "He isn't talkative. But he is kind and good."

I saw her worry-frown again, heard her courteously formal, "I do hope he will be happy here," before her face lit up. "Would you like to see his room? Mommy has just finished it."

She took my hand again and led me down a wide, carpeted hall. "Mommy's room is there. And her bath and dressing room. Daddy's room is there. And his shower and his exercise room." We turned an L. "The dining room is here. The butler's pantry. And our kitchen there."

Past the kitchen, off a narrow, linoleum-covered corridor, we came to a green door whose lintel held a shiny tin mezuzah. Ilene pressed a switch button on an inside wall. A naked twenty-five-watt bulb illuminated a room smaller than a cell in our county jail. I smelled shellac and paint. The room had been freshly done in dentist's-office green. A maple single bed, a maple bureau, an upholstered armchair, maple frame, all pristine from the store, were dovetailed like jigsaw-puzzle pieces, leaving barely space for sidling through. The bed had a white spread, the floor a sliver of braided rug; the bridge lamp was behind the chair, a price tag dangling from its parchment shade. The window curtain was tied back, to frame a triangle of scaly brick building wall and rusty fire escapes. Straining upward, you could glimpse a patch of sky.

"Mommy is buying him a little radio. He can keep it on his dresser and sit in his chair and listen to his programs without disturbing Daddy's guests."

Unexpectedly, unbidden, my eyes blurred. I am no weeper; a reporter dare not be. Mankind's sorrows have to leave him dry-eyed, a fact-collector who types the story, double-spaced. I turned away from Ilene to give my surge of emotion time to ebb. I opened a door and saw a closet, gussied up with chintz. On the shelf were Ida's candlesticks, glistening with lacquer. I shut the closet, feeling worse, and turned another knob. I saw a cubicle, holding toilet and washbasin, neither tub nor shower. Celia, your father is a clean old man. He bathes. He also breathes. He's lived in several rooms, looked out on grass and trees and sky. This is a coffin you've prepared for him. I shook out a handkerchief and blew my nose.

"Do you have a cold?" Ilene tugged my sleeve. "Oh, your eyes look crying. This room made you sad." She looked distressed. "But we couldn't let him have the bigger servants' room." She tried to explain. "Our couple sleeps there. And Mommy says it's hard to find a couple to take care of a big apartment, serve at table and stay in nights with me. She couldn't let *them* go. She didn't feel so bad about the cook. Anna kept mixing up the milk and meat dishes, and Mommy's *very* strict. And when they entertain we have a caterer, so a part-time cook is really all we need. So Mommy called Salvation Army to take Anna's furniture, and we had this room for Grandpa Weiss."

I tucked my handkerchief up my sleeve, took the armchair and raised Ilene to my knees. I hugged her, something I had wished to do from the minute I had seen the girl.

"Uncle Sam." She tried to comfort me. "He won't have to stay in here unless he likes being by himself. He's welcome to come in my room any time he wants. And even in the drawing room when Mommy isn't having company."

"Sweetheart, he won't complain. He's not a complaining sort.

And having you will make him very happy. Yes, I'm sure it will."

Her worry-frown eased off. "I'll go walking with him in the park. I'll take him to the museum, to the zoo. I'll play dominoes with him, Old Maid." She paused, the thumb punching her soft chin. "But what will he do while I'm in school? Or dancing class? Or the Schelling concerts Saturday? Or summer when I go to camp?"

"He'll pray," I said.

"All the time?" she asked.

A Negro maid poked her head in. "Miss Ahlene, youah mommy was wonderin' wheah you was. Youah daddy has come home."

Ilene slipped off my knees. "We'd better hurry. Daddy hates to wait." She held my hand again, hurrying down the halls. "I'm glad it's you that's company because I'm eating in the dining room with you. Most times when they have dinner guests, I eat in my room. I guess Grandpa Weiss will, too."

Joe sat behind a battery of bottles on a wagon table, a room's width away from Celia's couch. "Hi, Sam! How're you?" he rumbled. An ice cube clinked into a glass.

"Fine. How're you?"

"Alive and not kicking."

Had I met him on the street, I wouldn't have recognized Joe Slomowitz. The acne-pitted youth had become the reasonable replica of a gentleman. Good tailors and good barbers can work miracles. His suit, discreetly pin-striped navy, had padded shoulders, wide lapels, precisely fitted sleeves, eased just enough to slide back to show his gold cuff links; his four-in-hand necktie bore a black pearl, his kinky hair was slicked and aromatic, his cheeks lightly powdered.

Celia, beneath herself in oils, simpered, "Ilene, darling, Daddy's waiting for his kiss."

Joe filled a jigger with Scotch, letting Ilene stand while he poured whisky on his ice. He tasted it before he drew her to him, slid his fingers down her spine, nuzzled her throat, smacked her cheek. "Aaah, my sweetheart, my darling!" Her lips touched his forehead. He held her off and beamed at me. Celia nodded, approving. I got the feeling this tableau had been staged for me.

"Take a load off your feet, Sam. What do you drink? Martini? Manhattan? Scotch on the rocks?"

I said I'd have rye and ginger ale. Joe's glance was faintly derisive. Ilene carried the highball glass to me.

"My wife will have her usual." Joe filled a wine glass from a green bottle with a Saratoga Water label. Ilene delivered it.

"Thank you, darling. Mommy has to mind the doctor's orders." Celia turned toward me. "I'm paying the price for this summer's strain and agony."

The maid carried in a tray of snacks: smoked salmon, sturgeon, olives, black and green.

I raised my glass. "L'chaim!"

"Cheerio!" said Joe, an Englishman from way, way back. "You stay around, we'll have you drinking Scotch."

"Who's staying?" I took a sturgeon canapé. Joe took two of lox. Celia took nothing. She sipped her Saratoga Water, smiling secretively.

"Have another, Sam?" Joey asked.

"No, thanks," I said.

"Joe, will you have another? Yes, I will," Joe said.

His hand was on the bottle when Celia snapped, "Joseph, please!" I saw their glances clash.

Come to think, I'd not seen these two together since their wedding. What they were, who they were, to one another, after a decade, I couldn't guess, though I noticed Joe did not pour his second drink. "She's the boss," he said, apologizing lamely. "My wife don't want me to get fat."

"Dinner is served," the maid announced.

Celia rose languidly, taking Ilene's hand, and led us into a baronial hall. It had a beamed ceiling, shining woodwork part way up the walls and a lot of gold: in fleur-de-lis embroidered on rose-colored silk that lined the walls; on the crystal, china, candlesticks and cutlery; spread on lace on the banquet table. At either end—I found it hard to credit what my eyes beheld—were high-backed thrones. Celia halted beside her throne, looking expectantly at me. I marched resolutely past. I met you behind the herring barrels; pull out your own chair, girl. Ilene faced me across a gilded horn of plenty that was spilling flowers and fruit.

Extremely grand. Sure, Celia, I'm impressed, though not how you think.

The maid and butler carried in cut fruit in crystal bowls in silver bowls of ice, set them on the gold-trimmed plates, snatched them off when Celia signaled with a buzzer beneath the rug beneath her feet. They set down cups of chicken soup, deftly, swiftly, like magicians doing tricks.

The fruit was ordinary, the soup lacked salt and body. No one commented; we weren't talking yet. Celia pressed the buzzer. The magicians removed soup cups and fancy plates. Then, while the room was briefly clear of hired help, Ilene spoke. "Mommy, I showed Uncle Sam Grandpa Weiss's room."

"Your grandfather's home," Celia corrected her.

"No more butter with the meat," Joe growled from his throne.

"You know we never have," Celia said tartly. She caught my glance at a ridged yellow ball on my bread and butter plate. "Margarine," she hurried to inform me. "This is a kosher home. I have kept it so, not merely from respect for the laws of our faith but out of respect and consideration for my father. I don't want him to hesitate to eat at his daughter's table. You should realize, Samuel, there is as much of the true spirit of Judaism on Park Avenue as there was on the Hill. I am rearing my daughter to revere our heritage." What she'd lost in weight, obviously, she'd gained in pretentiousness.

Joe grunted; Ilene fidgeted with forks.

The butler placed a standing roast of beef in front of Joe. "How is Herman?" I asked Celia while Joe honed the carving knife.

"Father is healing nicely. We expect him for the Holy Days."

Joe scowled above the ribs of beef. "My wife thinks I should build a shul next door to accommodate my father-in-law."

"The synagogue may be a little problem," Celia conceded. "We may have to persuade Father to use the car—that's one of the adjustments he may have to make. And of course, it would be so helpful at the beginning, till he gets adjusted to his new surroundings, if he could see a familiar face." She looked pointedly at me. I couldn't imagine why.

The butler distributed slabs of beef, the maid offered vegetables and rolls, warm under damask, the butler decanted burgundy from a cut-glass carafe.

"I hope you're enjoying your dinner, Samuel," Celia said. "We're treating you like family. As you see, we live simply." With crystal bowls of tepid water in which a slice of lemon and a water lily's floating, with sleight-of-hand by which the bowls, their underpinning lace doilies, are whisked off and triangles of frothy lemon pie expertly centered on glass plates?

The butler set a silver coffee urn before Celia. Madame poured with grace. Where, now, had she learned these elegances? She must, again, have had private tutoring.

Joe mopped meringue from his lips. "Just you and me will be going to the meeting," he announced.

"It's not that I am not interested or vitally concerned," Celia assured me. "But the present state of my health forces me to limit my public activities."

Ilene, bless her, looked worried.

"We'll get there early," Joe continued. "Feller I want to introduce you to: Wullstein, the press agent. I sent him a memo, told him you're my personal guest . . ."

Hey, what is going on? This feast, this personal-guest business, is making much too much of our relationship. Pay me my ten bucks, say thanks for everything, I'll say thanks for the dinner and pleased to meet Ilene, take the subway to the Garden, join Walter and my delegation, tout fini.

". . . he should save a seat for you at the press table, you'll meet the newspaper boys. You'll introduce yourself, start in making contacts. And if Baumberg should happen to be available, which I doubt he will be, Wullstein is to introduce you." Joe grimaced. "Baumberg is the king."

I thought you were, I thought, saying nothing.

The butler entered, bearing cognac, snifters and a humidor.

"You may excuse yourself, darling," Celia told Ilene. "Mommy will be in to say good night."

The child folded her napkin and stood. "Excuse me, please. Uncle Sam, it was so nice meeting you. I do hope you'll visit us again."

"Kiss Daddy good night, darling."

Obediently, Ilene went around the table to brush Joe's pitted cheek with her soft lips. "Good night, Daddy dear." Drilled, disciplined—and exploited—I decided, another showpiece in this showy place.

"G'night, baby." Joe had a Corona Corona between his teeth. He did not remove it.

"Hey, sweetheart!" I spoke too loudly; I couldn't help myself. "How about a kiss for Uncle Sam?"

Celia flushed, glancing from me to the butler, silently begging me to act refined in front of him. Ilene blew a fingertip kiss across the table. She departed without a backward glance, her small scene finished, her part played in this exhibition of the home life of the Joseph Sloans.

The butler lighted my cigar. Celia coughed delicately, signaling me to puff the other way. "That will be all," she told the man. He left the room. She leaned toward me. "Joseph has something to discuss with you. You'll be surprised." She awarded Joe a nod, me a thin-lipped smile.

Joe rested his cigar on a saucer. "Well, Sam, no use me dragging the suspense out. I guess you been wondering why we asked you and not Walter and the gang. Well—" He hitched his throne to the table. "Ceil found out when she was out there, nursing her father, you weren't crazy about your job on the paper. Getting pushed around. Sadie—Sylvia, excuse me—told her you'd been talking to Walter, maybe he could cook up something, you could make a change. So Ceil got the idea, I got the idea, we both got the idea, you'd like to get the hell out of that one-horse town. Hypocrites. Anti-Semite bastards." He took his cigar up for a puff. "Sure, you bet, New York has its share. Only here they get lost in the crowd." He flicked off a quarter inch of ash and blew a smoke halo. "Moreover, we have a very active organization. On the ball, what is happening in Germany shouldn't happen here." He drew deeply on his cigar, laid it down, inflated his chest. "Sam, right now, our J.A.C., our Jewish Aid Committee, is expanding its staff. We are in need of good publicity people. For writing news releases, statements, pamphlets, speeches. What you could handle with two hands tied behind your back. I am in the position to recommend. Sure, Baumberg hires, but who pays his

150

salary? Me." He thumbed his breastbone. "Victory Steel. Number one contributor." He blew himself another halo. "Alongside of us, the German-Jewish bankers, the Yahudim, are stingy pikers. Take for an instance, Adolph Simon. . . ."

I was startled; he amused by my startle.

"Ah huh, my sister-in-law's father-in-law. For whom the Weisses weren't good enough."

"Blanche Simon is a very gracious woman," Celia informed us. "We serve on committees together. When I think of how Jessie behaved toward her, it positively makes me ill."

"Anybody been in touch with Jessie?" I put in.

"Hell and gone to Hollywood and let her stay," Joe said. "How'd she sneak into this? What I started in to say, before my wife interrupted, is the German-Jewish crowd is scared shit-less. . . ."

"Joseph, please!"

"Please yourself!" he barked. "No guts. Hush-hush. Maybe we shouldn't demand Roosevelt should let in the Jewish refugees, they'll take the jobs away from Goy-Americans, make more rishes here. Maybe we shouldn't antagonize that Hitler, it could start a war, American boys go out and fight to help the German Jews. Who's afraid of a war? Not me." He saluted himself with his cigar. "They argued maybe we shouldn't even hold this meeting in the Garden. Maybe only just send a committee down to Washington, leave a memorandum for the President. Sure, I said, that's genius, only just be sure you typewrite it on tissue paper, so he could wipe his ass. . . ."

This time, the "Joseph, please!" was not sufficient. Celia, eyes modestly lowered, had to interpret for the guest. "Joseph feels all this so deeply, he gets carried away. It isn't necessary to be vulgar, really, Joseph, it is not, especially when you happen to be men-tioning our beloved President. I have no doubt he feels this just as deeply as you and me."

"In a pig's eye!" Joe brandished the cigar at her and turned a baleful glare on me. "Who's afraid? Of who? Of what? We're Americans. I ask you, do we need to be afraid?"

Max in the shanty in the junkyard had cringed, an old-world Jew, with pogrom terror in the marrow of his bones. And I, in my

151

own way, had felt the genetic dread. Yet here was Joe, the sow's ear, the horse's ass, with steady guts and bold big mouth. He, the ignoramus, was telling off the aristocratic old Yahudim who, since the day when Peter Stuyvesant let in the first shipload of Holland Jews, had looked after the needy; he, the parvenu, was pre-empting their prestige. Because they were timid, he was brave? Or because he had the gall and the purchase price of leadership. Sam, be fair, if possible. You may be underestimating Joe. Times produce the men they need. These years demand tough characters.

So preoccupied was I with my speculations, only half an ear heard the preamble to what Joe was telling me. ". . . if you would be interested, and if you ask my personal, frank opinion you would be crazy not to be, we could offer you a nice position"—I came alert—"with a future, starting right away. Serve your people. In a small way make a little history. And earn a decent salary, say five thousand a year for the start. How does that strike you?"

Timing is the essence of all moves, this offer in the hour of my discontent, of my disgust with Barry Neale and Steve Durgin. And for twice my present salary. Maybe Joe expected me to dicker, ask for six, which I might have, had I had an inkling of the cost of living for bachelors in New York. Instead, I stammered, "Strikes me great." The ten bucks, bread upon the waters, was returning icing on the cake.

"Of course"—Celia leaned in my direction—"this means cutting ties. Just like Papa must. But maybe"—her voice softened—"you and he could keep each other company. Maybe go to shul together. Maybe now and then go walking in the park. Maybe play a game of checkers in the evenings. We had thought of hiring a companion for him, but you can understand how much more it would mean to him to see a friendly face from home."

Quid pro quo. We get you a well-paid job, you help us look after Herman. Fleetingly, I regretted I'd said yes so fast; then I thought, What the hell, I saved Herman's life, he's my responsibility. Old Chinese custom, isn't it? Moreover, coming here to visit him, I'd also see Ilene, tell her a few corny jokes, bring her a small present of laughter.

"It was Ceil's idea," Joe conceded. "Sometimes my wife does

use her head." He glanced at his wrist. "If we're going we better git. Car's downstairs. I told him half-past seven."

By my reckoning, we had time to spare, but Joe was the boss—my boss, now, in a way. I shook hands with Celia, who looked replete with raw canary, received my hat from the butler, and followed Joe into the elevator. The chauffeur acknowledged our previous acquaintance with a half wink when he said, "Good evening, sir," as I climbed into the rear seat of a familiar Cadillac. Joe gave him an address. It was not the Garden. We pulled up beyond the marquee of an apartment house in the West Fifties. "Be just a couple of minutes," Joe told me.

We sat, the chauffeur and I, in the darkened limousine, he stiffly erect in the driver's seat, I slouched in back, chain-smoking and brooding. Had I been precipitate, snatching up an offer that might change my life? Would I enjoy press-agentry? What little I had seen of it, I had deplored with a newspaperman's snobbishness. It's crawling into newspapers through a cellar door. And would I enjoy living in New York? I'm a small-town guy. Walk down any street in Grady's Mills, somebody waves, "Hi, Sam." Here I'd be a stranger, Mr. Nobody; address: a furnished room. So what? I have lived here before. When there were open trolley cars. And I a wide-eyed hick, discovering the theater. Well, Broadway is still here. And I do not have two heads, I can make new friends. "The fault, dear Brutus, lies not in our stars but in ourselves that we are underlings. There is a tide in the affairs of men. . . ." This is my tide. And my chance to help my people. That should be the main consideration. What little I had tried to do in Grady's Mills had come to nothing there. I had too much to lose and so I shut my trap. If Joe's committee makes its protests loud enough, they'll be heard everywhere, even in Grady's Mills.

The chauffeur's head swiveled. "Would you mind, sir, if I turned on the radio? Game at Ebbets Field. Starting about now. I'm a Dodger fan."

"Me, I like the Yanks." From his sniff, I gathered I'd mentioned the wrong team. "Go ahead, I'm not prejudiced," I said.

"Thank you, sir. And may I ask were Madame's jewels found?"

"Madame's jewels were not there," I said.

"I feared as much," he said. "She was rather upset." He clicked on the car radio, and while Red Barber drawled the pre-game warmup, I continued mulling. Uprooting is no cinch. Yet I must have been ripe for it, else why had I removed my tallith from the rack? What is there for me in Grady's Mills? A big nothing, kid.

The radio and my watch agreed on twenty after eight when Joe loomed under the marquee. The chauffeur silenced the radio, stepped briskly out to open the car door. I caught a furtive movement, the chauffeur handing Joe a folded handkerchief, Joe rubbing cheeks and mouth, returning the handkerchief, a practiced sleight-of-hand. A whiff of musky perfume entered the limousine with him. Joe settled back in the seat, ordering, "The Garden." I didn't say a word to him or he to me. Prosperity had not changed Joey Slomowitz.

He fumbled in an inside pocket of his jacket to draw out a folded sheaf of papers. "I'm making a few remarks tonight." His tone was self-deprecating. "Give this a quick look, will you, Sam? Maybe you'll have some suggestions I can incorporate." He switched on the car light. In fancy phrases, unlike his usual speech, Joseph Sloan was pledging, by his faith and honor, that Hitler could be blasted from the globe, provided all within the hearing of his voice stood shoulder to shoulder and opened up their wallets to the Jewish Aid Committee. Stripped of decorative verbiage, it came down to what Hymie Rogoff had pointed out to me: first you organize a committee; then you raise money.

"It's a little—well, strong."

He bridled. "Strong is what's called for. No pussyfooting."

"And after the money's raised?"

His stare rebuked my ignorance. "Without money there is nothing. Fighting Hitler is no dime-store proposition, Sam. There's big expense involved: the office rent, the telephone, the printer, not to mention salaries and the carfare to send the delegations down to Washington. And you think we get the Garden free?" He folded the speech and whacked his knee with it. "Hand it to them strong, they give. . . . Wullstein wrote this, following my ideas, of course. Maybe later, when you catch the knack of how I like to talk, you'll write me stronger ones."

I drew away, into my corner of the wide back seat. You might say I cringed.

There was a mob outside the Garden. A mob has a blood-congealing sound, boos and yells and growls and groans blended into a sullen roar. A mob has motion without movement, the massed bodies milling, no direction, all directions. A mob has a pulse, a throb of fever rising. A mob is frightening.

The mob converged around a thin line of youths in brown-shirts, holding signs that bore the swastika. I heard "Heil Hitler" shouted. I saw police nightsticks flailing. I saw police horses rearing and, on the curb opposite, men and women, watching, waiting, cheering, like those Parisian harpies around the guillotine.

I saw Jewish people streaming, heads ducked down, through the main entrance. Turn around, go home, I wanted to shout to them, Jews can get killed here.

Joe, beside me in the limousine, chortled, "Some turnout! Great publicity!"

The Cadillac cut in toward a side entrance. Stolid bluecoats flanked the door. A harried-looking man sprang forward, opening the car door. "Mr. Sloan! The Mayor is coming!"

"Some crowd!" Joe answered him. "We showed the bastards, didn't we!"

The harried man seized Joey's elbow. "This way, please, Mr. Sloan."

"Wullstein, this is Rosenbaum. . . ."

"Pleasetameetcha." My hand was pumped.

"Wullstein, I sent you a memo. . . ."

"Received, contents noted, sent to Baumberg. Got a press card, Rosenbaum? Good. Anybody tries to stop you say Leo Wullstein sent you. Have to escort Mr. Sloan."

News-Record press card in my hatband, I walked cement corridors lined with cops. I was bumped by scurrying men and women, waving colored tickets. My head filled with excitement and the smell of grilling frankfurters. In the vast arena, row on row, tier on tier of seats soared to a distant roof, faces, human semblance, blurred by the fuzz of smoke and lights. Strangers or my brothers? Who can tell?

Floodlights drenched a platform in the center of the floor, a stage that held a lectern, dripping wires, bearing a microphone and a white shield, blue-lettered: "Jewish Aid Committee. Your

155

Bulwark Against Hitler"; four standing flags, the Stars and Stripes and the blue and white banner of the Zionists, paired at either end; and a semicircle of armchairs. A fight ring, stripped of ropes and canvas, rigged out with flags and empty chairs.

Bluecoats, shoulder to shoulder, made a barrier, an aisle, to the platform's steps. In the arena's center aisle, a contingent of war veterans, uniformed, trench helmets gleaming, paraded with a band. The band was playing, of all things, "The Blue Danube Waltz."

Below the apron of the stage, I saw half an acre of green felt, spread on a mammoth trestle table that was cluttered with manila envelopes, mimeographed white paper, cameras, spent flashbulbs, and ash trays. Around it, on yellow wooden folding chairs, sat three score of my peers. I found a chair and straddled it.

All I remember of that evening seems so trivial now I hesitate to set it down.

I remember a red neon sign, high up, on a balcony rail, advertising "Billy Taub, the Clothier."

I remember Joe Sloan marching across the stage, chin up, belly in, taking his chair, crossing his knees, pinching his trouser creases. One pants leg hitched up. A bright blue garter, a hairy calf, was visible. I remember Leo Wullstein at the lectern, drawing the microphone toward himself, beginning, "Ladies and gentlemen, our national anthem," hearing a gargantuan howl, an ear-splitting squeal, going white with panic, waving frantically for help. A shrimp, in coveralls, strode cockily across the stage to adjust the gadget.

I remember the voluptuous soprano in green satin, singing the national anthem, stirringly, I thought, though some guy at the press table kept making sotto voce cracks about her bosom. And I recall the warm gush of my embarrassment when she started the "Hatikvah," since never before had I heard that Hebrew hymn of hope sung with Goyim present. I was astonished when the *New York Times* reporter hummed along with her.

I remember, too, a rabbi, with a white beard down to here, who gasped and wheezed the invocation and shook with age and fervor at the microphone. And a wild-looking character in a front row seat, who rose in the middle of someone's speech to pound his chest and hoarsely shout, "Ich bin das Yiddishe Folk." I expected cops and ushers to come rushing to toss the interrupter out. Instead, I heard the press table's laughter. "That nut! No Jewish meeting is official without him."

Of the interminable speakers and the speeches, I remember one—and of this, just the man and not a single word he said. He was swarthy, stocky, shrill. He pounded the lectern so emphatically the painted shield jiggled; we were afraid it would fall off. The crowd stamped, clapped and whistled when he finished, not so much for what he'd said as for what he was: the Mayor of the City of New York. And I recall the wild applause for him, particularly because it had been perfunctory for all the other orators. The audience seemed apathetic, lulled and drugged in the vastness of that arena, where the message reached them, if it did, dehumanized by amplifiers.

Oddly, I have no recollection of appeals for funds or of resolutions offered, and this may be because this meeting merged with all the meetings I attended after it, so that my brain's recording lobe failed to keep notes of routine procedures.

I do recall, however, how the Garden cluttered gradually and inexorably with discarded programs, handbills, newspapers and stragglers in the aisles, and how cigarette smoke drifted toward the ceiling, settling like a gray box lid atop the auditorium.

And I remember that my coccyx ached after four hours on a wooden folding chair and that I was bored when I'd come to be inspired. And with pleasure I recall an earth-brown face, leaning cater corner to read the press card in my hatband, saying, "Aha! Grady's Mills! We had a little article about some trouble in your town. I am Gershon Rothman of the *Jewish Morning Journal*. How's things? Any change?" He and only he had made me feel there was a solid reason for my presence in the Garden.

A rabbi was pronouncing a benediction, the crowd was oozing out, the reporters scooping up their mimeo sheets, when Wullstein appeared, beaming behind his perspiration beads. "Everything okay, boys? Got all the speeches? Everything?" He handed me a slip of paper. "Here's the address. Eleven sharp tomorrow morning. Baumberg will see you."

I started to protest, "Have to find my delegation. We're driving home tonight."

Rothman tapped my shoulder. "How's about a glass of tea?" I said I ought to try to find my friends. Rothman disagreed. "You're lucky if tonight you find yourself. Come with me."

The tide had caught me up. I grabbed my envelope of speeches and drifted beside Rothman out into the lobby, wading ankle deep in paper rubbish, past platoons of cops, into a tepid night. I caught a tabloid headline: "New York Jews Defy Hitler Terror." Presumably, in the Reichschancellery, Adolf was quaking in his boots.

We subwayed and walked to the Café Royal, over on Second Avenue, where the Yiddish actors, journalists, poets and philosophers congregated, to resolve the world's affairs each night. Rothman steered me past the crowded tables to a quiet corner at the rear. "Tonight I want you for myself," he said. "Some other evening I could share you."

The waiter squinted at the press card I'd left in my hatband. He removed it, read it poker-faced, handed it to me, with a mocking little bow. We ordered tea. "Rothman will have apple strudel," the waiter informed us. "The gentleman is a stranger. We give him a prune Danish."

"In the Royal," Rothman advised me, "the waiter is the only one you do not contradict. . . . So talk, let me hear. How did the meeting impress you?"

Rothman had sympathetic and intelligent brown eyes, a warm, candid quality. I could trust him with the truth, I felt, and so I said, speaking for myself and only for myself, the meeting was a bore.

Speaking for *himself*, Rothman agreed with me.

The waiter brought our pastries and our tea. The glasses were too hot to touch. While they cooled, I confided to Rothman I'd been offered a job with the Committee and had snapped it up, though at this moment, let down by the meeting, I was reconsidering.

"Stop considering," he advised me. "Why did the meeting let you down? What were you expecting? Trumpets? Cherubim and seraphim?" He sampled my prune Danish. "Rosenbaum, what we have we use. We have men. And only men. Men willing to stand up and be counted. I do not ask their reasons. Each man has his own. For one it is plain fear of Hitler; for another, he knows it is the Jewish destiny to fight to live; for some, it is ego, pure and simple. To be a big shot, get the picture in the papers. Which it is I do not care. All that matters is the man speaks up. So they speak with the tongues of ordinary men. Not angels, not prophets. To how many angels, to how many prophets, have you listened in your life? So let me tell you, for your future, exactly what to do. At a mass meeting disconnect your ears. Turn on your brain and think: Why are we here? What more must we do?"

We tried our tea. Rothman got a mouthful down. I had to wait.

"So, Rosenbaum, let me tell you what I will do tonight when I get to my office. I will spread out the bullshit Wullstein has mimeographed—and for him my heart bleeds, the poor shlimazel must put statesmanship and correct grammar into the mouths of jackasses—I will pick out from here one paragraph, from there one paragraph, that has a little zaft. And the story I will write, this I guarantee, will make whoever reads tear out his hair because he stayed home to play pinochle with his upstairs neighbor in the Bronx. Such a meeting he missed! Historic! Inspiring! This, you understand, is my responsibility as a Jewish journalist. From the kvatch in the Garden, I must make a call to arms." He paused to fork up strudel. "You read Yiddish, Rosenbaum? A pity. This is my eternal sorrow. So many whom I would like to impress cannot read one word I write. You speak Yiddish, perhaps?" He washed the strudel down with tea. "Good. Then you know the word galuth? Exile. You have been living in galuth. Now, come home to us. I think—yes, I am sure and positive—you will not regret." He pressed my hand that dawdled on my glass. "Look, Rosenbaum, here a Jew is a somebody." His voice had deepened with a kind of urgency. "A Jew is the Governor of the State of New York. He is half the Mayor of the City of New York. That fellow with the Italian name had a Jewish mother, did you know? An Italian name, a Jewish heart. Here you will not need to keep looking behind your shoulder, listening with one ear, what will the Goyim say? Why, in this place, in this Café Royal, the Sanhedrin sits." His head wagged, half mocking. "Sages, judges, masterminds, knowing all, deciding everything. And on the Committee you will find good people, brainy people. Sure, positive, you will also find the shtunks, like in any place and every place. We are people. We are good and bad. The people do not matter. The purpose is what counts. Rosenbaum, come. But do this not for others. Do it for yourself. You'll inscribe it in your book of life. You'll brag to your grandchildren, when the crazy Hitler threatened my people, I came forward and defended them." Then, in a quieter way, he concluded, "Long ago, one of our sages said: 'If I am not for myself, who will be for me? But if I am only for myself, what good am I? *And if not now, when?*' That is the whole proposition."

It was the best speech I had heard all evening. It had common sense as well as eloquence and a useful, apt quotation. It sold the bill of goods.

Rothman helped me find a medium-priced hotel, where, having no luggage, I paid in advance for a room. He shook both my hands. "I have done a good job, I think. Shluf gesundt."

Sleep well. Who could, on the brink of changing worlds? I sat at the hotel window, smoking endless cigarettes, looking down on the lights of other insomniacs, watching dawn pearl the awakening city of New York. I breakfasted early, got a shave and shine as soon as the hotel barber came to work. Having time to spare, I strolled to Macy's, bought a shirt and, neat and polished, at five of eleven turned up at the address on the paper Wullstein had given me. It was a drab suite in a midtown office building.

"Sam." Wullstein went straightaway to my truncated first name. "You are about to meet a personality and you will hate him at first sight because he will treat you like a dog. But don't you sell him short. He is a dynamo, a whiz, unique. A king. A legend in his own lifetime. He got where he is because he knows exactly what he wants. And he'll pull out your fingernails, one by one, till you give him what he wants. And you will come across, because he inspires. By hate. Today, he'll give you the hot treatment, tomorrow the cold. One day you're the fair-haired boy, next day you're a bum. He will drive you nuts. But show him you know your stuff, do a decent job, you'll never lack a pay check so long as you live. It's like a Jewish civil service: you're in, you're in for life. But once you try to doublecross Baumberg—or he thinks you did, which in his mind is the same—out you go, out, out, on your ass. No two weeks' notice, no reference, no matter which lay leader is your friend. Vershtehst?"

He rapped discreetly on the opaque half-glass of a door. A smartly tailored woman of indefinite age opened it a crack. "Mr. B. will see you in a few minutes. He is taking a long-distance call."

We waited in the corridor. Wullstein paced. He looked more nervous than I felt. After all, I still had my job in Grady's Mills. The King could take his Jewish Civil Service, stick it up.

The door opened. "Mr. B. will see you. Go on in."

Venetian blinds were drawn against the late morning sun. Thin bars of light filtered into a large corner room, prison-striping a slender, dapper man with hair and mustache black as ink. He perched behind an oversized desk that was blanketed with newspapers, within walls adorned by framed, glossy photographs. I recognized newsworthy faces: F.D.R., the President; Eleanor, his wife; Albert Einstein, the physicist; Chaim Weizmann, the chemist-Zionist; Stephen Wise, the rabbi-Zionist; Herbert Lehman, the banker-Governor of New York, each shaking hands with a someone whom I didn't recognize. In every picture, slightly off center, like an usher or an alter ego, was the popinjay who ruled this littered desk. "What's with your *Daily News?*" Thus he greeted us. "Where's the Mayor's picture?"

Wullstein blanched. "That was taken by the *Journal*. I'll send out for first editions right away." He lunged for a phone on the desk.

Baumberg brushed the reaching hand away. "And who is this character?" His eyes stabbed me, sharp and cold and colorless as icicles.

"Sam Rosenbaum. Mr. Sloan sent me a memo. I sent it in to you."

The newspapers rustled. "Miss Markowitz!" The secretary, waiting at her desk, pad and pencil at the ready, sprang to her feet. "It's on your desk, Mr. Baumberg." She riffled the newsprint. "I know I put it here." She held a sheet of paper up, triumphantly.

The cold eyes raced down the sheet. As far as I could judge

from my standing position, other side, eighteen inches to the right of the wide desk, the memo was brief. Baumberg studied it at what seemed interminable length, after which he studied me, without an eyelid's blink. "Sloan recommends you. He must have a reason. We'll give you a chance."

"Thank you, sir," was on my tongue-tip. I held it back.

"Six-day week. Seven when we're busy, which we are. Be available evenings. Salary five thousand."

"Yes, sir," I said.

I was hired and, as Wullstein had accurately predicted, with hatred at first sight.

"Expect you Monday nine A.M."

"I have to give notice, at least one week. Can't just walk out."

"Why not?"

The telephone buzzed. He lifted the receiver, "Baumberg speaking. Put him on. . . . Good morning, Mr. Sloan." He waved an exit-signaling hand at us.

Beyond the closed door, Wullstein released his breath. "Went better than I hoped. Usually, he rips new guys to shreds. Don't worry, you won't see much of him unless he likes you, which doesn't happen ordinarily."

*   *   *

I wrote a "Folk You Know" about my new job. Barry Neale made a separate item of it, headlined,

"Local Man Takes Jew
Propaganda Position."

He illustrated it with a single-column cut of me in the A.E.F. uniform. Walter Leeds phoned me when he read the paper. "So that's why you ditched us. Sucking around the Sloans. Out for number one." There was nastiness in his tone. "You won't lick honey, working for those New York allrightnicks."

I'm not sure Mama and Papa understood what I was doing. I believe they got the impression I'd enlisted in an army and was going off to war, which in a way I was. Mama dropped tears on my shirts while she ironed them. Papa took my measurements for a new winter suit and overcoat. I left my tallith in my bureau drawer, a guarantee, I told my parents, they could expect me for Yom Tov.

I took the Sunday morning train to New York, bought newspapers, marked the classified ads, rode the subway uptown, down, till I found a furnished room which suited me. It was on the West Side in the apartment of a German refugee. It had a stunning view of the Hudson and was near a crosstown bus, to get over to Sloans' readily. When my plump landlady learned I was employed by the Committee, she volunteered to put a down quilt on my bed and proposed, for an extra dollar a week, to provide breakfast daily, one egg, coffee, rolls, as well as homemade küchen Sunday. She also said she knew a lovely girl whom she wanted me to meet.

Seven

Miss Markowitz buzzed me on the intercom. "Mr. Baumberg wants you. In his office. On the double." The King, at last, had summoned me.

For half a year I'd drudged, ignored by him, in a sunless, airless cubicle, grinding out news releases, statements, pamphlets, speeches, couching in orotund prose the composite wisdom of the bankers, brokers, manufacturers and merchants, C.P.A.s and lawyers who were functioning as seers and statesmen in a debacle beyond mankind's previous experience or imagination. Sheaves, reams, carloads of white paper fed our mimeograph machines. Hands, paid overtime, stuffed nine by four envelopes, glued on miles of three-cent postage stamps to speed appeals and resolutions, declarations and rebuttals, to wastepaper baskets in newsrooms from Florida to Oregon.

There had been no briefing for me when I came to work, no indoctrination lectures, no laying down of formal propaganda lines. You're a Jew, aren't you? You learned Jewish tsoris along with Mother Goose. So you know: About Pharaoh, Haman, the Spanish Inquisition, the Kishinev pogroms. The front page of your morning paper will bring you up to date.

Afternoons, the Committee's Policy Committee met in Baumberg's office, smoked cigars, deplored, debated and decided whether Germany's newest outrage was to be denounced in a ringing public statement or respectfully called-to-your-attention in a diplomatic memo to the blind and deaf in Washington. Wullstein got the word. He passed it on to me to implement. My compositions were nit-picked, every comma weighed. Is "we protest" too mild? Why not "we demand"? What difference will it make? *This* difference: one excessive syllable, one nuance too much, might bring the madman's fury down on more of us. How naïve we were!

As I look back now, what is most incredible about 1938 is that though so many of us worked so hard, mailed out so many news releases, statements, memoranda, published so many pamphlets, passed so many resolutions, orated so fervently in hired halls and on the radio, sent so many delegations to confer with influential people, raised and spent so many dollars and were so morally, ethically and historically right, we achieved nothing whatsoever. We whimpered while the whirlwind howled; we wrung our hands while millions of our kin were rounded up for massacre. Possibly the fault was ours. We placed our trust in Presidents, Prime Ministers and Popes, good Christians all, when we should have cried out to Jehovah. And we sent forth tons of paper instead of Maccabees.

Our staff had been growing, our offices mushrooming through an entire floor. Carpenters hammered partitions, typewriters clacked, phones rang, desks were pounded, edgy hirelings yelled at one another. I lived and breathed Committee, neglecting Broadway, dames and correspondence with my folks. Often I was fed to the teeth, sick of my own words, yet, all in all, I was contented; though I was small potatoes in this shop, the deal was global and historic. Big. Inside me, a bulb of self-importance glowed.

And Leo Wullstein was a decent boss. At first he'd tried to make a gopher out of me. "Sam, go for a roast-beef-on-white, no lettuce, no mustard, a container of coffee, cream and sugar."

I looked him in the eye. "Nix, Leo, I'm a big boy. Send a kid."

He looked me in the eye—"My error, big boy"—but mopped his forehead with his palm. "I'll be better off I don't eat lunch. The doctor said don't eat when you're overtired." Without one extra word I went down to the luncheonette, brought back roast-beef-on-white (no lettuce, no mustard), a container of coffee (cream and sugar), and placed it on his desk. He glanced up. "Thanks, big boy, I appreciate," and though he never asked again, I asked, whenever I was stepping out for lunch, "Bring a sandwich back for you?"

Leo worked like a dog. He was a plodder, methodical and mediocre, making up in sweat what he lacked in flair. Though he serviced a nation's daily press, he'd never worked inside a newsroom, his entire journalistic background having been a two-year stint on an Anglo-Jewish publication where the editorial approach was "Is this good for the Jews?" rather than "Is this newsworthy?" He'd gone to City College, night school, without attaining a diploma. Young Judea and B'nai Brith had educated him. An organization man, a career functionary, limited, parochial, but dedicated, heart and soul and ulcer. I could show him how to slant a news release to get it past a city desk; he could show me cards and spades in what's what? and who's who? in the Jewish world, which was the only world he was acquainted with. I doubt he'd ever had a social cup of coffee with a Goy.

Baumberg I knew only through hearsay and mythology. Two legends had considerable washroom currency: one that, like Minerva, he'd sprung full-grown and armed from the aching head of Jove; the other that he'd crawled out from beneath a cold, wet stone. At various times I was told, in strictest confidence, by one who knew from nameless sources (unimpeachable) that Baumberg's father had been the alcoholic janitor (Polish) of an East Side tenement; that he'd been born out of wedlock to a chorus girl, sired by a Don Juan (Muscovite) of the Second Avenue Yiddish Theater; that he'd grown up on Brooklyn's Pitkin Avenue, eldest of the numerous progeny of a Chassid (Galitzianer); that he'd taught Hebrew School in the Bronx, sold life insurance in New Jersey, building lots on Staten Island, haberdashery at Gimbel's, done social work among immigrants on Ellis Island, but somewhere, somehow, had seen the Burning Bush. No one had ever read his résumé; I doubt there was one in our office files. Miss Markowitz guarded his door and his mystique, declining to reveal whether he had wife or child or human parentage or with whom he went to lunch.

Leo took a fearsome bruising from the King, yet he did not pass it on to me. His paper work never was caught up, because all day Baumberg kept him hopping to and from the corner office or fielding fast ones on the intercom. Evening after evening, I'd leave him, gray with fatigue, hunched over his desk, the last man on the floor, the cleaning women emptying wastepaper baskets and sweeping around his chair. One night he introduced me to his wife, who was waiting on the hard bench in the entrance foyer to go out to dinner. (It was their wedding anniversary.) We chatted while Leo was washing up. She did the talking, venomously. "Leo is heart and soul wrapped up in this. Baumberg's out for Baumberg, his ego, his glory. A monster, nonhuman positively."

The Wullsteins were human. They had a little house in Queens with a garden and two bright kids, a boy and girl. They asked me out to dinner. Mrs. Wullstein invited a girl friend, a moderately attractive, amiable spinster. The meal was good, though underseasoned because of Leo's ulcer. We played bridge afterwards. The girl friend was my partner. We lost thirty cents. I said good night after two rubbers, not offering to see the girl friend home. They had tried—every bachelor is a challenge—but they didn't press. The hefty, earthy clerks and stenos at the office—it was surprising how many resembled Sylvia's cousin Ruthie—were haimish, fun to kid around with, knowing marvelous Yiddish jokes, though none were what I'd ask out on a date. I didn't seem to need a personal life. Nor, as far as any of us knew, did Baumberg, who was nonhuman, positively.

I rapped lightly on his office door. Miss Markowitz opened it, smiling benignly. "Come in. He is waiting." I stepped to the side of his desk. The King was reading *Variety*. I stood, eyeing a recent framed photo on the wall, the Mayor shaking hands with Joseph Sloan, Baumberg, offside, facing camera.

While he read, Baumberg barked, "Sit down. You make me nervous standing."

I slid into the chair beside his desk, considered lighting a cigarette, decided not unless invited. At last, he gave me his attention.

"You come from Grady's Mills? Correct?"

"Correct."

"Did you by chance know a woman named Jessica White?"

"Jessie Weiss," I said.

"Then she *is* Jewish?" He sounded disappointed.

"Litvak. Orthodox background."

"Can't tell your Jew without a pogrom." He frowned. "I wish she was a Goy."

"She's Sloan's sister-in-law," I said.

The King smiled, a feat I'd have believed improbable. "I'll be

167

damned!" He tapped a front tooth with a pencil. "Then Sloan can ask her," he decided.

"Whatever you want Sloan to ask, he can't." That was reckless; the King, like the waiters at the Café Royal, is not contradicted.

He scowled and gnawed his lower lip before he asked, "How well do you know the dame?"

"Old, close friends," I said. "Grew up together."

"No kidding." The smile returned, broadened. He opened a silver cigarette case, offered me a smoke, snapped and held his lighter for me.

"What's Jessie up to now?" I asked.

"Why don't you read *Variety?*" He thrust the paper at me and I skimmed.

The Arsonists, a drama in three acts, by Jessica White, had opened in New Haven, and *Variety*'s reviewer had gone overboard for it. *"Miss White, author of two successful Broadway plays, has enhanced her prestige in the theater with a stunning drama on a stirring contemporary theme. 'The Arsonists' treats of the malignant disease of our times, the plague of anti-Semitism. . . . With eloquence and intensity, she has drawn a more searing indictment than Sinclair Lewis' 'It Can't Happen Here.' It has happened, it does happen in this typical American small city (could Miss White's native Grady's Mills have been the model?), of which the playwright has written with a pen dipped in fire and acid. Here are people whom we can identify: well-meaning average citizens, immobilized by indifference; public officials, morally obtuse, fundamentally biased; and native hooligans to whom Hitler has given a green light. The inevitable victims are respected, trusting local Jewish citizens who fail to recognize their peril till their synagogue is in flames. . . . With remarkable insight Miss White has limned the dignified old rabbi who is the vandals' intended victim and the confused newspaper reporter who. . . ."*

I flung the paper down and blew my stack. "The bitch!"

"Watch it," Baumberg said, watching me. "The dame may cop a Pulitzer."

"Over my dead body."

"Move the carcass," he said coldly. "This may be the gimmick I've been hoping for. The dame is a genius."

"Genius, my ass! A vulture." I could see Jessie's gray eyes, studying me across a table in the Hotel Grady bar. I remembered her odd withdrawal while I talked, the feeling I had had that she had left me, gone off into a world of her own. This must have been the instant of conception of the play. I recalled her disconcerting, silent probing from a bed in St. Luke's, her spying on my soul, and her mean crack on the courthouse steps, "You went along for the ride."

"What's griping you? You couldn't make the dame?"

"You flatter her. I never tried."

"Looks like the rear end of a truck horse, eh?" His cheerfulness was as irritating as his glower. "Well, what difference how she looks? Her name alone will pull the customers."

"Where? For what?"

"For the testimonial dinner we are giving Joseph Sloan, where we hope to raise one hundred thousand bucks. In May. Which will be just about when *The Arsonists* will be the talk of the town. Sam"—he used my first name for the first time in our non-relationship—"contact her at once and sign her up. Guest speaker at the Sloan dinner." He leaned across the desk; I caught the glint of gold inlays. "If she wants a fee, okay. Up to one thousand, not a dollar more. My hunch is she'll do it for publicity, maybe for the Cause. Could be even for the family yiches. Mrs. Sloan her sister? That the relationship? . . . Nice woman, Mrs. Sloan, organization-minded."

I kept silent, seething.

"Get on the ball. Waterhouse and Windom are producing. Contact the press agent; he'll tell you where to contact her." He waved, dismissing me.

I got up to go.

"Don't let me down," Baumberg said. "Or else" was implicit. "Pick up a few first-night passes, hear?" he added as I was leaving.

Wullstein said, when I reported to him, "The King's a genius; what did I tell you? Who else would hop on this so quick? Sam, to me you can tell the truth: do you really know Jessica White?"

Like the creases in my palm and that's what makes me leery. This dame is a heller, and totally unpredictable. I smoked my cigarette pack through, nerving myself to phone Waterhouse and Windom and ask for the press agent. His name was Morton Stein, one of ours, which usually is helpful. He went for the idea. As a matter of fact, he said, he'd been planning to contact us and a few other organizations to ask how's about buying up some benefits, to give the play a financial cushion before its Broadway opening. Not that he thought *The Arsonists* would need a cushion. Had I seen *Variety?* But who knows how New York critics will react? And say, could we cooperate by hetzing up the Bundist crowd to picket the theater? That would get a front-page break. . . . Oh, you want to meet Miss White. No sir, we can't give out her address. Respect her privacy. Creative people go nuts when strangers want to yak with them. . . . "You're no stranger? . . . You're from Grady's Mills? . . . You both come from there? Well, all I can say is it must be a great place to come from. Let's have your phone number. I'll contact her for you."

I left the phone number at the apartment where I roomed. If Jessie did call me, I wished the conversation private, no switchboard eavesdropping in case it became acrimonious, which, the way I felt, it was more than likely to. Around 11 P.M. when I was abed, catching the news on my radio, the landlady, in curlers and kimono, rapped on my door. "A Mrs. Weitz is on the telephone. Talks like a man."

"Hi!" A familiar throaty voice came through. "Understand you're paging me."

"I need to see you. Where and when?"

"Tomorrow. Five o'clock. Algonquin lobby. See you then." I heard the click of hanging up. Strictly business, both parties.

*   *   *

Being nervous, I arrived early to watch celebrities and their sycophants wheeling in a lobby that resembled the parlors on the Hill: squashy sofas, mismatched chairs. At five, precisely, Jessie came through the doorway, swinging a briefcase and swiveling her hips. The maroon velvet beret she wore jauntily was neither fresh nor seasonable, her coat wasn't recent, yet men and women ogled her. Had fame already stamped "celebrity" on Jessie Weiss? Or was it the indefinable something known as personality?

She came straight to where I stood, pulled down my head and kissed my mouth, instantly and totally disarming me. "Dahling, what *are* you doing here in town?" The inflection pseudo-Alabama.

"I work here." I mentioned for whom.

Her eyebrows rose. "Goody-goody! Let us sit. My feet are killing me."

We found a love seat in a corner, against a wall. She dropped the briefcase and kicked off her pumps. "Beat. No sleep in a week," she told me.

"You look in the pink," I said. Her eyes were brilliant, her cheeks rosy.

"Done with mirrors. Rewrite has worn me to the bone. Still, nobody's pleased."

"*Variety* was."

"Reviewer was a Yid. Play hit him where his worries live." Her hand's heel tapped a bell on the table before us.

I came to the point. "Jessie, why did you do this to me?"

Her eyes rose, meeting mine. "All characters in this work are fictitious. Moreover, you were nothing but a catalyst."

"Balls," I said.

"Watch your language, there's a lady present."

"Anyone I know?" The acrimony was standard opening for the two of us, except this time I had a full head of steam. "You cash in, you exploit every situation. Turn everyone and everything to copy."

"Tut, tut, child. What's a modern writer to write? Grimm's *Fairy Tales?*"

An aged waiter shuffled over. "Scotch, water chaser, no ice," Jessie ordered and turned to me. "Beer? Or mother's milk?"

"Go to hell," I told her. "Rye and ginger ale," I told the waiter. He tottered off.

She banged the bell to recall him. "A couple of peanuts or pretzels, son. I need nourishment. Missed my lunch." She rummaged wildly in the alligator satchel I had seen in Grady's Mills. "Brother, can you spare a butt? Why is it I always run in to you right after I've run out?"

I lit a pair of cigarettes. She settled back, one leg tucked under,

171

the way she used to sit when she was a kid. "Okay, let's have the pitch. Morty wasn't clear: something about a personal appearance at the Waldorf at a dinner honoring some big shot. Who he?"

I stalled, savoring the shock I was about to hand her. "Your brother-in-law," I said, grinning. "The honorable Joseph Sloan."

She stared in disbelief, then threw back her head and howled. "Priceless! This'll kill Celia. She knows, doesn't she?"

"Up to now, probably not. My orders were make contact, bring you back alive."

"They want *me* to praise *Joey Slomowitz?* Stand up, straight-faced, tell the world he's nature's nobleman!" She produced an inelegant Bronx cheer. "Who thought that one up? Did you?"

"Give me credit for some sense. The man I work for thought it up, in ignorance of who you were related to. You're a gimmick, it's a gimmick, to draw a crowd and raise a chunk of dough for propaganda against Nazis and for saving German Jews. What you say is up to you—recite the alphabet, anything—just so the customers can tell their friends they saw Jessica White."

"Crass, isn't it?" she muttered. "Now who's exploiting what?" But went on to add, quite sensibly, "Be fair to Jessie W. She knows how to make a speech. Especially about something she cares about." She tapped my arm. "Us two from the Hill in Grady's Mills, fighting for the Yids. A remarkable coincidence."

The waiter brought our drinks, along with a dish of pretzels. I grabbed the check. She slapped my wrist. "Expense account," I said.

"Pish! Gone up in the world. Public money buying the girls drinks!" but clinked her glass to mine.

"L'chaim," we both said.

The sniping was over, the armistice ratified. She stuffed pretzels into her mouth, chortling while she chewed. "Gorgeous! Family reunion at the Waldorf!" Suddenly, loudly, alcoholically, she burped. "Goddam indigestion. Eating on the run." Her hand pressed her middle. It seemed to me she was in pain, though almost at once she was laughing. "Do you realize we three haven't broken bread together since our transatlantic crossing? And how I've missed Joseph!" Her smile blinked off. "I should have gone up to their place, seen Papa, made sure he's okay. Joe's chauffeur took over in the Catskills, trundled Papa to New York. Exit Jessie." She cradled her chin on her hand. "Do you know I've never been invited to their place?"

"I have. Repeatedly."

"Lucky you." She banged the bell again. "Let's have another drink on that." While we waited for the waiter, I told her I went over to visit Herman whenever I had a chance, and last fall, while the weather was mild, I'd taken him strolling in the park several Sunday afternoons but I'd sensed he was uncomfortable; people kept staring at his face.

"I know." Her eyes grew somber. "Sam, it's more than that. Something's eating him. Is he comfortable up there?"

"The steam heat's adequate, the windows close tight, no rain or snow comes in. His mattress is firm, his linen's changed. . . ."

"Wise guy." Her brows quirked. "You know damn well what I mean."

I pretended I did not. "Nobody serves him ham, nobody calls him 'sheeny.' Or hits him with a stone. Nobody, but nobody, ever is around to bother him, you see. Celia and Joe use the place for changing clothes and entertaining guests. The only one who lives there is Ilene. Your niece. A lovely child. Who is also busy as a bee, with private school and dancing school and Hebrew school and you-name-it school. She has the best intentions in the world, but she hasn't reached first base. Herman doesn't seem to know that she's alive."

"What does he do all day, all night?"

"Lies on his bed, sits on his chair. Broods, prays, sleeps."

Her shoulders drew together, shuddering.

"You ought to get to know your niece," I said.

"I should. Make a date. A foursome. You, me, Papa and Ilene. In Central Park. Spring is busting out all over. We'll sit on a bench and eat Crackerjack."

The waiter brought our second dose. She sipped her whisky, this time didn't fling it down, then glanced at her wrist. "Goddamit, ten of six. Expecting a call from the Coast. MGM is nibbling." She groped down for her shoes. "Have to run. Leave you with the tab?"

"Where can I reach you without a middleman?"

"Here. The Algonquin's home till May fifteenth. Then Westport, Conn. I've rented a shack. Come up and swim. Also, I will send you tickets for the opening. We do owe something to a catalyst."

I told Baumberg the lady had agreed. "For how much?" he asked.

"Money wasn't mentioned. She'll do it pour le sport."

"I don't trust amateurs," he said. "I suppose we'll have to write her speech."

"Forget it. She's an orator from way back."

He humphed. "High school debating team?" And darted a sharp glance at me. "Not a Commie, is she?"

"I never thought to ask," I said.

"We'll have to take the chance. I still wish she was a Protestant; better yet, a Catholic." There was no word of thanks or praise. However, a slip attached to my next salary check informed me that come the first of May I'd be paid at the rate of $5,500 annually. Also Wullstein laid a key on my desk. "The private washroom," he told me. "For executives."

Joe Sloan rang me up. "Sam, I understand from Baumberg you made a deal with Jessie to speak at the dinner where the Committee is honoring me. Baumberg thinks he has a million-dollar idea. Maybe yes, maybe no. Ceil is worried Jessie might embarrass us."

"I'll police it. She listens to me."

"Glad she listens to somebody. Ceil told me to remind you it's a long time since you came to visit Mr. Weiss."

"Baumberg keeps me hopping."

"Makes you earn your money, eh? Not a bad idea. I hear you got a raise. Well, it would be in the line of business if you stopped over to discuss my speech. And maybe play a game of checkers with my father-in-law."

We never made the foursome date for Central Park. Jessie, when I finally reached her at the Algonquin after a half dozen "call-back" messages, said she was exhausted—rehearsals, and feeling lousy generally—but do not worry, Buster, she'd send my tickets and she'd keep her date to make the speech if she had to roll in on a stretcher. Be damned if she'd miss that golden opportunity to upstage sister Celia.

Mort Stein sent a pair, house seats, fifth row center, orchestra. I passed them on to Baumberg, not to curry favor but because I didn't want to see myself refracted through Jessie's spectacles. Baumberg received the tickets as his due; again, no "thank you."

I was reading the reviews, all raves, when the King buzzed for me. "What the hell's the matter with your prima donna?" he greeted me.

I was nonplussed. "The show's a hit, isn't it?"

"So far, so good. But where the devil was she? The audience kept yelling, 'Author, author.' The dame never showed."

I read his mind. If she was capricious enough, or shy enough, to duck out on her opening night, could we positively count on her appearance for the Sloan dinner?

"Hold everything, I'll check."

I called Mort Stein, the press agent. "How you like, sweetheart?" he crowed. "Line started forming ten A.M. By now, it's all the way around the block. We're taking reservations for Yom Kippur night."

"Where's Jessica?" I asked.

"Poor bitch. Cast had champagne at Sardi's; she got glucose, intravenous."

I caught my breath. "What's up?"

"Minor surgery. No, not an abortion. Gallstones. Held out through the dress rehearsal. Went in yesterday. Took it like a trouper. It'll be in Winchell tomorrow."

"Which hospital?"

"I didn't tell Winchell, I cannot tell you. The dame needs quiet, sweet repose. You realize she wrote *The Arsonists* in two months only? Speed record for the track. White heat. Burning up with it. Then rewrote, before New Haven. After. Perfectionist. All the while climbing walls with a bellyache. Heroic is the word for Jessica. Go ahead, mail your invitations out. Don't forget to send me one; if I can't go I'll send my secretary. And

175

copies of your news releases, please—you don't have to clear with me, yet it might be better. Just quit worrying, will you? Her kind of stamina, she'll be winning the six-day bike race long before your clambake. . . . Nope, I repeat, where she lies in pain and retching is a secret. Nobody gets the place or the name she's signed in under."

Locating her was duck soup. I knew what Mort Stein didn't realize I knew: all her names before her fame. I phoned the hospitals: Lenox Hill, Harkness Pavilion, Doctor's Hospital, Mt. Sinai. Bingo! Mt. Sinai had Mrs. Jessie Simon. The switchboard connected me with the patient's special. "Her condition is good," the prissy voice informed me. "She will not be permitted visitors until the fifth day. That will be Monday."

On Monday, telling Wullstein I had a lunch-hour conference, I subwayed to Mt. Sinai, bearing roses about whose color I'd deliberated until the florist turned sarcastic. "Mister, settle for a plant. A fern or a pot of ivy."

"Roses," I said stubbornly. "Mix 'em. Pink and white and red."

They were coals for Newcastle. Mrs. Jessie Simon, small and sheeted in the high hospital bed, lay embowered by baskets, vases, buckets, jardinieres and floral horseshoes.

"A swain bearing posies," she greeted me. "Exactly what I need."

A man in a long white coat who was seated at the bedside bent down and kissed her forehead. "I'll scram, you have company."

"Pu-leeze! I want you boys to know each other. Mark, this is Sam. Sam, this is Mark. Sam is my best, oldest friend. Mark was my cut-up. Regardez les delicate surgeon's hands."

The man who stood to greet me was tall, well-fleshed, vigorous-appearing, cheeks healthily pink, hair graying at the temples, the sparkle of a sunlit sea in keen blue eyes, a pleasant, friendly male of middle age.

A nurse entered, snatched the box of flowers, vanished.

"The rest of the name is Bishop, Mark Bishop," the surgeon informed me.

"M.D.," Jessie chirped from the mattress. "Diplomate American College of Surgeons."

176

"Samuel Rosenbaum, guy from across the street," I said.

"Mark's madly in love with me," the patient announced. "Became enamored of my pupik. I have a very deep navel, Sam; you'd be impressed. I ought to join Salvation Army. It's great for carrying the flag."

"Stick out your tongue," the doctor ordered.

A bright pink tongue popped out.

"Rapid." Dr. Bishop smacked her backside lightly through the sheet. "Behave, or we'll put you on sedation. I leave you two to reminisce about old times while I tend to the sick. This woman is so fascinating," he confessed, "I've neglected all my other patients." He winked at her. "You clown!" but said, low-toned, to me, "She's in fine shape, but it's difficult to make her rest." He shook my hand. His grip was firm; nothing delicate about the surgeon's hands.

"Isn't he an angel?" Jessie breathed when he had gone.

"Good bedside manner. Pleasantly paternal. Bet he takes his kids to ball games, helps them with homework."

"Bet he does," Jessie said. "Continue the summation."

"A competent butcher, of that I have no doubt." Then, prompted by a spasm of uncalled-for jealousy, I went on to add that surgeons don't appeal to me, they know the inside story, the twisted gut, the festering appendix. . . .

The patient thumbed her nose. "You won't have to live with him. I'll be delighted to."

"Isn't it polite to wait until you're asked?"

The nurse came in with my roses in a brown bucket. Jessie smiled enigmatically. "How you give yourself away! Never can make up your mind. Well, sit. Mark warmed the chair. Miss Kates"—this to the nurse—"show the gentleman my jewels."

The nurse held up a jar, containing what resembled chunks of coal.

"Genuine gallstones," Jessie informed me. "Mark's present to me. He wished they were emeralds."

"And you were Helen Hayes," I said.

She laughed. "Should have known you read the theater sections, too. Mistake to borrow gags. Miss Kates, remove the horrid things. 'Twas just to prove this was not a hysterectomy."

"Who asked you?"

"Someone might ask *you*," she said. "Someone like my sister Celia. . . . Well, Sammy dollink, how you liked the play?"

"All I know is what I read in the papers."

"Didn't Mort Stein send you tickets? I told him to."

"I gave them to my boss."

"You shmuck!"

I crossed two fingers on my lips. "A lady present," meaning the starchy Kates. "Went chicken, couldn't bear to see myself as you saw me."

Her expression turned sly. "Oh, but you have, time and time again."

"What else is new?" I said.

She pulled the sheet to her chin, eyeing me mischievously, saying nothing, waiting for me to carry the ball of conversation.

"Where do you go from here?" I asked, finally.

"To Westport. To eat a low-fat diet and bask in the sun."

"Spiritually. Professionally, I mean. You've hit the top, Jessie. The big success. Now what are you after?"

She stayed silent, her toes wiggling beneath the sheet, her eyes hooded, through a long moment, in which I heard a loud speaker clamoring for physicians, including Dr. Bishop, before she said, softly, "A little companionship, a little joy."

"I remember . . ." I began.

She interrupted, mocking. "I remember, I remember, in September. . . ."

". . . your three wishes," I went on. "To sing like a bird, turn handsprings, be blonde and willowy. . . ."

"Wasn't I a dope?"

"Mahneshtana? Where is it different?"

"Oh, I've changed. Spectacularly. Social values, human values. . . ."

"What you want now should be a cinch."

"You know, you never were too smart," she said.

I thumbed *my* nose. "Situation normal, and on that note I leave."

"Thanks for the visit, pal," she said. "Next time kindly omit flowers. Pair of dice, preferably." I was at the door. She called after me. "Sam, do me a favor. Bring my family here. Papa and the kid, I mean. Miss Kates tells me it's illegal to have a major operation without the kinfolk hovering."

No matter what, my relationship with Jessie didn't change. She welcomed me, insulted me, asked a favor afterwards. And Sam, the shnook, hurried to oblige. So the surgeon finds her fascinating. I could tell him where that fascination leads. Exactly nowhere, Doctor B.

I phoned Celia, told her Jessie was in a hospital, not telling which.

"Oh! Is it serious?" She sounded optimistic.

"Not particularly. Gall-bladder surgery."

"Who did she have?"

I named the surgeon.

"He's supposed to be very good—and quite expensive," Celia said. "We met him at a cocktail party."

"Have you seen her play?" I asked.

"My sister hasn't had the courtesy to send us tickets, which is the least she could do, since Joseph is giving her all that free publicity. . . . Well, thank you for telling me." A three-second silence. "Is there anything she needs?"

"She'd like her father . . . and Ilene . . . to visit her."

"Now, is that not ridiculous? And just like Jessie, I might add. If she had any interest whatsoever in her father, she'd have come to visit him, found out he is in no condition to go traipsing around. A serious depression. And as for Ilene, I don't wish her to visit hospitals, be exposed to infections, to a morbid atmosphere. However, I might drop in myself. Which hospital?"

"You'll meet her at the Waldorf," I said. "Skip the morbid atmosphere."

*   *   *

The creamy paper was deckle-edged, the flowing script engraved:

Joe brought in his mailing list—and Celia's. "Our personal, close friends," he told Leo Wullstein. "Tell me who you don't hear from; I'll have my secretary follow up." The lists included all the officers of every organization to which Mr. and Mrs. S. belonged or contributed, every scrap-metal dealer in the telephone company's Yellow Pages, building contractors, heads of shipping-trucking firms, Joe's lawyers, accountants, doctor, dentist, podiatrist, tailor and jeweler. As far as I could judge, none of the relatives who'd appeared at the wedding at the Astor were $100-couvert prospects.

The reservations came in nicely, from Grady's Mills for Mr. and Mrs. Walter Leeds, from Miami for Mr. and Mrs. Max Sloan, and the Misses Marian, Geraldine and Beatrice Sloan—Minnie, Goldie and Bessie Slomowitz gone all-American.

Using the pretext of requiring glossy photos for publicity, I phoned Mort Stein, the press agent, asking how Miss White was getting on, how soon she'd be leaving the hospital, and whether he could spare one ticket for this Saturday's matinee. He said Miss White had checked out of the hospital, gone out of town for convalescence—don't ask him where; strict doctor's orders she's not to be disturbed—and all Saturday matinees were sold out to July, but if I didn't mind standing—And say, had I heard the news? Paramount has taken an option.

I came out of the brilliant sunshine of a May afternoon into a murky auditorium, to stand behind an orchestra full of perfumed, gabbing women in flowery spring hats, to see myself through Jessie's eyes. *The Arsonists*, it pains me to report, had no resemblance whatsoever to reality, truth, or source of inspiration.

The town, as she portrayed it, was a snake pit, the Gentile natives Ku Klux Klansmen without robes, mouthing racist obscenities; the Jews all noble, mild and pious. Black or white, no gray whatsoever. She'd entirely missed the crucial point, the fetid undercurrent of racial animosity that you could never reach and touch, drag to light and extirpate because it wasn't overt, the two-faced politeness that segregated Jews, made them walk on tiptoe, make nice-nice, like Walter when he tried to buy a cottage at the Lake, the de facto second-class citizenship that custom had imposed on Jews in all the little towns and cities that are the backbone of this republic.

And the protagonists: the victim was a venerable, white-bearded rabbi, given to Old Testament quotations in a British accent; the hero an Epworth League idealist with a Charles Atlas torso, a nitwit, drawing down a pay check on the local daily paper; the heroine a svelte Jewish blonde, home from studying singing in Munich (first-hand observation of the Nazis, see!). She tries to do a Paul Revere. Who listens? Nobody, not even the reporter, who might have read some wire service cables. No, it cannot happen here, it is not happening; the desecration of a Jewish hero's grave is a prank, kids playing with a can of paint.

The third-act fire was offstage, a backdrop of orange zigzags. The rabbi is trapped in his blazing synagogue, trying to save the Scrolls. Our hero, at long last catching on, dashes in and staggers out, naked to the navel, cradling Rabbi and Torah in his arms, into which, before the final curtain, our heroine nuzzles lasciviously. You have saved our Torah, take my lily-white body (with its deep pupik) and my hand in marriage.

Claptrap! Junk! Phoney-baloney! Jessie Weiss, how could you? Anything to make a buck—plenty bucks, judging by the sold-out theater and the way the ladies clapped. (Wasn't it Mencken who once wrote it's impossible to overestimate the low taste of the

American people?) What this play had—all it had, as far as I could force myself to be objective—was vitality, Jessie's own, that made the hokum come alive.

Since it is my intention to be fair and honest, let me admit that what most sickened me was the so-called hero. The muscle-boy, who got the girl, could not have lasted one full week on any daily paper. No eyes, no ears, no sense of smell. And no common sense. Phone for the hook-and-ladder, Dumbo; we pay them to do the fire rescues.

But Miss White's plays are always personal history, autobio, including her childish fantasies. So here's a Jewish heroine, blonde, slender as a reed, coloratura-in-training. It's all there except the handsprings. Cut out before New Haven, possibly. Can I then assume that muscle-boy is what she wished I'd be so I might get the girl? Life tosses Jessie Weiss a cue; her imagination builds on it. Each person sees himself with his own eyes. That is his privilege. Jessie sees herself as this all-wise and fascinating Judy. However, when she looks at me, her astigmatism's serious. She ought to see an oculist.

I would have fled screaming. The lobby congestion trapped me and I had, perforce, to listen to some cogent drama criticism.

"I liked it all except the ending. She shouldn't have said she'd marry him. I don't believe in intermarriages."

"He saved the rabbi, didn't he?"

"But he didn't say if he'd convert."

"In his heart, his feelings, he's Jewish, just like her."

"Miss White, you mean? She's not Jewish. She must be a wonderful woman, a Christian, to understand the Jewish people good and do for them something like this."

Leo Wullstein whistled when I showed him the glossies Mort Stein had sent over. "Hey, she's a looker, too."

"A good retoucher. That is mercy, not justice."

"Come on, come on, the eyes are gorgeous. And the nose. That nose positively is not Jewish."

"Her mother brought it from Vilna."

He looked at me oddly. "You sound so cynical whenever we talk about her. Do you really hate her?"

"On the contrary," I said. "It's just she works too hard at not being likeable."

"I think you ought to get in touch with her again," he said. "Get an advance copy of her speech. Maybe she wants a little help with the material."

I shook my head. "She's a ham, a complete and total ham, but I guarantee you she will knock them dead."

"I'm doing Sloan's remarks," he said. "He felt you might not catch the spirit of the thing."

* * *

Miss Markowitz, in evening gown and rhinestone drop earrings, had charge of the girls who checked the reservations and issued table-numbered place cards in the corridor outside the Starlight Roof. Wullstein and I, in tuxedos, offered mimeographed hand-outs to the press and led them to the bar outside the "greenroom" where the "head table" people were assembling. Baumberg circulated, with measured cordiality, among top-of-letterhead officials who rated dais seats, keeping sharp, cold eyes on everyone and everything. Henry Eisenberg, a hair tonic and slickum manufacturer who was emcee for the evening, sat in a corner, jotting down cues for jokes with which he hoped to enliven the proceedings.

The banquet hall's padded chairs were filling with a dazzling turnout, the entire scrap-metal trade in fine raiment and fettle and an upper-strata crowd from the general population. Ordinarily (this much I had learned by now), when a business concern reserves a table for a fund-raising dinner, the stenos and their boy friends occupy the seats. By the bald heads and the penguin shirt fronts of the men, the jewels of their ladies, I saw that Jessica White's name had brought out the principals.

Dashing to and fro, I missed the arrival of the guests of honor. When, at quarter after seven, I inspected the greenroom, Celia, hair golden as wheat, gown low cut, of pale blue satin, throat encircled by a diamond and sapphire necklace that must have emptied the mint, was holding court for Sloan (née Slomowitz) relations, three tanned, overdressed young women and Max, brown, beardless and not too freakish in a tux. Ilene, in frothy pink, a crown of rosebuds on her hair, stood beside her mother, flushed and starry-eyed. Joe, somewhat disheveled, was pawing a flashy red-haired female.

"Hey, Sam!" he called to me. "Looka Mama!"

Mama stroked his cheek, saying coyly, "Not nice in public, Joey!"

Celia, pretending not to notice, twittered, "Ilene, darling, wasn't it lovely of your aunties to come all the way from Florida to honor your daddy?"

"Isn't Aunt Jessie coming?" Ilene answered. "Do you think she forgot?" She spotted me. "Oh, Uncle Sam, Mommy let me come, just to meet the family. The chauffeur has to drive me home."

Max sidled over. "You remember me, Sammy? Some difference, heh? My Lena and Ida Weiss, they should rest in peace, they should have lived to see this naches, the pnai come to honor Joey with a banket, Celia dressed up like a queen."

Baumberg tugged my sleeve. "So where is your prima donna? Why didn't you arrange to call for her?" The King was right, as always. If Jessie didn't show, I'd be unemployed tomorrow.

At half-past seven, precisely, a couple entered the greenroom. Jessie looked stunning, whittled down, poured into a maroon dress, low enough to reveal half-moons of white breasts, garnets around her throat, at her ears, head carried regally. Beside her was Dr. Bishop, a fine figure in dinner clothes, beaming as though he had invented her. I heard "ohs" and "ahs" and Celia's sucked-in breath. Joe disengaged himself from the redhead.

"Well, Jessie, I heard you had been ill. It must have been a false rumor." That was Celia's greeting. "Dr. Bishop, I believe." She extended her hand to him. "We have met, socially. I am Mrs. Sloan. Is your charming wife here, too?"

"This is professional, Mrs. Sloan. I'm looking after a patient. She needs watching."

Tartly, "I'm sure she does."

"Is Papa here?" Those were the first words Jessie had spoken.

"He doesn't go out nights, you ought to realize. . . ."

Ilene, who'd been watching, big-eyed, an eager smile trembling on her lips, edged forward. "Aunt Jessie, I'm—"

"Don't tell me, let me guess. You're my niece, Ilene. And you

184

are pretty. Puss, we ought to get acquainted. Look, I've rented a summer place in Westport. . . ."

Celia's arm encircled Ilene, drew her, proprietarily, against her side. "Ilene will be in Camp Ganeden. Joseph and I wish her to acquire a good Jewish background."

I saw Jessie's spine stiffen and her jawline firm. She wheeled around. "Sam," she cried, "you look incredible in the monkey suit!" before Joe enveloped her with octopus arms.

"Jessie, my first love! When'd you get so gorgeous? How's about a kiss?"

"Slomowitz, no chiropractic," Jessie growled.

And I heard Celia saying, saccharinely, "Ilene, darling, your Aunt Jessie doesn't care for children. Talk to your other aunties, dear."

Baumberg yanked my sleeve again. "Bring Miss White a drink. What's her usual?"

Dr. Bishop wagged an index finger. "Uh, uh. No alcohol."

Baumberg leaned to me, whispering, "Did she tell you she was bringing him? Does she expect him on the dais?"

Dr. Bishop caught the whisper. "Don't worry about me," he said amiably. "I'll sit anywhere. In the kitchen."

"That will not be necessary." Celia, poise restored, was acting hostess. "Sylvia and Walter Leeds couldn't make it. Walter has the flu. You might place him at their table." Then, to put an end to all embarrassments, she informed whom it might concern, "Yes, this is quite a surprise to Joseph and myself. You see, my sister was never active in a Jewish way."

Dr. Bishop raised Jessie's hand and kissed the back of it. "Be a good girl. Mind the doctor's orders."

She fluttered her fingers, bye-bye, see-you-later. Baumberg seized her hand and introduced himself.

"So you're the fiend who thought this up! Lead me to a chair. My feet are killing me."

Leo Wullstein said, with desperation, "Will Miss White and Mr. Sloan kindly step this way? The photographers are waiting."

Deftly, Wullstein straightened Joe's tie, smoothed his jacket lapels. Joe, displaying his teeth, offered Jessie his right hand. Mona Lisa smile a trifle crooked, she accepted it. Baumberg moved unobtrusively to Joseph's elbow, and the flashbulbs blinked. Wullstein lined the guests up, in their seating order. They marched in to dinner. From the press table, below the dais, I watched Henry Eisenberg holding Jessie's chair out gallantly, whispering something at which the guest speaker laughed immoderately.

The "Star-Spangled Banner" and "Hatikvah" were sung by a voluptuous brunette from the Met; the invocation was delivered by a rabbi from the Bronx. We broke bread; the waiters bustled, delivering fruit cups.

We were in the roast chicken, rissolé potatoes, green peas course when an agitated Miss Markowitz breathed over my shoulder, "There's a very strange old man outside and he will not go away. He hasn't got a ticket. He says he didn't come for any dinner—it's terribly hard to understand what he's trying to say—he says he wants to see someone named Weiss. He's got my girls all upset. What shall I do?"

I knocked my chair over, getting up. Baumberg, at the end of the dais, scowled threateningly at me.

In the corridor, Herman stood between two cops, looking terrified. He was wearing the summer suit Jessie'd bought for him and a battered panama hat. His relief, when I showed up, was piteous. "Sammy! Vot the police vant from me? I don't do nothing."

"Herman, why didn't you tell the family you wanted to attend this dinner?"

"Vot dinner? Tonight I see in the *Morgen Journal* Jessie's picture, she is on the Starlight's Roof by the Valdorf-Astoria to make a speech. So I go on the subvay. . . ."

"Come in, come in. Miss Markowitz, please check the gentleman's hat. You have a yarmulka? Good. The dinner is kosher, you can eat."

"I had already supper, the shvartze gave me. Only to see Jessie I come. The grandchild told me she vas sick in a hospital."

We threaded a maze of chairs to the table where Mark Bishop sat beside a chair left vacant by the absence of a Leeds. "Doctor, this is Mr. Weiss, Jessie's father. Will you take care of him?" Bishop rose. His glance, simultaneously sympathetic and professional, swept the blotched, beardless face. Courtly and solicitous, he pulled out a chair for Herman. "I'll look after him," he prom-

186

ised, and I hurried off to scribble a note, *"Your father is here. Next to Dr. B,"* to place it, folded, on Jessie's service plate. Joe, being occupied with a lady on his left, never noticed me. Nor did Celia, who was fussing with a floral arrangement that cut off part of the audience's view of the sapphire and diamond necklace.

From my seat at the press table, I saw Jessie searching for the table where her father was, though remaining expressionless while Henry Eisenberg engaged her right ear. Was she indifferent? Resentful? Her face showed not a thing, except the mildest boredom, while several orators detailed the plight of the Jews of Germany and mentioned how tirelessly the guest of honor, Joseph Sloan, had labored to alleviate it. She covered up a yawn while Joe stumbled through Wullstein's paragraphs, humbly accepting a plaque of bronze affixed to wood, for convenient hanging up: "My dear good friends, it is hard for me to find words tonight to thank you all for your presence here. I am deeply moved, I am profoundly honored, to receive this expression as well as this token of your high esteem. But it is undeserved. Many of you have done as much, nay, more than I. But all of us have done no more than our duty toward our suffering brethren in this battle for the ideals of justice we hold dear. I shall hang this plaque on my office wall. And every day, when my eyes behold it, it will remind me—fine, okay, you did good, Joe Sloan. But what have you done for them *today?* I must do more, you must do more, we must do more. Now—" He glanced toward Baumberg and inhaled heavily. "Well, my good friends, when I was a small boy in my father's house, I learned a sterling principle, which should be engraved in gold: it is more blessed to give than to receive. And so tonight, on this beautiful occasion which I shall remember all my life, on behalf of Victory Steel, of which my father, that young kid with the Miami tan, four seats down to the left alongside Mitzi, his very charming wife, is the founder and President while I am only the Chairman of the Board, on behalf of our firm, I pledge ten thousand dollars to our cause. . . . Wait, don't applaud, it's only a come-on. I expect from each and every one of you, my good friends and business associates, a present too. And believe me, I will not be insulted if you top our pledge."

Eisenberg arose to remind the guests, who were fidgeting unhappily, that there were pledge cards on their tables; young ladies would pass among them to collect the checks and pledges. "Write them out quick. Though the hour is late, a big reward is yet to come."

Jessie had been saved to hold the diners till their arms were twisted. It was close to eleven o'clock when Eisenberg rose to introduce her. "And now it is my privilege to present the distinguished guest speaker for whom we have all been waiting patiently. The famous little lady who has so graciously consented to lend her tribute to our incomparable Joseph Sloan. The celebrated author of an immortal drama that every critic of the most important papers in this city has lauded to the skies. This play, I can say without fear of contradiction, will be the *Uncle Tom's Cabin* of the Jewish people. I remember well what Abraham Lincoln said when he met the author of another immortal work, Mrs. Harriet Beecher Stowe. 'So this is the little lady who made a great war.' "

Jessie gnawed her lower lip, looking faintly sick.

"I give you another little lady who has stirred all New York to action against the vicious enemy who threatens our people everywhere. Her message, I have no doubt whatsoever, you will carry away locked inside your hearts and it will inspire you to double your labors—and your contributions—on behalf of our oppressed brethren. Ladies and gentlemen, I am privileged to present to you a gifted, courageous and—this you can see for yourself—charming young lady, the author of Broadway's sensational hit, *The Arsonists*." His bow, his upward hand wave, urged Jessie from her chair. "Miss Jessica White."

Chairs scraped back. The audience rose, dropping napkins to the carpet. The applause was thunderous.

Jessie got up slowly, moved toward the lectern slowly. She drew the microphone down, adjusting it to her height, hooked on her horn-rimmed spectacles, spread papers before her on the lectern, taking time, building suspense.

"Ladies and gentlemen." Her voice, always resonant and rich, was deepened to a sexy huskiness by the loud-speaker. "As you see by these papers, I have written a speech. However, before I begin my prepared remarks, I wish to make an introduction. There is, in this audience, a gentleman whom you should meet. A great gentleman who bears upon his fragile body the scars of the fires of hate. The gentleman whose personal ordeal inspired my play and whose noble character has been my lifelong source of inspiration. And I venture to say, an inspiration, also, to my sister, Celia Sloan. . . . Will our father, Herman Weiss, please stand up."

There was silence, then a bang, Joe's chair bowled over. I saw Celia changing colors, flushing, growing pale, before I slued around to watch Herman cowering in his seat, Dr. Bishop bending over him.

"Stand up, Papa dear, don't be afraid." Jessie's voice was like a caress. "These are good Jews; these are friends."

He rose, swaying slightly, unsteady on his feet. The applause began tentatively, a spatter here and there, before it swelled into a storm. For a second or so, Herman stood erect and dazed, looking toward the distant figure at the lectern, before he covered his scarred face with his scarred hands and dropped back on the chair.

Wullstein smacked his fingertips. "What a ham! That act, believe me, will be worth easy another hundred thousand bucks. Sam, if you planned it, if you cooked it up with her, the King will positively kiss your feet." Joe and Celia wouldn't. You could take a bet on that.

As was my habit, I picked up the finals of the evening papers and the "bulldogs" of the morning papers to check our publicity breaks before I went to bed. The "bulldogs" were carrying in past tense the release Wullstein had sent out, the finals reporting, via the United Press, that Franklin Delano Roosevelt, President of the United States, had asked Congress to appropriate $72,500 to assist Jewish refugees who had escaped from Germany, and also that Major General George Van Horn Moseley, Commander of the Fourth Corps Army Area and holder of the Distinguished Service Medal, had proposed, "If any such refugees are to be shipped to us, it should properly be with the distinct understanding that they all be sterilized before being permitted to embark. Only in that way can we properly protect our future."

None of the papers had gotten around to reporting that Miss Jessica White, the playwright, had stunned a glittering audience at the Waldorf by showing them the gruesome scars of the fires of hate in these United States.

Eight

Jessie's Westport summer rental was a shack on a wooded rise near Compo Beach. From the screened porch, through trees, you could glimpse white sails on Long Island Sound. The living room had a fieldstone fireplace, the bedroom a double bed, the lean-to kitchen a greasy range, using bottled gas, and a musty refrigerator, using ice. The plumbing leaked and clogged. The fact that a successful playwright had chosen this struck me as a showing-off, a pro-proletarianism, in its way as ostentatious as Celia's Palace of Versailles.

Primitive or no, I'd been delighted when, at the end of June, she phoned to invite me out for Friday night to Sunday afternoon. Westport had salt-water bathing and "interesting" people, I had heard. Stupor grips New York when the temperature zooms; weekends the city's dead. All I could do was read Sunday papers on a bench on Riverside Drive, take cold showers, sprawl on the bed in my furnished room, listening to the radio and reproaching myself for not crossing town to visit Herman Weiss. It was wise, I told myself, to avoid the Sloans till they recovered from the Starlight Roof.

Since that spectacular night, Jessie and I had not been in touch. I'd mailed her a note, care of Waterhouse and Windom, saying, "After that performance, I forgive you everything," thinking she might write or phone to ask, "Forgive me for what?" so that I could answer, "For writing a lousy play that libels me and turning your back on Ilene." Vain expectation. She wasn't even curious, though in the invitation phone call she did say, "Payment on account to catalyst," adding she'd meet me at the Westport depot, take the 5:15 from Grand Central Station.

Driving to her place, she offered another dubious reason for inviting me. "When the evening sun goes down, a shack in the woods gets lonesome as all hell. Eerie, scary. A dame needs protection from night crawlers and chipmunks."

"Rodents and bait."

"Correct," Jessie said. "Of what else are working girls afraid?"

"Who protects her in the middle of the week?"

"Her faithful servant, valor," Jessie said.

There was a cot in the living room, reeking of spilled gin, and one on the porch, neither fit for laying out a corpse. "Choose," my hostess said. "I do not recommend the porch. The screens have holes. Mosquitoes. Sheets and blankets in the hall closet. No maid service. The hostess is a convalescent."

You'd not have guessed that from the way she looked. Surgery and dieting had slimmed her, the sun changed her complexion to the color of ripe peach. With bobbed hair and in the shorts she wore driving from the station, she had a charming gamine quality, though in the slinky, silky cerise house coat she put on after supper she looked ridiculous, a sunburned kid playing femme fatale.

We'd had a store-bought supper, cold ham, potato salad, cheese, after which Jessie taught me what every Boy Scout knows—how to build a fire: Crumple newspaper, criss-cross kindling, leaving space for air to circulate, lay a single log atop, don't pile on more wood till the log is burning briskly. Since her manner was mild and friendly, I figured the moment was propitious to offer drama criticism. She flared like the tinder. "So my play didn't please you! And I must bust out crying. Why is it every amateur thinks he knows more than the professionals?"

Being the acknowledged catalyst gave me privileges, I said.

"Buster," she retorted, "I was writing a three-act drama, not a sociological survey. And what else is new?"

Desultorily, we discussed the latest headlines till the log shattered into embers and the hostess yawned. "Time to retire. Should you be of the breed that gets up crack of dawn, kindly tiptoe to the toilet and piss quietly. And should you decide to make coffee, I prefer it strong enough to support the spoon."

I am also of the restless breed that reads itself to sleep. Rummaging in a stack of magazines, I came upon a medical journal, with the mailing sticker of Mark Bishop, M.D. So what? Can't Jessie invite other guests?

Early birdsong woke me. I tiptoed to the bathroom and got the flush-box ball unstuck before the noisy gurgle was prolonged. Looking for a place to park my Barbasol and razor, I discovered that another guest had left his grooming items on the shelf. Again, so what? It's no secret that the lady enjoys sex.

The coffee was perking by the time she emerged, hair and pajamas tousled. "Ummmmm." She sniffed. "Smells heavenly. You *are* useful. I'll let you join the club."

We had coffee on the porch. She bummed my cigarettes. "The gang arrives elevenish," she said. "I think you'll like them and, since they have peculiar tastes, they may like you, too."

They called themselves the Westport Chowder and Marching Society. They were screenwriters, actors and directors whom Jessie had met on the Coast, magazine writers, an illustrator, a ballet dancer, the kind of "creative" people I'd long craved to meet. They were "name" people, too, though they were introduced to me as Kay, Paula, Lisa, Ann, Bob, Bill, Eddie, Ernie, Lou, no surnames or biographies appended, and I was Sam, accepted with an ease that said any friend of Jessica's is okay with us. It was the beginning of a sequence of wonderful weekends.

They assembled haphazardly at Jessie's shack each Saturday forenoon, tumbling out of Fords and Chevrolets and Teddy's station taxi, couples, singles, trios, the men in beat-up slacks or shorts, the women in dirndls, carrying paper bags and baskets, pooling sandwiches, cold chicken, fruit, piling back into the cars, sitting on each other's laps, because the taxi'd been dismissed and Jessie didn't want to take her car—she hated driving on weekends. Off we went to Compo Beach to spread blankets on the sand, set up beach umbrellas, dole out the picnic lunch, sunbathe, swim, sunbathe, snooze, plod across the burning sands to the pavilion for cokes and ice-cream cones. At five o'clock, toasted, salted, we packed up the gear and piled into the vehicles. One car was designated to run over to a farm for Golden Bantam corn and beefsteak tomatoes, plucked to order and ambrosial, another to stop at the Compo Grocery for buns and butter, pickle relish and chips while Jessie and the rest headed for the shack to start a charcoal fire in the outdoor grill, chip ice, set out glasses, gin and Scotch. One drink, two, no more, while the corn was boiling, the hamburgers charring, the coffee bubbling. We feasted on the porch, chins dripping melted butter, cobs and crumpled greasy paper napkins piling up. Sated, we straggled indoors to build the fire in the fireplace, sprawl on the floor and drink—the hostess, under doctor's orders, nursing a single light highball, as abstemious with liquor as with buttered corn—and talk, wonderful talk, about everything except how we earned our midweek bread. No shop. Verboten. Jessie had made the rule, and my suspicious old eppes told me this probably was because her friends shared my low opinion of *The Arsonists*. Let's not mar our friendship, kids.

Before that fireplace we retried the Moscow trials, cursed the Johnson Act which embargoed aid to the Spanish Loyalists, grieved for Barcelona and Madrid, vowed the march of Fascism must be halted by all means short of war. War was the unthinkable, civilization's failure, its demise. But where was civilization? Surely not in Germany. The Nuremberg Laws, the Krystallnacht, were appalling, the failure of the Evian Conference to come to grips with the problem of the Jewish refugees was a disgrace to all the nations, including the U.S. But let us keep the Jewish question within the broader context of the rise of Fascism. I remember someone—Paula, I believe, though when a group is yakking, you can't be sure of who said what—saying, "There is just one country, only one, that has no anti-Semitism." And someone—Bob, I think—replying, "The Soviet Union. The true democracy." And a woman (Ann or Lisa?) saying, gently, "What we have to try to do is make the world just and safe for all people." With that last you couldn't disagree.

At the beach on one of the early Saturdays, Bill or Ernie, offhand, had asked me what I did and Jessie'd answered for me. "He slays Nazis. Mows 'em down. With rhetoric. For a weekly stipend." There'd been general laughter, Jessica is so-so-witty. I decided not to clarify.

"Writer. Ghost," I told them, which was also true and within their frame of reference.

Some of them were Jewish, that I knew, but since no one wore the Star of David, wrong guesses were unavoidable. Lou, for instance. His profile was classically Semitic, though his ancestry was Castilian, born in Uruguay to Catholic parents. And Ann, red-haired, blue-eyed, nose tip-tilted, Maid of Killarney, turned out to be a Galitzianer, born in East New York. Whatever their genetic origins, they spoke a common language: cosmopolitan. Some, I had reason to surmise, were card-carrying Party members, though since this, too, wasn't advertised I never knew precisely who was which, politically.

Their marital statuses were blurred as well. Some were married to one another, some living felicitously in what is known as sin; most had been divorced at least once, several were mattress-hopping, none homosexually, as intolerant of fags or Lesbians as they were of Nazi-Fascists.

Occasionally, during the Saturday-night world news critique, I'd catch a bemused expression on Jessie's face, a condescending Mona Lisa smile. Children, how you talk! I imagined the woman saying to herself; I licked the Nazi-Fascist-Anti-Semite problem in three brilliant acts. Wrong, as usual. What we saw on Jessie's sunburned countenance, I learned in due course, was the dreamy contentment of a woman remembering the pleasures of the double bed.

On Sundays, the Chowder and Marching Society turned up at high noon for scrambled eggs, bacon, burned English muffins and coffee on Jessie's porch, where the afternoon was spent eating fruit and gossiping about the famous folk they knew. No beach, too crowded with one-day trippers. By midafternoon, when the grape stems, plum and peach pits had been dumped into the garbage, the dishes rinsed and left to drain, the bag of gossip emptied, it was "See you next week, Sam."

They took for granted I was Jessie's current lover. I did not deny it. Or affirm. That was how the lady wanted it.

By the mildest kind of snooping I'd found out why I had been tapped for the Chowder and Marching Society. Emptying a wastepaper basket into the fireplace, I'd noticed several torn-across envelopes, addressed to Dr. Bishop at a Park Avenue address. Add this to the medical journals, the dwindling tube of shaving cream in the bathroom cabinet, and her firm announcement of intentions at Mt. Sinai Hospital.

"Your doctor makes house calls," I remarked.

"Daily, after office hours." She eyed me to see how I received the news. "No Friday, Saturday, Sunday. In Vermont with the kiddies and Francine, the wife."

"Naturally," I said, playing cool as well as candid, "a surgeon who plans to operate next day requires a sound night's sleep. It wouldn't do to park him on a lumpy cot."

"Naturally," she said.

"Quite a stallion." I decided to get rough. "Seven nights a week."

She dimpled. "Vermont is where he recuperates." Then, softly, "It is love. And do not laugh."

"For how long?"

"Sufficient unto the day." And, hoarsely, "I will kill you if you breathe a syllable! The man has a position as well as a wife."

"And I'm the camouflage? The eunuch outside the door?"

She touched my arm, placatingly. "Come, come, Rosenbaum. Don't you fergin me happiness?"

I couldn't say yes, I couldn't say no. Jessie *is* my friend. I want her to be happy and, by the looks of her, she is. What she craved she has: companionship and joy. She radiates. She's almost beautiful. If the Chowder and Marching Society gives me credit for the light in Jessie's eyes, is that good or bad?

Question: What have I to lose? Answer: Manly pride. Question: Whose fault is it I've never made the Beautyrest? Answer: Mine. The invitations have been there, but I've always walked away. Why? Because whenever I start thinking this is quite a dame, Jessie slaps me down. True, and don't deny it, I love the woman. Half in love. Not totally.

Put it this way: I admire her accomplishments, her independence, her humor, the freewheeling way she lives. She's exciting to be with. But how often, for how long? Admit it, Jessie seven days a week could drive me absolutely nuts. Okay, so I'm not prepared to make a deal of bed *and* board. Why not bed alone? It takes two to make that bargain. She's not buying either. Sam's a good guy, he's a friend, he's the old reliable. But, let us face it, he hasn't got the stuff to tame the shrew.

Then why do I come running when she crooks her little finger?

195

Why don't I find myself a steady girl? What's great about bachelorhood? Furnished rooms and one-night stands aren't paradise. Look around. The world is full of well-stacked girls who would make good wives. Nu? The answer's simple. They aren't Jessie Weiss. Go figure these things out.

Moreover, the M.D. is a passing fancy, like the Seventh Regiment. He has a legal wife; she has a legal husband. By summer's end, Mark Bishop will be gone and I'll still be around. And what will be, will be. Thus, I reasoned, this, I concluded, was why I rushed to catch the 5:15, built the fire in Jessie's living room, fetched and carried, washed the dishes, slept on a cruel cot, frolicked, drank, palavered with a stimulating crowd and served as red herring across the trail of a romance. Sam, the loyal shnook, never was too smart.

* * *

On a Friday evening, a few weekends after my debate with myself, I saw Horace Simon at the Westport depot. Jessie was meeting both of us. Horace had taken the same train out. I hadn't recognized him, he had changed so much. Hair prematurely white, he resembled a mean rabbit.

Jessie had a fairly decent dinner waiting, a chicken casserole— she wasn't a good cook, though she was trying to improve—and the before-the-fire conversation for once was shop, a pro talking to a pro. What shows had he been working on? What plans had he for the fall? Did he know the Waterhouse and Windom people? Would he like an introduction? And had he seen *The Arsonists?*

He had. Its theme had interested him only mildly, but he regretted he had not been asked to do the sets. (His speech was slow, a trace of stammer, none of the brash glibness he had had when young.) The background of the town, for instance; he could have made it realistic. After all, he'd known the kind of place she had in mind. And that orange zigzag fire backdrop was atrocious! He could have done a fire scene so realistic they'd have stampeded to the exits.

To my amazement, Jessie listened, nodding vertically, yes, I agree, horizontally, no, you're wrong, without dogmatism or hysteria. At ten o'clock, she yawned. "Toss a coin, boys, who sleeps

196

where, living room or porch," rose, retiring, and slammed her bedroom door.

We tossed my quarter. It brought me luck. I got the living room cot whose lumps I was familiar with. I showed Horace where the linens were, warned him about the flush-box ball and put on my pajamas. Horace loitered in the living room, desiring conversation. I switched off the lamps. Reluctantly, he trotted to the porch. The springs of his cot kept creaking. He was wakeful, listening, I was sure, to hear me tiptoe into Jessie's room.

I'd figured him wrong. Mosquitoes had kept him up. At breakfast Jessie noticed the bites. "Something *must* be done about those screens. They're full of holes. Horace, you're so good with your hands, there's some wire netting hereabouts. Up, boy, let us find the tools."

She signaled me to stay put, not to follow, and so of what she said to him and he to her, in the lean-to or elsewhere, I got only fragments when her voice was carried toward me by prevailing winds—"Forget it. He's like a brother"—and later, shouting, not caring whether all of Fairfield County heard, "I want it *now*. Immediately. For reasons I don't care to state, I can't make the trip to Nevada or Mexico. You will have to go. . . . Okay, Mexico, if you prefer. If your old man won't put up the fare, I will. . . ."

What he answered, I don't know. He came back without tools or netting and announced he was leaving for New York. "H-h-have to s-s-see a m-m-man about a d-d-dog."

Jessie phoned for the station taxi. "Let me know if you want a check," was her farewell to him. After the cab had rattled off, gone before the Chowder and Marching Society turned up, Jessie rubbed her hands, dry-washing them. "Clearing decks and none too soon," was all she said. In her father's kitchen years ago, she'd told me she wouldn't bother with divorce, she never intended to remarry. Never, in her vocabulary, means till I change my mind. Ho hum, Dr. Bishop has a wife.

Briefly, a wild fear struck me that Horace might bring suit in the state of New York, charging infidelity, with me as co-respondent. I'd have the name without the game. How much more does Jessie Weiss expect of me?

Plenty, as it turned out.

197

On a Sunday noon in August, eight of us were settling down to breakfast after Bromo-Seltzer had settled us. Saturday night had been more bibulous than political, the talk for once lighthearted: about Edward the Seventh and the "woman I love"—let's drink to them; about the disappointed other women in Edward's bachelor life—let's drink to them, wish them luck elsewhere; about "Wrong-way" Corrigan, bright spot in a world of gloom and doom—by all means drink to him. The morning after found the women frowsy, surly, the men unshaven, bleary, a crummy-looking bunch.

"More company! Jesus Christ!" Jessie cried in the kitchen. "You're up, Sam. See who it is."

I emerged from the shack to find Celia and Joe emerging from the Cadillac, Joe in plus fours, Argyles and plaid cap, Celia in trim skirt and blouse, white gloves and just one string of pearls.

"The family. Yours," I yelled into the house.

"Shit!" Jessie's voice, as usual, carried well. "Somebody come in here, moosh these eggs."

Celia offered me gloved fingertips. "Samuel, what are *you* doing here? We were told Jessie wished seclusion, to recuperate."

"You have time to kibbitz here," Joe rebuked me. "Not one Sunday you can spare to visit my father-in-law."

Celia stepped inside the shack. The living room was a sty, empty liquor bottles, unwashed glasses and my unmade cot. "Bacon!" Celia sniffed, sounding horrified. Surprising, she who was strictly kosher recognized the smell.

"It is indeed, and will one of you be good enough to drain it." Jessie came from the kitchen in the bedraggled cerise house coat. I caught her fleeting grin at Joe's get-up, before, "Why the surprise party? This place does have a telephone."

"Don't worry, we're not staying. We wouldn't dream of spoiling your party," Celia said. "Joseph's playing golf at Longshore. We decided to stop by, save a special trip."

"Where's paper to drain bacon?" Paula yelled from the kitchen.

"Excuse me," Jessie said. "I'm the cook. Had breakfast? Sam, dig up some crockery. Squeeze together, gang. Make room for the duke and duchess."

Celia swept the table with a frigid stare and announced she

didn't wish to intrude, she'd be more comfortable waiting in her car. Joe thought he'd join us for a cup of coffee. Lou and Ann slid closer on their bench to leave space for him. "Do the honors, Sam," Jessie said before she scooted to the kitchen. A man for all services.

"Joe, Jessie's brother-in-law." I mentioned first names up and down the table and squirmed into my place.

"And what does Joe do?" Lisa drawled, breaking the standing rule.

"Makes money," I said.

"Doesn't everyone?" she asked.

Jessie, carrying in the eggs and bacon platter, chose to amplify. "Junkie, Scrap metal."

"How quaint!" Kay murmured.

"Steel," Joe said, bristling. "Preparedness. Defense."

"Sugar and cream?" Lisa drawled.

"Cream's curdled, me and it," Jessie said. "Have a muffin, Joseph. More blessed to give than to receive."

The Chowder and Marching Society caught the storm signals. They finished breakfast silently and swiftly, then announced, one after the other, that they hated to eat and run, but they had to get to the beach—the tide was coming in or going out—or meet Aunt Tillie at the depot, or make an urgent phone call to the Coast or do some shopping at the Compo Grocery. I discovered I also had to rush, to buy papers before the store sold out; we'd sent out a release for Sunday's newspapers, I had to check on the coverage we'd received. No one suggested clearing up. We ducked away and stayed away around a bend in the road till the Cadillac had driven off. When we straggled in, Jessie was pacing the porch, white as a sheet, her stop-tears fist rammed against her mouth. She removed it to growl, "Get the hell away from me."

The party was over. Kay and Ernie washed the dishes, I stripped my cot, tidied up the living room, announced I'd take an early afternoon train, I'd call the taxi, no one needed to hang around to drive me to the depot, and, in a pack, they left. I put my shirt and bow tie on, hasped my small valise, went out to the porch. "I'm phoning for the taxi. Anything I can do for you before I leave?"

She glared. "Fine friend. Running out, when I need you. Yes, there's something you can do. Should of thought of it yourself. Get me a drink."

I measured a jigger of Scotch out of one bottle that had not been drained last night and brought it with a water chaser. She gulped it, the old lebensmittel. "The mob gone? Good. Sit down. . . . Sam, it's Papa."

"Dead?"

"Bite your tongue. Spit out. We have to make a decision."

The "we" gave me pause. I lit a cigarette for her and while she smoked, in hard, angry puffs, I watched the scudding sails on the sparkling Sound. It was a glorious day, cloudless, not too hot, a shame to waste it sitting here in gloom, wrestling with problems that were not my own. But, back in Grady's Mills, I'd been caught on the hook of caring. On the Hill we knew—out of nosiness—everybody's problems, and we tried to help. Abe Finkel put up my college tuition money, I compromised my conscience to help Max Slomowitz, Sol Katz tried to get me promoted to the city desk. And the women all had worried about Herman after Ida died. All Jews are brothers. I'd been raised that way.

Jessie finished the cigarette, helped herself to another from my pack, lit it from the stub. "They want to send him to a Home." She paused, waiting for "Oh, no" from me. I didn't make a sound.

"I knew it wouldn't work, it couldn't in a million years. But this was how my sister wanted it. *She'd* give him a home, *she'd* take care of him, *she'd* be the good daughter, let me be the bad, selfish one. Well, she got it, she has it, they have it, up to here. And to be honest, there's something on their side. It's like having an infant in the house, only worse. You can dress a baby up and show it off. But old men are unpresentable. Sam—" She leaned to me. Smoke blew in my eyes. I squawked. She set the cigarette on a clamshell. "They're ashamed of Herman. Ashamed! *Of my father, Herman Weiss!* And since that affair at the Waldorf, they've been burning up. (By the by, they blame you for bringing Papa there. Did you? Joe said his first impulse was to get you fired, till somebody explained it was a great fund-raising gimmick. *Gimmick! Papa! Me!*) Well, since that night, Herman is a tourist attraction. Friends of theirs drop in. They say, 'We understand your famous father lives with you, we'd just love to meet him.' Most times, he balks, won't leave his room, and when he does, it's worse. Shlumpy bedroom slippers, tsitsis showing underneath his vest, and like as not his fly's half zipped." She was talking furiously, growing short of breath, while the cigarette burned to an ash string in the clamshell. "It's summer, they'd like to close up the apartment, get away to the mountains, the shore, wherever it is rich people go, but for him they have to keep the home fires burning. Somebody to market for his food, cook it, serve it, wash his dishes, make his bed, wash his underwear and socks. Oh, I tell you they spared me no details. And, I hate to admit it, there was right on their side. Can't get away, even for a weekend, unless the help agrees to hang around. And the help is human, too. They might enjoy a trip to Coney Island to cool off. Last week Joe and Ceil drove up to see the kid in camp. When they came back, they found the maid and butler'd skipped, left the old man with a little lettuce and tomato, a can of sardines, to see him through the weekend. They'd figured when he came, he'd find himself some pals. There were cousins, landsleit, in the New York area. Or maybe he'd pick up a crony from a bench in Central Park, or maybe you, you wouldn't be a shtunk, you'd come and keep him company. But no, not a soul. He's depressed, they're depressed. And it can't go on like this. They want to get it settled before the kid comes home from camp. Unwholesome for her having him around. And you were right, she's a sweet kid—the little I saw of her. She feels she has to be his playmate, cheer him up. But, I ask you, is that fair? I wouldn't want *my* little girl to spend her childhood playing dominoes with an old man. She should be free to sing and dance, run wild—"

As if her "run wild" was a stage direction, she stomped up and down the porch, arguing with herself. "Celia said either I take Papa or they arrange to put him in a Home. Now, how can I take him? You know the way things stand with me. First, he wouldn't eat a drop of food in my house, it's trefe. Then Mark. The man I've searched for all my life. So it's my tough luck he has a wife. Maybe she'll divorce him, maybe she will not. She likes being Mrs. Doctor Bishop, it's prestige. So, for the present, the time being, the other woman, namely Jessie, takes what she can get and thank you very much. Well, maybe Papa wouldn't say a word about the sleeping arrangements in this place, but I can bet and you can bet he'd add the score and it would hurt him terribly. He's old-world, Victorian, a prude. Why, before I went through that meshugas under the canopy with Horace, Papa wouldn't let my fiancé sleep under the same roof. Oh, Mark knows a little of my problem. He and I have discussed Papa. Mark's kind, a kinder man you never met. You noticed how sweet and tender he was with Papa at the Waldorf? We've talked about the possibility of plastic surgery on Papa's face, so that being seen by strangers wouldn't upset him so. But Mark thinks, at his age, it's hardly worth the torture that's involved. . . . And can you see me setting up a kosher menage in New York, next door to a synagogue? Ménage à trois, Papa, Mark, and me." She drew deep breath, let it slowly out. "No sir, give up my love to make latkes for my father? A king, may I remind you, gave up his throne, his country for the woman he loved. But I'm expected to discard my love, all because there was a fire in Grady's Mills. Is that fair, humane, just? Or sensible?"

A yes was on my tongue. We make decisions glibly about what other people ought to do. Sister, you're raking in the shekels because there was a fire in Grady's Mills. Pay something back, make a sacrifice, you've had it all your way for years. Herman sacrificed for you, financed a college education, set you free. Now, give him a couple of your years. The argument was all there, in my head. I didn't speak a word of it, since what occurred to me was that I was fortunate. My parents were healthy, self-supporting, self-sustaining, making no demands. Yet suppose, suppose, tomorrow the situation changed, how would I handle it? I pulled a shutter down and put my blinders on.

"A Home!" Jessie was storming. "A leper colony for society's untouchables. A city dump, for worn-out, used-up, human souls and bodies. The old shapeless women in their wigs and baboushkas, with their bunions and their fallen wombs, the old hunchbacked men leaning on their canes, with hands with swollen veins, like sleeping snakes, underneath the rusty skin. In rows in rocking chairs, staring at nothing while they wait for death. The sticky, dripping eyes, drained of every human spark, the bony claws, groping, clutching, wanting to hang on. To what? To a piece of herring, a stale crust of sour rye to dunk in watery coffee. Sam, have you ever been in one of those places? They stink, of Lysol and incontinence. The pre-mortuary stink." She spoke with such intemperate rage, I had no doubt she stormed at, strove to exorcise, a profound terror of her own, the unvoiced fear in everyone of us, of growing old, unwanted, alienated from the rest of humankind. Nevertheless, she hadn't touched the real and present problem, the relocation of Herman Weiss.

"Why'd you move your father out of Grady's Mills?" I asked.

She all but spat. "Because he wouldn't stay. That's why."

"He didn't need to be *that* scared. It happened, but it wouldn't happen twice, you could be sure. You might have found a room for him with one of his old friends."

Her head shook violently, impatient with me. "You think I didn't urge it? I'm no fool. I knew from the start Celia's fancy-shmansy setup was no place for him. I was prepared to pay his room and board. But honestly, and I believe I've mentioned this before, he gave me the impression he was ashamed to stay. Not afraid. *Ashamed*. Ashamed to face his friends. Remember he wouldn't say goodbye to them? But why? Maybe being a victim had, he felt, degraded him. One guess is as good as another. Maybe this is how Jews in Europe feel when they've taken the full treatment from the Nazi gangsters, robbed of dignity, subhuman." Her voice was running down to a wheezing whisper. "I don't know, I can't think. . . . Sam, squeeze the bottle, see if there's another jigger. . . ."

I was in the kitchen, wondering whether a post-gall-bladder patient in a highly emotional state ought to have a second Scotch, when I heard the shuffling footsteps. Jessie must have heard them, too, for by the time I reached the door, she was on its threshold, hugging her father. He was pale and panting, soaked with perspiration, and his shoes were white with dust; he'd probably hiked from the depot. Jessie's hug had dislodged his Panama hat and the two brown paper bags that he was carrying. Half a pumpernickel and a heel of cheese had spilled from one, a bedroom slipper and the fringes of the tallith from the other. From the evidence, he had come to stay a while.

"Papa, I'd have met you at the station. Why didn't you phone you wanted to visit me?"

"I didn't know if you have a telephone. I vanted to see you, Jessie, it vas necessary. They tell me last night they going to send me to a Home. The whole night I didn't sleep a vink."

Her color rose and went. "Come in, Papa. Sit down on the porch. Rest. Cool off. I'll fix you a cold drink. Or hot tea."

"Or a shnapps," I butted in.

He noticed me. "Ah, Sammy, our friend! You live here, too, in Jessie's house? She got rooms?"

"Sam!" Jessie pulled me aside. "You drive, don't you? Good. Hop in my car, drive over to South Norwalk. There's a Jewish grocery. Get some sour cream and farmer cheese, anything you find that he can eat. And paper plates and cups. . . . Papa, take off the shoes, the coat, the vest."

He removed his coat, slid out of his dusty shoes. She knelt to put his slippers on. Thus, I left them, on the porch, Jessie kneeling at her father's feet, to drive off to buy farmer cheese and sour cream, sweet butter, eggs, a rye bread, seeded rolls, a matjes herring, radishes, a cucumber and paper plates. Herman wouldn't starve here or violate Kashruth.

He was in carpet slippers and yarmulka, padding from porch to living room, picking objects up, putting them down, replacing a book on a shelf, centering an ash tray on an end table, putting things to rights, his pleasure at being here obvious and innocent. "A nice house, Jessie, only small, old-fashion', Mama wouldn't like. It is near the votter. Maybe it is for you damp. You vas sick. You feeling all right now? . . . The landlord you should ask he should put a vasher in the sink. . . . How much you pay for rent? . . . Five hundred dollars! . . . Gevalt, a tief, a robber, that landlord!" I got the impression he believed he'd arrived opportunely, to manage his daughter's business.

We supped on the porch. He ate with excellent appetite. "Papa, it's so funny how this happened." Jessie's voice had the wavy edge of hysteria. "Sam and I were sitting, talking, we were too lazy to drive over to the beach, it's a good thing we decided not to go this afternoon, or else you wouldn't have found me here. . . . Wait, I'll ring the Longshore Country Club. Ceil and Joe are there; they'll pick you up and drive you home."

He shook his head stoutly. "There is not mine home."

"They'll be worried, Papa, they'll call up the police."

"They vouldn't vorry. Lotsa times, whole days, they don't look in the room to see am I alive. Only the schvartze comes to say, Come in the kitchen, mister, I give lunch, I give supper. Or the child to ask could I play a game vid her." His face contorted with an unexpected anger. "All my life I am a businessman. Now I am good only to play games vid a child."

Poor Ilene, I thought, so well-meaning. And he'd rejected her. But Jessie'd also turned her back in the greenroom at the Waldorf. Blame Celia for that. Why always blame Celia? After her fashion, she means well, too.

Jessie went to the phone. She called the Longshore Club. "They've left," she returned to announce. "You'll go back on the train with Sam."

Herman didn't answer. He was murmuring a prayer of thanks for his food.

She waited, her mouth tightening with resolve, until he was finished. "Papa," she began, "it's a coincidence. Sam and I were talking about you just before you came. We were saying it was a mistake you went away from Grady's Mills. We decided you ought to go back."

His spinal column stiffened. "*You* decided. Vot am I, a little child? And if I decide I do not go back, who vill make me go?"

I'd never dreamed he had this firmness in him. Mild, docile I had figured him, leaving all decisions to his womenfolk. We had, indeed, been underestimating Herman. He had, as he'd pointed out to Jessie and to me, all his life been a businessman, which meant buying, selling, paying taxes, managing his own affairs. He'd had enough intelligence and resourcefulness to find Jessie's Westport address and get here by himself. Yet, with the arrogance of adult children, we'd been thinking of him, speaking of him, as if he were a semi-idiot. Jessie stared at me, with shame and a kind of despair, her expression plainly saying, Find the answer, work this out, for us.

It was fortunate Sam Rosenbaum, in youth dubbed Sir Shmulke Galahad, was on these premises.

"Mr. Weiss, I have a proposition. I am now living in New York; my room in Grady's Mills is standing empty. You and my parents always were the best of friends. Mama, I am sure, would be happy—"

Jessie leaped at it. "Why, that's a marvelous idea, a perfect solution!" Her eyes began to sparkle. "Papa would have a kosher home, his shul, his friends." There was something shameless in the way she'd snatched at the suggestion.

We eyed Herman, she avid, I curious. "I have no friends," Herman answered us.

"Now, Papa, isn't that ridiculous! There's nothing to be afraid of any more."

"Not afraid. Ashamed," he said.

"Of what, Papa? You did nothing, you owe nobody."

"I owe." He faltered and glanced at me as if he wasn't certain he could trust me with his secrets. "I owe for Mama's diamonds," he said, finally.

"In God's name, what are you talking about?" Jessie cried. Her fingers edged stealthily toward my cigarette pack. After a timorous glance at Herman, they edged back, wiggling, pretending all she'd meant to do was brush away some crumbs.

Herman spread his hairless, rust-splotched hands, palms down, on the table top, the fingers splayed so that we saw the deep burn-groove between the thumb and index finger of the left, and the truncated right hand—both stigmata of his painful history—while he braced himself for talking, which always had come hard to him. "You remember, Jessie tochter, ven you and Celia, bot of you, vanted to go in college and ve sent the bot of you, did you stop and think from vere comes the money for two colleges? Ve are poor storekeepers, ve have a small grocery, ve have no money in the bank for two colleges." Color was draining from his face; perspiration pearled his forehead. "So Mama takes the diamond earrings and the pin and she says to me, I should make a pawnshop loan on them, ven the college girls is earning nice money, ven the business picks up good, ve pay back the pawnshop loan. Then, ven the girls is married, to Jessie goes the earrings, to Celia goes the pin. I do not like this, Jessie. To the Hill it is like I make believe I am a velty man, I can send two girls in college. I am a faker. To be a faker is a lie, a shame. I am always an honest man." He paused to hawk up phlegm; since the fire, there'd been some congestion in his chest. "So Mama talks, she hollers—You remember, Jessie, how your mama hollers? Maybe you remember, too, Sammy? You vas like from our family. Ida Veiss, she should rest in peace, thought from you like a son—'Mister Veiss,' she said to me, 'this is no fakerei. So long you have mine diamonds you are a velty man. Do I need them in the grocery? No. So vere do I go ausgeputst? To shul. So Yom Tov, I vill be like the odder vimmin, plain, vidout the diamonds. Ven ve have in the bank safed up the money, ve bring to the pawnshop the tickets, ve take home the diamonds, in the pawnshop they don't spoil.' By her grave I make the promise—you vas dere, Sammy, you vas a vitness—I tell my vife I vill do vat she asked from me. It is hard to safe up money. The business is not good. Perlzweig opens up his store. I cannot tell young peoples they should buy from me, not Perlzweig. He must make a living also. So I am glad ven Jessie, mine tochter, sends me Chanukah gelt. I bring it in the bank to safe it up, to keep mine promise to mine vife. Then, in the fire, in mine own hand, the tickets they burn up. I can no more keep mine promise to mine vife. I cannot be a honest man. . . ."

He was ghastly pale and a-sweat. This must be how it is, I realized, when you spill your secrets on an analyst's couch. And this was why Herman Weiss had almost died. When he realized his house was burning, he didn't rush to save his life. He had to search for pawnshop tickets for diamonds, beyond a doubt long since unredeemable. He had to save his self-respect before he saved his life.

Jessie had her arms around him, hugging him, choking off his flood of explanation, expiation, covering his face with kisses, cooing, "Papa darling, poor, proud Papa darling, what a foolish Papa! Who needs diamonds? Celia? Me?" cradling him and rocking him as if he was a child, which in a way he was. And so was she. An adult of cool head and common sense had to straighten out the two of them.

I called my mother, long distance. "Hello, Mom, it's Sam. Your Sammy. . . . No, nothing's wrong. . . . Yes, I'm well, feeling fine.

. . . Yes, I get enough sleep. . . . Yes, I eat three meals. . . . No, I don't smoke so much. Don't worry, Mama. I never felt better in my life. . . . No, I don't have ham sandwiches for lunch. There's a kosher delicatessen on the same block where my office is. Wonderful hot pastrami. . . . No, not every day, I'm not constipated, don't worry. . . . How are you? And how is Papa? . . . Tell him not to worry about business. If he needs cash, he has a son can help him out. . . . Listen, Mama, I called you up for something special, important. Who is sleeping in my room these days? . . . Well, how would you like a boarder? . . . No, not a woman. . . . Yes, women are a bother, using up hot water, washing stockings, underwear. This is a man, a gentleman, somebody you like. And he likes you. No, I won't tell you the name. I like stringing you along. . . . An old friend of yours is here with me, I'll put her on, she'll tell you all about it. . . ."

"Hello, Mrs. Rosenbaum, this is Jessie Weiss. Remember me? That fat kid with the pigtails. . . . No, I keep it short, easier to take care of. . . . I'm sorry I couldn't accept your invitation to supper last summer. It was so hot, I had such a lot to do, I was so tired. . . . Yes, I was in the hospital. How did you know? It was a little nothing. Nothing to speak about. . . . Oh, I'm fine now. And yourself and Mr. Rosenbaum? . . . Yes, Sam and I are still good friends. As a matter of fact he has been spending this weekend with me, at my little country place. . . . It's in Connecticut. . . . That's near New York, an hour on the train. . . . No, dear, we aren't planning to get married. That isn't why we called. . . . Thank you very much, and if I were looking for a mother-in-law, you are just what I'd pick. . . . Yes, you're right, I have a husband. . . . No, he isn't here with us. He's out of town. On business. . . . Well, I hope it isn't monkey business. Anyway, your Sam wouldn't marry me, I don't know how to cook, you spoiled him, you're such a wonderful cook. Besides, I'm married to my work. . . . Well, I make a living. That's what counts, isn't it? . . . No, it's not a steady salary, I guess you'd call it piecework. . . . Oh, I couldn't be a teacher, I never graduated." (Hand over the mouthpiece: "What is she, Sam? Mrs. District Attorney?") "Listen, Mrs. Rosenbaum, it's my father, Herman Weiss, your old friend, we're calling about. . . . Yes, he's well, completely recovered. As a matter of fact, he's also here with me. We just finished supper. . . . No, it wasn't a lot of bother, just a little farmer cheese and cream. Mrs. Rosenbaum, we were talking and Papa told us how he hates New York, the subways, the rush and so far to walk to shul. So Sam, your Sammy, got the idea maybe you'd consider taking him for a boarder, you were always such good friends. . . . Sure, I'll put my father on. . . ."

"Hal-lo, Mrs. Rosenbaum, it's Herman Veiss. . . . Vere am I? By Jessie. In Connecti-cut. . . . How is it? Nu, a small place. Ida, she should rest in peace, vould call it a shanty. I think Jessie should get a better place; maybe she can't afford. It is by the votter, I think maybe it is damp for her. She vas sick in the hospital after Pesach. . . . Yeh, the second time. I didn't know, who tells a fader? . . . Yeh, yeh, now she looks healthy. . . . How do I feel? I live. The Abershter decided I should live. . . . Vell, I vant to come back and I don't vant to come back. Jessie talked me in. Maybe she knows the best. . . . Yeh, smart she alvays vas, the best marks in the school. . . . You could give me Sammy's room? It's not for you a big bodder? . . . Maybe I could find a little something to do, not sit all day on the stoop. . . . Yes, I vas alvays an active man. . . . Sure, positive, your schav is vonderful. Sure, vid cucumber. And sour cream. Not sveet."

He laughed. Not in all my years had I heard Herman laugh; it never had occurred to me he could. Nor heard him talk so freely. The only other lengthy conversation attributed to him, I'd had secondhand from Horace Simon and I'd doubted its authenticity.

"Ven I come? Jessie vill decide. She'll call you up, long distant. . . . Yes, the best friends ve alvays vas. You do a big mitzvah, Mrs. Rosenbaum, to give an old Jew a home. Tank you very much."

There were tears in his eyes when he hung up. He brushed them with his wrist. Jessie's face was on the verge, sad but triumphant. She'd showed Herman which daughter cared most for him, would do the most to make him happy. And all it would involve was money, and not too much of this.

She returned to the phone to make another call. "Celia! I wanted you to know Papa's here. . . . Yes, in Westport, with me. . . . He came around four o'clock. . . . How'd he get here? The New York, New Haven and Hartford. And he does speak English. And in case you've forgotten, he's an adult, used to run a retail business. . . . Were you worried? Aw, go on, I'll bet you never even opened up his door, to see if he was alive or dead or in there with a chippie. . . . Yes, I know the problem; you spared me no details. But relax, take it easy, everything is solved. All the problems. Even Mama's diamonds. . . . No, he did not bring them. They are gone forever from our lives, pawned to send you to State Normal, me to Emerson. And the pawn tickets burned up in that fire. So get the family heirlooms off your mind. You won't miss them. Those rocks Joey buys you. . . . Sure, I'm jealous. Why should I not be? My speed is garnets. And earned by the sweat of my brow. . . . Yes, we'll settle this some other time. Listen, about Papa, he's going home, to Grady's Mills, to live with a friend. The name is Rosenbaum. Yes, dear old Sammy's mother. Yes, we've talked to her, she's willing, she has a big, sunny room. Not like that closet you have kept him in. . . . Okay, okay, you meant well. It did not work out. Let's leave it at that. I'm going to keep him here a couple of days. Don't worry, I won't feed him pork and beans, I'll give him fresh air, sunshine, loving *personal* care—he looks terrible. What you could do, if it isn't too much trouble, is send your chauffeur out here with his clothes, then drive him to Grady's Mills. . . . I'll pay for his board and lodging, I'll be delighted to. . . . No, you need not go fifty-fifty. You have done your bit."

Herman tweaked her sleeve. "Jessie, if you can't afford, I find a buyer for the lot."

"Papa dear, I can afford. And believe me it's a bargain."

I made noises about calling Teddy's taxi to catch the late train.

"Stay over, Sam," she begged. "The situation's still so new I don't trust myself with it. Help me change my bed for him. Papa rates the royal suite." While we spread the fresh muslin, she said, "I'll phone Mark at his office in the morning, let him know what's up; he'd best not come out while Papa's here." Then, "Sam, light a butt for yourself and let me have a puff. It'll darn near kill me, but I'll kick the habit while he's here. If I smoked, he'd be convinced I was a prostitute."

At daybreak Monday morning when I tiptoed to the bathroom, I saw the bedroom door ajar, the double bed empty, and I went into panic. Had Herman changed his mind and run away, possibly, in despair, thrown himself into Long Island Sound? I hurried to the porch where Jessie occupied the cot. She was sleeping soundly but at the far end Herman stood, tallith on his shoulders, phylacteries binding arms and forehead, facing east, toward the memory of a temple in Jerusalem, praying soundlessly and with such an air of contentment here, close to his daughter, I was sorry we'd decided he had to return to Grady's Mills.

*　　*　　*

During the winter Jessie dropped another relocation problem in my lap.

Our office receptionist sounded gaga when she buzzed me to announce that Jessica White was on her way to the Rosenbaum cubbyhole. Stenos and file clerks, alerted by the outside desk, lined the corridor to get a glimpse of the glamour girl of the Sloan testimonial banquet. Her highness did not nod or wave. Preoccupied, if not arrogant.

"To what do I owe this honor?" I bowed her to my desk-side chair.

"To the bastard who is U.S. Consul in Berlin." She unbuttoned her coat. I helped her off with it.

"You are speaking of a man we love," I said.

She caught my sarcasm. "And with good reason." She took a sheaf of clipped-together papers from the old alligator satchel. "Look and puke," she said.

The one on top was handwritten, in Yiddish. "You read?" she asked. "Me neither. Took doing to locate a translator. Papa got it in October. Note that it's addressed to his wife. Papa read it, shed a tear, mailed it on to me. 'What can we do?' 'We,' natch, meaning Jessie. First, I was suspicious it might be a phoney. The snapshot that came with convinced me otherwise. Spitting image of Ida. Read."

"*Dear and respected Cousin Chaya,*" I read the typed translation. "*This letter is written by your cousin Sara who is the daughter of Rochel, the sister of your sainted mother, Yenta, may she rest in peace. My mother, who is also many years departed from this life, spoke often of the clever cousin, Chaya, who went with her husband to the United States. It was our sorrow you did not write to*

211

your devoted family, only one letter to tell your mother your husband had established himself in business from which it is our hope he made much money. You did not write us if you gave birth to children and how you are in health. We ourselves had much trouble with sickness, from my parents and my brother, Zalmon, who became in both legs paralyzed when a small child and lives in Vilna with a family of cousins on my father's side who take care of him. I myself moved from Vilna when I married my husband, Shimon Cottler, because after the big war it was hard to make a living in Lithuania. It was fortunate I learned to sew when I was a young girl. With my needle I helped to earn for us our bread. Since twelve years we have lived in Koenigsberg. My husband is a bookkeeper and till now he has made for us, thank God, a living. Only because of the troubles, of which you have no doubt heard, he has now lost his position. And our son, Mendel, can no longer attend school. He is a delicate boy, the situation is hard for his nerves. We have decided it is better for us to move to the United States, and my husband has a letter written to the American consul in Berlin. From him we have learned to get a visa we must have affidavit from relations in the United States saying they will be responsible for us.

"*Our brother, Zalmon, kept the letter you wrote to your sainted mother. He thought one day if God is willing he will travel to the United States, where there are many professors of medicine who can cure his legs. He was sure the cousin Chaya would receive him and find the best doctor. From him, I have obtained your address. You forgot us, dear Cousin Chaya, but we did never forget you. My sainted mother, your aunt, spoke often of your high intelligence. Now, dear Cousin Chaya, I would ask from you the important favor that you send for us the affidavit to the American consul in Berlin that you will receive us in your home and then the consul will give to us the visas. The money for ship's tickets we do have and our living we can earn, not to eat like guests in your home. My husband asks this be quickly done. We are in danger. . . .*"

I laid the paper down, feeling numbed. Koenigsberg was at the Polish border. How soon would the plague infect the East?

"I sent the affidavit. I didn't know the people, never heard their

212

names. Even if they were strangers, I'd move heaven and earth to get them out. Wouldn't you?"

What else was my job all about? My mind paused to wonder whether in some Lithuanian town or village there were kin of mine, strangers with the same blood stream, who one day soon would write, "Save us." All Jews are brothers is the legend. A cousin Sara is for real.

"It was a goddam nuisance," Jessie was telling me. "Photostats, notarized documents, income tax returns. Bank accounts. So yesterday this."

"This" was on the letterhead of the American Consulate General in Berlin. "*Subject: Immigration Visa Application of Shimon Cottler. Madam: In reference to the affidavit submitted on behalf of the registered applicant Shimon Cottler, wife, Sara, and minor child, Mendel, this department finds the affidavit insufficient in several respects. We note that the name of the visa applicant is misspelled in these papers, thereby creating doubt of the claim of relationship, which is not adequately explained. The affidavit of support includes a copy of an income tax return for the year 1937 which demonstrates a net income of $6,475. The notarized statement of income for 1938 is incomplete, covering only a portion of that year, to the month of October, but indicating a substantial drop in earnings. It also includes the statement that you support an aged father. From the two statements submitted, it is apparent that there is no regular or fixed source of income. You have also submitted evidence of bank accounts totaling less than $2,000. It is therefore believed you are not reasonably in a position to guarantee the support in the United States of three additional persons. Additionally, no evidence has been presented that you maintain a household adequate to furnish living quarters for this family.*

"*It is therefore the opinion of the Consulate General that these aliens are likely to become public charges if admitted to the United States for permanent residence, and the application for visa is refused.*"

No doubt many anxious families in the United States had received letters resembling this, and from the same source. Up to now, I'd known about them by hearsay. True, our consulates abroad had been besieged but helpless, hog-tied by archaic immigration quota laws. Yet seeing the rejection coldly typed on high-grade bond made it altogether different. Three human beings were denied a chance to save themselves because a second cousin, a famous woman in New York, hadn't sufficient money in the bank. It was heartless. It was evil. It was *us*.

What shocked me, almost as much, was finding out how little Jessie had. I'd been under the impression she'd been raking in the dough in Hollywood. Perhaps, before 1937, she had, though obviously she'd spent as if there'd be no tomorrow. And go explain to the consul in Berlin that a writer's income tax return is like a traveling salesman's swindle sheet, deductions for a cab ride around the block (transportation), a drink bought for a friend (entertainment), a bedroom on the Super-Chief (travel). And go tell him that midway through the year of 1937, Herman's Grocery burned down and Herman's daughter, Jessie, dropped what she was doing on the Coast to rush to him and get the inspiration for a play that she wrote and rewrote while she lived off capital. That's why the bank balance is small. Go tell him, too, that *The Arsonists*, a critical success, had not turned out to be a bonanza. Paramount had dropped its option; no other studio had nibbled. In July, business had fallen off, as is normal on Broadway in summer; by autumn, the play had serious competition from the press-association cables. Who'd spend three bucks to see a hoked-up version of small-town racial prejudice when, for a nickel for a daily paper, he could be harrowed by details of big-league bestiality? The show closed after Thanksgiving, the management figuring business usually was off during the Christmas shopping weeks and the home-for-the-holidays young crowd wouldn't care particularly for *The Arsonists*. These are facts, Mr. Consul-in-Berlin. These are the realities. A reputable citizen of the U.S.A. offers to rescue second cousins who're in mortal peril. You, the agent of our big, rich and humanitarian government, decide to let them stay to perish.

"Well?" Jessie's lips were tight. "What do we do now?"

I offered her a cigarette and drummed my desk while she smoked.

"It humiliates me, sickens me," she said.

"Me, too," I said.

"*Our* man in Berlin." She sent a withering glance around my cubicle whose dingied walls were hung with clipboards of releases, posters, pamphlet covers. Her arm swung in a gesture of contempt. "Kindershpiel!"

"Leave the papers here with me," I said. "I'll get another affidavit."

Her lips thinned. "Joe?"

"Joe," I said.

There was a long silence. She pressed out the cigarette.

"Money talks." Her tone was gall-bitter. "Money rescues."

"That's what counts," I said. "Rescue."

"I hate to give that s.o.b. another gold star for his crown. Sam, he's a dirty man."

"You don't know the half of it," I said.

She scooped up her bag and gloves, rose, buttoning her coat collar high. "Well, I tried. Credentials were inadequate. So, now I shall go and cultivate my garden and leave the Jewish problem to the affluent."

Joe snickered when he took the papers. "So Mrs. Big-Shot-Genius had another flop." He inflated his chest. "We'll see some action now, you bet."

In March he phoned and asked me to go down to the West Side docks, meet a certain Dutch steamship and welcome the family of Shimon Cottler; Celia had the sniffles or the pip, she couldn't go to the pier; he was tied up at his office. Bring them to the McAlpin, his secretary had reserved a room; tell them he and Celia would get over sometime in the evening.

I met a buxom dark-haired woman who did resemble Ida Weiss, a thin nervous man and a skinny hyperthyroid boy, conveyed them to the McAlpin, bought them Swiss on rye and coffee, and left them, grateful though confused, in a modest twin-bed room. What seemed to confuse them most was me. I wasn't even a cousin.

Within the week, Shimon Cottler turned up at the Committee's office, bearing a note from Joe to our office manager. He received a job in our mailroom, stuffing envelopes. When I ran into him at the water cooler, he wanted to know whether it didn't shame the wealthy cousin to have him doing this sort of work; also whether I could speak to Mr. Sloan and ask him to find a better flat for them. The one on Washington Heights Mr. Sloan had sent them to was four flights up. He was not complaining—the cousin was paying the rent—but for a heavy woman like his wife, the steps were a strain on the heart. And if, for instance, they might get a ground-floor apartment, she could put out a sign for dressmaking.

There was nothing I could do. Joe was boasting he had rescued his wife's cousins. He'd given them life, liberty and a chance to pursue happiness. It wasn't up to me to ask him to increase his benefactions. I did, however, advise Shimon Cottler not to speak too freely at the office of his relationship to Sloan. This might get back to Baumberg and, the King's suspicious nature being what it was, he might jump to the conclusion Joe had planted a spy.

I phoned Jessie at the Algonquin, where she'd holed up again after Westport, to tell her the cousins had arrived. "That's fine," she said coolly. "I presume the rich relations are looking after them." She went on to tell me she had leased an apartment on Gramercy Park and was busy buying furniture. She'd have me down, she added, as soon as things were settled, by "things" meaning, I gathered, the relationship between her and Dr. Bishop.

Nine

Dr. Bishop was a competent persuader. He convinced Francine, who'd been his wife for nearly twenty years, that it was in everyone's best interests for her to take the cash and let the husband go. As I heard it through the interested third party, his line of reasoning was that Francine and he had dragged along in double harness out of a sense of duty toward their two sons and deference toward psychologists, who maintained that divorce was a shattering experience to kids, whereas, if you used ordinary common sense, you'd realize that living in an atmosphere of strain was far more damaging to children than a clean break would be. The boys were old enough, intelligent enough, to be told, without rancor from either side, that their parents were unhappy in their marriage, even though, unhappy as they'd been, they'd respected one another and had been devoted to their sons. Divorce was not a crime; fathers and mothers loved their children no less after the elders agreed to live apart. He and Francine needed—nay, more, deserved—a chance to enrich their mature years. The woman he had had the luck to meet had renewed the vigor of his body and his mind and opened vistas of a true companionship. He sincerely hoped Francine would be as fortunate.

It wasn't altogether a surprise to Francine Bishop. Mutual acquaintances had let her know that Mark had escorted a certain public figure to a certain public gathering on an evening when the doctor had left word he was detained at the hospital—touch-and-go with a postoperative patient. Also Mark's receptionist, to whom the doctor's wife had given generous Christmas gifts, had made available the phone number of the Westport love nest—the doctor had had to leave it, in case a patient hemorrhaged or raised a fever. Had she so desired, Mrs. Bishop could have hired detectives and gotten a New York decree. However, since the tabloid headlines might have shamed her adolescent sons, she deferred to Nevada and in April filed in Reno, charging mental cruelty. The financial settlement had been worked out and signed. She'd made the terms, and they were harsh. Mark was to continue to support his sons in the style to which they were accustomed, meaning a comfortable apartment on New York's gold coast, the Sixties between Madison and Park, two in help and private schools, and to set up a special fund to guarantee their higher education at Ivy League universities. Also, he was to transfer to her one half of all his stocks and bonds and cash in savings banks as well as the deed to the cottage in Vermont and to maintain his present life insurance policies without change of beneficiaries. Also, as a personal indemnity for that mental cruelty, his lawyers were to mail her one thousand dollars every month, this to be continued until she remarried, which, she assured him through counsel, would be never, her best years having been squandered promoting his career, her health and nervous system shattered by his shocking infidelity. In return for his signature on the surrender pact, he might see his sons one Saturday each month, provided the meetings did not take place on premises occupied by that neurotic bitch, that home-wrecker, that sloppy whore, that phony idealist who was his paramour. Few men would have paid as steep a price for a not-so-young, not-so-pretty girl from Grady's Mills.

Further, Mrs. Bishop, being the injured party and having a wide acquaintanceship, broadcast the news and, simultaneously, everyone was telling everyone that Dr. Bishop, to whom so many women had entrusted life and chastity, was sex-crazed, a middle-aged Don Juan, chasing Broadway floozies; decent women should insist the nurse stay close at hand when they stripped in his examining rooms. This repelled one type of patient but attracted another, so that, for the time being, his practice didn't change numerically. The future might be another story: Colleagues and hospital trustees had wives, suffering menopausal insecurity. "If you let Bishop get away with this—" "Would you refer your own sister to an immoral lecher?" Such domestic nagging well might jeopardize Dr. Bishop's income and his hospital affiliations.

"Sweetheart, money is the least of our worries," Jessie assured him. "I'll earn packs for us. Work my fingers to the bone."

She didn't. Happy women do not write.

At the end of May, twenty-four hours after Francine Bishop received her decree, Jessie and Mark were married by a clerk at City Hall. There were no attendants, no wine, sponge cake or stuffed derma, no engraved announcements or write-ups in a daily paper, just Mark's name pasted above hers on the mailbox and door of a second-floor apartment in a remodeled red brick on Gramercy Park. The doctor kept his Park Avenue office, three blocks from his former residence, though he hired a new nurse-receptionist.

On a Sunday afternoon in June his friends and hers were invited for cocktails. A Negro maid answered the bell, took hats and wraps. It was a warmish day. The living room's casement windows, flung open wide, framed the green enchantment of the fenced park across the road. The host and hostess, he more than a head taller than she, stood, backs to the open windows, at a long table turned into a bar, shaking hands, making introductions and offering libations. It was an awkward yet, in a way, amusing situation.

When there is divorce, inevitably mutual friends take sides, and the injured wife pre-empts most loyalties. Yet in the practice of medicine, one hand washes another. To spite a second wife, it is hardly politic to cold-shoulder a colleague who may order a fifty-dollar cardiac consultation or split a surgical fee. And so you come to wish them well with muted affability, drink their liquor, and retain the professional goodwill. Your wife comes, too, bringing her cat's claws and curiosity. Next morning, early, she is on the phone to her best friends. "Guess who I met yesterday? Jessica White. The playwright. She's no Brenda Frazier. I can't imagine why Mark left Francine for *that*." Someone is sure to pass this on to the previous Mrs. B.

I waited my turn in line behind some M.D.s and their wives. "Dr. and Mrs. Martinson, this is Jessie." Mark was introducing, as well as mixing drinks. "Dr. and Mrs. Levine, this is Jessie." Not "This is my wife" or "This is Mrs. Bishop," both of them blandly cheerful, not discomfited by stares or hollow well-wishes. Scraps of conversation drifted over shoulders back to me.

Man's voice: "How are the boys, Mark?"

Mark: "Full of beans. Had lunch together yesterday. Went shopping. How they exploited me! Cameras, catchers' mitts, tennis racquets. We bought out Abercrombie's. Their mother, thank heavens, is buying the basic camp equipment. . . . Daiquiri, Estelle, did you say?"

Woman's voice: "Yes, daiquiri. . . . So they're going to camp this year. Which?"

An Indian name I didn't catch.

Second woman's voice: "Not Ganeden? The Sloan child—what's her name—Irene? . . ."

First woman's voice: "Ilene."

Second woman: "Oh, yes, Ilene. She went there last year. Had a lovely summer, Ceil told me."

First woman: "By the way, isn't Jessie—aren't you?—somehow related to the Sloans?"

Jessie (dryly): "Somehow."

First woman: "I ran into Ceil at a luncheon last week. She was saying they'd just brought a whole family over from Europe. Distant cousins she never knew existed. Joseph's supporting them. Isn't that just wonderful!"

Second woman: "They're so generous, both of them."

Not a sound from Jessie, not a Bronx cheer or a grunt.

Man's voice: "Where you going for the summer, Mark?"

Mark: "Right here. Park key comes with the flat. We may take a short motor trip, drive down to see Jessie's father."

First woman's voice: "Are Ceil and Joseph coming today?"

Mark: "I believe not. Martini for you, Phil?"

First woman: "I'll tell Ceil I met you. By the by, when you do those windows, why don't you consult Ceil? She has such perfect taste."

It was my turn. Jessie clasped my hands. Mark clasped ours.

Mark: "Glad you could come."

Jessie: "He always comes. My kin. Better than."

Mark: "What do you drink?"

Me: "Rye and ginger ale."

Jessie: "Be adventurous. Mark makes fabulous martinis. That's why I married him."

Me: "You used to be a Scotch and water girl."

Jessie: "Before I knew the finer things of life."

Mark: "Rye and ginger ale it is."

Me: "Here's to both of you. Congratulations and good luck."

Jessie: "The kalah's side is second sofa. Mill."

Glass in hand, I milled, and I inspected. The room had sixteen-foot ceilings, ornate with plaster curlicues; an imposing fireplace, framed by bookshelves floor to nearly ceiling; two long couches, parallel before the fireplace; a few rush-bottomed chairs; hassocks and fat cushions, red and blue and purple, on the floor; small tables holding large ash trays; a redwood screen, fencing off a corner that held a desk—a room not yet completed, lacking ornaments and pictures, yet already having character. The uncurtained, opened windows told me much: Jessie wanted all the world to look in and share her happiness.

The guests were divided, as at a Jewish wedding, the groom's adherents on and around the first sofa, the bride's opposite, eyeing one another curiously and with hostility, wondering, Is he good enough for her? Is she good enough for him? Several of the Chowder and Marching Society regulars clustered around the second sofa, the women surprisingly attractive in city summer dresses, the men looking civilized with white jackets, collars and neckties. I saluted with my highball as I passed. The kitchen behind the living room was a windowless galley with walls of white-washed brick, an immaculate gas range, a Frigidaire, and a shelf of cookbooks. The maid was arranging hors d'oeuvres on trays—anchovies, smoked salmon, sturgeon, caviar, fat olives—upper-class comestibles.

I wandered down a long hall. The door at the far end was shut. Off limits, mind your business, Rosenbaum. My glass and I returned to the second sofa. Ernie collared me. "Stiffs!" His head jerked toward the first sofa. "Bloated bourgeoisie."

Paula fingered my lapel. "Perhaps *you* understand this, Sam. Of all people, an M.D.!"

"Father image," I replied.

"A surgeon's a perversion of the image, don't you think?"

"Madam." I donned my dignity. "In old-fashioned Jewish families, including Jessie's, marrying a doctor (any specialty) is the highest yiches."

221

"And what is yiches, pray?"

"Status. One up on the peasants."

Kay stroked my arm. "You carry it off so gallantly. Are you badly hurt?"

"Why should I be?"

"Why, after last summer. . . ."

I smiled, enigmatically, I hoped.

"How long do you figure this will last?" Lou wanted to know.

"Unto eternity," I said. "It's love."

Lisa pivoted into the conversation. "Will she give up her career, do you think?"

"Broadway will survive even that," I said. "So will she. What she wanted most she has: companionship and joy."

"How poetic!" Kay stroked my arm and gave me a tender glance. "How beautifully put!"

I failed to mention I'd been quoting but went on to elaborate: "Fame was not what Jessie wanted most. Fame came easily to her. It was acceptance she craved, of all she was: bitch, angel. . . ."

Kay shook her head sympathetically. "And you couldn't give her that. Poor Sam, we know how you tried."

"She's happy. Look at her," I said. "Happy people, like happy nations, have no history." That was good going on a single highball.

*   *   *

I was a better prophet than I realized. Jessica White's name vanished from the entertainment pages and the gossip columns. She was happy; it showed in her glowing eyes, in her complacency about gaining weight. Accordingly, she had no history. Nor, for that matter, did the rest of us, after September, 1939. History was outside, beyond, and all around us, submerging personal drives and vanities. We existed, numbed and dazed, while Amsterdam and Rotterdam, Coventry and London were bombed, while panzers raced across the fields of Holland, Belgium, France, while the Hitler-Stalin pact was signed and broken and the Nazi hordes invaded Poland and Lithuania.

On one of the days of our stunned confusion, I ran into Shimon Cottler in the corridor—he'd been promoted to assistant bookkeeper, had put on a little weight and a neat American suit. "My wife is sick with worries," he told me. "The brother is in Vilna. He is paralyzed. How can he run? I called up the cousin, Mr. Sloan, on the telephone. He says he can do nothing. If he, a big important man, can do nothing, who can?"

Who indeed? We lived and worked in nightmare, immobilized by fear. Are the Jews of Eastern Europe, Western Europe, living, dying, dead? Is there no way to bring them out, no country which will give them sanctuary? Do something. Anything. What? How?

On a Sunday afternoon, into the broadcast of a Philharmonic concert, the news of Pearl Harbor thundered. I clicked off my radio. "The Yanks are coming," I hummed. "We won't come back till it's over, over there." I hunted up the name of Shimon Cottler in the phone book; I had to talk to him. "How old is Mendel?" I asked.

"The boy has fifteen years," he said, surprised. "Why do you ask?"

"Too bad," I said. "If he were older, we'd put him into a uniform, to save his uncle Zalmon."

"What are you talking about?"

"Turn on your radio."

"We have no radio. The cousin did not provide."

"We're in the war," I told him. "Our Navy has been bombed at Pearl Harbor."

"My God, we will all be killed," he gasped. "Here we came to be safed."

Could you blame the man? Survival is what matters.

I got to the office at half-past eight. Wullstein and Baumberg were already there. We huddled in Baumberg's office, the three of us gray-faced. "My son's going down this morning to enlist," Baumberg said, his mustache quivering. "He was eighteen three weeks ago."

Wullstein and I looked at one another in surprise. We hadn't known the King had a son.

"Mine's only twelve," Leo said. "Preparing for Bar Mitzvah." We stared dully at each other. I'm sure their thought was mine: Please God, let the boy live to Bar Mitzvah. "I'd enlist in a

223

minute," Leo said. "Believe me, I wouldn't hesitate. But with my ulcer—"

I, healthy and a bachelor, said, "I've gone to one. I'd gladly go again. This one is ours."

Baumberg seesawed a pencil in the crotch of his hand, seeming all-absorbed in watching it, while we watched him. At last, he raised his pale eyes, meeting ours. "Alte kackers," he jeered. "Hip, hip, hooray! Johnny get your gun! Come down to earth, you guys. Yours, is it? Then hear what else is yours." He got up, strode to the door, making certain it was tightly shut. Then, low-voiced and grave, he told us something he had learned in confidence from one of the distinguished men whose picture graced the office wall, that the Nazis had set up extermination centers for the systematic murder of all of Europe's Jews. "We have got to save them. God alone knows how." His thin hands covered up his face. The King, we realized at last, also was a mensch. "Ours is a war within the other war," he went on to say. "We'll send our sons to win the Allied war; we older men must fight the other war. Our survival's on the line."

We went to war. We recruited fighters, armed them with lead pencils and secondhand typewriters. We recruited press agents, field organizers, stenographers and clerks. The military, the Pentagon, the war industries were scooping up the able-bodied males. We scraped the bottom of the manpower barrel. Slonim, a half-ass poet hired to assist Leo and me, said we were like the French Foreign Legion, the last refuge of scoundrels. That wasn't so. What we recruited were mediocrities, not villains or adventurers, uninspired, nice guys exempt from military service because of disabilities or dependent families. Which of them had, like me, been propelled into this work by a goad of anti-Semitism, personally experienced, I never knew, because this wasn't talked about, since we ceased to be individuals when we became full-time employees of the Jewish Aid Committee.

Ours was a strange war, compounded of desperation and futility, lacking beachheads, communication lines, warriors and weaponry. Like camp followers, we'd need to trail the Allied military. A vagrant message from some "underground," a cryptic sentence in a correspondent's cable, gave us hints of the horror that was happening. Normal minds refused to take it in. And on land and sea and in the air, the big war was being waged. It crowded out the special Jewish agony.

"Lay leaders," whom now we rarely saw, did our thinking, improvised and shaped our policies, and wrought a faint embarrassment in each of us: we were earning bread and butter out of the Jewish catastrophe. The men who ponied up the cash that paid our salaries deplored us even while they utilized our skills. We were "paid professionals," mercenaries; they, dedicated volunteers. Between us was a social chasm, never to be bridged, no matter how well you knew each other when. Like the other army, we had a caste system and a code of protocol.

Assume, for example, that a "lay leader" who is a former personal acquaintance invites you to his house. Baumberg must be informed before you go, reported to in detail afterwards, lest he suspect you've been blabbing office secrets (i.e., the purchasing agent favors an expensive printer who is his wife's brother-in-law) or brown-nosing and by subtle hints undermining the King.

Similarly, no letters or memoranda may be sent to "lay leaders" by "professionals" of the lower echelons, no phone calls made to them directly, through the office switchboard, save by authorization of the King.

On the other hand, a "lay leader" may invite the King (with or without wife) to his home for dinner, at his whim—a command performance. Baumberg is to sit below the salt, speak when spoken to, then to the point, and brilliantly.

The King may never invite "lay leaders" to *his* house. That would be chutzpah.

In conferences which may last all hours, in shirt-sleeves, in a smoke-filled room, any "professional" below Baumberg's rank may be used as gopher, laying out petty cash for sandwiches and coffee and accepting reimbursement, like a lowly office boy, though never thanked or tipped. And his deference must not falter to the point of addressing a "lay leader" by first name. So thorough was my indoctrination that, once, when I encountered Joe at our executive's urinal, he greeted me, "Hi, Sam!" and I answered, "How are you, Mr. Sloan?"

We didn't protest, march with placards demanding to be considered persons, for several reasons, one of which was that each of us was easier to replace than a "lay leader" was; another that the job, the work around the clock in the atmosphere of crisis, Baumberg's temper shortening as his nerves tightened, left us too debilitated to revolt. In addition, every man and woman there was emotionally involved, and dignity is a minor sacrifice when your survival's on the line.

Whenever I found myself, unexpectedly, with a free evening, I'd invite one of the office secretaries out to dinner and an early movie, not obliged to see her home, since both of us had to be at the office on the dot of nine o'clock. Other nights, I'd listen to the radio in my room, ears to the globe, and after midnight read myself to sleep. *The Arsonists* was the last Broadway show I'd seen.

And only intermittently did I see Jessie and Mark, though Jessie phoned me frequently to say that a few people were dropping over for cocktails or a buffet supper and would I stop by, too? The friends were hers—whether Mark's acquaintances were also entertained, I do not know, since I was invited only with the remnants of the Westport crowd. They were talkative, though not as much so as before, bibulous, but not as much so as before, since not as much was being served. A man who's paying heavy alimony becomes a careful host. Usually, there was a fire on the hearth, warmth in the welcome, but only desultory interest in the work I did. Let's talk about Corregidor, Guadalcanal and Stalingrad, instead.

Usually, Mark was present; frequently he excused himself, after an urgent phone call. Recruiting for the war had drained off so many doctors that those too old to serve in uniform worked like dray horses in the hospitals. When Mark was home, he mingled amiably but unobtrusively, looking slightly baffled by the conversation—Jessie's pals, I gathered, weren't quite his dish of tea—though his face invariably brightened whenever she pre-empted a discussion, her eyes and wit flashing. Between them, it was good. You could tell that by their exchange of smiling glances, the impulsive reaching, touching, of their hands.

How Jessie filled her days, I guessed by changes on the premises. She was furnishing and with antiques, which requires patience as well as flat-heeled shoes. She had gone early American, bought a

Boston rocker, a pair of lithographs by Currier and Ives, a steeple wall clock with a brass pendulum, a loud tick and a sweet chime for the hours, and a wooden cradle, Pennsylvania Dutch, cookie-cutter hearts carved into the foot and headboard. She labored over the cradle till her fingertips were raw, scouring with steel wool, sanding with emery paper, soaking in linseed, polishing with lemon oil. I twitted her about preparing for a blessed event. She gave me the Mona Lisa smile. The cradle, smooth and shining, wound up before the fireplace, stuffed with newspapers and kindling.

She haunted the copper and brass shops down on Allen Street and brought home a Czarist samovar. She hung a colored map of Europe, place names in Spanish, above her fireplace mantel, announcing it had been carried from Barcelona by an Abraham Lincoln Brigader. She also combed the secondhand bookstores on lower Fourth Avenue. The floor to nearly ceiling shelves were filled. Her windows stayed uncurtained.

For a spell she went in for haute cuisine with intensity and grim determination: prowled among the greengrocers under the El for mushrooms, artichokes, endive, pomegranates; exercised her charm (and small cash bribes) on the butcher to wangle a tender porterhouse, a pair of squabs, a pound of fresh calves' liver. She became a steady customer at Trinacria, a Third Avenue treasure house of exotic foods, spices and kitchenware from every accessible corner of the globe. Copper pots and moulds hung, gleaming, on her kitchen wall; earthen casseroles piled up. Hers was the first table on which I ever saw a wooden pepper mill or tasted cumin, cardamon and capers.

Unfortunately, she hadn't the palate and the true passion for food which makes a gourmet cook. Yet she racked her brain, burned her hands, calloused her feet, trying to delight Mark, who most evenings was too weary to notice what was on his plate.

She talked about starting a play—only talked. Her days were taken up with wifely piddling, bringing Mark's shirts to the laundry, his suits to the cleaner, and her kitchen was too crowded with casseroles to leave space for an Underwood.

One evening in the spring of 1943 she phoned me to say Mark was tied up at the hospital, would be there till God knows when; if I wasn't busy, she hoped I was not, would I come by and have a drink, maybe we'd go out and eat; come early, if I could. She sounded edgy. I heard the echo of old bugle calls.

As soon as I arrived, she proposed we have our drinks at the restaurant, she wanted to get the hell out of the flat. I began to wonder was she tired of playing house. She suggested Pete's, the old saloon on Irving Place, where O. Henry used to tank up to write his folk tales of Manhattan. It was just around the corner; we wouldn't need a cab. We walked there in unaccustomed silence, not even an agreeing grunt from her when I observed that the park was beautiful with its tulip beds abloom.

We ordered drinks and food that turned out to be dreadful. What with meat rationing and kitchen help conscripted for the war, most restaurants served wretched food. She lighted one cigarette from another, a noisome brand dredged up from some dung heap, before she blurted, "Sam, who do you know in Washington? V.I.P., I mean."

My eyebrows rose. "Who wants what?"

"Me," she said. "I have to find a safe spot for Bill."

"Who's Bill?" I asked.

She seemed surprised I didn't know. "Mark's eldest. His pride and joy. Yale freshman." She pressed out a cigarette, half-smoked, took another. "I've met the boy. He has spirit. Not afraid of Mama; comes to visit us. Adores his father. It is mutual." Her flaring match brightened one eye, left the other in shadow. She drew the smoke into her chest and coughed. "What drek do they put in these? Rips your lungs apart." I took the coffin nail and stamped it out, handed her one of my Camels. "It will just about kill Mark," she went on to say, "if anything happens to his boy. It's awesome to care this much."

"I didn't know you did," I said. "About children, I mean."

"Me? Children?" She shook her head. "Mark is what I care about. What makes him unhappy makes me; what worries him, I carry here—" She pressed a hand to her bosom. "This is what is known as love. The beloved's needs, the beloved's happiness, come before your own. That's something you wouldn't understand."

Oh, no? How often had I received her needs, her demands, and gratified them? How often received her slaps? Call this love. Or greediness, my own greed of giving. I was getting mad. "You're an unnatural woman, you hate children so."

Her eyes opened wide. "What makes you say that?"

"Kindling, not kinder, in the cradle."

"Idiot! From nothing you draw conclusions."

"Do I? I remember and I'll not forget how you treated Ilene at the Waldorf."

She paused longer than she should have before saying flatly, "Thou shalt not covet thy sister's possessions. First amendment to the tenth commandment."

"It's no skin off my back, but why haven't you had children of your own?"

She laughed. "With whom? Horace? Forked-tongue monsters, conceived in carelessness. With Mark? At this time of our lives? Can't you see me pushing a go-cart?" Then, throwing back her head with arrogance, "I've been creative, don't you think? Three plays are not sterility." She tapped off cigarette ash. "Answer my question. Who do you know in Washington?"

"Not a soul." Then I said, "Don't try it, girl, this war is ours. The last thing Jews should try to do. . . ."

"Rosenbaum, the Maccabee!"

"Who was it wrote *The Arsonists?* I forget the woman's name." I sipped coffee, waiting for her to simmer down.

"Mark would be furious"—her voice dropped—"if he knew I'd been trying to pull strings. He is a man of absolute integrity."

I held my tongue. To small-towners like me, two-timing by married men isn't absolute integrity.

Jessie made as if to rise—"Why am I wasting breath on you?"— but settled back, pressing hand to cheek. "My brother-in-law. He likes saving lives. I could ask. . . ."

"The conference is over. Thank you, Mr. President," I said.

I dropped her at her door and flagged a cab, riding to my furnished room, full of rancor and mixed metaphors. The woman is an octopus, I thought, stretching out her tentacles to pull favors out of me. And doing favors is a morass. Sucked in, sucked under, slapped. It would be years before I fully grasped the peril of the shnook. Only now, with hindsight's clarity, can I firmly say,

229

though the abnegation shames you, pains you, avoid the pitfall of trying to be kind.

I don't know whether Jessie spoke to Joe, or whether, if she did, he couldn't or wouldn't lift a finger, since she stopped phoning me. And Joe I saw seldom these days, even professionally. In wartime, scrap-metal dealers become tycoons. They haven't time to attend rescue-philanthropic meetings. Fortunately, it takes only seconds to scrawl a signature on a contribution check. Okay, your money's what we need, and thank you very much. Celia had stopped inviting me to dinner since Herman no longer was around, pining for companionship. My mother was looking after him and very well, indeed.

Mama's letters kept me informed. At first there had been discomfiture over his appearance; old friends couldn't help staring at the scarred face. *"Mr. Weiss was eppes not the same without the beard."* Mama put it tactfully. *"But we got used."* His health was good, except for a morning cough. *"The German doctor said don't worry, give him a thicker pillow, he should sleep high up, and keep the windows closed nighttime. The air is poison."* He puttered in the backyard garden, pulling weeds, staking tomato plants. He helped Mama carry out the furnace ashes. The salvage in Walter Leeds's garage had been moved over to the Rosenbaum cellar when Herman took up residence, and with coarse steel wool and patience he scraped and polished the charred metal. He conferred with Mama about what might be sold, what given away to whom. He helped the shamas in the shul, sorted out the dogeared books in the Beth Hamedrash, aligned them neatly like merchandise on shelves, and responded on the double to a summons for a minyan for a kaddish. He consulted with real estate brokers about selling his lot on the Hill. They advised him to wait; after the war there'd be a building boom, prices would go up. *"For who must he provide?"* Mama asked. *"The girls is well off, no?"* He was pleased, though not excited, when I wrote that Ida's kin had been brought safely to New York. They, after all, were strangers and to Herman just in-laws. *"Who heard from them before?"* my mother blustered. *"Not a shonatava even, when the husband was earning a good living. He loses the job, so they on-come to the cousin in America. Maybe they could ask before, does Ida have a piece of bread? Thanks God she didn't need."*

My father taught Herman pinochle. Evenings they played on the kitchen table. Herman turned out to be sharp, practically a cortesnick, Mama wrote. He took long walks, usually to Ida's grave, and he received visitors on my mother's stoop. They were frequent and given to congratulating him on how successfully his daughters had been married off. Dr. Bishop, driving there with Jessie the first summer of their marriage, had impressed everyone. Joe was local-boy-got-rich but nonetheless—this was by no means forgotten—merely the son of Max Slomowitz, the junkie, and he hadn't finished high school. *"A doctor! A educated gentleman! So refine!"* Mama's awe was in her exclamation points. *"I was surprise Jessie said the wedding was by City Hall, not a rabbi, but Mr. Weiss don't say nothing. He sees this one is more unshtandig than the skinny-herring Reformer. And from always he knows Jessie is a little bit meshuga. Who would think a wild girl like her, nicht kain shaine, would make a shidduch with a doctor? Ida, she should rest in peace, she never had the luck to enjoy. A smart woman, Ida, she knew send the girls to college, they get married high-class."*

Mama, I gathered, basked in the refulgence of Herman's daughters' marital successes. Just once did she complain, and mildly then. *"Semmy, if you get the chance, maybe you could talk with Jessie, she should make a little more the check for Mr. Weiss. By me, if I could affoder it, he would be a guest, only today meat when you get it with the points coupons is dear like gold. And Papa's business now is off. Who orders tailor-made? Alterations, pressings, is all comes in the shop."*

Since at the moment Jessie and I weren't on the best of terms, I mailed my own check, writing, *"Mama, your son is a first-class stinker. Here he is earning a fat salary and does he send a penny home? I'll send this every month. In case you need more, just drop me a postal card."*

Her thank-you note was gushy, which led me to believe my financial help was what she had been hinting at. That letter ended, as all her letters to me did, *"Mr. Weiss sends you his regards."*

In the summer of 1943, even this communication faltered. I flew off to Lisbon, North Africa and London to try to rescue Jews. The Allies had dug in on the northern rim of Africa and were advancing toward the toe of Italy. We could inch behind the armies, scoop up survivors, herd them into temporary shelters, until we got them visas to some place, any place. I had asked for the assignment and I'm not sure why I did. Possibly, I was bored with writing news releases; possibly, like Walter Mitty, I had hero fantasies. Possibly, I was fed up with the sidelines, with getting, secondhand and watered down, the biggest story of my century. To Baumberg I said, sounding bold, I was an experienced reporter who knew his way around, resourceful and, when necessary, brave. Also, I was Yiddish-speaking and unmarried. How about sending me abroad? Not for an instant did I dream that he would call my bluff. The first contingent the Jewish Aid Committee sent overseas comprised two 4F social workers and me.

Gershon Rothman, the *Morning Journal* reporter whose earth-brown face and eloquence had sold the Committee job to me, came to the press conference Leo set up to announce our imminent departure. Rothman embraced me proprietarily. "You remember, we sat, you and me, drinking tea in the Café Royal after a certain meeting and you were asking, Should I, shouldn't I? I take the credit; I am responsible, personally."

There was a farewell luncheon, too. Joe Sloan and a few other "lay leaders" turned up at it. Joe read a few Wullstein-written paragraphs, telling us how privileged we were to have been selected for an historic mission, after which he drew me aside and slipped a folded hundred-dollar bill into my hand. "Sam, I understand some places you boys will be allowed to buy in the army PXes. Good perfume, I understand, is dirt cheap. If you could find a bargain, a half-dozen bottles Christmas Night, or something else high quality—" He caught my glower and he gulped. "For Celia. She asked me to give you her best wishes. She couldn't make it today, some affair of the Red Cross. Did anybody tell you she's high up in the Chapter? In a rishes place like Greenwich, where we bought a house, that's a big honor."

I shoved the bill into his pocket, saying loftily, "This is not a shopping expedition." Since I was risking my life, I could afford the hauteur. Moreover, I'd be damned if I'd be purchasing agent for his stable. His mistresses—brown, black and white—were an open secret.

Shimon Cottler also handed me a folded paper. "The address from my brother-in-law. Maybe you can find out where is Zalmon." I put that in my wallet. For years I was to carry similar slips of paper.

The flight to Lisbon on an army bomber was my first air trip. I caught a cold that turned into pneumonia and I almost died. I moved on to North Africa, got dysentery and wished I was dead. In London, a buzz bomb landed near the Lyons shop where I was taking tea. A medic wasted several hours pulling glass splinters out of me while I bled like a pig.

Whenever I had a chance, which was seldom, I air-mailed a note to Mama and Papa saying I was very busy and felt fine. This was true. Never had I brushed so close to death and never felt as much alive, for I'd discovered I had a talent for criminality.

The world into which I had been dropped was not merely the world of a shooting, bombing war against life and real estate but the indecent world of unclean war against accidents of race and faith. Saving a single life, a dozen lives, demanded the skills of illegality: how to forge or purchase passports and visas, bribe frontier guards or cabinet ministers, smuggle currency and quaking bodies over borders, neutral and hostile, "liberate" food and transport, operate boldly in the dark of night, look mild and innocent by day. Without exaggerating, I believe I helped at least one thousand Jews. I escorted them across borders, said a few reassuring words, saw to it they were fed and hidden, and in darkness shepherded them aboard leaking ships, some to wade ashore in pre-dawn darkness on the beaches of Palestine, most to land behind barbed wire on Cyprus as Great Britain's prisoners. A handful I managed to ship off to the United States, with visas legally—or illegally—procured, and one of them, a lad of fourteen who'd tramped alone across the Pyrenees after he had seen his father shot before his eyes, his mother raped and dragged off by Storm Troopers, I sent to Baumberg with a forged visa and a note: "While your boy's in the army, you might enjoy having this one around the house. He's a gutsy kid." It was presumptuous, but eppes told me Baumberg wouldn't mind.

233

Considering that my previous experience with illegality had been limited to paying off the cop, Durgin, it can be said without fear of contradiction that my performance in Europe was remarkable. Also it taught me much: that the human body may be frail and susceptible to germs but the human spirit is indestructible; that Christian nations, including ours, were indifferent to what was done to Jews, all except the Germans, who were dedicated to destroying them. Strangely, I had progressed beyond hate for *them*—a chilling acknowledgment. They were the avowed enemy. My greater bitterness was for our friends, our democratic allies, who turned their backs and closed their ports.

I moved so fast and furtively that mail from the States seldom caught up with me. After Paris was liberated but before the Rhine was crossed, Baumberg reached me with a cable, ordering me home. It took finagling to get space on an army cargo plane, returning from London's Bovington airport.

When I reached New York, Baumberg closed his office door and said he had a new assignment. I was to travel again—the United States this time—talk confidentially to well-heeled groups, tell them a little, just enough, of what we had been doing, how we had been doing it, and plead with them for money—only money—to buy bread and shoes and vitamins but principally to buy ships —old excursion steamers, rusty rumrunners—to be loaded to the gunwales with survivors, destination Palestine. I protested I had never made a speech. Orators were dime a dozen, Baumberg said, nobody listened to them any more. A reporter, with eyes and ears and sense of smell, relating personal experiences, would hit them in the gut. Tell it straight, and make them give until they bleed. But no interviews, you understand, not a line in any papers, anywhere. I understood. In 1944, being humane was another illegality.

"And by the by, you sent us a good kid, though we didn't exactly have an empty house. Don't suppose you ever bothered to find out I have six. Why else do you think I work like a dog?" Yes, he said, you can have the weekend off to see your folks. From all of this, I gathered he thought well of my work.

From the mid-Manhattan hotel where I had been billeted, I telephoned my mother, said I'd be home Friday on the five o'clock, she could start preparing the gefüllte fish. Yes, I was feeling fine, and how are you and Papa? Before she could tell me, Leo Wullstein yanked my sleeve. "Don't shmoos. You'll see her Friday. You and I have work to do." I said, "Mama dear, we'll talk on Friday. My three minutes are up." Mama respected the three-minute limit on phone calls, as she did the ten-words-only for a telegram.

The train was filthy and crowded, as all rolling stock, stateside, was that year, and Grady's Mills was so intact that I walked from the depot filled with incredulity. Why, there's Rogoff's name on an awning, Perlzweig's on the delicatessen's plate glass window! Jewish names. Jews are doing business here, openly and unafraid. Our shaded street on the Hill (leaves starting to turn, a snap in the air) is unchanged except that sumac and goldenrod have sprouted where Herman's Grocery used to be.

Mama heard my footsteps on the porch. She came from the kitchen in a rush, hugging me, slobbering kisses, before she held me off. "Semmele, you look terrible. Skinny like a herring and sores on the face."

"Mama, you forget, I was never beautiful."

"In my eyes you was."

"You look fine. How's Papa?"

"You'll pick up the telephone, you'll call him up, tell him he should close the shop, come home, we have a guest."

"How's the boarder?"

Her mouth corners drew down. "You didn't hear? Nobody told you? Herman Weiss, he should rest in peace, is passed away. Five months already. . . . Come in, Semmele, don't stand on the stoop, I'll make a glass tea. A piece strudel you can have, a small piece not to spoil the appetite."

We sat together at the white-topped kitchen table, she bobbing up between sentences to fat-skim the chicken soup and turn the veal cutlets.

"I don't know for sure, Semmele, maybe we didn't do the right thing. After Pesach comes werry warm weather. I say, okay, Papa, we let go out in the cellar the furnace. Coal is dear. And we carried out already enough ashes. Now is beginning summertime. Mr. Weiss is sweating in the fleece-line underwear. We are

235

sitting in the kitchen, me and Mr. Weiss, talking should he change the underwear. And Papa, your papa, he should live and be well, sometimes he is a buttinsky, Papa begins to nag Mr. Weiss he should take off the fleece-line, put on the beeveedee. 'Because now is snow on the ground in Shnipishok, you need to shvits in fleece-line here in Grady's Mills?' So Mr. Weiss he don't like arguing, he is a quiet gentleman, he puts on the beeveedee. Next week is a little chilly, raining, windy. Mr. Weiss starts in with a cough. A little chorchle he always had, so coughing by him is nothing special. I make him hot tea with raspberries. I give him hot milk with honey and two aspirins. He don't get better, he coughs more, so I say I will call the doctor. He says no, in his life he had already too much doctors; the German doctor we called before says the cough is nothing to worry, so we shouldn't worry. I make him chicken soup. I give him two more aspirins. He says, 'Thank you werry much, mine friend, you do too much for me. Now, I go upstairs and sleep, I feel better.' In the morning"—her apron tip mopped her eyes—"he don't come down for breakfast. I send Papa up to see. Mr. Weiss is laying"—her tears were streaming—"like a kotinka, a dove. Quiet. A zaddik's death. No pain, no sufferings. And, Semmy—" The tears stopped. "Such a funeral! Everybody from the Hill, from Brookfield Heights. And in the paper, a fine write-up, not so good like you would write. . . . Wait, I get. For you I cut it out and saved."

"I'll see it later. Go on, talk. Did the girls come for the funeral?"

She waxed indignant. "What you think? They have no respect for the father? Both girls and the doctor-husband from Jessie. And the daughter from Celia. Pretty like a picture. Shlank. On the train they come, right away, so soon Walter Leeds, he calls up on the telephone. The people was expecting they will come with the big car and the chauffeur. Celia explains it is too hard now to get the gas coupons. I was thinking maybe Joe, the big shoot, will come, since I-don't-know-when he was not here. Celia explains he has to be in Washington, helping the President to win the war. Pish-pish! . . . So what can I tell you, Semmy, it breaks the heart to see those fine educated daughters standing crying and the parents laying in the ground, not to see their naches that they sacrificed so much.

236

Like the olden times it was, the two girls togedder. They're good friends in New York, no, Semmy?"

"No," I said.

She looked shocked. "Why not? One don't need to be ashamed from the other. One don't need to come to the other for charity."

"That's a long story, Mama," I said. "Go on with yours."

"So-o-o." She exhaled the long sigh of the confident narrator. "Here in mine house I fixed the hard-boil eggs and bagel, and the herrings and the lox. Where else? This was the home from Herman Weiss. And the two svell daughters and the doctor and the grandchild they is sitting eating in mine dining room. You can believe me, Semmy, I made the table nice, you wouldn't be ashamed. When your mama wants she can be stylish . . . No shiva, Semmy. Where could be? In the Hotel Grady, by Goyim, you can't sit shiva. And the doctor-husband must go back, is many sick people in New York. He left a nice sum money in the shul they should say the kaddish for the year, and he thanked me I took care on Mr. Weiss. If he was here the doctor, I betcha Mr. Weiss would be living, healthy."

I slept fitfully in the bed where Mr. Weiss had died like a kotinka. The phone started ringing early on Saturday. Tell-a-woman, our speed communication system, had spread the word I was in town. Barry Neale called, saying he'd been hearing I was overseas; he'd like me to stop by the office, make it soon, early go-to-press on Saturdays; he'd like some local angles on the war from me and inside dope on how soon we'd be in Berlin. I was delighted to say, No thanks, just a social item, if you must, for "Folk You Know": Samuel Rosenbaum, formerly of this city, now of New York, is spending this weekend visiting his parents, Mr. and Mrs. Isaac Rosenbaum on Sixth Street. And, Buster, this is all.

It was otherwise when Walter phoned to ask would I drop in in the evening; he'd like to ask his parents, Sylvia's parents and Sol Katz over; maybe I could tell them a little of what was going on. I said I'd call him back as soon as I was sure about my plans, meaning, though he didn't have to know, I needed Baumberg's clearance before I could tell anything to folks in my home town. I reached Baumberg at home—I heard kids squabbling in the background while he told me, sure, but in strictest confidence, and try to pick up a few bucks. "Those characters are loaded. They haven't learned to give. And I doubt you'll be the one to teach them. Home-town boy. Prophet without honor."

You'd be surprised. When I boarded the New York train Sunday, I carried checks totaling twelve thousand dollars, along with an apology and a sepia-tinted photograph, vintage post-World War One. The apology was Walter's for misjudging my character. The radio station deal hadn't materialized; the owners had got down on their knees, promising to soft pedal the anti-labor stuff, and the F.C.C. had let them keep their franchise. It was just as well. The local air had cleared; there was no overt anti-Semitism, no Hitler-heilers around. Adolf's boys were killing Protestant Americans; he was everybody's enemy, one nation, indivisible, against the common foe. Walter's kid, Harold, that pipsqueak who'd squirted a hose on me, was in the Navy, in the Pacific, "which is worse," and had already earned two battle stars. Walter looked worried and sounded proud, a combination known as bravado.

The photograph came from Sol Katz, a family group, a plump, pompadoured wife, a portly, black-bearded husband, one girl, two boys, teen-aged. "My brother Yossel," Sol told me. "Gittel, his wife, my niece Pessah; my nephews, Berel, Simcha. They lived in Lodz. In nineteen thirty-nine, before the momser, Hitler, marched, I wrote to him, 'Yossi, get out, come to us, I'll send affidavits, tickets, what you need. Save your family.' He answered me, 'How can I leave my factory, my house, everything I worked for my whole life? I am not young, Solly, to go with empty hands to America.' So, Sam, you are going back, carry the picture with you, please. Maybe you will meet some persons who will know what happened to the family Katz of Lodz. Whoever is alive, I want them. I will bring them here. My house is big, we have parnosse. . . . Sammy, you remember I was a customer peddler with a horse and wagon? You remember my horse, Jenny? When you was a little kid, I used to let you drive and hold the reins in your hand. You remember also my small dry-goods store? Smaller than the bathroom in my house. Today the Bon Ton is the finest store on First Street. America has been good to me. I appreciate. I want to share." Tears stood in Sol's eyes. He wiped them with

238

a monogrammed handkerchief. "One foot in the old country I still have. My brother Yossel, my flesh and blood. It drives me crazy, thinking. . . ."

I asked Mama whether she and Papa didn't have relatives in the old country. "Sure, we have, sure," she answered, looking indignant. "Who knows from them? Old-fashion people in a little shtetl. Fifty years we are in America, not a postcard they don't write. I think they got mad we went away to America."

As usual, she wept when I prepared to leave and she gave me good advice. "Semmele, take care the health, that's the main thing. Get plenty sleep, don't get wet the feet, eat good, take in the mornings a couple stew prunes, it should move the barrels. And don't smoke so many cigarettes." I'm sure neither she nor Papa understood what my job was abroad. How could they since I'd been forbidden to explain? Mama, I believe, was under the impression that somewhere in Europe I was sorting mail.

In New York, I tried to pay two condolence calls. With just one day available, I managed to see only Celia. Leo Wullstein knew the Sloans were quartered in a Manhattan apartment hotel, gas rationing having made Greenwich inconvenient. A switchboard operator took my message; Mrs. Sloan rang back at five o'clock. "Samuel, this is telepathy! I've been thinking about you all day. I do need your advice in a most important matter. . . . You're free this evening? Excellent. Joseph won't be home. He mentioned when he left this morning he'd be tied up. But you may catch a glimpse of Ilene; you used to be so fond of her. Get here before eight if you can; Ilene's going to the theater."

Jessie's phone hadn't answered, morning or afternoon. I did ring Dr. Bishop's office. The answering service said the doctor would not be available today.

Both Sloan women greeted me at the hotel suite door. Seventeen isn't chronologically a woman, yet when I saw them side by side it struck me Ilene was the mother, all solicitude, and Celia the dependent child.

Celia offered me a cold-fish hand. She was in total black, though her hair had been dyed again, this time a sort of salmon pink.

Ilene kissed my cheek. "It's permissible, Uncle Sam." She'd

grown tall, with shapely breasts, slender hips and flanks. Her face was, as in childhood, exquisite.

We sat on a sofa, in a row, I the middleman. The hotel parlor was too hot, the odor of cut flowers overpowering. Celia worried a handkerchief, waiting to receive my opening words of sympathy.

"I didn't hear about your dad till last Friday," I began. "I've been abroad, out of touch, you know. It hit me hard. He was part of my life, too."

"Poor Papa," she quavered. "It was such a shock, a tragedy. If they'd only called a doctor. I suppose it was a matter of who would pay the bill."

"It's a lucky Jew these days," I said, "who gets to die in a clean bed."

Her eyes went blank; she didn't get the implication. "If only Ilene could have been with him at the end. She loved her grandfather so. I'm so happy we had him with us for that little while." She wrung the handkerchief. "Our mistake was to let him go. If my sister hadn't lost her head, made that irresponsible decision. I should have insisted, yes, I should have been firm. But once Jessie gets on her high horse. . . ."

I coughed to camouflage my bubbling anger.

"Would you like a drink of water?" Ilene asked.

As dispassionately as I could, I said, "Celia, your father's chest had been affected by the fire, his heart was strained. And he wasn't young. Comfort yourself, his last years were happy."

"Were they? Among strangers in a furnished room? Not one person, not a soul, with him when he passed away. Suppose he'd had a final message. . . ."

I kept control and spoke the set piece of condolence. "It was God's will. Herman's with his wife. May they rest in peace."

"I envy them. At peace, side by side." The handkerchief was at her eyes.

"Don't, please, Mother dear," Ilene begged.

She stroked her daughter's hand. "This angel is my only comfort. This is what I live for." And snuffled genteelly. "I have buried myself in Red Cross. I am needed there." Then, all grieving done, she said, "Ilene, dear, please bring me the clipping and the sheet of paper on my desk."

The girl rose docilely; she'd been trained in obedience. Celia passed the clipping to me but held the other paper on her lap. "Samuel, I want your honest opinion. What do you think of this?"

It was Herman's obit, out of the *News-Record*. My mother had shown it to me, I said; it was a creditable sendoff.

"And you noticed nothing peculiar?" Her voice thinned. "There!" A pink fingernail tapped the final paragraph. " '*Mr. Weiss*,' "—she snatched it from me to read aloud—" '*is survived by two daughters, Mrs. Celia Sloan and Mrs. Jessie Bishop, both of New York. Mrs. Bishop will be remembered by many local people as Jessica White, the playwright, author of several Broadway hits, who delightfully addressed our local literary ladies at the Hilldale Country Club.*' That sister of mine!" Her cheeks had flushed, her throat cords distended. "Can you imagine using her own father's death for personal publicity!"

"Please, mother, please, I don't believe she wrote it," Ilene said gently. "It's possible she's never even seen it."

"Dear child, you do not know your aunt. She is capable of anything. Now, Samuel, I wish you to see how differently Papa's other daughter acts." She fingered the sheet of paper but didn't read or offer it to me. "Papa left a small insurance policy. My sister and I were joint beneficiaries. Joseph and I have decided, from my share we'll pay for perpetual care of the two graves and for the stone—Jessie'd never think of that, I'm sure. Then, to what was left, if anything, we'll add my share of the proceeds of the sale of the lot—that piece of ground on the Hill was all Papa had— and we'll add our own money to it—actually, most of it will come out of our pocket—and we'll endow a bed in the Hadassah Hospital in Jerusalem."

I said I thought that was splendid.

"What my sister plans to do with her inheritance, I do not know. Or care. Each does what the heart dictates. Now, this is how I think the wording of our plaque should read: 'Donated in reverence and loving memory of our sainted parents, Ida and Herman Weiss, by their eternally devoted children, Celia and

Joseph Sloan of Greenwich, Connecticut.' You're a writer, Samuel. How does the wording strike you?"

I thought it was fulsome, self-promoting. I said it was rather long; it would require a large chunk of bronze or very tiny type. She frowned, reviewing the writing. "But what could we cut out? Every word is important."

The doorbell rang. Ilene rose to answer it and ushered in a hunk of beef in a De Pinna topcoat. Celia donned a measured smile.

"Uncle Sam, this is Michael-David Eisenberg. Michael, Mr. Samuel Rosenbaum. When I was little I named him Uncle Sam."

"In civvies tonight," I said. "Sent the cutaway and stovepipe to the cleaners."

He gave me the supercilious stare whippersnappers turn on oldsters trying to be cute.

"Skip it," I said. "Uncle Sam wears O.D.s nowadays."

It's hard to tell on florid complexions, but I believe the young man blushed.

Celia glanced at her wrist watch. "We'd love to chat with you, Michael, dear, but you two will have to hurry. It's an early curtain, I believe. They're going to *Harvey*. Joseph got them tickets."

Michael-David helped Ilene on with her coat. "Pleasetameetcha, Mr. Rosenfeld," he grunted, his manners better than his ear for names. "G'night, Mrs. Sloan."

Ilene kissed me again. "I've missed you, Uncle Sam." She hugged her mother. "Good night, Mother dear. Do try to get some rest."

"Have fun, my darling," Celia said. "Michael, take good care of her." Her eyes followed till the door was shut, her fingers fluttering goodbye. "I've told Ilene she doesn't have to observe the year of mourning. These are her glorious days; she mustn't waste a single shining hour." She sighed. "I want her to have the pleasures that I missed. Growing up in a grubby little town, helping in the store, the flat, teaching school; there was very little fun." She looked hard at me as if expecting I'd take some blame for the drabness of her youth. I glanced at my watch. Her chatter hurried to deflect my evident impatience. "They make a handsome couple, do they not? His father is Henry Eisenberg; you remember him, don't you? He was emcee at that dinner honoring Joseph. Oh, so

242

long ago, before this awful war. Ilene met him at Ganeden. He was an assistant riding counselor. He's been in love with her ever since. And the Eisenbergs are crazy about Ilene. I suppose we must steel ourselves to losing her. But she *is* so young."

"And he?" I asked.

"Twenty," Celia said.

"Why not in uniform?"

"I believe he has some allergies."

"Walter's son has two battle stars," I said.

"How harrowing for Sylvia!" she cried. "Joseph says he's glad he never had a son."

Knowing other people's secrets is not recommended. It inhibits conversation. Also, it's a warning signal: get the hell out of here. I said I was sorry I would have to run; my appointments started very early in the morning. She looked desolate. Apparently, she'd counted on an entire evening, tête-à-tête. "I understand you have become quite important, Samuel. And getting a large salary. Joseph did a nice thing for you, didn't he?"

*   *   *

All next day I tried to reach Jessie. Her phone wasn't answered. Then I had to rush to catch the Twentieth Century to Chicago, to start six weeks of traveling on filthy trains, jam-packed with G.I.s, sailors, marines, airmen, their dufflebags, their wives and babies, of hanging around drafty airports, waiting endlessly, of being bumped at Hotseplotz by army brass or big-shot businessmen who'd wangled priorities. It was worth the trouble. I brought back nearly half a million dollars. Baumberg was surprised and, though he didn't say so, pleased.

Fund-raising is a cinch, I boasted rashly. You tell people why for what, they take out the checkbook, skim off a little fat, their hearts aren't stone. And they feel a kind of guilt; they're safe and not too much afraid because a father or grandfather had the gumption to cross the Atlantic in the steerage of a ship. Also, there's no man living who doesn't relish hearing hush-hush inside stuff.

I was listened to and banqueted by wives who used up a month's ration points—or black-marketed a bit—to get a leg of lamb, a standing roast of beef. And when they learned I was a bachelor the family eligibles were trotted out, nice girls with money, all of them. But, excuse me, please, I have to rush to make a plane. We understand; you're dedicated to your noble work. They treated me like a hero. It was heady stuff. Not before or after have I felt as big.

Along with the checks, I collected names and addresses of brothers, sisters, aunts, uncles, cousins, for whom, please, Mr. Rosenbaum, make inquiries and send us word if they're alive. Over all of the United States there were Jews with one foot in the old country.

Winter had set in by the time I returned to New York, wartime winter, Broadway's lights browned out. A sleety rain was falling, taxis were slithering dangerously, the night I rang Jessie's bell. She met me at the apartment door in a maroon wool bathrobe. Behind her, in the living room, I heard the fire crackling, the steeple clock ticking. She took my hat, dropped it on the vestibule table atop the telephone. "Keep your overcoat. Landlord's out of oil. There's a war on, you know."

It was the same room, casual and comfortable, the cushions strewn about, the casements uncurtained, yet it was not the same, an air of neglect, and the fire shallow, light wood, snapping, sputtering, not the steady glow of logs. Jessie waved toward the fire. "Crates. I scrounge, beseech the groceryman. Fireplace logs are platinum. Sit, Buster, sit." At the far end of the sofa, she indicated. She herself took the end nearest the fire, wrapping the robe tightly around her, tucking her feet under. On the coffee table was a cognac bottle, snifters, the usual overflowing ash tray, a crumpled, empty cigarette pack. We took a moment to reconnoiter with our glances. "You look Lincolnesque," she said.

"You look twelve-year-old Jessie Weiss," I said. "Not a day older."

"Have a brandy. Warm your gizzard." She poured into two snifters. "Where you been?"

"In hell," I said. "Where I shall return."

"I said Lincoln, not MacArthur. Be specific."

"Europe and North Africa, trying to save Jews. And cross-country, raising money to buy ships."

"Hurray for you!"

A burning slat dropped, scattering sparks to the fire screen's edge. She rose to take the poker, push the embers in, banged her ankle on a rocker of the antique cradle and swore with vehemence.

"If I hadn't been on the road, I'd have come sooner," I said. "To offer condolences for Herman."

"Thank you. Superfluous." She resumed her corner, rubbing the bruised ankle. "An old man died, peacefully and full of years. For myself I'd ask no worse."

She sipped brandy. The clock chimed nine. I sipped brandy. "Understand you're an heiress," I said.

"Big deal," she said.

"Celia and Joe are endowing a hospital bed, with plaque, in Jerusalem."

"Hurray for them! I gather you have seen my sister. When?"

"About six weeks ago."

"Oh!" Her mouth pursed.

"Tried to get you on the phone." I felt I needed to explain. "No answer. Then I had to catch the Century."

She showed more interest in the snifter than in me.

"Have any plans to use the windfall?" I was merely making conversation.

"Uh huh. A winter coat. Fur."

"A Jewish doctor's wife has to have her mink."

"How'd you get so smart so young?"

"My line," I said. "Used it on you years ago."

She smiled, but meagerly. "Mink looks tacky on me," she went on to say. "I'm a Hudson seal. And I hope you're carrying cigarettes."

I took out the pack. "Like old times, you bumming my butts." I held my lighter to her cigarette.

"Like old times," she snapped, "you drinking my liquor. Did you ever think of bringing a bottle to my house?" She inhaled deeply and set down the cigarette. "Believe me, Buster, I need a winter coat more than Papa and Mama need a plaque."

My brows shot up. "Things that bad?"

She swirled the brandy in the glass. "The pitcher has gone to the well too often. Papa's board and keep. Francine's alimony."

245

"Where's Mark? The hospital?"

Her fingers tightened on the snifter's stem. I heard the clock tick loudly before I heard her. "At Francine's."

"Oh, no!"

"Not what you think." She picked up the cigarette. "Not yet." She puffed, shook off ash. "Bill's dead," she said.

"Bill who?"

She stared at me with a growing anger. "William Bishop, aged twenty, turret gunner, United States Air Force. The boy for whom I pleaded with you. The one about whom you lectured me on my patriotic duty. Shot down in a flaming plane over New Guinea."

I took a few seconds to listen to the clock. "Jessie, the young are dying everywhere, the young, the middle-aged, the old."

Her lips thinned. "*This* was Mark's boy," she said. "We buried the cinders six weeks ago, probably the day you couldn't reach me on the phone."

"Let's have another brandy," I said.

Her hand trembled as she poured. "There were services." The brandy heaved in the glass when she handed it to me. "He sat next to Francine in the chapel. I was two rows back. He had his arm around her, walking out."

"He was *their* child, wasn't he?"

Her anger grew with every word I said. "Sam, he left with her, rode with her in the limousine to the cemetery, went back with her to her apartment. I found a taxi; I came home, here, alone; I waited, went out to the movies, sat and cried. Cried alone. Yes, I cried; you won't believe it but I did. Not for the boy, not for me. For Mark and me. This was the worst, the hardest, deepest hurt Mark Bishop ever suffered. And I couldn't share it. Francine could. She can. I had no memories of Bill with which to comfort Mark, no how good and bright and wonderful he was, how fortunate we were to have enjoyed him for those twenty years." She shivered and huddled into the red wool robe. The fire was dying. She made no effort to revive it. "What Jessie must remember till the day she dies is she cheated Mark out of a couple of those years. But Francine's the repository of every shining hour. The most important part of Mark, his fatherhood, his creativity, I can never reach."

This was a different Jessie. This was the one I'd never seen or heard. She was muted, humbled, and she sounded desperate.

"Sam, she phones him here. I try not to listen but how can I help? The phone's there in the vestibule and out back between our beds. 'Yes, Francine. Take a phenobarb, try to get some sleep. . . . Well, don't you have some chloral hydrate in the house? There used to be a bottle in the cabinet. . . . I'll have a prescription filled and send it up. . . . Please, Francine, please. . . . Yes, I'll bring it up myself. You mustn't talk that way.' What's she trying to do, blackmail him back by threatening suicide? That's where he is tonight, out in this pneumonia weather, drying Francine's tears. . . ."

While Jessie, his second wife, sat brooding, stewing, boiling over, jealous of another woman's right to grief.

She pounded her fist against her mouth. "Oh, I'll have him. I will have him back and I will keep him. He loves me too much to give me up. But Sam, oh, Sam, I want to be the one, the only one, in sickness and in health, for richer or for poorer." Her tobacco-browned fingers dropped into her lap. She stared at them. With bitterness, she said, "Do you realize I've been second all my life? Second fiddle from the day that I was born. Never first."

In a way, this was not to be denied. "Isn't it time you went back to your typewriter?"

"A play? What in hell would I write a play about?"

It was a fair guess that, when Jessica White again sat down to work, the opus would be entitled *Second Wife*. I didn't tell her that. "Something will come up," I said.

247

Ten

Julia Rakosch was her name. The children
called her Yuli. We met in darkness at Bratislava, on the Czech-
Austrian border in the first winter of peace. I was waiting for a
convoy, boys and girls groping out of Hungary toward the
American Occupation Zone of Austria. The wind had a razor's
edge; the ground was frozen hard. Within a flashlight's circle, I
saw her upright in a truck, bulky, in a man's army overcoat, white
hair framing an opalescent face. Blanket-muffled kids surrounded
her. We exchanged brief words: my directions where to bed the
group down for the night, her "thank you" in English with a
Gabor accent. The truck rolled ahead. I remained, waiting for the
next load of "illegals."

On Christmas Day, I saw her again, in Vienna, at Rothschild
Hospital. That hospital had taken two direct hits, from whose
bombers let's not ask. One wing remained, unshattered, not intact.
Its window glass was gone, its tiled floors were cracked. The
windows had been boarded up, the dark wards were Frigidaires.
Here, our occupation army, wishing to be merciful but without
equipment or authority to be, had provided cots with filthy mat-
tresses and ragged blankets for illegal transients, for children
who'd survived the death camps, who'd been sent back to the
towns and villages where they'd lived, been left to wander seeking
kin—not a mother or a father, this would be too much to expect, a
third cousin or a fourth, maybe, who'd be glad they were alive.
We—the Committee—were trying to round the children up, smuggle them into the American Zone of Austria and send them on to
Palestine. Vienna was a way station on an underground railway.

The woman called Yuli sat on a cot in a cold, dirty ward, reading aloud to a group of girls and boys. I went close to see which
book. It was *Hamlet* in Magyar. Her hair, I noticed then, was

248

silver-blonde, not white, her complexion pink, not opalescent as it seemed at night, and she was singularly beautiful. The children's faces, listening, were so lovely I wished I had a camera. In the way a mind plays hopscotch, I thought of a fat, homely kid named Jessie Weiss, breathless with rapture. "Such words! Like beautiful music!" Judging by the exaltation on the faces around the cot, Shakespeare sounded good in Magyar, too.

Steaming pails were carried in, set on the broken tiles between the cots. The woman shut the book. "Come, children. Food." The boys and girls lined up. Soup was ladled into metal bowls. The kids were hungry, they began to slurp. I watched their anger blaze. One girl made as if to dump her soup. The woman gripped her wrist. "You will eat." She had authority as well as looks.

"But, Yuli, it is garbage."

Garbage. Literally. In every American army mess, signs were posted asking G.I.s not to dribble ashes on their trays because left-over rinds of fat, spoonfuls of mashed potato, dregs of gravy, were scraped into a vat and water added to make soup for *them*. Believe me, in those days of chaos and of nothingness, the army couldn't have offered better even had it wanted to. I told the woman so. "Vienna's the end of the supply line," I explained. "The rations will improve as soon as we get trucks to haul in food."

"We have eaten worse." She raised her arm to spoon the noisome brew. Her sweater sleeve slid back; I saw the green-blue brand. I'd seen that tattoo often, and each time it had harrowed me. This was done to *people*, to people like myself. To bridge the moment of dismay, I asked, "You're going to Palestine?"

"No. I need to stay in Europe." She didn't tell me why. "I will be with UNRRA. It has been arranged. I take charge of the hostel in the Count's Palace." She rested her spoon and smiled. "From the Konzentrationslager to the Palace. Is it not funny?"

Funny-ironic. Not funny-haha. "I'll come to see you there," I said. In my job, those days, you didn't wait for invitations. *They* hadn't yet attained the luxury of saying come or don't to would-be visitors.

On New Year's Eve, I drove my jeep to the Palace, a marble shell, artillery-pocked, stripped of fine furnishings, heatless, stink-

249

ing of disinfectants, and housing one hundred refugees. I came bearing gifts: a half-dozen chocolate bars, a pack of cigarettes, and a bottle of slivovitz. She wouldn't accept the cigarettes; she didn't smoke, she said, though, improvident woman, she could have sold them for ten dollars or traded them for woolen underwear. The chocolate she squirreled in a drawer, for the children, she said, but since I'd been so generous, would I stay and have a drink with her? She fetched two metal cups and set them on the trestle table she was using for a desk with such an air of graceful elegance she might have been the countess of this marble palace.

She was large, statuesque's the word, though now running to fat, the unhealthy bloat of the survivors who these days were being fed chiefly grease and starch. Her features were delicate and her eyes dark blue, like lapis lazuli. Shiksha, she looked; shiksa, I guessed. As it turned out, she was as curious about me as I was about her.

"Which nationality do you have?" she asked while I uncorked the bottle.

"American. American-born."

Her pale-blonde eyebrows rose. "You have been long in Europe?"

"Since nineteen forty-three."

She took the bottle to decant for us. "Where have you been?"

"Everywhere."

"But not where I have been?"

"My jeep knows the roads to Belsen, Dachau and Auschwitz," I said.

Her hand, pouring, trembled. "You saw the railroad tracks?"

"They were not bombed," I answered. "Nor was Farben's compound in Frankfurt."

She gave me a steady look. "I think we can be friends," she said, and held out my brandy cup.

I raised it. "To a happier New Year."

"Thank you," she said, not returning the toast.

I tried again. "L'chaim," I said. To life.

"Thank you," she said and tasted the slivovitz. It was raw. She grimaced and set down her cup. "Since we are friends," she said,

"I can tell you why I do not go to Palestine. I need to try to find my children."

They'd been taken—the whole family removed together—from their flat in Budapest, herded into a cattle car for Auschwitz, separated at the death camp's gate. Her husband, a professor of mathematics, was Jewish. She had been born and baptized Christian, though converted when she married him, technically a neophyte, flung headlong into the violent and bloody stream of Jewish history.

There had been no struggle over change of faith: her parents were dead, there was no question of rejecting them by renouncing their religion, the young man with whom she'd fallen in love wished his Orthodox parents to accept his bride as a true daughter. "And so it was. We were a Jewish family."

Her voice stayed level when she told me this, a control, mastered and deliberate, as if her mind had set these details all in order to provide a future documentary. Her husband was dead, murdered; this her own eyes had seen. (Those blue eyes glazed but did not spill.) From across barbed wire, from the women's section of the camp, she had seen his naked body dangling from a hangman's rope, an example execution, for what infraction she was never told. The children's fate she surmised but did not know for sure, and when you have not proof you cling to hope. She added, with a gentle urgency, that perhaps, when I traveled about, I might come across someone who knew what had happened to Lilli and Rosika Rakosch, eight and ten when last their mother kissed them and brushed their golden braids. Or possibly, miracle of miracles, I might find the girls alive. Her eyes filled again. She drained her cup of slivovitz.

A long shot. For two years I'd carried the photograph of Yossel Katz's family, the address of the crippled Zalman, the names of other brothers, sisters, uncles, aunts and cousins, and hadn't found a one. Yet tomorrow, a gaunt, ragged man or woman with the numbers on an arm might produce a scrap of paper that had been treasured like a gem. "Do you know this name? My cousin in America." So, too, tomorrow or tomorrow, I might come upon a wraithlike child, cowering in the toilet of a beat-up train, on a futile journey to a vanished home, or a withdrawn little girl hidden in a peasant's cottage who desperately denied her origins, because she'd sensed to be a Jew meant death, yet, because the memory of a mother's hand, a father's voice, remained, reluctantly admitted she used to answer to the name of Lilli or Rosika Rakosch. Such miracles were possible in this winter when all of Europe was in flux.

I poured brandy to give the woman's tears a moment to recede. "And how did you survive?" averting my head, not to see the numerals when she received her cup.

"Luck. No matter what else you have been told, luck decided who would live. My luck was I had for one year studied nursing. They could use me in the infirmary. The food was better there." She lowered her voice and eyes, staring into the cup. "You will not believe what was done there. No one will believe it, so it is better not to speak of it. Some day, perhaps; now it is not possible." She shook her head decisively. "No, look forward, only forward. A new life for the children. We must help them to forget and never more to be afraid. Each child who has no mother today is my child."

I marveled at her compassion and her strength. I told her so.

"Please speak about yourself," she answered. "What has brought you here?"

I managed to laugh. "That's a switch. We're the ones who ask the questions. It's our privilege, collecting the case histories."

"But I am curious. You see, I have never before met an American like you. Your military, yes. They are army. They are ordered here. They have given me food, advice, though person to person we have never sat to talk. But you are civilian, volunteer, and that is different. I find you in this broken city, far from your comfortable America, and I wonder what it was that brought you here."

"Drift. The tide," I said, and paused, realizing that a flippant answer wasn't right for her. "I'm a Jew from a small town in the United States, an insignificant newspaper reporter, not even what you Europeans call a journalist, caught up by the tide of history, swept along in it." Then, being unaccustomed to speaking about myself, I went on to tell her about a big shot I once interviewed,

252

who, straight-faced, said to me his dying mother had commanded him, "My son, go forth and become a leader of men."

She didn't get the humor. "And did your mother send you forth to help the Jewish people?"

"No, ma'am. My mother is a simple woman, a Jewish mama, typical and average. She neither urged nor held me back. All the advice she ever gave me was, Eat well, sleep well, keep your bowels open. I doubt she understands what I've been up to overseas. And do you know, if I wrote her how I've been living, working, all she'd say, I swear, is 'My, my, Semmele! That's why you're skinny like a herring. Come home. With chicken soup and knoedlach, Mama will build you up.'"

This time she smiled, with eyes as well as lips, then said with an air of wondering, "But you came during the war?"

"Natürlich. I came when it was possible to come. Wars don't frighten me. I was in the First World War, in France, came through without a scratch. Hired an angel to sit on my shoulder and look after me, a most efficient angel. Except for the blitz in London, this one wasn't really dangerous for me."

"But you didn't need to come, to take the risks." Her gaze was disconcerting.

"Please! Don't try to make a hero out of me."

She waved aside my protest. "But why did you come? Out of pity, charity?"

Those are condescension words. This is my peer. I cannot tell her pity for her brought me overseas when guilt might be closer to the truth. *We* let this crime be done to *you*. *We* Americans. And I was of the cowards. Too timid to cross a Goy in power, a Barry Neale, a Steve Durgin. Multiply me by the thousands who sent the memoranda, made the futile speeches, breaking wind, fearing to demand the ports be opened up, the rail lines bombed. Okay, guilt brought me here. Then why are there few of me?

"I came because I was needed," I said finally.

She seemed to like that, though it didn't satisfy her altogether. "Are you a nationalist? A Zionist?"

"Not particularly. My home is not Jerusalem. It's a town called Grady's Mills."

"Was it for the pay? The good salary? Or are you what we call adventurer, soldier of fortune?"

I reached for the brandy bottle. Her questions were bothering me. She placed her hand over her cup; she'd had enough.

"It was drift, I tell you, chance, a series of accidents. I'll give you the sequence, so you'll understand. One summer night was very hot, I couldn't fall asleep. So I happened to be the first to see a fire in a Jewish grocery store across the street from where I lived. I called the firemen. I helped to save the groceryman. He had a daughter. She was married to a rich man in New York. He happened to be a big shot in the Jewish Aid Committee. Out of gratitude or what, he offered me a job doing propaganda for his Committee. The salary was double what I had been earning. I was fed up with my reporter's job. I saw no future for me in the town. And also—this I won't deny—being Jewish, I was troubled about what was going on in Germany. Well, while I was making up my mind, a Yiddish journalist I happened just to meet—these are all accidents, understand, all part of the drift—recited a few lines to me. When you're undecided, words can give the push. 'If I am not for myself, who will be for me? But if I am only for myself, what good am I? And if not now, when?'"

"A good saying; I have heard it"—offhand, dismissing it.

Let me not be fancy. This isn't the kind of answer the lady's looking for. "I took the job. The Committee needed men to serve abroad. The war was on. Healthy men without dependents happened to be scarce. So they sent me. They learned, I learned, I was suited to this work. And so I stayed. And that's my story, all of it."

She had been listening carefully, her chin propped by a hand and elbow, the numerals facing me. "And you like yourself better since you do this work?"

"I've never given that a thought," I said.

"This is not good enough." She was stubborn as well as beautiful, I'd come to realize. "You do not speak like an adventurer. You are not a nationalist, you say. You do not speak of idealism, pity, saving lives. And I find this modesty—you will forgive me—somewhat false. And this behavior abnormal. To live without comfort, in danger, to take risks as volunteer. . . ." She inched her chair closer. Her gaze was too intent. "Now, selfishness is the normal way. It is as normal as the wish to stay alive. It is the how to stay alive. Do you know I have seen, with my own eyes, fine women, honorable women, steal from one another a small crust of bread, to stay one more day alive. This I could understand more than I understand you. Why have you preferred self-sacrifice? Is it you wish to have a high opinion of yourself? To think yourself a saint? Forgive me if I sound impertinent, but I am very interested in the why of things."

"Must there be a why?"

"There always is," she said.

I set down my empty cup and began to hum a Yiddish song, one of Mama's favorites. " 'Gott veiss vos er tut und sein mishpet is gerect.' " Not knowing whether she knew Yiddish, I translated it. "God knows what he's doing and his judgment is correct.' I'll pass the buck to Jehovah," I added.

"Why did he wish my family to die?" she asked.

I raised her hand and kissed the palm of it. There was not another word to say.

The drift carried me from Vienna to Constanza, Bari, Marseilles, to send "illegals" up the gangplanks of "illegal" ships, "illegal" still because of Britain's Middle East oil politics, "illegal" still because a victorious allied world regarded Jews who'd stayed alive as nuisance rather than as miracle. In the spring of 1946, I drifted back to Vienna. I asked about Yuli. She was in France, the UNRRA people told me, running an orphanage. As far as anybody knew, her children had not been found. I hoped our paths would cross again, for, increasingly, this statuesque woman with the blonde-silver hair and dark blue eyes was in my thoughts. And in my memory she had become radiant, unique, a woman unlike any I had known, beautiful and strong, intelligent and brave, enduring sorrow without drowning in tears. Yet, to me, her uniqueness lay in something else. She was the first person who had ever asked me to identify myself. Who are you? Why do you do what you do?

The drift carried me to the fetid sties of Cyprus where the British penned "illegals" with barbed wire and to the shores of Palestine in the week of Israel's birth. Sam Rosenbaum of Grady's Mills, on May fourteenth of 1948, leaned against the rear wall of a room in a Tel Aviv museum while Ben-Gurion read the proclamation of the state. ("Local Man Attends Meet in Palestine," Barry Neale headlined my firsthand account, and with it he used that one-column cut of me in the A.E.F. uniform.) Then, under Jordan and Iraqi fire, I traveled the dangerous road to Haifa to wait for ships, *my* ships, *my* people, coming off, coming home, kissing the dockside muck and grit as though it was hallowed ground, hearing the mortars of defiant Arab states but not listening, marching straight ahead, to receive a primus stove, a blanket, a cot and cooking pot, to rest a night or two before they joined the struggle for the nationhood.

In the Negev, in Jerusalem and the Galilean hills, other Jews were fighting, dying, to safeguard this tiny sanctuary. I know that a number of those whom I brought home fought and died in the battle for the heights above the Jerusalem road. I like to tell myself they felt their deaths were not as senseless as they might have been at Dachau, yet I am not sure, since the dead can't speak for themselves. It may well be that having tried so hard to stay alive, they would have preferred not to die so quickly on the battlefields of Israel.

I scanned the lists of new arrivals, searching for two golden-haired young girls, Lilli and Rosika Rakosch, praying a long shot would come in and I might be the one to take the news to Yuli that her children had been found. And after we had shared the joyful news, I might explain myself once more and we come to an agreement on the validity of drift. Truly, I believed and I do believe our routes are designated so. God's will, the firm believers call it. Beshert, they used to say on the Hill.

Curiously, while I mooned about the woman who was called Yuli, it was Ilene Sloan who drifted back into my life.

Eleven

I was on the terrace of the Kaete Dan Hotel in Tel Aviv at the end of an October day in 1948. My lodgings were across the road, at the Armon, where the war correspondents stayed, my frayed *News-Record* press card having given me the right to fraternize with the A.P., U.P., Reuters, *New York Times* and *Herald-Tribune*, and buy whisky-soda at the Public Information Office bar. To hold the franchise, I'd airmailed some feature articles, cleared by the military censor, that Barry Neale ran, by-lined "By Our Special Correspondent in Palestine." Keeping my hand in for a cent a word, payable to Papa and providing fuel for the oil burner I'd purchased for the folks after V-J Day. However, mainly, I was winding up the job for which I'd left New York in 1943. Now, my own time to go home was near. I was wrapping up some souvenirs.

Like sundown on the Mediterranean, where the sun doesn't set but plummets, a fiery disc, racing to be extinguished in the sea, no afterglow, no lingering rose or mauve, just instant dark before a canopy of stars is spread. The phenomenon fascinated me. We don't have sunsets like these in the States.

The view from the Kaete Dan terrace was unobstructed west. The Armon desk had instructions to page me there in case a call from Rome came through. I'd had a cable telling me to expect a group of V.I.P.'s from New York, flying in for a once-over-lightly of the war.

I'd found a vacant table on the terrace, signaled an evasive waiter, appealed to him in the name of our mutual heritage and pride, please be kind enough to bring me one cognac, sat waiting for the sun to plunge, listening to the lively guttural Hebrew of a coffee klatch of stylish matrons meshing with the rhythm of the surf, watching the shell-riddle hull of the Irgun ship *Altalena*

257

bobbing on the waves, and wondering whether Yuli had remained at the orphanage in France.

"Uncle Sam!" My head jerked up. There stood Ilene Sloan, in a white form-fitted gown, black cartwheel hat, long black gloves, black patent leather handbag, a New York fashion plate, incongruous in a city where her contemporaries were in O.D. shirts and shorts and over-the-shoulder Stens. Her arms swept around me. "How wonderful! How marvelous to see you!"

I disengaged myself to draw out a chair for her. "What in the world are you doing here?"

"Honeymoon." Her voice went flat. She drew off the gloves. I saw the diamond circlet on her hand. She yanked off the big hat, dropped it on the table. I saw purple shadows under her gray eyes. I asked the banal question, "Who's the lucky man?"

She looked toward the sea. "Michael-David Eisenberg. I believe you met him."

I checked an impulse to pinch my nose. "Mazel Tov. When was the happy day?"

Her shadowed eyes grew vague. "Two weeks ago, I think."

"And here he brings you for a honeymoon! Now, there's a loyal Zionist!"

"Daddy's idea." Her fingers ironed the fingers of her gloves. "Michael's with the firm. Daddy thought he might work up some business contacts. Get in on the ground floor here. The country's going to need steel."

"Right now guns and ammunition, food. And would you like a drink?"

She seemed relieved the subject had been changed. "I'd love a Coke. No such in Tel Aviv. Only mitz and"—her small nose crinkled—"that abomination they call lemon squash."

"The brandy isn't bad." I tapped my glass.

"Coffee," she decided. "Turkish. Sweet, thick, hot."

I wigwagged to catch the waiter's eye. "Chaver," I pleaded. "The young lady is perishing. Would you be kind enough to bring two Turkish coffees, hurry up?"

Hands on hips, akimbo, he challenged me. "Two thousand years we waited for a state; coffee he must have hurry-up." That tickled me. I laughed. The princess was not amused.

"Where's the groom?" I asked.

"In the bar. Teaching the bartender to mix martinis. They do not have the least idea—"

"Nor the ingredients," I said. "The country's very young. And how do you like it?"

Her gaze veered toward the dark sea. The sun had dropped without my admiration. We listened to the surf and the radios behind the blackout curtains, until she said, woodenly, "I know I should be feeling something; I'd like to be feeling something." Her shoulders rose. "I've been raised with this, you know: Mother in Hadassah, Daddy in his organizations, the trees for Grandma Sloan, the hospital bed for the Weiss grandparents. That's a kind of roots here, isn't it?" Again, the restless fingers smoothed the gloves. "Oh, Uncle Sam, I want to go home!"

I heard my name—"Adon Rosenbaum, Adon Shmuel Rosenbaum"—being paged; my phone call had come through. "Sit tight," I told Ilene. "Don't pay when he brings the coffee. I'll be back in a jiff."

When I returned, bearing tidings that my delegation was due on tomorrow's early flight from Rome, the hat, gloves, the bag were gone, Ilene was gone, two tiny cups of Turkish coffee were cooling on the table and the waiter, lounging near, was glowering. I paid him, doubling the legal tip on the chit, and waited on the terrace for Ilene to reappear. Eventually, I drank two cups of cold coffee and departed, irked. A hell of a way for an American girl to act after she has found her Uncle Sam.

My V.I.P.s kept me busy; they wanted to go everywhere, see everything, meet everyone; transportation was difficult to scrounge; Rosenbaum was expected to arrange. We took a bone-breaking junket over the "Burma Road" to spend a few hours in beleaguered Jerusalem, drove up to Galilee, down to the Negev, and, endlessly, we conferred, drank coffee, tea and mitz with the new bureaucrats of a new government. All this left me no time to watch the plunging of the sun or catch up with the honeymooning Eisenbergs.

It was Thanksgiving—the American Thanksgiving—before I saw Ilene again, at the dinner the correspondents had arranged. A national holiday (ours) evokes nostalgia in Americans who're far

259

from home. They yearn to feast traditionally. Though out of a consideration for the hardships of a gallant newborn nation, involved in a war, we refrained from griping publicly, most of us were desperate for a decent meal. How all the world's worst cooks had managed simultaneously to get to Tel Aviv, I shall never understand, but thanks to Thanksgiving some of us, for once, intended to eat well. By pooling our expense accounts and our standing with the Armon management, a banquet was arranged: turkey, candied sweets, cranberry sauce, the works. Bringing guests was permitted if you could manage the tariff, which was steep. I couldn't manage; *Life* and *Time* and A.P. could.

Across the crowded dining room, I saw Ilene and Michael-David, someone's guests. I didn't recognize the individuals either side of them. The bride seemed thinner than when I'd seen her at the Kaete Dan, her cocktail dress so low-cut that the bony clavicle was visible. I wormed my way to them. "Mrs. Eisenberg!" She looked up, startled, as though not accustomed to the name. "I shouldn't talk to you," I said. "Women who run out on me. . . ."

"Oh, did I? I am sorry." She seemed to be groping to remember when. "Oh, yes, I remember. But we had a dinner engagement, didn't we, Michael?" The large man beside her eyed me suspiciously. "Michael, it's Sam Rosenbaum."

He got up clumsily; the chairs were jammed so close a thinner man would have found it difficult. He loomed broader, taller, than I remembered, though not as crudely beefy, his light-brown hair slicked, his cheeks close-shaven, powdered, a well-groomed young man of Manhattan's upper middle class. I offered my hand. "Dr. Livingstone, I presume."

It drew a blank, a stuffy, "I'm Michael Eisenberg."

We shook hands over the skulls of a press-association stringer and his French girl friend.

"Good to see you again, sir," Michael said. His manners had improved, likewise his girth. "My wife did mention she ran into you. We thought if you were staying at the Kaete Dan, we'd run into you again."

"I'm here, at the Armon," I said. "And traveling hither and yon."

"Mind if I sit down?" he said.

The turkeys, brown, mouth-watering, were being carried in.

"Eat hearty, enjoy," I said.

"See you later, I hope," he said.

Ilene said nothing.

I waited for them at the door to walk them back to their hotel, to ask did they want me to bring regards to their families. The blackout was complete, the roadway pitted by shell scars. I held Ilene's arm, helping her across.

In their lobby, Michael asked, "How about a nightcap?"

Okay with me, I said.

Ilene rubbed her forehead. "That room was so stuffy, I've a horrid headache. Will you excuse me?"

Michael scowled but didn't protest. I did, in a way. "Your last chance, baby. Six A.M., this coming Sunday, I depart Air France. Friday, Saturday, a million things to do before the wanderer leaves for home."

"Home!" Her rouged lips trembled on the word. "How I envy you!"

"Don't. I've begun to hate to go. This country's quite an experience!"

"Is it?" with polite indifference. She pecked my cheek. "I'll see you before you go; I'll manage, I promise." She didn't kiss Michael-David, nor he her.

The barroom was all but empty. The commercial and Zionist characters who lodged in the Kaete Dan were wine-with-dinner, cognac-after types; serious drinkers patronized the Public Information Office bar. "Chaver!" The bartender rubbed his hands. "You will have martinis, gentlemen?"

"Whisky-soda," Michael said. He picked up my glass and his, carried both to the far end of the bar.

"L'chaim," I said.

"Skoal," he said. His drink went down the hatch in one swig. I drank slowly, savoring. Whisky, being an import, was scarce and expensive here. "Freshen?" Michael asked.

"No, thanks," I said.

"I will," he said. This time he toyed with the highball. "You'll be seeing Ilene's parents," he said.

"Not necessarily, unless you wish me to."

"Don't. That's what I'm afraid of. You or somebody will tell her mother how goshawful she looks."

"She does. Been sick?"

"No more than you or me. Shil-shul. The national disease."

"Curable. Sulfaguanidine. Strong tea. Scraped apple."

"I beg her to see a doctor. She says they can't help her. That's nonsense. I hear some of them are pretty good, American-trained, I understand."

"She's homesick; take her home," I said.

His ponderous shoulders drooped. "Don't I wish I could. You think I like it here? Think it's any fun for me, sitting in this goddam lobby, waiting for phone calls. Takes forever to get appointments with these characters."

"A war keeps them busy," I said.

"Mind if I have another?" he said.

"No skin off my nose," I said.

He signaled for the bottle, poured a he-man's hooker, omitted the soda. "You married? . . . Tha's too bad. Y'wouldn' unnestand." His speech was getting slurred and loud. An amateur drinker, he was having trouble with hard stuff. Instead of bracing his backbone, it was turning him to glop. The bartender had moved down, propped his elbows on the wood, all ears and big mouth. I talked fast and hard to convince young Mr. Eisenberg it was too hot here; let's get out and get some air. I gripped his arm and dragged him down to the deserted beach. We mushed across the sands. He was on a talking jag, couldn't stop, so desperate to spill his guts, the bartender might have got the details had I not been there. What he told me I'll set down, third person mostly, only slightly paraphrased. It is Michael's story; I was just an ear. All I said was an intermittent "Uh huh," a "Go on, go on." My silent observations were personal and, by and large, irrelevant to what bothered him.

He'd met Ilene when he was a junior counselor at Camp Ganeden. His parents, maybe I knew, maybe I didn't, traveled with the Sloan crowd, belonged to the same organizations, though not by any stretch of the imagination were they in the same financial bracket. Ilene was one of the rich kids at camp whose parents paid for all the extras, like horseback riding and overnight trips. Usually, junior counselors were assigned to the toddlers, wipe their noses, tie their sneakers, button their pants, pick bed-wetters up at night, supervise the swimming crib. That summer the riding counselor pulled a tendon in his calf and Michael got a chance to teach riding. The kids thought he was the Lone Ranger, and the mothers, when they came to visit, made a big fuss over him; a strapping lad looks romantic in the saddle. I wouldn't believe it, but it's the truth; some of the mothers actually tried to make him, a sneaky trick of reaching up, just accidentally, you know, getting their fingers on his crotch. You have to be darn careful—and darn tactful—in a spot like that.

Well, he taught Ilene to ride and her father slipped him a twenty-dollar tip. No need to do that; he'd have been glad to teach her free. She was the prettiest, sweetest kid in camp. And after she'd passed all the swimming tests, he got permission to take her out in a canoe after supper, just the two of them alone, but no fooling around, not in a canoe if you have half a brain, no matter how well you swim. After they came back to town, he'd call her to go riding in Central Park or to the movies Saturday afternoons and she'd phone him to be her escort to parties. He got his first tuxedo—bought, not rented—for her sweet-sixteen dinner party. "I figured she really liked me or she wouldn't have had me around that much. But, you know, I never so much as kissed her, not even good night. Not that she was cold or anything like that or she didn't have a sexy build; she was wearing brassieres, needing them, before most girls in her crowd. It was she was a lady and that was how you treated her."

He got into N.Y.U. It was hard plugging; he wasn't the world's greatest student, he was frank to admit. Ilene made noises about college; actually she applied to Vassar and Wellesley; her mother made her do it. Her father blew up quite a storm when they turned her down, Jewish quota, anti-Semitism, but Ilene was sure it was because her marks weren't good enough and it didn't matter to her anyway; she'd applied just to please her mother. "That was one of the nice things about Ilene, the way she always tried to please her mother." Did I know Mrs. Sloan had been a college graduate and a career woman before she got married? Pretty advanced for those olden days. Ilene said she supposed a career was all right for someone like her famous Aunt Jessie, who had no domestic or maternal instincts, but what she wanted for herself was a normal life and at least half a dozen kids. She took some courses at Columbia General Studies, marking time, Michael figured, till he was ready to supply the home and kids. Saturday nights they had a standing date to go dancing at the country club her parents belonged to, or a show; her father got them seats for all the hits. Quite often, when he drove her home, he'd sleep over at their house to play tennis on their court on Sundays or swim in their pool. But no necking. Part was on account of her attitude, part on account of her dog. She had this little white dog—poodle-terrier, a mixed breed, shaggy, cute—that she took along when they went driving and kept on her lap in the house, cuddling it and kind of jockeying it between them, so he could never get too close. Besides, the damned dog's hair made him sneeze. Allergies can drive you nuts. That was why the army didn't take him, he wanted me to know.

His parents thought Ilene was wonderful and they bragged to their friends their son was practically engaged to Joe Sloan's only child, an heiress and a gorgeous girl. Then, about a year ago, she began to make excuses for not seeing him, and he began to wonder was she dating someone else. But none of their mutual friends reported seeing her dancing at the country club. He wondered was the new guy taking her to sophisticated places like the Persian Room, though as far as he could find out there was no new guy. He tested her a couple of times, called her house on Saturday evenings when she'd turned down a date with him; she was home alone, she said, watching television, she said, but no, she didn't want him to drive up.

He wondered was she trying to ease him out without hurting his feelings. What was the point in dating him exclusively when he wasn't asking her to marry him? And Christ! if he didn't even try to lay her, he must have decided she had no sex appeal; lots of girls get insulted if you don't make the pass. Christ! he sure wanted to; the broads who were hauling his ashes were nothing to write home about. It was all he could do to keep his hands off her, but you do not treat a princess like a broad. But how could he propose, he just out of college, and what he earned couldn't buy her shoes? He tried dating other girls. No dice. It was driving him nuts. He itched all the time, couldn't sleep, had to take phenobarb every night. What bothered him most was she wouldn't even make a date to talk it out, what he'd done wrong, what she was mad about. That's no more than fair, isn't it? So he called up again, and the butler answered the phone and said Miss Sloan was out of town. No, he was not permitted to give out the address. No, he couldn't say when Miss Sloan would be back. After a couple of weeks, he tried again and got the same malarkey. So he asked his mother to call up Mrs. Sloan and kind of beat around the bush and find out where Ilene was and when she'd be home. His old lady wasn't smart enough. All she got out of Mrs. Sloan was some drool about the Hadassah Donor Lunch. Got hooked for a table, too. "And how is your lovely daughter, Mrs. Sloan?" "Quite well, thank you, Mrs. Eisenberg."

Well, you want something bad enough, you have to fight for it. He decided to have a talk with Mr. Sloan. Ilene's father was a self-made man; maybe he remembered what it was like before he made his pile, when he couldn't work up nerve to ask a girl to take a chance with him. He worried he'd have trouble getting through to Sloan, switchboard and secretaries, you know, but the great man came right on the wire and said hop on your horse and get over to my office. Well, it was easier to talk to Sloan than to his own father. "Sir, you know Ilene and I have been dating for years. She's the one and only girl for me. But something's happened, and I figure she's giving me the air because I can't propose. Christ! There's nothing I want more, but I guess she doesn't realize I can't because I don't earn near enough to keep her in the style she is accustomed to and lord knows when I will. Sir, would there possibly be an opening in Victory Steel, something with a future? I'd work like a dog to make sure Ilene won't lack a thing." Well, Sloan knocked him for a loop, practically fell on his neck, said he and Mrs. Sloan had been wondering why Michael'd been neglecting Ilene. Was it something they had done? Some remark they'd passed? They'd always considered him the ideal son-in-law, his family background, his college degree, his personality. And it so happened there was an opening in the firm. Selling. Perfect, with Michael's personality. Twenty thousand salary to start. Plus commissions. Did he think they could manage on that? "What a guy! Direct. Decisive. Is it any wonder he got to be a multimillionaire?" He and Mrs. Sloan would buy them a house and furnish it. And what would Michael say to a honeymoon in Israel, combine business and pleasure, work on the top-level government contacts Sloan had through his organization work, open some new markets for Victory Steel? Naturally, the condition the country was in, it wouldn't be a luxury honeymoon like Bermuda or Palm Beach, but Mr. Sloan, through his connections, would make sure they got the best accommodations available. Interesting, eh? Exciting, eh? He wished he was young enough for an experience like that. Come up for dinner tomorrow night, seven o'clock. We'll be delighted to see you. One and all, including Ilene; you could take his word for it.

There was something about the evening he couldn't put his finger on, an artificial quality. Look, he was accustomed to the big productions the Sloans put on at dinnertime, three kinds of wine, the English butler, and that business with finger bowls, but this production seemed to be rehearsed, everybody watching everybody for a cue, everybody careful not to muff a line, and the parents being so damn nice, how pleased they were to see him, how much they had missed him, all the while watching like hawks, smirking whenever he looked over at Ilene, like how thrilled we are he finds our daughter good to look upon. Christ, was there something wrong with her, they were trying to palm her off? As far as he could see, she was as sweet and pretty as she'd always been, and as polite, asking had he been riding much lately, and how his parents were. Right after they got up from the table, her father announced he and the missus were expected at the club. He kissed Ilene on the forehead before they went out and said, "Now, be Daddy's good little girl!" *"Daddy's good little girl!"* What else? All the years he'd known her, he'd never heard Ilene contradict her parents or criticize them when they were not around. Respectful. Brought up right. One of the things he admired in her was how she treated older folks. Even his mother, who could be a shlock.

He asked Ilene if she'd like to go dancing. She said she would, then said she wouldn't. Well, he had his car, how about a drive?

She said she would, then said she wouldn't. He mentioned he'd phoned a couple of times and the butler had said she was out of town, thinking she'd talk about her trip. All she said was, "Yes, I was away." Before he could ask more questions, she asked would he care to go down to the rumpus room and watch television. He said he would; anything she wanted was okay with him. Besides, his family hadn't yet acquired a set, it was a sort of novelty to him.

Well, he couldn't remember precisely how it happened, though he was certain he didn't get down on his knees and ask, "Will you marry me?" and she had that damned dog on her lap, so he couldn't lunge, but he did remember saying, "Babe, do you really like to watch that junk? Don't you want to hear me say I keep thinking about you night and day, I can't sleep for thinking how I want you, there's never been any other girl for me since I laid eyes on you. I'll do anything, everything, turn myself inside out to make you happy." He wasn't sure he said all that but, anyhow, that's what he was thinking. And he did remember she laid her hand on the back of his, just that, and it set him on fire. "This is a hot number, mister, make no mistake, she is." It was all he could do to keep his zipper closed. But she wasn't putting out, and when she did talk it wasn't about wanting to go to bed or even about love, but practical things, like there was no need to buy her an engagement ring, she didn't care for diamonds, and, besides, her mother had enough of them to sink a battleship; she'd be passing them along eventually. She supposed their families would want a big wedding; she didn't care one way or the other. He said he didn't care one way or the other; all he cared about was soon. Then she smiled, sort of crookedly, and said, "It's all right, now, isn't it?" and put the dog down and puckered up her mouth and let him give her one short kiss. And, whoosh, before he knew it, engraved invitations were out for a wingding at the Pierre and she was so busy with dress fittings and showers and stuff he barely got a chance to say hello on the telephone.

At this point, Michael plopped on the sand, came down hard, while I stood over him, wondering would I have the muscle to haul him back to the Kaete Dan. He stretched flat, eyes closed, mouth shut finally. Having no choice, I squatted alongside and wondered was that moving light high in the sky a falling star or an enemy reconnaissance plane. We were in a country that was in a shooting war, though in Tel Aviv you frequently forgot. Jerusalem, the Negev, was where the action was. This cold, dark, deserted beach gave me an eerie feeling that Michael and I were the last human creatures left on earth. The *Altalena*'s ghostly hulk—I could just about make it out—intensified the desolateness. In June, I'd seen that ship alive with young men and flaming ammunition. And here it rocked, a coffin shell.

Boy, this has been a peculiar war, I told myself, a human war, if war can have humanness. What I saw in the Negev on that trip with the V.I.P.s pretty much sums up what this one is. We stopped at a kibbutz where farmers, out of Eastern Europe, had lived for half a year in bunkers underground and fought off Egyptian tanks and planes with Molotov cocktails. We drove on to Beersheba, for a concert out of doors, the Israel Philharmonic, Leonard Bernstein, guest conductor. The war-wounded lay on stretchers, the soldiers sprawled on rooftops, listening, and just before the sun started down Lenny played Gershwin's *Rhapsody in Blue*. This I shall remember till the day I die, so beautiful, so stirring, so unsuitable and so appropriate, it was. And next day, driving back, when the sun was high and searing hot, I saw something else I shall not forget. In a parched field a soldier lay. His grinning skull was white, picked clean by the buzzards, even the eye sockets. He wore the uniform of Egypt, and he was alone.

I was brooding about the lonely death of the Egyptian when Michael-David Eisenberg sat up, blew his nose and began again to talk. About his wedding and his bridal night. What he blubbered was so embarrassing I was grateful for the dark.

He remembered—this was all he remembered—Ilene coming down the aisle on her father's arm, swathed in frothy white, "like a dream walking," and her warm mouth receiving him when the rabbi said, "Now kiss your bride." And he in a sweat and becoming more horny by the minute and hoping to God it didn't show. And mobs of people, and champagne glasses being passed. It was all a champagne bubble, big, getting bigger, like it would explode. He was drinking, Ilene was drinking, too, and come to think of it, whenever wine was served at her family's table, she barely tasted it, and on their dates she ordered Coke or ginger ale. They had a suite reserved in the Pierre; their flight to Rome was tomorrow evening. More champagne was waiting in an ice bucket upstairs, but they never opened it. One thing, just one, was on both their minds: get on the mattress, quick. He believed he tore her dress getting the back zipper down, but he remembered he kept saying to himself, Take it slow and easy, don't hurt her, don't scare her, this is not a broad. But by jeezus, she was more hot than he, if that was possible.

As I now recall, I did grunt, "Cut it out," and squeeze his arm to shut his mouth. Voyeurism is not my dish; a bridal night deserves privacy. There was no stopping him. She was not a virgin. No, this you can't blame on horseback riding; that girl knew what it was all about. Experienced. "She wanted it and wanted it and I thought, Gee, this is terrific. I got myself a babe. But jeezus Christ, a dame can take it; a guy has to rest in between." He dropped off to sleep. When he woke, Ilene wasn't on the bed. He heard water running. The bathroom was full of steam. She was in the shower and she was crying. "Ilene, baby, darling, did I hurt you? Ilene, sweetheart, what's the matter?" He reached in and tried to shut the water off. She slapped his hand away and screamed, "Don't come near me, don't touch me!" "And I swear it, she hasn't let me touch her since that night. Nothing. Absolutely nothing. You won't believe it; we have separate rooms. She does her nails, fixes her hair, changes her get-up, walks this goddam beach. And looks through me as if I wasn't here. Now I ask you, be honest, what the hell kind of a honeymoon is this?"

The absurdity—not the tragedy—hit me so hard I all but laughed aloud. Here in a newborn country, fighting for its life, a New York Yid was blubbering because he couldn't screw his bride. One man, one problem. One tiny bubble in the seething cauldron of history. Let's have priorities on what's important when. Chaver, your problem, all personal problems, have to wait till we stop making history.

"I'd like to kill her, kill her, kill her, strangle her with these bare hands. It's driving me nuts. Why? What did I do to her? Tell me, tell me what?"

Chaver, because your in-laws were my landsleit on another planet, you do not hold a lien on my omniscience. Those who

269

know me are aware—and I agree—that I'm a doer, workman, craftsman, not a philosopher. Yuli asked me why about myself. "There always is a why," she said. I passed the buck to Jehovah. He decides what's right. Even when six million of his children are destroyed? Well, look at it another way. That was the price of Jewish nationhood. Too high? Find me a man in Tel Aviv tonight who'd call the bargain off.

Michael was plucking at my sleeve. "What shall I do? Advise me, tell me what to do."

"Lay off the booze for one thing. That sure as hell won't help. And get Ilene home, and to a psychiatrist."

Maybe he was hoping I'd promise to speak to his wife, in loco parentis, take an avuncular hand. No dice. Also no time. I pushed and pulled at him, urging him to stand, and I led him back across the beach to the Kaete Dan. At the hotel steps, I told him, "You're a husband, be a man," and added cheerily, "I'll be godfather to your first-born."

I was up early on Friday, to brief my successor for the nth time, verify my flight, get my papers cleared and sealed by the military censor, reclaim my other suit from a dilatory dry cleaner. It was a hectic day, and exasperating, because everyone I had to see went home for lunch, took a siesta afterwards, and closed early to prepare for Shabbos. Saturday, I packed and went the rounds to say goodbyes. I had a lot of friends in Tel Aviv; we'd shared a meaningful experience. You're leaving home, not going home, they said.

"Shalom," I said.

I got to bed late, high on emotion and local wine and brandy.

The Armon's night porter woke me at half-past four. The hotel had arranged for a taxi to pick me up at five. I staggered down to the lobby with bags in my hands and under my eyes. The porter who was swabbing the lobby's tiled floor said, "A lady is waiting for you," and nodded toward a curtained alcove at the rear. I drew the drapery aside. Ilene was on a banquette behind a little table, her eyes red and swollen, cheeks flushed, hair and dress disheveled.

"Been waiting all night," she whispered. "Didn't want to miss you."

I thought of Michael. "Your husband must be frantic."

270

She ignored what I'd said. "Uncle Sam, you're going home, please take a letter back for me." From her shiny handbag, she took an envelope. Complaint, I thought, to Papa and Mama: I hate it here, tell Michael to bring me home. S.R., as usual, the middle-man.

"They've censored and sealed my papers," I told her. "There's a war on."

"I know," she said. "But the censor reads outgoing mail, and I've heard he sometimes gossips. Read it, so you'll know it isn't military secrets."

The single sheet lay between us on the table, its distinctive penmanship easy to read, its import just as legible. *"My dearest, I have tried so hard but I cannot forget you. Each hour, each day, each night, you're in my thoughts and in my heart. I walk alone on the beach and pray for a miracle, you appearing out of the sky or sea, as you appeared out of nowhere, in our driveway. I need you, I want you, we belong to each other. I do not know how long I shall have to stay here. It already seems like an eternity. Send me word, some word, somehow, quickly, that you want me, you'll be waiting, that you are forever mine as I am forever yours."*

She tucked the sheet into its envelope, saying, "I'll leave it unsealed, so you won't have trouble with it. Please buy a U.S. stamp in New York; I can't get one here," and stroked the envelope, caressing it, before she held it out to me. "Please, Uncle Sam."

I didn't take the envelope. "Does anybody know about this?" I asked.

The answer came too fast. "Why, yes, Aunt Jessie," Ilene said.

The consternation on my face must have been eloquent.

"But I had to talk to someone," she protested. "Someone worldly and experienced."

The porter raised the alcove curtain. "Slichah, excuse, Adon. The taxi is waiting. He says if he does not leave right away, you miss the airplane."

She thrust the envelope into my hand—"Please, Uncle Sam!"—with such tear-choked urgency, I could not refuse. I leaned over the table to kiss her forehead, saying not a word, not even the

271

"Shalom." In the cab, I put the letter into my wallet where for years I'd carried all those lists of lost persons.

It was a long day's flying. The aircraft stopped at Nicosia, Athens, Rome. Up to Rome, I slept. Between Rome and Paris, I was wakeful with hard thinking, arranging myself, getting my emotions all in order.

I thought about the country I had left and wondered why I'd left. I loved it and I felt that I belonged in it. Yet I had kept part of me reserved, alien and foreigner, Jew, American passport. Yes, America's my home, not that sliver of the Middle East. Come, come, what home are you returning to? A furnished room, four walls and a radio, doing crossword puzzles, reading the *New Yorker* and *Time Magazine*, taking girls on dates, buying a lay with two martinis and a three-fifty table d'hôte? Is that living? Is it life? What are you, Sam, a stone?

Do you ask nothing more, nothing better? What is better? "A little companionship, a little joy." Jessie wanted that. She snatched, she took the risks. Last time you saw her she was full of pain. Like Ilene. Would either of them say it wasn't worth the risk? Giving and receiving love. Suppose tomorrow there is grief? They've lived, haven't they? Even Michael-David Eisenberg has given love and received its pain.

This is one world you never made. Why not? Because you've been afraid? Of disappointment? Hurt? Or because your woman never did turn up? How do you know? How hard have you tried? *If not now, when?*

By the time the plane reached Paris my mind was made up. Baumberg had expected me to fly right on to New York. I went A.W.O.L. without cabling him, checked into a hotel and made inquiries. Oui, Madame Rakosch is at the orphanage. The village is not distant; a train from Gare St. Lazare will bring you there.

I walked the Rue Rivoli and the Rue Faubourg St. Honoré until I found a ring of antique gold, set with an oval lapis lazuli. I bought it and took a train to continue a conversation begun in Vienna on a New Year's Eve.

The orphanage was in an old chateau in countryside which in summer might have inspired Corot: graceful trees, placid fields, a mossy stream. Today it was bleak, the leafless trees shivering

272

under the white, icy fog in which France seems to specialize. The damp chill was in the hall where I waited, nose red and dripping, for Madame Rakosch.

She greeted me without surprise, since a man who's termed himself a drifter may drift here as well as there. She shook both my hands firmly before she led me to her spartanly furnished office. A small stove warmed it; a coffee pot was on the stove.

She hadn't changed; the blue eyes, the tendrils of silvery hair, the contours of her face were as I remembered. Yet she had changed. For one thing, her tall figure was slender and as lovely as her face. For another, the sleeves of her school-mistressish gray woolen dress were tight to her wrists, hiding the numerals.

"You will have a coffee?" She brought cups of decent china from a shelf. The coffee was the best I'd drunk in years, no ersatz or burned cereal, not even the bitterness of chicory. I praised it. She smiled. "It is American. Americans come here. They ask many questions. They take away our life histories. They leave us good coffee." Spoken matter-of-factly, though I sensed, rather than heard, a trace of cynicism behind her words.

I set my empty cup down on the edge of her desk, warmed though a trifle wary. It had been easier to talk to her when I'd met her softened by her sorrows, her defenses down, and my authority in evidence. I hitched my chair closer. "Well," I began, a useful word for all situations.

"Quite well," she answered. "The country air, the good food of France, have helped with the healing."

"I asked everywhere," I said. "No one knew."

"*I know*," she replied, her voice and eyes steady. "I am no longer searching for my children."

I fumbled for a cigarette and lighted it.

"I may soon leave this place," she went on to say. "The children's need for me is no longer great. Nor mine for them. We can move on, I and they."

"Where will you go? To Israel?"

"That is not yet for me. I need a placid country. Denmark, perhaps, or Switzerland."

"Why not the United States?"

"The Hungarian quota is filled for many years."

I laid my cigarette down on the saucer's lip and pulled my courage up. "If you were married to an American you could get a visa quickly."

There was a moment of silence, in which I felt the quickened beating of my heart, before she answered, gently, "For everything there is a time. For me it is not yet time to build a new relationship."

I groped in my pocket for a little box, wondering should I venture to offer her the ring. Let's have an end to cowardice; the worst that can happen is that she'll refuse. I took out the box and opened it upon my hand. "I saw this in a shop in Paris. The stone reminded me of the color of your eyes. I took the liberty of buying it for you."

"Oh!" Her color heightened. "It is very beautiful." A slight sparkle came into her eyes, but she made no move to take it. "You Americans are generous," she said.

"I'm not doing this for my country." I heard my voice, rasping. "I'm doing this for me. It's a gift of selfishness. Take it, please. Wear it. For remembrance, friendship, or just because it's pretty."

Still she hesitated.

"No strings attached. No obligations. I wanted to see you. I couldn't come empty-handed. Do me the honor to accept this gift."

There was another long, thoughtful look before she reached to take the ring. She held it up, turning it on a fingertip, admiring it, before she thrust it down the fourth finger of her right hand. She held the hand out and smiled at me. "It is a beginning," she said. "I have one beautiful possession. That is a starting to be normal." Then, folding her hands in her lap, the ring concealed by the bare hand, she said as she had in Vienna, three years earlier, "Talk about yourself."

"I've been here, there, everywhere," I said. "In Europe. Israel. A drifter as I was before. But now, I'm also starting to be normal, to want something for myself. Something—someone—beautiful." My words sounded stilted. I do not have the knack for romantic speech.

"The time is not yet for me to think of things like this," she said.

"I'm leaving for the States," I said. "I don't want to lose you."

Her color rose again. Her hands clasped, unclasped, on her lap.

"If I write, will you answer?" I asked.

"Of course. I would not like to lose you."

"A slow start, but a start," I said.

"Would you like to see the orphanage, the children?" she asked.

I got up, saying, "No, it was only you I came to see."

She extended the hand that wore my ring. I raised it, turned it over and, like a European, kissed the back of it. I would have liked to kiss her mouth. She didn't offer it.

If not now, when? I returned to Paris, angry with myself. Night had dropped a shroud of icy fog upon the city, fuzzing the amber street-corner lights. I sat over a cognac in a crowded, steamy bistro. At the table next to mine, a young man kissed a girl full on the mouth. I could have strangled both of them. A frowsy whore wriggled past. I snarled at her. She pursed her painted lips to spit. I got up, paid, walked out alone into the horrid night.

American, go home. To what? To whom? Why, to the King. Baumberg's waiting for you, Sam. He and no one else. A hired hand, a non-person, is coming back. A man returning from a couple of wars wants a welcome from someone who belongs to him, to whom he belongs. Mama. Now, isn't that ridiculous? Flying home to Mama at my age? Mama's boy. So what? Is this a disgrace?

I found the cable office and sent off a wire to Grady's Mills, asking Mama and Papa to take the Sunday afternoon train to New York, register at the Hotel Commodore next door to Grand Central Terminal, take a taxi Monday morning to La Guardia airport and meet my Air France flight. Papa will be flabbergasted, I thought; he'll have to close the shop, and if Mama has the least idea how much this cable cost she'll have a conniption fit.

I flew at night and slept soundly, a babe returning to his mother's arms. At daybreak we circled New York. The rising sun blazed on a million window panes, unbroken windows in a place untouched by bombs. We came down smoothly on cement and coasted to an easy stop.

When Immigration asked to see my passport, I pulled out Ilene's letter, too, licked the flap, sealing it, and dropped a coin into a machine to buy a postage stamp. Gluing on the stamp, I glanced for the first time at the name and address on the envelope and went stiff with shock. I saw a junkman's shanty; I saw a dark-haired boy baby on a doorstep in the Flats. Red flames and shooting stars exploded in my skull. Rage all but blinded me. I ripped the envelope across, across, and into shreds, and dumped them into a can of trash.

For the name on the envelope was Sgt. Jody McCarthy, and someone had to end this thing.

Home from two wars, I was filled with fury at a worldly and experienced woman named Jessie Weiss who had—of this I had no doubt—abetted this affair out of sibling spite.

Twelve

I spied them as I came from Customs, leaning on each other, Mama under a monstrous purple turban, Papa in a garish overcoat that might have been the balmacaan he'd sewed for me a million years ago.

"Semmele!" Mama squashed me with a hug, plastering kisses on my face. "You got so old!" she wailed.

Papa embraced me, whacked me on the shoulder blades. I caught a powerful whiff of camphor. "Nu?" Papa jabbed my ribs. "Show us already the kalah."

Mama beamed. "Why else would you sent the telegram?"

I pinched her withered apple cheek. "You're the only woman in my life. Come, let's find a taxi. We'll have breakfast at the Commodore."

Mama nudged Papa. "Go make number one."

"Sha!" he hissed at her. "No water closets here."

"They must got. Semmy, dolling, please go find."

I guided them to their respective doors and stood beside my baggage, chuckling. Back to basics, down to earth; life begins again with number one. Mama, flushed and furious, opened her door. "Semmy, costs ten cents." I fished out a dime. "The pocketbook is for style," she apologized. "I don't carry nothing. Only the handkerchief."

Eventually, we occupied a cab. I sat between my parents. Across me, they jabbered about the outrage of paying to do number one.

"Same price I could do number two," Papa said morosely.

"In a strange place!" Mama cried.

"Sammy, you didn't go," Papa said. "For my ten cents I could hold open the door for you. You didn't need?"

"I went on the plane," I said.

277

"In the sky!" The shock on Mama's face was marvelous. Ah, well, other people wonder, too.

"Look ahead," I suggested. "There's New York. Magnificent, isn't it?" Mama ignored me and the skyline. "The place was werry clean," she said, thoughtfully. "Charge ten cents, gets a better class pishers."

The cab scooted through the drab Queens streets.

"Papa, did you turn down the thermister?"

"Up. I turned up," Papa said.

Mama rocked her head. "Gevalt. The house will be a shvitzbod."

Papa blanched. "I turned down," he stammered. "You told me down, I turned down."

"I don't believe. Semmy, your papa is in trouble. He has little swindles in the head. He mixes up. Down is up, up is down."

We crossed the Fifty-ninth Street bridge, wheeled into Second Avenue.

"How you like the hat, Semmy?" Mama straightened the ugly turban. "From Katz. The Bon Ton. The salesgirl said is stylish for New York. Your mama didn't shame you?"

"You rekonize the coat?" Papa added. "The goods from Leeds I made for you. Mama kept in kemfer, upstairs in the closet."

Neither one had asked me what I'd seen and done abroad, why I'd stayed so long, or where I planned to go from here. They were my parents, weren't they? Then, the world in which they lived was my world also, wasn't it? What had the world in which I'd spent five years to do with them?

They stood behind me while I signed the hotel register, frowned distrustfully when I gave a bellhop my room key, coat and baggage. They looked horrified when I proposed they give him their wraps, too. Three abreast, we entered the dining room.

There was crisp damask on the tables. A deferential waiter offered menus.

"Mama, Papa, what would you like?"

"Notting, Semmy dolling, we already had," Mama told me. "My husband and me, we sit with the son for company, you don't mind?" she told the waiter.

"The orange juice fresh?" I asked.

278

"Squeezed to order, sir. Large or small? . . . Yes, sir, double orange juice."

"Two fried eggs. In butter, please. Turn 'em over. And toast. Butter on the side."

"Yes, sir. Marmalade or strawberry jam? . . . Yes, sir, both. . . . Bran or corn muffins?"

"Corn muffins and sweet rolls, if you have them. A pot of coffee, cream and sugar. You do have cream and sugar, don't you?" Still not believing I was in a world of no shortages or ersatz.

"Yes, sir. Now what can I bring the lady and gentleman?"

"Mama, Papa, what would you like? Order anything you want."

"I am full only looking on you, Semmy dolling."

"Order something, Mama, please."

Mama, to the waiter, coyly, after deliberation, "A couple stew prunes, if you have. And a cup hot water."

"She is constipate from the train," Papa whispered.

"You, Papa. Maybe pancakes, some French toast?"

"He will have a cup tea," Mama decided. "With lemon."

"Bring a double order of sweet rolls," I told the waiter, and he winked at me.

"We didn't need," Mama whispered after the man had headed for the kitchen. "Upstairs in the room we got a coffee cake, I baked for you, with tzinamin, white raisins, like you like. Delicatessen from Perlzweig. And apples and bananas."

"Mama knew by New York hotels is not kosher," Papa whispered.

"We are zat looking on you, Semmy dolling," Mama said.

The waiter brought Mama's stewed prunes and hot water and my tumbler of orange juice. Mama tried a sip and smacked her lips. "Not sour. You want a taste, Papa?"

"Eat the prunes," Papa said huffily. "Let Semmy enjoy."

"Bring two more orders of orange juice," I told the waiter.

My eggs were served. Mama leaned over, sniffing. She forked a morsel of the white, tasted it, nodded, approving.

The waiter winked at me again. "Two more orders," I said.

"Too much!" Mama cried. "One egg for me and Papa is enough.

279

We are old people," she explained to the waiter. "We don't have big appetite no more. We eat to keep our son company. He comes now on the airplane from Palestine where the people is very poor, they don't have what to eat."

The waiter tsked sympathetically. "Have to fatten him up, eh, Mother? One fresh egg apiece for you and Papa. In butter."

Mama had corn muffins with her egg, Papa sweet rolls with his tea. I had poured my second cup of coffee when Mama started her report on the folk I used to know. "You remember little Kerel, the daughter from Sylvia?"

"Sadie Finkel," Papa muttered.

I lit a cigarette.

"You smoke too much," Papa told me.

"After Sukkos she got married. With a dentist," Mama said.

"He made for Mama the new teeth," Papa said. "Show Semmy."

Mama exposed the teeth; I admired them. "They made by the Temple a beautiful wedding," she went on. "Everybody was inwited. For the kiddush in the Temple also. Not for the dinner. This was only for the both families."

"You remember Bobby Rogoff?" Papa asked.

"The grandson from Sophie," Mama amplified. "The son from Hymie, that was with you in the high school? He goes in Harvard's College. Hymie says it's a werry big honor."

"We got a new rabbi in the Litvak shul," Papa broke in. "A fine man, edel."

"With such bad trouble," Mama added. "A boy, the third, born with a clubs foot. An operation could maybe fix it, the rebbitzin told me. Who has so much money for big operations?"

"The German doctor moved away," Papa said. "To Chicago. In Grady's Mills he couldn't make a living."

Mama lowered her voice. "Anti-Semitin in the hospital."

"Solly Katz," Papa said. "He called up on the telephone. When was it, Mama?"

"After Pesach. No." She counted on her fingers. "After Shevuoth."

"He said we should buy the paper," Papa continued. "Your picture was in. Some writing from you about Palestine. He said it was a big honor, a man from Grady's Mills was by a big meeting with big Zionists."

"I told him what's the surprise?" Mama said. "My Semmy, when he was only just a kid, a young feller, he was by General Pershing in the headquarters."

I was right back where I started from. My small share in history hadn't registered on Sixth Street. Yuli was light years away. Ilene never wrote a letter.

The waiter hovered with the check. "Everything okay, folks?"

"Everything was tasty," Mama said. "Thank you werry much."

We went up to my room. Mama took off the atrocious hat, Papa the abominable coat. They stood over me while I unpacked, Mama clucking over the condition of my clothes. "You'll come home, I'll wash, I'll press." I took out the presents I had brought: from Israel, for Mama, doilies of Nazareth lace and a Yemenite pin; for Papa, a mezuzah of silver filigree; from Paris, a Rodier satin scarf for Mama, a soft woolen ascot for Papa.

"You shouldn't spend so much," Papa scolded. "Old people, what do we need?"

"From Palestine you didn't bring the small bag earth, for the graves?" Mama complained.

I hugged her. "You'll live and be well to a hundred years," I said.

She sighed, a long, deep sigh. "Not when you go always in a war. The worry makes me sick to death." It was the first intimation that she'd been aware my years abroad had been dangerous.

"I'm home," I said. "Stop worrying."

"Who could stop, you come back skinny like a herring? Papa, go up in the elevator. Bring down a couple apples, a banana. Maybe a small piece cornbeef. Semmy would enjoy a nasch."

While Papa was upstairs, I phoned the office to check in. Leo Wullstein bellowed at me. Where in hell had I been? They'd been expecting me for days, Baumberg was having kittens, get over on the double, no kratzing around. "My folks are here," I told him. "They've come in from Grady's Mills. Haven't seen me in three years."

"You're a big boy, aren't you? Cut the apron strings."

Papa's chin dropped to his chest, Mama looked as if she'd cry, when I said my office was expecting me. "You didn't told us nothing," Mama complained, justifiably.

I tried to cheer them up. "This is only for an hour or so. Look, you go up to your room, rest a while, then go downstairs, get a taxi, tell the driver to take you to Radio City Music Hall. Go in, see the show, a movie, dancers, music, I promise you will like it very much. Here's money. Take it, Papa, it's my treat. . . . When the show is over, take a taxi back to this hotel; I'll meet you here. We'll go out to a kosher restaurant."

They pouted, sulked. Mama recovered first. "Come, Papa, I'll take out the teeth, lay down for a while. You'll maybe take a dremmel, too. Then we go to the teyater, be big sports in New York."

I walked to the office. The day was sunny, crisp, and Fifth Avenue was festive, shop windows sparkling with tinsel and glitter-studded artificial snow, store fronts hung with necklaces of colored bulbs and giant holly wreaths, Santa Clauses tinkling bells alongside cardboard chimneys. Mink-coated women, loaded down with green and red and gold-wrapped bundles, jostled me. The city looked prosperous and gay; not one cornice had been nicked. It was a treat for eyes that had been viewing rubble for so many years.

An office receptionist, blonde and new, asked my name, who I wished to see, and did I have an appointment with Mr. Wullstein? "Are you for real, sister? Tell Leo the prodigal is here."

Leo bustled out, harried looking, crow's-feet at his eyes, furrows in his brow. He pumped my arm. "How are you? How do you feel? Have a good flight?" Before I could reply, he said, "His majesty is waiting," and led me down the hall. On the way, he did manage to ask, "What delayed you?"

"Sex," I said.

"At your age, kid?" he said.

Baumberg, lean as a matchstick, top hair and mustache grayed, growled, "Hi. Couldn't tear yourself away from Paris, eh? Sit down, sit."

And this, so help me, was my welcome. In minutes, the harness was yoked on as though I'd never been away.

"What you're to do first," the King informed me, "is address a

282

few parlor meetings in the New York area. Big gifts. Give them the inside stuff on the war, the army, not too much, one or two details they haven't read in the press. Then, the refugees, the immigrants, the rachmonas stuff. Lay that on with a trowel, thick. Your first appointment is tomorrow at Joe Sloan's."

I tried to keep a poker face; I wasn't good at it.

"Turn down your nose," Baumberg admonished me. "Sloan's crowd is good for half a million if you goose them right. Sloan wants you while you're hot; he's been primed for a week. I got him on the phone the minute you called up. He bitched about the short notice; only as a personal favor to himself would his pals turn up." To mollify me, Baumberg added, "If you've acquired an interest in art, he has some first-class stuff: Matisse, Chagall, Picasso." He studied my get-up. "You look like what the cat dragged in. Stop in at Wallach's, pick up a couple of suits. Own a tux? You'll need one on the road. We're booking you to the Coast." He pressed a buzzer on his desk. He had just time enough to tell me, "That kid you sent, he's in Columbia, on a Regents' scholarship," before two young men, brisk and brusque and carefully tailored, came in. We were introduced without biographies. They pulled up chairs and talked, to Baumberg and each other, about quotas, pledges, increases, pace-setters, advance gifts, card-calling, problem communities. Now and again, they glanced in my direction, and I gathered they were briefing me. Their vocabulary was strange and their attitude baffling. Rosenbaum is back from where the action is. Ask him about the people who believed and served, the humble, tired, earnest men and women who endured and fought because they had no choice. They're our partners in this deal. They've given us prestige. Money didn't win that war; people's courage did. Ask me about them. Did I knock my brains out, run my ass off, just to help you raise your quotas here? Apparently, I did. You cannot feed and clothe and heal the immigrants with peanuts. You can't defend and build a nation with your kind regards. But have rachmonas for Sam Rosenbaum. He needs a little time to change his skin.

"Get going, Sam," the King decreed.

It hurt to tell my parents they'd have to go home alone. Previously, when I'd returned from a war, I'd gone straight back to the

Hill. And the last place in the world I wished to see was the residence of Joseph Sloan. Yet not for an instant did it occur to me to rebel. The old mantle of non-person came with my new suits.

One of the fund-raisers drove me up to Greenwich, adding advice on the way. "Make them, each and everyone, feel he did it personally."

The Sloans had exchanged the Palace of Versailles for a Tudor mansion. In the darkness I could make out just its bulk that was girdled now by limousines. Beside a stately, gleaming oak staircase in the entrance hall two portraits hung, Joe and Celia, side by side, large as life and many times more beautiful, Joe in hunting pinks, Celia in a garden frock, arranging petunias in a Wedgwood bowl, the squire and lady of the manor. Somewhere, behind heavy doors of oak, I heard the yipping of a dog, the one, perhaps, that had made Michael-David sneeze. I'd rather not have heard the animal.

An English butler took my hat and coat; the Sloans converged to greet me, Celia with her limp-wrist handshake, her mincing, "Samuel, how nice to see you!" Joe with a slap on the back, "Hi, kid! We did great, didn't we?" and "I did my part, like I promised Baumberg. A fine crowd inside. I can tell you each and every one is proud about our victory."

In a ballroom-sized living room, hazy with tobacco smoke, I saw two dozen men and women, cozy on deep sofas and armchairs. I noticed a Chagall above the fireplace, recognized a Matisse on one wall and, on the grand piano, a handsome bridal couple, three poses within a gilded, jeweled frame. I averted my eyes and searched for the Picasso Baumberg had promised me.

"Friends!" Joe stood beside me in the piano's arc and clapped his hands for silence. "It is my privilege and pleasure to introduce you to a young feller I have known all my whole life. And confidentially, let me tell you, when he was growing up we never figured he'd amount to much. (Laughter.) But like I always say, give a man a chance, show you have confidence in him, he'll try his damndest to make good. (Applause.) He has just come back from a mission to our co-religionists, our brave and suffering brethren abroad, and I can let a cat out of the bag, it was me, myself, that sent him on that mission, me myself that showed him what he owed his people, gave him his big chance to serve. (Applause.) I did not guess wrong. I sent the right man for the right job. He's got no medals pinned on him, he's a bashful, modest feller. But after you listen to him tell in his own plain, simple words what he did and how he did his job, maybe you'll say he deserves a medal. He'll give you the low-down, the inside true low-down, not what you read in the papers, folks, the genuine article. . . . Ladies and gentlemen, my old friend, my close friend, my high school chum, Sam Rosenbaum."

"Thank you, Mr. Sloan. Ladies and gentlemen. . . ." I got this far before tension kinked my throat.

Joe took my hoarseness for something else. "Friends, could I ask a big favor for the guest speaker. Could you please put out the cigars." Sotto voce, he growled to me, "Get a hold of yourself. Don't let me down."

I got a hold. I told them about the ships, the wanderers coming down the gangplanks at Haifa, about the cream of the country's youth, fighting and dying to create a nation that would be a sanctuary. I spoke of what I'd seen—courage and pity were implicit rather than shmeared on. I described the people in the bunkers in the Negev, though I did omit the *Rhapsody in Blue* at Beersheba and the lonely dead Egyptian in the field. These, I felt, might not be appreciated here. There were snuffles, handkerchiefs dabbing eyes, and a diffident sort of applause, after I said, "Well, that's the story, folks." The fund-raiser put his middle finger and this thumb together. O: okay. Joe patted my shoulder and took the grand piano's curve, to do the arm-twisting. He did it through Ilene. His daughter, his dearly beloved only child, he told his friends and fellow country club members, had sacrificed the luxury of a Palm Beach honeymoon—"Look at that beautiful young couple, friends, feast your eyes on them"—to travel with her husband to a war-torn country, with its back to the sea, to share the struggles and the sacrifices of the birth of a nation. "I tell you this kind of idealism gets me so choked up, I can't hardly talk. So I ask you now, one and all, if these noble, idealistic kids of ours can risk their lives to build a homeland for our needy brethren, can we do less than give until it hurts. . . . Speak up, let me hear your pledges. Don't be bashful, we're all friends, we know each other's Dun and

Bradstreets. . . . Rifkin, one hundred thousand. Thank you, Morry. How's about some applause for the Rifkins? . . . I have some news for you. I'm matching Rifkin's pledge and I am adding another fifty thousand in honor of that wonderful brave young couple up there on the piano. . . . Don't clap, folks, I'm only doing what comes naturally. . . . How about a little friendly competition, Morry? Gonna let me get ahead of you? . . . You know when you're licked. Well, maybe we don't have the same kind of inspiration. . . . Okay, who is next? . . . Goldstone, fifty thousand. Make it seventy-five, Oscar. You had a good year. . . . Another twenty-five in honor of Mrs. Goldstone's parents, they are celebrating their golden wedding. May they live and be well and happy to celebrate their diamond. Let's have a hand for the Goldstones. . . ."

A lace cloth was spread on the table in the banquet-hall dining room. Silver tea and coffee service gleamed. Uniformed waitresses offered dainty sandwiches and cakes. The butler stirred highballs. The office fund-raiser and Joe, Scotch on the rocks in hand, totaled pledges in one corner. Celia edged me into another. "Samuel, did you by any chance run into Ilene and Michael over there? . . . Oh, I'm so glad you did! How did she look?"

"Beautiful."

"Of course. Aren't they a stunning couple! Such a perfect match! Of course, we miss her so, but this is what we wanted. All we ever wanted was our darling's happiness. We're so pleased she chose Michael. They were childhood sweethearts, you know. And our families have been friends for ages. . . . I'll tell Carrie Eisenberg you saw them; she'll be thrilled. . . . Did they give you any idea of when they plan to return?"

"Doesn't Ilene write?"

"Ilene's never been a letter writer," she replied.

*   *   *

Two weeks after that evening, while I was dressing in a hotel room for a dinner meeting, I clicked on the radio for the 6 P.M. news. I was plugging my shirt with studs when I heard: "The body of Mrs. Michael Eisenberg, bride of a young American businessman, was washed ashore on the beach at Tel Aviv this morning. Mrs. Eisenberg had left her hotel the previous evening for a stroll on the beach. Since she was reported to have been a good swimmer, authorities are investigating the possibilities of foul play. Mrs. Eisenberg was the former Ilene Sloan of Greenwich, Connecticut, daughter of Joseph Sloan, chairman of the board of the Victory Steel Corporation."

My stud dropped. I crawled on the carpet, groping for it. Thus Ilene must have crawled and groped into the sea. No, Ilene had walked, head up and tears streaming. I could see her walking, deliberately walking, desperately walking, west, toward Sergeant Jody McCarthy.

Somehow I managed to button my dress shirt, tie a black tie, shake a chairman's hand, stumble through a speech, hearing not applause or pledges, hearing just the pounding of the surf on a distant beach before I ducked out to make a long-distance call. To Baumberg I said I was taking the midnight plane to New York; I was sick, too sick to go on with the tour. That was true. I *was* sick. With guilt. If I hadn't torn that letter up, if I'd given the man a chance to send a word, any word—yes, I love you and I always will, but what's done is done, we have our memories to live on—Ilene still might be alive. Unhappy, yes, but living, growing scar tissue. Youth is resilient; she would, somehow, have managed. But, so help me, I was prepared to murder her Aunt Jessie, the worldly and experienced confidante.

It was four in the morning when my plane arrived. I dialed Jessie's number from the field. Mark Bishop's sleep-drugged voice answered. "Jessie's up in Greenwich, at her sister's. There has been a ghastly tragedy."

A word popped into my head, an ugly word I'd picked up in post-Nazi Germany, a word unique among the vocabularies of the peoples of the globe: *schadenfreude*, meaning rejoicing in the misfortune of another. So Jessie was at her sister's house, gloating, that at last they were equals: neither had a child.

*   *   *

The huge house, gray stone, half-timbered, resembled a medieval fortress. The gardens lay in formal patterns beneath ice-polished snow; the denuded trees shivered like the weathervane

287

atop the garage, trembling North by West. My breath, drawn painfully, came white. It was close to zero in this suburb.

The butler opened the door and barred it. "You are of the family, sir?" A lapse of memory or association; he'd seen me before.

"Practically," I said.

Not enough, his stern expression warned me. "You are not from the press?" Suspicion sharpened in his oyster eyes.

"Please tell Mrs. Sloan Sam Rosenbaum is here."

"Mrs. Sloan is receiving no one."

"Then Mr. Sloan."

"Mr. Sloan cannot be disturbed."

I stuck my shoe into the opening. The butler looked distressed. Being a gentleman, he hesitated to collar me and throw me down the steps.

"If you will telephone Mr. Sloan's office, his secretary will let you know when the family is receiving."

A Western Union messenger was plodding up the driveway. I, being cold, was getting cranky. "I don't intend to go away," I told the butler, "unless I know for sure that Mrs. Sloan refuses to see me. I rather think she'll want to. If she doesn't, I should like her sister, Mrs. Bishop—she's here, I understand—to tell me this in person."

He wavered, weakening. My tone had been imperious. "One moment, sir." He reached around me to accept a sheaf of telegrams. "Now, sir, kindly wait in here." Thanks for small acts of mercy. My nose and feet were numb. I sat on an oak bench in the entrance hall, thawing, keeping my eyes low, to avoid the life-size portraits on the wall. The house was stifling and muted like a hospital, the ringing of a phone muffled by heavy doors, the tread of a maid soundless, being rubber-soled. I heard no voices, no barking of a dog.

The butler descended the majestic staircase. "Mrs. Sloan will see you. May I take your hat, your coat? . . . Upstairs, turn right. Madam's room is at the front."

Celia lay, ash-white, in a canopied bed in a room whose blinds were drawn and mirrors sheeted. Her eyes were closed, her thin arms inert on the blanket. Jessie sat beside her, gray-faced, somber, stroking Celia's hand, a sister, the way sisters ought to be. Perhaps

God does know what He's about though His ways are devious. Consider Ilene's death not altogether wasteful if it had accomplished this.

"Celia, Sam is here." Jessie's husky voice was gentle, without a trace of schadenfreude.

"Samuel!" A drowsy drawling of my name, the eyelids fluttering, slowly rising, eyes looking at, not seeing me. Cold fingers fumbled for my hand. "You were the last to see our darling." Tears spurted from the dulled eyes.

Jessie mopped them with tissue. "Try not to, dear. Try to control yourself. . . . Here, I'll raise you up a bit." She fluffed and propped a pillow behind Celia's head.

Celia's hair was burnished copper and, even in the illness of grief, immaculately coiffed. Her fingers tightened on my hand, her tears dropped, scalding, on the back of it. (In the way a mind skips around, I thought of Yuli and her restrained sorrow on a certain New Year's Eve.) "Samuel, it cannot be true. You can't believe it, can you? It's a mistake, isn't it? She was happy when you saw her, wasn't she? You told me so yourself."

I'd told her nothing of the sort. And so I looked away, avoiding her beseeching eyes.

"Tell me everything, Samuel. I want to hear every single thing, how she looked when you saw her—the people all adored her, didn't they?—every word she said to you. Each little memory is a precious jewel; we have to treasure it." Then, again, insistence on denial of what the act itself proclaimed. "They were divinely happy, weren't they?"

"He loved her dearly." That much I could say.

"Then why? Then what? Joseph's sure there's something sinister—oh, my poor, poor baby, my innocent darling—Joseph's going to get the facts. . . . Tell me, Samuel, help us out. Tell me everything you know. Did she say anything, drop any hints?"

Jessie's eyes pierced me, warning. Don't worry, my eyes assured her, I am not an idiot.

"We didn't have much chance to talk. Just a few words on a hotel terrace, before I was paged, called to the phone. Then I met them at a dinner party."

"A dinner party! Which dress was she wearing?" Celia never does step out of character.

"Something purplish-blue, low-cut, as I remember, very low."

"Bergdorf," Celia murmured. "We chose it together. She relied on my taste. Go on, Samuel, please."

"Well, she did mention she was homesick, felt alien, a foreigner. She said she knew it wasn't right for her to feel that way, she did have a kind of roots in the country, all her family had done for it."

She nodded, agreeing. "Go on. I want everything, every bit of it."

"Well, she had some trouble with the food. Shortages you expected, but what they did with what they had was unbelievable. And as I recall, she detested lemon squash and she did say she was dying for a Coke. The main impression I got was that she was homesick. Very."

I couldn't have chosen my bits and pieces of the truth more shrewdly. There was a glimmer of triumph on Celia's ravaged face. "She missed us! Do you hear that, Jessie? She missed her mother and her daddy. . . . Oh, Samuel, Samuel, we tried so hard to make our darling happy, she was all we had, we gave her everything, just everything. . . ."

Jessie hooked a chair rung with her foot, pulled the chair toward me. "Sit, Sam, you look bushed."

I denied it, being past fatigue. Nevertheless, I sat.

"Samuel, you're an angel to come running here, to bring me those last precious memories: our darling thinking of her parents, of this home. Oh, she loved it so." She gripped her hands atop the blanket, the fleshless fingers seeming frail to bear the stone and metal burden of her rings. "Yes, many an evening she'd sit home, watching television, with just her little dog for company." The tears leaped again. Jessie mopped them. "Where is Skippy? Who's taking care of him? She looked after him so lovingly. Oh, she was so tenderhearted, Samuel. Always so considerate. Remember how she was with Papa?"

Jessie's fist was at her mouth, the stopper against tears.

"And there she was, far away and homesick. She'd never mention it to Michael, she wouldn't worry him. . . . Oh, if she'd only told him, if he'd cabled Joseph, Joseph would have cabled back:

290

Bring her home, forget about the business, we have enough. Enough . . . enough. . . ." Her voice had risen, uncontrolled, hysterical. Her nervous hands flicked the blanket off.

Jessie pulled the blanket up. "Celia, if you get so upset, we'll have to ask Sam to leave."

She shot an anguished glance at me. "Don't. Please don't, Samuel," and clutched my hand again. "You're our loyal friend. You always were. So kind, so patient, helping with my lessons. And our dear mother, may she rest in peace, Mama used to be so fond of you. She'd bring you all the best treats in the store. Mama! Mama! Mama, darling, we're sending you our precious baby. Take care of her, Mama darling, until I get there. It won't be long." Her voice dribbled out, all emotion spent, yet she clung to my hand. We heard her humming, wordlessly and sweetly, a kind of lullaby. Half asleep, she droned, "Such good days. So happy, so innocent." She roused herself. Her free hand groped for Jessie's. She laid Jessie's hand atop hers and mine. "Samuel, Jessie came to me. My sister came. And here, see we are together, Jessie, you and me, the three of us, the way we used to be." Her voice faded, her lids fluttered down.

"Sedation," Jessie whispered. "She'll sleep now, I think." She edged Celia's hand off mine, tucked it beneath the blanket and crooked her finger to lead me out into the hall. "You did okay," she said.

"I want to talk to you," I said.

"I want to talk to you," she said.

"Where?" I said.

She hesitated, thinking. "In Ilene's room," she decided. "No one's there."

The blinds were drawn. She pulled them up. The feeble winter sun sifted through curtains of fine lace. It was a virginal room, the walls, carpet, furniture white, with a modest touch of gold on picture frames and dressing table accessories. The mirrors were not sheeted, a singular oversight, as though the angel of death, passing through, was permitted to see his reflection here. White boxes, leaking shredded paper, cotton batting, trailing white ribbons—wedding presents Ilene probably had not seen—were stacked against one wall. The gift cards were piled neatly on a little table for the thank-yous that never would be written in Ilene's striking penmanship. Tight-lipped, Jessie said, "Someone will have to return the loot. A fifty-dollar berry spoon from Dr. and Mrs. Bishop, back to Georg Jensen."

Near the bay of windows was a white-cushioned chaise, on it, folded, a knitted blanket of bright-colored wools. I went past it to raise a window curtain's hem. Ice glistened in a blue-tiled swimming pool, leaves, brown and sere, dappled snow heaps on the tennis court. Ilene's playground, frozen, dead. I let the curtain down.

Jessie came to stand beside me at the window. "It was suicide?" she asked.

"What advice did you give her?" I replied.

She flared, in quick anger. "Your business?"

"It is. I need to know did you or I kill her?"

"What in hell are you talking about?"

"You know damn well. You were the confidante. You advised—"

"Crap. I listened. That was all."

"She wrote him a letter. A love letter. She asked me to mail it in New York." My mouth went dry.

"Did you?" She had hold of my lapels.

I wrenched away. "I tore it up," I said.

I heard her gasp, her furious, "And when did God die and leave you boss?"

I turned to face her. "Incest is a dirty word," I said.

She went white. "What in hell are you talking about?" she repeated.

"Jody McCarthy was Ilene's brother, her half-brother. Yet you encouraged it. Any whip to hurt Celia. . . ."

Her gray eyes widened, bulged.

"Son of Joey Slomowitz," I went on, "and Dolores McCarthy, who died giving birth."

Her breath whistled. "When?"

"When Joe and Celia were on their honeymoon."

"Did he know?"

"I believe he did."

"He married Celia, knowing?"

My stomach churned. That was *why* he married Celia, I could

292

have said. I had to wait until I'd choked this down. "Jessie, didn't you wonder why Joey in all these years hasn't set foot in Grady's Mills? Why Max moved out in a hurry? Some people knew."

Her gaze stabbed me. "How did you?"

"Don't ask," I said.

"I didn't know. You must believe me I did not. Ilene mentioned his name. It meant nothing to me. John Doe. Richard Roe."

True, she'd been in Paris at that time. Joe would not have blabbed to her. And if Celia knew, which I doubted, she'd not have told her sister, in a million years.

"He came looking for his father." Her hands gripped. "What tragedy! What drama!"

And then I caught a gleam in Jessie's eyes, a peculiar expression of withdrawal. Once, previously, I'd seen that look, in the barroom of the Hotel Hiram Grady. It was the look of the instant of conception of *The Arsonists*. "Jessie, I will kill you if you turn this into corny Broadway dialogue."

She flushed. I'd caught her out. "You wouldn't have a cigarette on you?"

I didn't have; I was laying off, I said, to protect my throat. At that point smoking might have helped us both.

"Let's sit," she said. "Standing screaming at each other is no good." She lifted the bright blanket to the bed to make room on the chaise.

"I want to know, I need to know," I said, "what Ilene said to you, you said to her."

"Why?" she demanded.

"Because I want to be able to trust you here on in."

I expected indignation. Instead, she answered quietly, "Relax. You will. I'll give it to you, as much as I remember, straight." And she began a fantastic narrative.

"Out of the blue, Ilene phoned me one November day last year. 'Aunt Jessie, this is your niece, Ilene. I wonder could I come and visit you.' I was flabbergasted but, naturally, I was pleased. 'Come tomorrow, for lunch,' I said. It was a chilly morning. As usual my lousy landlord wasn't providing heat. I made a fire in the fireplace. I fixed lunch on trays to eat before the fire. She came early, before the time I'd named, this bosomy and stunning creature in a veddy-

veddy Bergdorf outfit, leading a darling little white dog who looked, I swear, exactly like Professor Einstein. Well, we sat him on a hassock. She gave him a biscuit. And there he sat, sweet and shaggy and intelligent, looking so much like the Professor that I had to ask, 'Why do you call him Skippy? Why not Einstein and be done with it?' 'Oh, that would be disrespectful. Einstein is a genius. This is just a darling mongrel.' We laughed. We started our long-postponed friendship laughing. We'd gotten acquainted, just a little, on the train going out to Papa's funeral. But all we'd talked about was Herman. It was his occasion and she did have a lot of feeling for him. Well, she made a fuss about my place—'So warm, so friendly'—but I was sure she hadn't come to see my furniture. 'Aunt Jessie, you don't mind my barging in? It's cheeky of me. You must be awfully busy writing.' I assured her I was just a housewife, hadn't put a scene on paper in I didn't know how long. And I hoped she liked my Swedish meatballs. 'Oh, I do, I do, they're delicious,' she said, but she was picking at the food. 'You were so good to let me come. You see, I had to talk to someone.' "

"Someone worldly and experienced," I broke in.

Jessie looked at me oddly. "You took the words out of Ilene's mouth."

"So I did. Go on," I said.

"Well. . . ." She moistened her lips. "I said, 'You're in love and the parents disapprove.' 'However did you guess?' 'Eppes, the old Jewish witchcraft, told me. Moreover, it's written on your pretty face, the glow, the shining eyes. I know the signs. I've seen them in my looking-glass. I wasn't born middle-aged, you know.' She flung her arms around me then. 'Oh, Aunt Jessie, I'm so glad I thought to come. I knew you'd understand. They don't. They won't.' 'He's not rich,' I said. 'That's the least part of it,' she said. 'He's Christian. Catholic.' I said 'Uh, uh,' stalling. 'Aunt Jessie, are you religious?' she asked. 'Not particularly,' I said. 'Then you don't mind intermarriage?' We were getting to thin ice. 'That depends on who is intermarrying. How mature they are.' It must have reassured her; every pisherke thinks she is mature, like me when I picked up the Simon character. 'But Aunt Jessie, would I be betraying the Jewish people, after they've gone through all that suffering, if I married out of my faith?' Now, that was ridiculous. 'Who says you would?' 'Why, Mother. She says we lost six million people in Europe. And every one of us that's left has a responsibility to remain good Jews, faithful to our noble heritage.' It tickled me, it outraged me. 'My sister, Celia, has become defender of the faith!' I must have sounded nasty. She looked hurt. Hell, this was no time to add our hostility to the confusions the girl already had. 'Intermarriage can work two ways,' I said. 'There can be either gain or loss. Ruth, the Moabite, if you recall the Bible story, was the ancestress of David, the Jewish king.' She said, 'Why, that's true, isn't it?' And her face lit up. 'I wish my parents were as unprejudiced as you.' Then I said, 'If you want to tell me, tell me. But start from the beginning, not the climax of act two. Where did you two meet?' "

"In the driveway," I said.

"How'd you know?"

"It was in the letter," I said. " 'Out of nowhere, in our driveway.' "

"Not exactly out of nowhere. Let me tell it as she told it, please. It seems she'd just taken her car from the garage that morning—it was early September; she was going into New York to register for some courses at Columbia. She almost ran down this tall Marine. He was standing in the middle of the driveway with a slip of paper in his hand, looking at the house. She braked the car, let down the window. He came over. 'Hey, does Daddy Warbucks live there?' he asked and she laughed. 'Sure, and I'm Little Orphan Annie.' She did have a sense of humor. . . ."

"And an attractive giggle," I said.

Jessie touched my hand. "You always raved about her. . . . Well, that's how they began, giggling over a comic strip. She asked the Marine was he looking for someone. He said he was looking for a Mr. Joe Sloan. She said that was her father and he asked was this the Joe Sloan who used to live on Park Avenue. She said it was and he said, 'Then he's the one I'm looking for.' She said he was at his office in New York and could she be of any help? While they chatted in the driveway, she decided he was the best-looking man she'd ever seen, silky, curly, coal-black hair; eyes a kind of violet blue; small, straight nose. . . ."

Irish and Jewish genes combine agreeably, I'd thought about the little Jody.

"But manly, straight as an arrow, broad-shouldered, magnificent in the uniform, a rainbow of overseas ribbons with battle stars and medals on his chest. 'Aunt Jessie,' she told me, 'from the minute I laid eyes on him I was a gone goose.' "

I sat up, startled. "Gone goose" was what I'd said to Celia when I first met Ilene.

"He didn't know if she'd be able to help him," Jessie was saying, "but there was no harm in asking. He was looking for his family, he said, and he'd been told Joe Sloan would know where they were. He'd lost them years ago, he said. He'd grown up in an orphanage, St. Michael's. That was when she realized he must be a Catholic, so she explained, politely, that her Sloans were a Jewish family—with their name people sometimes thought they weren't— but they couldn't have had any Catholic relatives, so he must have been misdirected. He said he'd gone to a lot of trouble getting out to Greenwich; the super at the Park Avenue apartment house had dug up this address for him. It was tough luck, not only a wild goose chase but probably the end of the line for his search. He looked so crestfallen, she said since she was driving into New York she'd be glad to give him a lift back to town. No, she wasn't worried about picking up a stranger. During the war, she'd given lifts to any number of servicemen. Besides, Skippy was in the car, for protection. . . ."

From Michael-David Eisenberg, who had allergies and sneezed, I remembered.

"Besides, she wasn't worried about this chap. He had such a nice manner, open, courteous. Well, on the way in they talked, he talked, and a blue streak, she said. He wanted to, she wanted him to. This hunting for a lost family intrigued her. She'd heard about foundlings and abandoned children, and her fairy tales were full of changelings who turned out to be princes. He told her his mother was dead, though how she died he wasn't absolutely certain. He had a gruesome memory of her—he might have imagined it, he admitted—lying bloodied at the foot of a staircase. . . ."

"His grandmother," I said. "Fell or pushed."

Jessie gave me a hard look. "And a giant of a man who must

have been his father, slapping him on the mouth to make him stop screaming. . . ."

"His grandfather," I said.

"You knew the right people. He should have come to you," Jessie said.

"The grandfather skipped before the funeral," I said. "He was never heard from afterwards."

"Except in Jody's dreams," Jessie said. "And it gave him nightmares. He'd convinced himself those two were his parents and his father had killed his mother. And if that was so, he was the son of a murderer, wasn't he? It haunted him. The Fathers at St. Michael's—Ilene said he had a real affection for them—tried to console him, told him his mother was at rest in the loving arms of Jesus and, if he prayed to Jesus to guide him in the paths of righteousness, he'd meet his mother in heaven. And if his father had sinned and had repented, he'd be washed clean in the blood of the Lamb. Ilene said she was fascinated; she'd never heard anyone talk Catholic before." She paused, thinking, "Sam, what was she like, his mother, did you know?"

Bound to keep me involved, Jessie was, to worm from me what I'd hidden for so many years. "I saw the girl once. Small and blonde. Not particularly pretty." I added, "She was seventeen."

"Oh, how rotten!" Jessie said.

I said, "Skip past history. Tell me how he got to Joe's."

"See here," she said, with a trace of irritability. "You asked for all of it. I aim to please. This passion to find his family, he told Ilene, started while he was overseas. Other guys got mail, from mothers, sisters, brothers. No letters ever came for him. 'It's cruel to have no folks,' he said. 'You need to belong to somebody.' And then her heart turned over. She said she understood how it felt to be lonely, and he said, 'You?' and she said, 'Even when you have a father and a mother, you can be very lonely.'"

I saw a ten-year-old in a pink-walled room; I heard a grave, childish voice. "Ilene really had no one," I told Jessie.

She touched my hand again. She'd sensed I, too, needed sympathy.

"Well, when he came back from overseas," she continued, "he decided he'd make an effort to locate his relatives—oh, anybody, an aunt, an uncle, a second cousin—someone who'd be glad he'd come through the war alive."

Like the children Yuli brought into Vienna, I said to myself.

"He'd decided to stay in the Marines, make that his career, so he got a leave and headed for St. Michael's orphanage. The Fathers who'd looked after him were gone; the new priests had no idea of where the old records were. He nagged till someone located a register that had his name and the name of the town he came from. *Grady's Mills.* That knocked Ilene for a loop. And he got terribly excited when she said she knew the place; she'd been there for her grandfather's funeral. Her mother'd been born there, taught high school in a town nearby. Wasn't this a coincidence? The world's small, isn't it? But the Sloans, she told him, were a Florida family. I let that pass. Why upset the girl? She told him her mother had gone to New York for a Christmas holiday, had met her father who was in business there, and it must have been love at first sight because they got engaged that week and married two months afterwards."

"My stomach can't take crap today," I said.

"Nor mine," Jessie said. "But can you imagine my sister raising a child on such bullshit? Florida family! Love at first sight! Well, Ilene said she could ask her mother whether she'd known a McCarthy family back in Grady's Mills, but she doubted her mother did; Jewish and Christian people didn't mingle there. She felt she might have offended him with that, but he said, with a smile, he hadn't mingled with any Jewish people either, till he got in the service, and then he got along fine with them. He said it, she felt, as if he meant it, not just to be polite. Well, he went to Grady's Mills. But you can't go knocking on people's doors, asking, 'Are you my aunt Tillie?' So he went over to City Hall to see if there was a birth record. The woman clerk couldn't find one. She said he needn't be surprised at that; a lot of records got mislaid or thrown out when they moved from the old Town Hall; try the County Courthouse. He tried. And if you remember, Sam, how I sweated blood trying to find Papa's tax records, you know what he was up against. Well, somebody, one of the old creeps that hang around courthouses, said the retired police chief had a remarkable memory, he might know. . . ."

298

A chill ran down to my fingertips and toes.

"Sam, are you sick?"

I denied it with a headshake. Through gritted teeth, I growled, "Son of a bitch!"

"Did I know the man? Yes, I believe I did. I called on him, didn't I? Unpleasant character. Well, at least he tried to help Jody. And from what Jody told Ilene, he acted glad to see him. 'You're a treat for sore eyes, son. Turned out right handsome.' And when he heard why Jody'd come to him he said, 'You come to the right place, boy, and if your family has any sense they'll be proud to own you.' Jody asked him did he know his father. He said he couldn't exactly say he did; he never met the chap."

I muttered, "True."

"Well, this character told Jody, 'You get on down to New York and see Joe Sloan. You tell him Durgin sent you!' " She gave me the probing look. "Sam, how did *he* know?"

"Don't ask, tell," I said.

Her stare was demanding. I shook my head and clamped my lips. She had to continue. "Well, from some New York phone book he had propping up a shelf he copied out an address for Jody. 'There must have been other Sloans in the book,' Ilene decided. 'He probably copied the wrong one.' And Jody said the way this had turned out, he meeting her, he had no right to be sore about it. Then he asked if he could buy her lunch, and right away they had a problem. He was a stranger in New York, he'd been eating in Automats and hamburger joints, he didn't want to take her there. And all the restaurants she knew were expensive, she didn't want to embarrass him by suggesting a place he probably couldn't afford. Besides, she had Skippy and most restaurants wouldn't admit dogs. Then, she got a brainstorm, the zoo cafeteria in Central Park. That's where they went. It was divine, she said, absolutely perfect, the terrace, the sun, the trees, the birds, and Skippy lying under the table like an angel (that darling little professor! They shipped him off this morning to a vet's to board, afraid his barking might upset Celia more) and Jody kept traipsing back and forth, fetching franks in rolls and chocolate ice cream and more and more coffee, always afraid he wasn't being generous enough. And between trips, he talked, about the war,

299

his buddies, his experiences, and how he felt about all he had gone through. Ilene said her heart ached when she realized how starved he'd been for a listener, for someone interested exclusively in him. Sam, that is the saddest thing, not to have a soul who knows or cares about your human worth."

And this, I thought, is why I love that woman with the dark blue eyes. She wished to know the human worth of Samuel Rosenbaum.

"They were so absorbed in one another, they didn't come up for air until five o'clock, and then she had to grab Skippy and head for her car. She wanted to ask Jody to drive back with her but eppes warned her Mama and Papa would be less than pleased, picking up a serviceman, asking him to dinner. He said he had only a few more days of leave, and could he see her again? She said, 'Of course. Tomorrow, noon, this place.' He walked her to the car. They kissed. Like brother and sister, she said."

Jessie shuddered, I shuddered.

"She told a lie that night. It was the first lie she'd ever told her mother. She said at the registrar's office at Columbia, she'd met a McCarthy girl who came from Grady's Mills. She wondered had her mother known a family of that name. Celia said there might have been McCarthys living in the Flats; Jews never went down there. Besides, Irish kids went to parochial, not public, schools, so Jewish children had no contacts with them. When she told Jody her mother hadn't been able to help, she didn't tell him why. The Jew-Goy business had begun to bother her. For instance, when he begged her to talk about herself, how she spent her time, what it was like living in the mansion, she hedged. She didn't want him knowing a Jewish family was *that* rich, she said. It's the damndest thing, I told her, this cockeyed fear of stirring up anti-Semitism. You don't know the fear is in you, until in the middle of a relationship that's going normally you begin to get sensitive. 'How wise you are,' the sweet kid said. 'I knew we were in love. I was petrified this was going to spoil it.' Well, he kissed her on the mouth when they said goodbye, no more sister-brother stuff. And it was 'Same place, same time tomorrow.' She didn't sleep that night, she said. She was trying to decide which nightgown to take; she wanted to be gorgeous for the big event. 'Aunt Jessie,' she told me. 'I've met a lot of boys, young men, but I never felt this way before. I didn't have to ask myself, should I? I knew this was right. I've always been sure love would come to me like this, out of the blue a handsome stranger was going to sweep me off my feet. Do you understand what I'm trying to say?' I said I believed I did. The body chemistry was acting up, the glands act in mysterious ways. She said, 'It's more than sex. We belong together.'"

So she'd written on the sheet of paper I'd delivered to a trashcan at the airport. Dully, I stared at the white boxes of wedding gifts, wondering how, if Ilene's belief was so strong, she'd let herself be dragged to the "wingding" at the Pierre. "Daddy's good little girl." That answer is not good enough.

"She packed her prettiest nightgown and her fanciest negligee into an overnight bag," Jessie was saying. "And Sam, she blushed when she admitted he wouldn't let her put it on, wanted her stark naked, no fool he. She'd left Skippy in his kennel, told the butler if she wasn't home for dinner, he was to tell her mother she was meeting a friend in New York, they might take in a matinee, have dinner and, if they finished dinner late, she might spend the night in town, Daddy didn't like her driving alone after dark. And that was exactly how it was. It was raining by the time she reached the zoo. They had their hamburgers indoors, got in her car, drove west. She garaged the car, took out the little suitcase, and they went to Radio City Music Hall. That was *his* idea, he'd heard about the place, she'd never been there either. She couldn't remember what the picture was and it didn't matter, something more important on their minds. When it got too hot to handle, they ducked out and ran through the rain. To the Waldorf. That was *her* idea. The rain must have cooled her off, because she said she was perfectly calm and collected when she stood beside him while he registered, and, of course, she was wearing gloves, so the room clerk couldn't guess she had no wedding ring. And in the room, on the bed, it was the divine rhapsody. I bowed low, congratulating her; if this was her first try, she'd had extraordinary luck. She gave me a doesn't-everybody? look. 'With most virgins,' I said, 'it's great expectations, some pain, practically no rapture.' And she looked at me so smugly that for the first and only time I felt like smacking her." Jessie laughed, a short, harsh laugh. "Sam,

301

when Mark came home that night, I told him about my visitor and we kidded about the virgin's ecstasy and Mark said, 'Either the lad's a genius or the girl's a horseback rider.' "

I saw a beach in Tel Aviv and heard Michael-David's drunken voice. I shuddered again. The echoes had become unbearable.

Jessie eyed me, anxiously. "You'd rather not hear this?"

I dredged up spittle, swallowed it. "Get to the morning after," I said.

"You're right. This is neither time nor place for my vulgarity." She stroked my arm, once more extending sympathy.

"Well, in the morning he begged her not to leave him. 'I'll be back,' she told him. 'For keeps, I mean,' he said. And she said she expected her parents would have some objections, but when they met him, when they realized this was true love. . . . 'They want me to be happy and I am,' Ilene said. Well, all hell broke loose as soon as she got home, and it started with a petty thing. Celia's car had developed carburetor trouble, she'd needed it to drive to some luncheon in Stamford. Ilene had promised to go, too, but it had completely slipped her mind, which was understandable. Celia had counted on going in Ilene's car. When, by one o'clock, her daughter hadn't showed, she had to have the butler drive her in his little Ford. She was furious when Ilene turned up. 'May I ask which friend of yours was so interesting you forgot your obligations?' "

Jessie had grown hoarse with talking. She tapped my arm. "Wait. Let me get a glass of water. Want one, too?"

I didn't. Until she returned, I stared at the knitted blanket, thinking, This is out of place here. The colors are garish, like a G.I.'s overseas ribbons.

She came back saying, "I wish I knew where Joe hides his Scotch. Both of us could use a drink. You look like warmed-over death. Where was I? Oh, yes, Celia's tantrum. Well, this time the girl didn't lie. She couldn't and she didn't want to, and she came right out with it. And Celia screamed, 'You spent the night with him? Are you a tramp?' And Ilene said, 'I'm going to marry him.' And Celia said, 'Your father will have a stroke.' And Joe damn near did. Ilene said she tried to talk quietly, rationally, to them, to explain how this man had swept her off her feet—why, it wasn't so very different from their own romance; that had been love at first sight, hadn't it? Sam, for God's sake, take it easy, don't die on my hands. She told them how wonderful he was, and even, poor chick, tried to butter up that miserable Joey, saying, 'He looks a little like you, Daddy, maybe that's what first attracted me, though he isn't Jewish. He's Irish, with wonderful blue eyes.' My sister gasped, 'A Catholic!' My brother-in-law asked, 'What does he do for a living?' When she told him Jody was a Marine non-com, he barked, 'Are you out of your mind?' So she felt she had to get past the religious prejudice and the snobbery and she began to tell them how Jody had lost track of his family, how when she met him in the driveway he had a slip of paper in his hand, look-ing for a Joe Sloan who might tell him where to find his relatives. Joe asked his name. When she told him he went livid; she was sure he was going to have that stroke. He poured himself a stiff drink, a couple of drinks, and sat with his head in his hands, moan-ing, and Celia went to bed with a migraine. And Ilene realized there wasn't any use trying to talk to them right now. By morn-ing, she'd decided she was a woman, she'd do what she had to do, which was be with Jody, sleep with him and make the most of whatever time was left. She packed her bag, drew some money from the bank and off she went." Jessie moistened her lips with her tongue. "I'll spare you the details of make-the-most-of; I got it play by play. . . . When she came home from New York, her parents didn't know how to treat her. They were cold, they were hurt, they were angry. They talked too much to her, or they didn't talk to her at all. They looked ashamed whenever they looked at her. They made noises about sending her to Florida, to California, to a psychiatrist. And when his letters began to arrive, they badgered her ferociously. The more she tried to explain how much she and Jody meant to one another, how instinctive and complete their attraction to each other was, the more furious Joe became. He was like a raving maniac, she said. 'And why, Aunt Jessie? Because he isn't rich? Because he isn't Jewish?' She was sure and I was sure it was entirely the difference of religion and the finances. I was thinking *Abie's Irish Rose;* she was rewriting *Romeo and Juliet,* with a happy ending. Neither of us for a minute guessed it was Greek tragedy. Those weeks must have been a nightmare to the girl. It's a miracle she didn't crack. But love

303

conquers all, as they say, and apparently that kept her on her feet. She said she took up knitting to calm her nerves, but Celia ragged her about the afghan she was making—must be that one on the bed, gay, isn't it?—'Taking up with riffraff, you've even lost your refined taste. Such loud, common colors!' Can you imagine that! Well!" Jessie breathed in, heavily. She must have been as tired as I. Surely she, too, had had no sleep. "The story's almost finished. Ilene said, 'Aunt Jessie, he'll be here Christmas week. He wants us to get married then, he say's he'll convert, do anything to please them. But I don't know what to do. Mommy keeps having her migraines; she looks dreadful. And Daddy raves. He says if I don't break off with Jody, he'll report him to the F.B.I., put him in prison, do something terrible to him. Why? Because he loves me? Is that a crime? I'd go down to City Hall and marry him, but I just can't bring myself to hurt my parents so. After all, I'm all they have, I'm their only child. But I can't give Jody up. We belong together, don't you see? So please advise me, Aunt Jessie. I'll be guided by what you say. I know you're worldly, experienced.' " She glanced at me, self-conscious. She drew a deep breath. "And here I go, Jessie, the oracle. This is what I said to her and this is all I said. 'I wish I could advise you. I'm flattered you came to me, but it's too late. You see, I never had the chance to get to know you, and so I have no right to tell you what to do. Not knowing you, I don't know how much you have to invest, how much strength and guts, how much capacity for inflicting pain on those you love, how much for creating your own happiness. All I can do is wish you wisdom and good luck.' Then, I said, 'He'll be back in town; you'll sleep with him again. Suppose you get pregnant. What contraceptive information do you have?' 'Why, he takes care of that,' she said. 'The Marines provide things.' 'For the prevention of disease and the inhibition of pleasure,' I said. 'One thing I can do for you. I want you to go up to see my husband, Dr. Mark Bishop. His office is on Park Avenue. I'll tell him why I'm sending you. It's out of his particular territory but he'll see you're fitted with a pessary.' " She halted, bowed her head, sat silent, fingers tightly knotted on her lap, before, suddenly, she cried, "Sam, kick me in the ass. I'm the one responsible. I killed that sweet girl."

I stared. Had she gone off her rocker?

"Sam, don't you see? I had the whole thing in my lap. I could have saved the girl, if I hadn't been so goddam smart, so non-interfering, if I'd said, 'Kid, you love this man, he loves you. Go to it. Take your chances! . . .'"

I put my hand on hers. It was my turn to offer sympathy. "You're talking like a fool. Joe couldn't have let it continue. He'd have done something drastic—to him, to her." I stopped. "Did he?"

She gaped at me. "What do you mean?"

"I'm not sure what I mean. But Michael-David told me in Tel Aviv there was a long period when he couldn't reach her on the phone. Out of town, the butler said."

"A hospital? A crack-up?"

"I wouldn't be surprised," I said.

She shook her head. "That I wouldn't know. All I know is she didn't turn up at Mark's office and she never got in touch with me again. Next time I saw her, she was floating in tulle, so I assumed blood will tell after it cools. She was being the dutiful Jewish daughter, marrying a clean-cut Jewish boy. I thought she looked a little hectic at the wedding, which might have been champagne; they were pouring it from spigots. She let me kiss her cheek, a cool thank-you to my Mazel Tov, never letting on that she and Einstein had spent an afternoon in my living room. And being invited had amazed me, too. Maybe Ilene had suggested it, her way of showing me she no longer needed my advice. Maybe Celia was mellowing, who knows? I did phone when I got the invitation to say Mazel Tov and try to get a line on what led up. All I got was a dither. 'The young people surprised us. Oh, we shouldn't have been. They've been sweethearts since they were children. And our families are friends. His parents are giving Ilene her flat silver—we're buying their house and furniture—service for twelve. Jensen, the pattern's registered. You might fill in some serving pieces.' Not a whisper, not a hint, there had been anything amiss. That poor kid, that sweet kid. . . ."

I leaned over and I kissed her forehead. It was my apology for the word I'd brought along to tag her with, the ugly schaden-freude. "Everyone acted with the best intentions," I said. "And at

305

least one good was accomplished. It brought you and Celia together."

The tension snapped in her. "Someone in this family has to be a mensch," she cried.

The bedroom door opened. The butler stood there, stern and disapproving. "Mrs. Bishop, we have been looking for you. Mrs. Sloan is awake. She is calling for you. Mr. Sloan has been informed Mr. Rosenbaum is in the house. Mr. Rosenbaum, will you be good enough to join him in the library." Frowning, he crossed the room to let down the blinds.

Joe, haggard, in a robe of purple silk, sat behind a massive desk of wormholed oak, riffling telegrams and cables. The Eisenbergs, she large and rawboned, he skinny, gray of hair and mustache, huddled on a prayer bench like apprehensive patients in a dentist's waiting room.

"Sam!" Joe greeted me peremptorily. "What was the idea of shmoosing with Jessie when you knew I needed you? Why didn't you come straight to me?"

Excuse, please, the "lay leader" was kept waiting. I was too tired to answer.

"What's the name of the Chief of Police of Israel?" he roared at me.

With all the things I needed to remember—and remember to forget—this detail eluded me.

"Hurry up! I got to put a phone call through. Person to person."

"Why?" I managed to ask.

"Why? Are you an imbecile?" he bellowed. "We have to run this down, to the ground. I demand an investigation. Thorough. After all I did for that country, that's the least they owe me." He pounded the desk.

Let the poor bastard bang and yell. He'd blow his brains out if he gave himself a chance to think.

"Till I have the facts, not one penny of my money, not a dollar of my pledge—you heard me, Sam, I pledged one hundred fifty thousand right here in this house—not one penny till they catch the murderers."

"Have you heard from Michael?" I asked.

"What has my poor boy got to do with this?" Mrs. Eisenberg had a loud, imperious voice, pitched for holding forth. "The Irgun killed her. The Stern gang gangsters."

It was preposterous. So was all of this. The truth was something no detective in Israel would run to the ground. I knew that truth. Now, through me, Jessie knew most of it. But Ilene's father also knew it and he did not dare acknowledge it.

"When I saw Ilene," I began, "she was homesick and depressed. Michael and I had a long talk. He was worried about her, sincerely concerned. He wanted her to see a doctor. She refused. I urged him to bring her home. He said he didn't dare, he had to show his father-in-law how good a businessman he was."

The Eisenberg expressions changed from relief, to gratitude, to glaring at Joe.

"When I was here a couple of weeks ago, I didn't tell you this because Michael begged me not to. He was struggling with his problem, trying to be a husband, be a man. . . ."

"My poor boy," his mother moaned. "What he had to live through."

"Ilene liked to walk alone on the beach. And when a young person is depressed. . . . I advised Michael to get her home, to a psychiatrist. . . ."

Joe slapped the desk, turning as purple as his robe. "You trying to tell me my daughter was crazy? She was well, in perfect health; the best doctors told us. Why, before she got engaged, she was two months in the country, resting in the sunshine. . . ."

He'd let it slip. He'd filled in the missing link. There had been a crack-up, and the cure had failed. Poor Ilene. Poor Michael-David. Let's settle for poor everybody, I thought wearily.

I said, "Look, Joe, call the Chief of Police, satisfy yourself. But if you want my advice, just bring her home. That's all she asked."

I turned to go. I hadn't realized Jessie had been in the doorway, eavesdropping. She linked an arm into mine. "You handled it okay. Now get the hell away from this loathsome family and stay away till we invite you to a funeral."

*   *   *

307

Last week's sooty snow blocked the gutters; the threat of fresh snowfall hung in the air, raw, marrow-penetrating. Mink cloaks streamed into the chapel where a white casket stood, blanketed with white orchids. It was the funeral home's largest chapel. Every pew was filled. I recognized the "lay leaders" who had been at the testimonial dinner for Joseph Sloan. I sat with the professionals. We listened to piped organ music before the family mourners filed in: the Eisenbergs, Michael between his parents, pale as death, with lusterless, bewildered eyes; Celia, tottering, heavily veiled, Joe, gripping her arm, his face gray and unshaven beneath a black homburg; Jessie behind them, erect, unveiled, solemn, Mark Bishop's arm around her; and after them, an old man whose white eyebrows bristled like mustaches, held up by a woman with henna hair and a wrinkled monkey face. Max Slomowitz, by God. I thought, What a tragic thing it is for an old man to outlive a grandchild. Then I thought, Max, you bought this tragedy. You paid for it. Then, I thought, Rosenbaum, you handled the transaction, you were the paymaster. There was a beginning. There had to be an end. Rosenbaum, the final touch. We can't pass the buck to Jehovah when we are interfering fools. Ah, but everyone had good intentions. Pave the Autobahn with them.

There was a eulogy; there were prayers. I didn't hear a word. Leo Wullstein had to nudge me to stand up when a rabbi, intoning, "Yea, though I walk through the valley of the shadow," followed the wheeled casket, leading the mourners out. We waited in our pews, each row emptying in turn.

At the rear of the chapel, where the procession veered toward the exit, I saw a young Marine, with a bowed head of coal-black hair. Jody McCarthy's father had passed so close he could have touched him with his hand.

Out of the crowd that was milling on the pavement, waiting for the undertaker's limousines, a man came up and tapped my arm. I recognized Shimon Cottler, whom Joe Sloan's affidavit had rescued. He drew a buxom woman through the mob. "I believe you have before met my wife." She looked so much like Ida Weiss, I got the creeps. "Mr. Rosenbaum," her husband said, "I have a question. They will be sitting shiva. My wife and me, we have never been invited to the house. Will it be proper if we pay the visit?"

"You see," the woman broke in, "there are so few of us now left, mir darfen zach tulenin." She spoke in Yiddish altogether and I leave the last of what she said, as is, because I love its quality. "We have to hold each close and lovingly" is as near as English comes to it. For me it says all I want to remember about Ilene and Jody.

"Go to Celia," I told Shimon Cottler's wife.

She thanked me effusively and went on to ask if I would honor them by coming for a Sunday dinner at their flat. I said yes, maybe yes, I'll try, I'll let you know, full well aware I'd not turn up.

Thirteen

Celia clung. I was the thread, the link, the repository of a tiny string of pearls, the selected words of Ilene in the weeks before her death. Also, I was a crutch for the dark days when Celia stumbled through the valley of the shadow. One crutch. The other was a psychiatrist, who received fifty dollars for each fifty-minute hour. Mrs. Sloan, the doctor had concluded, wasn't a suitable candidate for psychoanalysis; we'll give her supportive therapy, i.e., sedative and antidepressant pills and conversation biweekly.

I gave her conversation, too, at my own expense. Celia used to phone me and suggest meeting her for lunch. On my salary, it's impractical to shell out twenty dollars for a snack for two and, with my temperament, uncomfortable to let a woman pay as if I were her gigolo. Hence, I stuck to hamburger at two twenty-five while she studied menus with absorption, as if she was planning the Last Supper. "Do advise me, Samuel, which shall I have today: the sweetbreads sous cloche or the blini with caviar?"

The tab ran high; the conversation ran to monologues, hers. "Samuel, what would I ever do without you? You're the only one who ever really understood me. Perhaps" (with a coy sadness) "you're the one I should have married." (Me, thinking, Ma'am, it's polite to wait until you're asked, and feeling queasy, since I had been the deus ex machina.) "Oh, I'm not criticizing Joseph. In his way he's wonderful—just see how generous he is! How much he gives! Oh, his heart is broken too. But men must never show it. They have to go on, be strong. He can't bear to discuss it. You know how he adored Ilene, though she wasn't his whole world the way she was mine. All I ever wanted, hoped for, prayed for, was Ilene's happiness, Samuel, I tried so hard. Why, I gave her everything, did everything for her. How could she have done this to me?"

Ask what *you* did to her. You and Joe and I. You won't, you do not dare. That's opening up Pandora's box. Moreover, if you blame yourself, you're guilty, you're condemned, deserving punishment. And punishment is painful. I know, I'm taking it. "Mir darfen zach tulenin," we who were partners in the crime against Ilene.

Helping her on with her sables, an accidental contact with Celia's nape could make me jump as if I'd touched a lizard, which was irrational and far from charitable. The woman needed pity. But it's easy to despise and hard to pity those whose lives are spent in vanity, acquiring show-off things. What more was Ilene to her mother than another display piece?

I told myself Celia didn't mourn the girl, she mourned the loss of her. And she was one of those—this I'd realized when I saw her after Herman died—who make the most of mourning, who grieve too long, too blatantly, needing this to claim attention. Undoubtedly, Herman's death had touched her, severance from the source leaves every orphaned child bewildered, lost. Yet her exaggerated grieving, then, had hinted at mixed feelings: self-reproach—why didn't I keep Papa in my house, provide a real home for him?—and guilt because there was relief, a burden lifted, a silent critic, censor, gone.

With Ilene it was different. The girl had been the compensation for all her disappointments and frustrations, her sublime achievement and her triumph over Jessie. "Samuel, you're the only one to whom I can talk. My sister doesn't come to see me anymore, she doesn't even call me on the phone. Too busy, I presume. Of course, she never lost a child."

"Nor had one to love."

"Whose fault is that?" The old waspishness, though less strident than before. "I'm sure I'm not the one who deprived her of motherhood."

One thing she never mentioned, nor did I, was Jody. She'd known he was her daughter's lover, Jessie's secondhand account had made that explicit. Did she sometimes tell herself, At least my daughter had this joy before she died? Did she shudder at the illicit relationship? *Did she know?* Perhaps the head-shrinker pried the truth from her. Perhaps she hid it from him, too. Much was at stake, not the least of which was the legend of the pure and innocent Ilene.

She used a trick to bind me to her self-deception. After every lunchtime session, a gift-wrapped package arrived at my place: monogrammed handkerchiefs, tortoise-shell-backed brushes, ties from Sulka's, with Mrs. Sloan's card and her E-for-Excellent penmanship: "In profound gratitude to one who understands." Out of politeness, I would phone and hear, "When shall we two meet again?" In thunder, lightning and in rain.

Jessie never phoned me—nor I her; we'd said all we had to say to one another that morning in Ilene's room. And Joe I never saw. I couldn't have borne the sight of him. Baumberg dealt with him directly and, being shrewd, induced him not merely not to renege on his pledge to the Committee but to make a new and larger one, as a starter toward the construction of a memorial to Ilene, a hostel for immigrant girls in Tel Aviv. Further, Baumberg suggested Mrs. Sloan might, as soon as she felt equal to the task, wish to plan the decor of the Ilene Sloan Memorial House. Mrs. Sloan's superb taste was widely known. This might be therapy for her. Successful fund-raisers have to be psychologists.

I respected Baumberg's talents though I wasn't crazy about how he applied them to me. Straight off the plane, he'd propelled me into the world of high-pressure fund-raising, a multi-million-dollar business that had been burgeoning while I'd been herding Jews onto illegal ships. It was as though the only point and purpose of my years abroad had been to raise the campaign quota in Hotseplotz.

Overseas, I'd been reasonably contented. That was a person helping people and these were people who might have been myself. With them I felt normal size. When Baumberg sent me out to shnorr for them it diminished me, as well as them.

Let's be clear about one thing: I am not opposed to charity. I learned it at my mother's knee. As far back as I can recall, Mama kept a slotted blue box with a Star of David on the shelf above the kitchen sink, and into it she dropped small change whenever she returned from Herman's Grocery. Itinerant collectors for

Yeshivas and orphanages in Palestine always got a glass of tea, a slice of cake and a dollar bill from her. Zadokah, she taught me, was a mitzvah that secured you standing room beside God's throne, and blessed are the poor; if they weren't poor and numerous where would you and I procure mitzvahs? And when I took that junket across the continent, during the war, talking hush-hush to small groups to get cash for ships, that also was person to people, to people who were scared. In the gas chambers all Jews are brothers, share and share alike. This now was altogether different. This was they the shleppers, we the benefactors, separate entities.

Europe had been the womb. The umbilical cord was cut by six million deaths. Overnight, the child, the Jewish American, became head of the family, a big man, with two feet planted on this continent, his stance firmed here at last by—this is sickening irony—the belated stirring of the Christian's conscience and his grudging admiration of a military victory against odds. The new man fed the children who were scattered over many lands or gathered into Israel. He provided clothing, shelter, paid the doctor's bills, like any head of family. However, since giving also is a greediness, he sought his status, built his stature here through misery and courage overseas. He functioned in a world whose yardstick for the measure of a man was, How much does he give?

In that world I spent my days and nights. Baumberg kept me on the road, telling the saga of the "illegals," reciting shmaltzy anecdotes, peddling rachmonas, peddling pride as well. *We* have won a war, *we* have created a state.

In all these travels I never met a poor tailor like my father, a humble groceryman like Herman Weiss, or any Jew out of lower-income brackets, or even of the lower middle, the haberdashery clerks, the bookkeepers, the school teachers, the four-, five-, six-thousand-dollar-a-year men. They existed, in shabby streets uphill, across railroad tracks, or in the brand-new ghettos for young couples starting out, in boxes of cement and shingle where the rooms were tiny, the mortgages big. I didn't find them in the hotel banquet halls or country clubs where the roast chicken, peas and carrots were dished out and the pledge cards signed. Out of a disaster without class distinctions, we had created caste.

313

But you cannot build a state with pennies in a blue box, nor feed the hungry, heal the sick, with sympathy and prayers. So forget that there are Yulis who read Shakespeare in the ruins, who have lost a world and slowly start to build another one, who enrich others with the richness in themselves and know that do-for-others also is a selfishness. And don't remind big givers that Jewish soldiers pause in the middle of a war to listen to the *Rhapsody in Blue*. Fear, starvation, degradation open up the purse.

I flew in fog and rain and blizzard while local chairmen stewed and made long-distance calls to Baumberg. "Where in hell is your speaker? What kind of sloppy outfit do you run? You're sure, positive, he'll show?" At airport snack bars, I braced myself with paper cups of coffee for a grueling day and after midnight coaxed myself to sleep, counting airports in lieu of sheep. See here, I tried to tell myself, you're the bridge. You have seen. Ergo, you must communicate. A sense of mission kept me going while I grew thin and testy with awareness of the self-aggrandisement behind the façade of philanthropy.

Let me be fair. I did meet men and women of worth and dignity who knew the full score, had known it since the Munich Beer Hall putsch, who, given choice, would have signed their checks "anonymous" and mailed them without fanfare, who graciously surrendered their head-table seats to parvenus, whom this *koved* might induce to increase a pledge. And there were individuals who revived my spirit intermittently.

Like the pants manufacturer who was the campaign chairman in a midwestern city, a lonely ex-New Yorker, who instead of dragging me to his split-level duplicate for coffee and tuna salad sandwiches, led me to a bar and discussed Montesquieu until 2 A.M. Now Montesquieu is one of numerous philosophers I have never read. I didn't tell him this. I drank my beer and let him talk philosophy. Bless him, he took me for an educated man, not merely a campaign utility.

Like the reporter, a skinny Yid, who turned up at my hotel to do a publicity interview and shyly asked my frank opinion, should he go to a kibbutz? Except he called it kibbitz and was painfully embarrassed when I corrected him, pointing out that kibbutz life was real and earnest, hard, dedicated work, no kidding around.

314

Whatever, he meant it, honestly he did, and if I gave the nod, he was prepared to walk out on central heating, ice cubes and T-bone steaks to till the fields and dodge the mortar fire to help to make a state. Since he treated me with reverence—I'd been there, I'd seen it happen, I was practically a national monument—I refrained from quizzing him, as Yuli had quizzed me, about his motivation: did he see himself as hero or as saint?

And there was Susan Rabinowitz, née Susan Jones, previously Jonas, who had a pixie face and a Southern accent so thick you could spread it on your bread. She came forward on the steps of the modernistic Temple where I'd just delivered my set piece. "I'm your airport transportation," she announced, and led me to a red station wagon bigger than the hook-and-ladder of my home-town fire department. "I enjoyed your talk." She used this standard opening while she switched the ignition on. "You made me feel like I was there. A deep, way-down Jew, not the Sue-come-lately that I am." Then, as she guided the station wagon dexterously past trailer trucks, moving vans and home-bound-for-supper motorcars, she spoke about her background: a daughter of the Confederacy, no foolin'; her great-grandfather had owned slaves—no plantation, just two for scut work on the premises; her grandfather had fought in Jeff Davis's army; and her father, who had a Georgia textile factory, had played footsie with the Ku Klux Klan, to get their cooperation in running union organizers out of town. Her mother, queen bee of the snobs, had had the family surname changed from Jonas to Jones, sent Sue to a finishing school run by high-church Episcopalians, made her bob her nose, and positively tore the roof off when Sue met Hy Rabinowitz of Russian-Jewish parentage, a liberal, a damn Yankee and a damn fine man, and declared she planned to marry him. "Couldn't have been worse if I'd chosen a Nigrah. We had to elope and never darken our door.

"Well, suh, along came Mister Hitler. And Hy said, 'Sue, the both of us have Jewish grandmothers. We're for burning, too.' And I decided now was when to find out what they'd burn me for. So I stole me a Gideon Bible from a hotel room and I read the Book. Fascinatin'. Found out where Hollywood got the plots for all those sexy pictures. Found out I had a family tree that was really what to brag about. And decided, like they say, if rape is inevitable, just re-lax and enjoy it." Her horn started braying at a farmer in a Model T. "Those poky drivers slay me. Hope he don't make us miss your plane. . . . Well, suh, you'd think I was corn-ball if I told you I found God, so let's just say I got interested in Him. I do have doubts He is all-wise, though I haven't yet found anyone that's smarter than He is. We did join the Temple, Hy and me, as a kind of act of solidarity, but we decided we would play the deal the way it gave us pleasure. Not think of bein' Jews as pain and sufferin', a cross to bear, if you'll pahdon the expression, but as somethin' extra-special excitin' and impohtant. Nothing borin', I can tell you, about bein' Jewish. Always something comin' up."

She tried to pass the Model T. The cars were coming fast and frequent in the opposite direction; she had to quit trying. "Hy and me, we talked about keepin' kosher. Hy said it wasn't fair to ask a Georgia girl to give up crab and shrimp because they didn't have refrigeration in Asia Minor four thousand years B.C. But I do keep the Sabbath holy and I light the candles and I feel a special quality comes in my house every time I do. Not sanctity, exactly. Continuity. The belongin' to history. . . . Well, well, here's that airpoht. Did you think we'd never make it? . . . I do want to thank you, suh, for comin' here to us. And I do wish if you get a chance, you thank those people over in Israel for needin' us, for cuttin' us in on their terrific deal." She braked at the terminal entrance. I grabbed my two-suiter and began to sprint. "Remember," she called after me, "just you re-lax and enjoy it."

These three helped, but not enough.

Passover week, when no meetings were scheduled, I decided to go to Grady's Mills, to sleep in my old bed and, perchance, to dream of Yuli. I'd written her; she'd written me. A letter from her had been waiting when I stopped off in New York. She'd left the orphanage in France, taken a position in Geneva, an administrative post concerned with refugees though not exclusively with children, and this, it struck me, was further progress in her healing. Her letters were friendly, warm, though never with a mention of coming here, to me. I didn't urge. Baumberg would have sent her on the road, exploited her beauty, her tragic personal history, to haul the shekels in, and it might have sickened her as it did me.

Many things sickened me in the early months of 1949, especially the messages I found whenever I checked into the residential hotel where I'd leased a furnished room and kitchenette, to park my clothes, my travel souvenirs and books. The desk clerk wore a smirk whenever he handed me my key and the sheaf of switchboard slips. "Mrs. Sloan called. Please phone her." He must have concluded Celia was my mistress, God forbid! I'd call, lamely explain I was between trains or planes or all tied up with conferences, sorry I couldn't make a luncheon date, dodging, and ashamed because I did, and furious with Celia because she made me feel ashamed.

This time I didn't phone but raced to make the train. A two-hundred-pounder shared the coach seat with me. He introduced himself. "I'm in auto accessories. What's your racket, Bud?" When I tried to tell him, his cheeks blew up like a red balloon. He opened his newspaper, fidgeted, folded the paper, got up, marched ahead to the smoking car without a word or glance. I stared at the Jersey flats, thinking, We haven't licked it yet.

My mood was sour when I reached Sixth Street, and my parents didn't sweeten it. They'd been on company behavior in New York. At home, they were just old folks with hardening arteries, cantankerous and quarrelsome, bruising one another with all-but-forgotten grudges, unsettled petty scores. Papa had retired right after the first of the year—I'd advised him to; his fingers were too arthritic for the needle and the pressing iron; my salary could take care of them. Mama's housekeeping had grown slipshod, her cooking insipid; only the quality and the goodwill remained. Add to this the fustiness of an old house and the stench of Passover borsht fermenting. Our Seder was painful. Mama kept shrieking, "So skip already, Papa, get finished; Semmy is hungry," then berating me, "What'sa matter you don't eat my knoedlach? You don't like? For you, special, I made double portion." Out of mashed granite.

The knoedlach were hard rock in my belly when, in the morning, Walter Leeds phoned to say Sylvia had learned, via the kosher butcher, that I'd be home for Yom Tov and would I come right

317

over to his house? Sol Katz was there; they wanted my opinion on a matter of policy. No use protesting I was incognito here; I knew and he knew I knew whence my pay check came.

Crossing First Street on the way to Brookfield Heights, a spare, gray-haired woman, going the other way, eyed me, continued crossing, veered, caught up and tweaked my sleeve. "You *are* Sam Rosenbaum. . . . You don't remember me?"

I lied and said of course I did.

The eyes behind her spectacles were shrewd. "You don't and I cannot blame you. You haven't seen me in I don't want to think how many years. Jane Ehling. At the library. You were my most voracious reader."

I reached for one of the thin, ridged hands that gripped a frayed straw shopping bag. "How could I forget you!"

"Easily." Her laugh was a self-conscious cackle. "All the exciting places you have been. I've read your articles in the *News-Record*. About Palestine."

"Israel," I corrected.

"Of course. I keep forgetting, it's so new. But so very thrilling. Do you know"—again, the genteel cackle—"I do believe I'm jealous of you people. Rising like Phoenix from the ashes. Fulfilling prophecies and making miracles."

"We paid a price in lives," I said. "And a modern miracle takes hard, grubby work."

"Oh I know, I realize. Sam—you don't mind my calling you Sam? You were one of my boys—it's a joy, a fulfillment, for a woman like myself, when one of those whom I helped to discover books, becomes a writer. . . ."

I blushed, mumbling a belittlement of my literary accomplishments. She patted my shoulder, there, there. "I'm proud of what you have been doing and know many people in this city are proud that one of ours has helped to make history. We have so few celebrities." She paused, her forehead crinkling. "We had a girl, a little fat girl, who went to New York and Hollywood, who wrote plays. I haven't seen a word about her in 'Folk You Know' in years. Where is she, do you know? What's she doing nowadays?"

"Housekeeping in New York," I said.

"What a waste! She should be doing creative things."

I didn't argue; I wasn't in the mood.

"Let me see, there was a sister, wasn't there? I don't believe I knew her well. She seldom came to the library. The other I recall distinctly. She wanted an adult card when she was just a tyke; her chin barely reached my desk."

My shoes shuffled, impatient to be on my way. Miss Ehling detained me, hand upon my sleeve.

"Sam, I would be so happy—and I know other people here who'd be—if we could have a small share in the great work you people are doing." She hesitated, fingering the straw handle. "People like myself, who have very little money, only goodwill and ideas. I've been thinking especially about the children, those children from the concentration camps; I've been wondering whether they know how to play, whether anybody's thought of getting toys for them. . . ."

I wanted to interrupt, to speak about priorities, blankets, shoes, powdered milk, vitamin pills. Her shining eyes, the eager quaver of her voice, stopped me.

"I'm sure if I tacked up a notice in our Children's Room, asking the youngsters to bring their dolls and games, their stuffed animals and little trucks, the toys they've outgrown, we'd collect a carload in no time. We could send it as a personal gift from the children of Grady's Mills."

"It's a beautiful idea," I said. "Why don't you discuss it with Walter Leeds? He's the Jewish Aid Committee chairman here."

"Oh, but that's a charity." She shook her head. "That isn't what I mean. My idea is sharing, children with children, the one-world idea."

I said I was on my way to Walter's, I'd speak to him about it, she'd surely hear from him. "The idea does you credit; the spirit, even more," I said.

"Bless you and thank you," Miss Ehling said.

Walter, bald and portly, met me at his front door. "What kept you? Sol has to get back to the store," he said as he led me to Sol Katz in the basement rumpus room.

Sol, it struck me, had grown smaller, shrunken, a wattled turkey neck above his four-in-hand, eyes rheumy behind owlish horn-rimmed spectacles, white hair thin across a speckled scalp, teeth years younger than his face, a kind of pathos in his trappings of prosperity, the hand-tailored gray suit, the zigzag of initialed handkerchief in breast pocket, the white carnation in lapel. He wheezed when, without rising, he stretched up a hand and said, "Welcome home, Sammy. I hear you did good work."

I dropped into the chair beside him.

"I was hoping to hear news from you," he said.

I spread my hands. "You know how it was."

"We lost them." Behind the thick lenses, his eyes filled. "I kept on hoping."

Walter sprawled on a settee, bit off the end of a cigar, spat, glanced tentatively toward Sol, struck a match.

"Smoke," Sol said, as if permission had been asked. "I gave up cigars. The last couple years since I started worrying about Yossi, my asthma got real bad. My Irwin—Isie, you remember him?— nags me to retire, move to Arizona; he could run the store. With Nina. Nina is his wife. She was Nettie Rogoff. You remember her? She advises on the ladies' fashions. Children, a big house, Hadassah, the Sisterhood, a head for business, too. Some girl!"

Vaguely, I recalled Nettie Rogoff had had a sister, Pearl, Isie a sister, Bella. I didn't ask what had become of them. I didn't especially care.

"I had a pleasant surprise walking over here." I got right down to business. "Ran into Jane Ehling, the librarian." I told them what she had proposed.

Sol looked over at Walter. "It's a good idea," he said, diffidently.

Walter scowled. "Great. And who will pack and ship?"

"The Bon Ton could pack and ship." Sol, I gathered, liked the suggestion, though by his tone and manner he deferred to Walter, even as Walter, in a way, deferred to him. Both of them were the machers here: Sol, the old settler with self-made success and the tradition of caring; Walter, the aggressive, ambitious newcomer.

Walter hooked his cigar into a standing ash receiver's clip. "Sam, for once use your head. Should we hold up a shipment of groceries Israel needs because we got a load of one-eyed Teddy bears?" His lower lip came forward truculently. "Listen, Sam, I will tell you exactly what this is. The Goyim want to ride our coattails. Be free-loaders on the Jewish victory. We win a war; we show the world what Jewish courage is. Now, everybody wants to get in on the act."

"Why not?" Sol asked mildly. "Before we had no friends. Now we have. What's the sense to push away?"

"Listen, Solly, you and I are partners. We run the drives together. Right? We make our quota every year. Right? We talk things over, you and me. We come to decisions. Joint. But here is where we separate. I say, and I mean every word, we shouldn't let these sentimental Goyim in the deal. They start this toy campaign, they louse up ours. They grab the newspaper publicity. A kid bringing in his Easter bunny rabbit. Appealing? On page one it goes. And our publicity is up the creek. No, sir, the Goyim want to help, let them contribute, pledge, to us." He rubbed his fingertips. "Money. Give us cash."

I was too listless to debate. Sol knew he was licked. Miss Ehling's lovely idea died in Walter's rumpus room.

"Enough shmoosing." Walter shook off cigar ash. "Let's get down to tachles, Sam. We have a problem, we could use your advice. Two weeks from today we have our campaign dinner. The Fieldbrook Country Club—this is since your time, Sam; wait till you see our golf course, finer than Hilldale's—roast beef dinner, baked whitefish for the kosher crowd. We have to decide should we call cards at the dinner."

"Hymie Rogoff," Sol put in. "He's the one against."

"Hymie hasn't grown up yet," Walter said. "He hasn't realized which century this is. Travels with the old-fashioned bunch up on the Hill. He raised hell when we started to build the country club; said we ought instead to build a new Jewish center for the kids. Hell, I told him, we can have the both, if you and your crowd loosen up. We go over the top, we can skim off for our local needs. Hymie talks poor mouth, but I know to the dollar what the produce business grossed last year. And, by God, if Hymie doesn't raise this year, I'll personally blackball him for Fieldbrook. Now we got it built, his Bobby is nagging Papa to get in."

Sol raised his hand, trying to stem the flood of Walter's acrimony. "Hymie isn't altogether a fool. He makes a couple of good points. The card-calling shames people, he says: their names called out in public, they can't sit like dummies, so they announce more than they can afford and in the end the pledge isn't paid; we're stuck, like me with deadbeats in the store. Walter knows and I know—I could name you names, but better Sam shouldn't know our shtunks—which guys made themselves big shots, standing up in the Grady ballroom, pledging a thousand dollars, and not one penny paid."

"We have some shysters, cheapskates, moved into town," Walter growled. "Since your time, Sam."

"Hymie makes another point," Sol went on patiently. "He says public pledging makes a bad impression on the Goyim: the names, the big amounts, printed in the paper. They start going around asking, How much do these same people give to the Community Chest, the Red Cross?"

"I give my share, I always have, you know that, Sol. And so do you. Not only money. Support. Your windows. Your ads."

"Goodwill," Sol said and smiled. "Good business, too."

"Hymie still thinks it's nineteen thirty-seven," Walter said. "We have to be afraid. Nah. We can hold up our heads. And why? I'll tell you why. Because we licked the shit out of seven Arab countries. We showed the world we weren't cowards."

"We?" I asked.

"Yes, *we*." He glared at me. "Sol and me, we got up a quiet campaign to raise money for the Haganah army."

"Got together a nice five thousand dollars," Sol added.

"What more do they expect from us?" Walter asked.

I thought of Jessie Weiss, dusting off her skirt on the courthouse steps, speaking of my name upon the tablet on the monument, of my participation in the First World War. "Aaron died. You went along for the ride." I didn't mention it.

"Speaking of cowards," Walter said, "Sol and I went personally to see Chief Durgin after you beat it out of town. He told us he investigated the fire in Herman Weiss's building; there was nothing like what you suspected. He didn't know why you got so bekocked; he told you he'd look into it. He was sorry you got him wrong. You were one of his best friends, he said. He wished you'd drop around when you were in town."

"Fat chance," I said.

"No chance," Sol said. "He had a stroke; died six weeks ago."

"Not one day too soon," I said.

Walter gave me a funny look. "Enough. No more shmoosing," he ordered. "Hymie says he'll have his crowd boycott the dinner if we decide to have card-calling. Not even if we get Georgie Jessel or some other big star for guest speaker. . . . Hey, by the by, Sam, could you get us Eleanor Roosevelt? They'd come for her, irregardless. How much does she charge?"

Sol tsked. "They shouldn't hire paid speakers. People don't like it. They ask questions—they have the right—how much of their money goes for expenses?"

Both of them gave me a hard look.

"Not excessive," I said. "I'm not getting rich on Jewish tsoris. Six days and nights a week, twelve-hour day, nine bucks per diem."

"My heart bleeds." Walter tamped out his cigar. "I remember what you earned on the *News-Record*."

"A certain amount expense is necessary," Sol said. "Fund-raising is a business, too. Overhead. Advertising. You don't spend it, you don't make it."

Walter stretched his long legs. "Okay. We told you the problem, Sam. Now what's the official attitude? Card-calling or no?"

I stretched *my* long legs. "Local problem," I said. "Settled locally. We never interfere." Everything they'd told me I had heard before in a dozen cities. I stirred to get up to leave. "You're no help," Walter said.

Sol rose when I did. "I don't see your father around since he retired. How your parents feeling?"

"Same address," I said. "Drop in. They'll be pleased to see you."

"You know how it is." Being a nice guy, he looked embarrassed.

I saluted both of them, goodbye. It occurred to me as I went up the steps that Walter hadn't even offered me a glass of sweet Passover wine. In the place where I was born and raised my status had changed. Walter and Sol were the lay leaders, I was merely a paid professional.

Sylvia, large-bosomed, matronly, a white streak in her raven hair, saw me out. "Sam, you owe me a Mazel Tov. Cousin Ruthie, that lovely girl I tried to fix you up with, got married in March.

To a wonderful man. In the Finance Loan business. A widower. Three children. They're just crazy about Ruthie; she's wonderful with children; you remember how nice she behaved with my kids? She didn't even need to furnish the home. He had the best of everything."

I grinned a "no comment" grin.

"So here you are, an old bocher, still eating in the restaurants, no home cooking, no home." At the door, she leaned to my ear. "Tell me, is it true Celia's Ilene committed suicide? We heard it on the radio."

So did I, I said, and that was all I knew.

"I wrote Ceil a condolence letter, very warm. All I got back was a printed card. And we used to be so close. It's a shame how you drift apart. Joe got too rich, I guess. They move in a different world, forget their old friends." She smiled a mean smile. "At least for one person Joe did something nice. He got you a good job."

Hymie Rogoff called right after I came back to Mama's house. This time I wouldn't run, and he had to ask me on the phone was it true I'd told Sol and Walter card-calling was official policy? Not at all, I said, we let local people decide what's best locally. Advised, not decreed, is our attitude.

"Another question," Hymie persisted. "What is the official policy if we take off from the campaign total for our local needs? To build a Jewish center, for instance."

"You have a Y, a country club," I said.

"Not enough. The club's for allrightnicks, to play golf. The Y's old-fashioned, it hasn't even got a swimming pool. We can't attract the kids. The kids from the Hill have no place . . ."

"To learn to be good Americans?" I asked.

"Nah," Hymie said. "To learn to be good Jews. We have to preserve our heritage."

"By the Australian crawl?" I asked.

He caught the sarcasm. "At you, I'm surprised. From you, what you've personally seen, the way you earn your living, I would expect encouragement. Maybe if we sat down together, chewed it over, how about that, Sam? I could ask Irwin Katz and Myron Finkel; they've got a little sense, even though they aren't leadership material. That's all that's left of our old gang. Say when. I'll call them up."

I said I'd see, maybe later in the week, after I'd won my battle with Mama's matzoh balls.

I couldn't have cared less about sitting down with Hymie and the residue of the old gang to talk about the preservation of the Jewish heritage through a swimming pool in Grady's Mills.

Mama wanted to know why Walter had summoned me. I'd just begun to tell her when Papa wandered in, sat down with us at the kitchen table, and diligently picked his nose. "Feh! How many times I told you leave the nose alone," Mama shouted. "You make a sore." What I was saying was swept under the linoleum. They began a loud, vituperative argument over how many times he'd picked his nostrils till they bled and how successfully she'd cured him with white Vaseline.

"Yellow," Papa screamed and stamped his foot.

"White. White is more pure," Mama yelled.

"Show me your doctor stiffticket, Mrs. Rosenbaum," Papa sneered.

It wasn't funny, it was painful. And the fermented beet borsht Mama served at second Seder was no nauseating that next morning I packed and returned to New York. A sheaf of messages was waiting. "Mrs. Sloan called. Please phone her."

Not being rushed, I phoned. "Samuel, where have you been hiding? I tried and tried to reach you. We wanted you for Seder, our first without our precious darling. Oh, I didn't want to have it, but Dr. Harris said I must make the effort. Oh, I tried so hard to make it a real family gathering, and I think of you as family, I do. I asked those refugee cousins of dear Mama's, those people Joseph rescued. Their son asked the four questions our dear darling always asked. That just about broke me up. But, Samuel, they were so out of place, their table manners were so crude, and he kept correcting Joseph's Hebrew reading. So tactless. She kept sobbing about her relatives the Nazis murdered. Total strangers whom we never even heard about. As if our loss was unimportant. Of course, I invited my sister and her husband. But their values are so different. Being Jewish doesn't mean a thing to them. They observe nothing. Why, Jessie, my own sister, hasn't gone to a

Seder since we went away to college. And he—he's practically a Gentile—doesn't read one word of Hebrew. From a very assimilated family. But he is a nice person. He lost a son in the war, he told me. So we had something in common. My sister's very lucky, after the first mess she made, to find such a sweet, kind man. . . ."

I let her babble on, poor thing, until all at once she said something that brought me alert and wary. "Samuel, though believe me, nothing is further from my own desires, Dr. Harris thinks I should start going out. You know, or perhaps you don't know, we have a box at the Opera. They're giving *Tristan and Isolde* this week. I wonder would you care to accompany me." The thought of listening to "Liebestodt" with Celia alongside made my blood run cold. I said I was sorry, I thought I might be coming down with flu. That was a mistake. She became solicitous. "Suppose I brought you down some nice chicken broth? Or better yet, let me send the car to bring you here. You could convalesce so nicely at our place. Sit in the solarium. Be waited on, hand and foot."

"The house phone's buzzing," I replied. "Switchboard must have a call. Excuse me. I'll ring you back."

I was frightened. Celia's clinging was turning into clutch. I should have stayed on the road. Or in Grady's Mills. Yet in this room, I felt a kind of sanctuary. My few possessions—the odds and ends of peripatetic bachelorhood—did embrace me. And it was a relief to be alone. I spent the evening without abrasion, writing to Yuli, listening to WQXR, and skimming a recent novel. I woke, feeling footloose, almost free. The office believed I was out of town, no one but Celia knew that I was in, and so if I moved fast, before she phoned to ask about my health, this day might be pleasant. I made and drank two cups of coffee, walked to Central Park, sat for an hour in watery sunlight, reading my morning *Times*, strolled over to Fifth Avenue and leisurely downtown, examining shop windows, reached the Public Library, sat again in brighter sunshine on the marble steps behind the lions, watching the pigeons pirouette and flutter, an agreeable idleness I'd not experienced in Lord knows how many years. Hunger caught up with me. I crossed to the Brass Rail, defiantly ordered baked Virginia ham on rye, strolled again, downtown, until I glimpsed the iron fence of Gramercy Park. I hadn't spoken with Jessie since that winter morning in Ilene's bedroom. Why should I not? We weren't enemies.

I stepped into a drugstore phone booth and dialed her number. "Remember me?" I asked the woman who said "hello" huskily.

"Where in hell have you been?"

"It's such a big United States," I said.

"Quote, Unquote," she replied. Her memory was flypaper. "How's about coming over for supper? Have a bite of chometz with us. Mark gets home sevenish."

It was only four o'clock, three hours to fill. I dropped into the neighborhood movie house. The picture didn't matter; my feet did. At seven I rang the Bishop bell; the buzzer let me in. Jessie opened the door upstairs, grasping both my hands. "The friend!" She was decidedly plump. Given time, she'd be a butterball.

A small fire was crackling on the hearth, the wall clock ticking rhythmically, books on chairs and tables in a friendly clutter, cushions battened down, the cradle heaped with kindling, the windows still uncurtained, a room unchanged, unchanging, yet subtly different, as if it managed to reflect the moods of those who lived in it. Last time I'd been here, during the war, it was cold and dismal, with Jessie in despair. Tonight it looked contented. A television set in the corner was rattling off the news. "Interested? Or turn it off?" Jessie asked.

"Off," I said.

"Mark's washing up," she said. "How about a Scotch?"

Sitting alone while she fixed drinks in the kitchen, I could imagine Ilene here, with the white dog that resembled Einstein perched upon a hassock. The image faded as soon as Mark came in, hand outstretched, saying heartily, "Good to see you. It's been years. How are you?" Mark looked worn, his trouble, other people's troubles, had etched his face. He sank into the sofa near the fire, exhaling his exhaustion. Jessie brought him a highball, stroked his cheek. He brightened instantly. So comfortable with one another, these two were, I was jealous of them.

Over dinner, which was simple—lamb chops, baked potatoes and a salad—they asked what I had been doing and received my reply with mild indifference. Jessie seemed more genuinely interested when I said I had just been in Grady's Mills. How did the town

327

look nowadays? Any new stores on First Street? Anything built on Papa's lot? Had I by chance gone out to the cemetery? I told her Jane Ehling, the librarian, had inquired for her. She was pleased. I told her Police Chief Durgin was dead. She clapped hands. "Gott sei dank." In her turn, she described Celia's Seder. She hadn't wished to go, she said; Mark had decided it was only decent to accept. The food was fine; Celia's chef had a light hand with gefüllte fish and matzoh balls. But Joey, in a yarmulka, mumbling the Haggadah in Bar Mitzvah Hebrew, was incredible and the refugee cousin had been the spitting image of Ida, with the same yak-yak about the Vilna yiches. She brushed off her hands. "That takes care of that. We've discharged our obligations to the Sloans." It was as close as either of us had come to Ilene's tragedy.

The phone rang while we were having coffee: Mark's answering service, an emergency; he had to go uptown. "Glad you're here," he told me. "Keep my wife company. And come again. Often."

Jessie washed the dishes. I dried and told her about Sol and Walter and Hymie, what machers they'd become, busy with fund-raising. She made no comment. We watched television for a while, a trivial drama. I told Jessie she could write better with both hands tied behind her back.

"Using my toes? Neatest trick of the week."

We drank after-dinner highballs. The clock ticked evenly. She said, "You keep nagging me about writing. Why don't you? You've seen so much."

"Seen much," I echoed.

Her eyebrows arched. "Not felt? Always the reporter?"

"The guest speaker, the shnorrer," I said.

She made a face. "You like that life?"

"You must be nuts," I said.

"Then why?" she asked.

"You can't build a nation with peanuts and sympathy," I said.

She stroked my arm, patronizingly. "Sam, the shnook. When will he—will he ever?—begin living? Truly living, in a house, a home, with a person. One and only, for better or for worse. Can it be"—in an offhand way, she threw a devastating taunt—"the bell doesn't ring because it has no clapper?"

I bared my teeth. "Cut that out."

"Well, Christ, a healthy, normal human being doesn't go through life on airline tickets! Why haven't you got married?"

"Mebbe," I said, "when the lady's ready and willing." The taunt had caught me off-base, made me indiscreet.

Her eyes widened. "Then there is a dame."

Yuli was a topic I had no intention of discussing. It was too iffy. I changed the subject. "Jessie, why haven't you asked me about Israel?"

Her expression took note of the sudden switch, though her answer played along with it.

"Like when? In Celia's bedroom or Ilene's?"

"Like now. Tonight."

She bent and tucked one leg beneath her, a posture that I've been told induces spinal curvatures. "Why should I? The information isn't classified. The papers, magazines, are full of it."

"But don't you have a special pride in what's been happening?"

"The 'oh, my glorious brothers!' bit?" Her head wagged side to side, emphatically. "Let Rand McNally be happy. I cannot get ecstatic because another little country's on the map."

That flabbergasted me. Everywhere I'd roamed they were ringing bells, hurray for us. Perversely, Herman Weiss's child was counting herself out. " 'If I am not for myself—' " I launched the well-known quote.

Her palm went up like a traffic cop's. "Dispense with chauvinism, please. The world—this is my absolute conviction—must offer bread and justice to all its people, brown and black, yellow, white, Christian, Moslem, Buddhist, Hebrew, Atheist."

"When does the next plane leave for Utopia?" I asked.

"No skeptics allowed on board," she said.

I can't leave well enough alone. I'd like to win an argument, just one, with the prize debater of Grady's Mills High School, class of 1918. It's a neurotic compulsion, a masochistic drive. "The Sermon on the Mount didn't save your crippled Vilna cousin. And don't you mourn for the six million dead?"

"I do. And for those who died at Lidice. And the innocents at Nagasaki, too."

No argument there, no real difference. Yet there was. "Jessie,

329

if Hitler'd won the war, the gas chambers, that would be us. What's happened to the dame who wrote *The Arsonists?*"

She let me count five ticks of the clock before she leaned to me, shaking her head, rebuking. "Bubi, if you hadn't been so snide—and so immodestly subjective, I might add—about that play, you'd have understood what I am all about. All men are brothers. Let us make a world where anyone and everyone can be whatever he is or he desires to be. And let us remember that the enemy is apathy and ignorance at home as much as mass insanity in Germany."

I applauded while I racked my brain, trying to recall whether this had been the message of her masterpiece. "Very noble, very fine," I said.

"Shtunk." She'd had enough of loftiness. "That's what gums the works, wise guys. Want another highball?" She started to untwist her leg to go for it. My "no, thanks" halted her. "Do I? Nope. Mark rations me, one before dinner, one after, keep a healthy belly, kid." She lunged at a cigarette box on the coffee table, opened it, banged it shut. "The cupboard's bare. My monster's sneakiness. Cut down, babe, I'm saving you for my old age." Not complaining, sounding pleased that her man cared enough to protect her from the minor vices, though inconvenienced momentarily, since she turned her big eyes on me, wheedling, "Maybe the guest can help out?"

I produced a squashed pack that held three flattened mentholated cigarettes. Her nose turned up. "So desperate I am not."

"In a pogrom," I said. She took. I flipped my lighter for her and placed the pack within her reach. She grimaced at the menthol sharpness, filled her lungs, coughed heartily and settled back to inform and enlighten me. "Bubi, I left the Hill to join the human race, not to be a willy-nilly, whining, pining member of a persecuted minority. And please do not remind me I was born a Jew so I had no choice. I *had* a choice. I *made* a choice. I left a narrow world to walk freely up and down whatever road I pleased. And it was quite a thing to learn that I could walk alone and stand alone and Jehovah's lightning didn't strike me dead when I ate steamed clams. And also that, no matter what, Papa still thought well of me." She stopped to unkink her leg, to thrust it out and shake it. "Dammit, pins and needles. Rub it, will you please."

At your service, ma'am, as usual. I massaged the calf. She grinned—"Same old Sam, no lechery"—propped her back against a sofa arm, stretched her legs straight, pulled her skirt down, ostentatiously. She puffed once or twice before, "Sam, you lived across the street; you watched the Weisses coming, going; you heard me and Mama yelling; you sat at our kitchen table. But did you know, could you guess, what it was like to be the child of Herman Weiss? The daughter of a saintly man who part-time ran a grocery?" Her tone was changing. The mockery was gone. "Don't get me wrong. I loved my old man. Did and do. But in that house Papa was a presence, not a human being. Remote, aloof. Wrapped up in his piety. Shul, morning, night, all day Saturday. What time had he for me, for us?" She waved the cigarette, dropping ashes on her knees. "Why, we never had a meal together, except Friday night, Shabbos, and the holy days. And then he was busy praying, before, during, after. When he sliced the chalah, when he poured the wine, when he washed his hands. Boruch attoh over the first muskmelon, over the new moon. Prayers! And in a language I couldn't understand. In Grady's Mills, if you recall, Hebrew wasn't taught to girls. So how could I learn what Papa's prayers were all about? By osmosis, maybe? Bubi, my eyes dripped grating horseradish for the Seder, but did Papa take the time to teach me about the bitterness of Egypt? Maybe if it had occurred to him to explain—But no, Mama never gave the man a chance to open up his mouth. Mama!" She spewed a long stream of smoke. "The right-hand woman of the right-hand man of God! Why, she used him like a club! 'Jessie, you go to the liberry Shabbos, you have no respect for Papa!' 'Oooh, Jessie, a Christian Christmas song you was singing, I'll tell Papa on you.' Honest, all I was doing was trying to hum 'Silent Night.' The tune. Without the words. 'Jessie, a frum man like your father should find out his daughter ate from the trefe bakery a cake it would positively kill him.' Hah! Don't do this, don't do that." She stopped to cough, pressed out the cigarette, took a fresh one, waited, silent, till I lighted it, then rested her dark head against the sofa. Her eyes were thoughtful, somber.

"Sam, it is thirty years since I left Papa's house. Thank God, I've purged myself of most of my childhood memories. Exorcised them in a play, you know, the first one I wrote. . . . Don't look so surprised, you must have guessed. Sam, mine was a lousy, lousy childhood, worse, believe me, than that kid's in the play. Drudgery, hard, dirty work: scrubbing floors, beating carpets, scouring pots, polishing the copper boiler, blacking stoves, scrubbing clothes. And hanging up the fleece-lined underwear, the flannel petticoats, in winter my fingers froze. While Mama yak-yakked downstairs with the women. And my sister—she was delicate, she was nervous—sat on her can, embroidering. Celia!" A drop of distilled venom. "Why, on account of her, just on account of her, Papa didn't even dare be proud of me. He was, you know. I could see it in his face when he signed my report cards. But not a single word of praise. And why? Because there stood Celia with *her* card. And you mustn't, you daren't, make Celia feel inferior. Which she was." Her chin came up, angry, arrogant. "And is." She knocked an ash string from the cigarette. "Sam, this is extraordinary, but you must believe it; I can remember just one time, only one, when my father said something personal and endearing to me. I was seven or eight. I was sick, running a high fever, mumps or measles or whatever, something catching and disfiguring, and Mama'd bedded Celia in the parlor and left me alone in the big bed. And Papa came into the dark bedroom and he put his hand on my hot head and he said, 'Shluf' "—Her voice deepened— " 'Shluf, mine tiere kind.' " She repeated the words, slowly, first in Yiddish, then in English. " 'Sleep, my dear child.' The only loving words my father ever spoke to me. That and the look when he signed my card was all I had, to tell me that he valued me. A growing girl needs more than a look and four words."

She shook herself, as if shedding the excess of her emotion, reached for the last cigarette, lighted it from the stub of the other and, unexpectedly, she laughed. "It's amazing, when you pull the cork, what silly things pop out. Just now, I saw them both, Papa and Mama, sitting at the kitchen table, counting, wrapping money. They did that every night. They'd lock the store, come upstairs together. Papa'd be carrying a canvas bag. They'd sit down, side by side; he'd empty the bag on the table. They'd take out the bills, tie a bit of twine around the paper money—that was for the bank. Then they'd sort and stack and count the coins and roll them in brown paper. Twenty dimes, twenty nickels, twelve quarters. Pennies last. They always had a lot of pennies. I'd offer to help; Mama'd shoo me off. She wouldn't let me say good night to Papa for fear he'd lose the count. Another sacred rite, another ritual. Counting pennies." Her chin tipped up again. "Prayers and pennies. And scrubbing clothes and scrubbing floors. And living in a strait-jacket, not to hurt Papa's feelings. Do you wonder I hated everything and everybody in that house? Yes, even Papa, whom I didn't want to hate. Yet he *was* to blame. If he'd been a real father and a master in his house, not submissive to God and Ida Weiss—" She balled the empty cigarette pack in her fist and hurled it toward the fireplace. "So there you have it, why Jessie Weiss walked out on Judaism. Have I made it clear?"

Clear as mud, as murky, as illogical, I thought, as the explanation of his shame Herman Weiss had given both of us in Westport ten years earlier, and as unreasoned, as subjective, as are most of the crucial decisions of most lives. Unhappy childhood is the alibi nowadays for every aberration from kleptomania to genocide. Why not for Jewish indifference?

Jessie was yawning, lightly. "Now, Bubi, let us go back to where we were before you started asking foolish questions. Who is the mystery female?"

The clock began to strike. I put my finger on my lips to hush her while I pretended to count. "Ten." I got up. "It's been a long day. You've worn me out."

"Brunette or blonde?" she persisted.

"The thing to keep in mind," I said, "is you can't resign from *being*. Good night, my Jewish friend." At the door I made a final effort. "If rape is inevitable," I said, "why not relax and enjoy it?"

"You're nuts," she said, affectionately, and rose tiptoe to kiss my cheek.

* * *

I saw Celia before I went back on the road. She insisted I be her luncheon guest at the Colony, where she told me I'd been very naughty not to let her look after me when I had the flu. She'd tried to reach me the next day, but the switchboard didn't know where I had gone. She'd been frantic, having visions of me in a hospital. She was glad I was well, though I did look somewhat peaked. Then she went on to inform me they were closing the Greenwich house in June to go abroad. Joseph needed a vacation and Dr. Harris approved, provided she'd resume her therapy when she returned. They'd do London, Paris (she dabbed her eyes)—Paris that she hadn't seen since their honeymoon and hardly seen that time since she'd been in bed, pregnant with Ilene —Rome, Florence, Venice and, if she found the strength, go on to Israel to choose the site for Ilene's memorial. Was there anything she could buy for me in London or Paris? Anyone over there to whom I'd like her to bring a message or a gift? I thought of Yuli, Yuli might help her, but decided no, Yuli might despise her and, hating her, think less of me. Would I accept a guest card for her country club, to get away from the hot city on weekends, swim, play golf, be with some nice people. She looked hurt when I declined. "You never let me do a thing for you. You've been so kind to me. I don't have anybody else."

* * *

After the Sloans sailed (Queen Mary, A deck suite), one of the better summers of my life commenced. It was slack season at the office, no traveling, no drives, just planning for the fall campaigns. And a New York summer can be quietly agreeable when you have friends who have a key to Gramercy Park and a car that knows the way to Jones Beach. I saw the Bishops often. At their apartment, occasionally, I met some of the Westport crowd, as talkative as before, yet with no interest whatsoever in quotas, big givers or card-calling. They drew me into heated arguments about should we have dropped the bomb on Hiroshima and Nagasaki when the Japs were making surrender overtures? Was Alger Hiss guilty, not of passing secrets but of lying when he said he didn't recognize Chambers? Did Faulkner rate a Nobel prize or a kick in his riding pants? And which was the better playwright, Arthur Miller or Tennessee Williams?

Jessie, her envy showing like her lace-edged slip, announced that both were flashes in the pan. Moreover, they were turning the theater into a nut house. Is there nothing to write plays about except the sickness of the psyche? Is there no drama in the way

334

people come to terms with life? Her own typewriter stood behind its screen, gathering dust and rust. Looking after Mark and the apartment, she insisted, took all her time and energy; a woman has only just two hands. Since the brass and copper weren't polished, the frayed cushions not recovered, it was a reasonable assumption Jessie used her hands chiefly for counting blessings.

One of those blessings was a spectacled youth named Frederick Bishop, a first-year med student at P. and S. who came around frequently. Possibly, his mother was no longer bitter; possibly she'd realized the doctor-papa could further Fred's career. Or maybe he'd become his own man, enjoying, for the pleasant thing it was, the companionship of Mark and Mark's second wife.

We had a good summer, Jessie, Mark and I. We even saw some shows. I took them to *South Pacific;* they took me to *Born Yesterday*. Pete's Tavern hired a new chef; we dined outdoors on the red-and-white checked tablecloths. We never talked fund-raising. Out of curiosity, I did check up on Mark in our office files, found out that since 1946 he'd been pledging, paying, $250 every year; an obligation, I concluded, like his A.M.A. dues, a token payment for membership in Jewish peoplehood.

After Labor Day, I resumed my flights to Buffalo, N.Y., Akron, O., and Hotseplotz, returned to find the messages that Mrs. Sloan had called. "Please call her back." I did.

"Samuel! Didn't you know we had returned?"

"I've been out of town. How was your trip?"

"Exhausting. And so, so heartbreaking. To see the beach, the spot. . . ."

Enough already, Celia. "How was Paris?"

"Joseph enjoyed it," she replied with asperity. Then, retaining the sharpness, "I spoke with Jessie on the phone—*I* called *her*—she said you'd been spending a good deal of time with them. I presume their bohemianism is more to your taste, all that drinking that goes on. For us, you never seem to have the time."

With that reproach, she hooked me. I agreed to take a train to Greenwich; the chauffeur would pick me up at the depot, we'd have a quiet dinner at the house and she had something wonderful to show me. She led me directly to Ilene's room and clicked on a switch. Mauve light flooded a frieze of photographic blow-ups on the unwindowed walls: infant Ilene in her mother's arms, baby Ilene in her pram, with nurse; the toddler taking her first steps, the three-year-old in snow suit in the park; the ten-year-old with whom I'd fallen in love, wearing leotard and ballerina slippers; Ilene at camp, in tennis shorts, bathing suit, and jodhpurs, on horseback; the sweet-sixteen party with Michael-David in his first tuxedo behind the birthday girl; the high-school graduation picture, a charming group in white formals; Ilene walking the little dog who resembled Einstein; the wedding photographs, the dream walking up the aisle on her father's arm, the groom raising the veil to kiss his bartered bride, two sets of parents holding champagne glasses to toast their offspring, Ilene's and Michael's hands together on the knife to slice the towering wedding cake. Then, small silver frames that held newspaper clippings, among them the birth announcement I'd written for the *News-Record*, and society-page descriptions of the wedding, out of the *New York Times* and *Herald-Tribune*. And last, a photograph of a beach in Tel Aviv with the ghostly *Altalena* in the distance and the clippings about a funeral. Beneath this was a marble stand holding a bowl of white orchids and silver candlesticks, with electric-lighted flames.

"I knew you'd want to see this," Celia said.

It was morbid. What kind of a psychiatrist did she have? Why couldn't he knock some sense into the poor bitch? Yet, oddly, she looked almost happy as she switched off the eerie light. She had her little girl, didn't she? And she kept her, thus eternally a child, a showpiece, surpassingly beautiful.

Joe joined us at the dinner table, the old Joe, full of bombast, holding forth about Israel to me. In spite of himself, he'd been impressed; they were really making progress, although certain know-it-all bureaucrats needed taking down a peg. They'd been positively obnoxious when he tried to point out, sure, the cement boxes they were putting up for immigrants were cheap, but in the long run they'd prove more expensive, deteriorate too fast. Build with steel, you build substantial, permanent. He'd have steel framework for Ilene's house, by God, if he had to ship it there himself; that building was going to last as long as Israel, let Baumberg make this clear to them. This much he could say for Baumberg, the boy had briefed the big shots properly. The Sloans were met at the airport, a limousine and driver were waiting, a conducting officer assigned, a red carpet spread from Dan to Beersheba, Cabinet ministers had them to tea, Celia's Hadassah women turned themselves inside out, though they couldn't make the trip up Mt. Scopus to see the plaque for Celia's parents, the hospital was cut off, just the U.N. convoy going up, and government people decided an important man like Mr. Sloan shouldn't risk the convoy trip. Joe also thought that now he'd seen the country he might go on the road for the Committee, to a few important cities like Miami and Los Angeles; American businessmen might be more responsive to one of their own than to a professional like me.

Celia had brought me presents, a cashmere sweater from London, a leather wallet, with matching eyeglass case, from Florence, a pair of silver cuff links from Tel Aviv. The gifts were handsome and useful; my thank-you was for real. "Now do something for me, Samuel," she said, looking wistful. "Ask my sister why she never calls or visits me. Did I say or do something to her? I can't imagine what. I wrote her—I hoped she'd meet us at the pier—it's so nice to be welcomed. Do you know, she hasn't even phoned since we got back."

I passed the message on at Jessie's dinner table, on Rosh Hashanah night, when she and Mark and I were dining on a shrimp, scallops and lobster casserole, one of the few dishes Jessie did well, since the recipe demanded no more than adding a can of mushroom soup and two tablespoons of cognac to the fish.

"Bubi, I did try and you know damn well I did. When Celia was in trouble, I ran, didn't I? And I stayed and coddled her and nursed her, answer me, didn't I? And I went up for their putrid Seder and let her chew off my angelic husband's ear. But honestly, I cannot stand the woman. And as for Joe, Sam, maybe you remember the evening and the hour when that s.o.b. first revolted me. So Celia chose to marry him. Her tough luck, not mine. Money can't buy happiness, though it can buy a lot of drek. Seriously, Sam, my sister and I haven't got one thing in common except mutual dislike. Our worlds are simply not the same. And Ilene I will not talk to her about. That story is fini; that book is closed. Other people have lost children. One is sitting at this table. You mourn, but you take it like a mensch: we were fortunate to have had the child as long as we did; who is to say how long a life-span is?" She paused to oil her throat with chilled chablis. "And look, see here, pay attention, if my sister really wanted to see me, I have a telephone; the number's listed in the book. She's in and out of Manhattan all week long. Does it ever occur to her to phone to ask me how I am? You know, I might just possibly have a cold, a fever, a bellyache; it would be nice to have a sister stopping by, maybe I am dying. Okay, so I'm healthy as a horse. But why not phone and ask, 'Jessie, can we have lunch together?' or 'Jessie, would you mind if I dropped in for a cup of tea?' Do you know my devoted sister has never set foot in this place?"

"Have you invited her?" I managed to ask.

She blushed and, being caught out, bellowed, "Listen, that Sunday morning when she barged in on me in Westport—you were there, you should remember, Sam—her nose went straight up in the air. The duchess and the bug. Good God, if she spent one single hour in this room, she'd run, quick, quick, to get herself de-loused."

Mark stroked her arm to calm her down. "Dearest, you exaggerate, you dramatize." And laughed. "It's part of your charm."

"Do I exaggerate?" She wasn't mollified. "Then let me tell you something, both of you." She banged the table with a fist. "You'll not believe it, I wouldn't either, if I'd heard it secondhand. During the shiva, when you thought and I thought everything was hotsy-totsy, hunky-dory, between us, after one of those ghastly evenings when the Sloans had been receiving condolences, I took Madame upstairs; lean on my shoulder, darling. I tucked her into bed, gave her Ovaltine and Nembutal. And out of the blue, she began to tell me a bobbemeise, how at my first wedding, I had smashed a shmate of hers, a plaster statuette she cherished, her 'Good Fairy.' And that night she swore to herself she never would forgive me, never, never. And maybe when she lost her 'Good Fairy' was when her troubles started; that was why she had so much sorrow." She slapped her chest. "Looka me, boys. The hex of the house of Weiss! Garbage!" By the rageful way she thrust back her plate, I realized to her it wasn't garbage. It was a deep-hurting indignity.

338

"Be a big girl, Jessie." I was doing my best. "The poor thing didn't realize what she was saying. She was half out of her mind."

"Out of her mind, my eye! Out of her sewer. Listen, Sam, that sister is no sister. She has never been. We were hatched by the same mama but we're totally different chicks. And I've always been the misfit, the disappointment, from the hour I was born. I should have been a boy, you know, to perpetuate Papa's name, provide the kaddish so he'd rest easy in his grave. And don't think Mama didn't let me know it and Celia rub it in. Who needed you? Who wanted you?" She was closer to crying than I'd ever seen her.

Mark cradled her hand against his cheek. "I did," he said.

We never spoke of this again. In fact, after that evening, we didn't have much chance to speak of anything. I was on the road continuously, and the job was getting tougher, week by week. It had been a big deal all along for communities to fill a hall with people willing to sit still and listen, with one ear, to what I'd come to say. They weren't exactly tired of giving, they were bored with why. "For God sakes, don't give us the six million dead," one chairman told me. "We've had them up to here." And as for Israel, the flush of pride had ebbed, the annual drive had become routine. Nightclub entertainers, not pride or pity, brought out the customers. I'd return to New York too beat, too disgusted, for any socializing. The twenty-first of April, 1951, was such a return.

"Mrs. Sloan called. Please call her as soon as you get in. It is urgent." The date on the message slip was yesterday's. My flight had been rough: rain, gale winds, nerve-wracking circling in thick fog to get down into La Guardia, after a disastrous meeting in a city which I chose to keep nameless. That was hostile territory, where Jews seemed more sympathetic to Arabs than to Yids. All the while I was making my pitch, I sensed I was butting a stone wall. The picayune pledges proved no one had been listening. Baumberg, I was sure, would not believe the circumstances had been beyond my control. He'd been giving me the cold treatment, the yes-but-what-have-you-done-for-us-lately?, sending me to smaller, less productive places—the big cities were demanding name personalities and movie stars. Even the shmegeggy chairman of this meeting had had the nerve to say, as I was leaving for the airport, "Tell New York next time they should send us a decent speaker, maybe we'll get out a decent crowd, Georgie Jessel, somebody that tells jokes. I was insulted reading your biology. You ain't even a college graduate." Right. Mr. Nobody. Sucked dry. And with a bellyful of card-calling. Baumberg could take this assignment, stick it. Twelve thousand a year out the window? Sure. Who needs it? Me. How else will Papa and Mama pay the water tax and road-paving assessment? There must be easier ways of making a living. The Committee's Geneva Office, for instance.

When a man grows older—not precisely aged, understand—the feet swell in warm weather, the staircases seem steeper, the valises heavier, there's a little shortness of breath chasing after trains, and the banquet chicken, peas and carrots have produced chronic indigestion. Comes the time when he dreams of sitting behind a desk, dictating to a secretary, signing letters, calling it a day at 5 P.M. That's the hour when part two of a fund-raising speaker's day begins. The Committee's Geneva office was low-pressure—coordination of its European activities, gathering and collating materials for public information, playing host to touring V.I.P.s—all of which I could handle with self-respect and the back of my hand. The man currently on the job was mentioning retirement, to Israel, to join a "dig"; he was an archaeology buff. Besides, and most important, Yuli was in Geneva, and time and work were readying her for a new life. I didn't need to read between lines in her letters—she was a forthright woman. "I should like to see you again," she had written.

I stirred a martini, drank it, kicked off my shoes, mixed and drank a second martini, took off my tie and shirt. Revived, I called Mrs. Sloan.

"Samuel!" She sounded agitated. "I wondered if you'd get back in time. I suppose you've heard the news."

"What news?"

"Dr. Bishop has had a coronary. His condition's critical, I hear."

"From whom did you hear?"

"Why, from a mutual friend, a doctor's wife. They have him in Mt. Sinai. I've been trying to reach Jessie. Her phone doesn't answer; she must be at the hospital. I keep phoning there. Can't get through to her. Samuel, if she would only call me back, say she needed me, I'd fly to her on wings."

I had to listen to some blather about what a sweet dear man Dr. Bishop was, and how uncertain life is—here Jessie had been riding high, her problems all solved with that man working so hard to provide for her—before she released me to put on shoes and shirt and tie and jacket, wash my face and grab a taxi to the hospital.

Jessie, looking two years older than God, and Frederick, the spectacled med student, were in an alcove at the end of a corridor. Jessie glanced in my direction, without a trace of recognition. She let me take her icy hand. The youth said, "I'm glad you're here. She needed somebody." Somebody who could put an arm around her shoulders, as he couldn't yet permit himself to do, having graduated only yesterday from acute hostility; somebody who'd know the steps to take, the practical details, in case the worst happened.

"We wait," Jessie said. "What else can we do?"

I waited, too. I lit a cigarette. Mutely, Jessie begged for it. She smoked it till it scorched her fingertips. I took the stub, found an ash receiver. She rose, walked slowly up the corridor, to stand, holding the knob of a closed door, not venturing in, returned to her chair and crouched, waiting, dreading.

A white coat, a poker face, approached. "You may see him for a few minutes, Mrs. Bishop. Please don't try to talk to him."

Fred got up, too. The doctor shook his head. "One visitor."

She hesitated, looking at the youth, possibly considering bestowing her few minutes on the son, but drew her shoulders back, head up, and walked swiftly to the room. Returning, she said, "He doesn't seem to be in pain." Only that. I lit another cigarette for her. We waited again. My wrist watch turned up six o'clock and seven. I mentioned there was a coffee shop downstairs; I was sure she hadn't eaten all day. "You go, Fred," she told the youth. "Food would choke me." Fred wouldn't leave. I went down, fetched a couple of packages of crackers and containers of coffee for the two of them. Fred drank his coffee, she started to sip hers, before we noticed activity around the room up the hall: a cart, a tank, hastily wheeled in, nurses, residents converging. We stood, holding on to one another, advancing with laggard steps, pulled toward the room.

The white coat emerged; the poker face was broken up. "We've lost him, Mrs. Bishop. I can't tell you how sorry. . . ."

She didn't crumple or cry out. Her fist went toward her mouth, pounding her bloodless lips, before, "Can I see him now?" The young man went in with her. I remained in the alcove. My supporting arm was ready when Jessie came from the room.

The youth, the surviving Bishop male, was admirable, controlled and practical, aware that there are next steps for the living, like passing on the word to next of kin, like transferring the deceased to professional custody. "Sir, if you will be good enough to phone the chapel—we used Campbell's the other time—I'll call Mother, ask her to find the deed for the plot where Billy—my brother—is. You don't object to that, do you, Jessie? I think Dad would want to be with him. . . ."

Her lips barely moved. "Whatever you. . . ."

"To whom do you wish me to telephone?"

"Whoever you. . . ."

"Your sister?"

"Why?"

"Won't you need her?"

"Why?"

He had enough sense not to push it. "Sir, do you have change for the phone?" Now that I think of it, there is a kind of symbolism, though I'm not sure what it signifies, in the fact that the first service I performed for Jessie after her husband died was emptying my pocket of small change.

Fred made the family calls. I phoned the funeral chapel, told them a new client would be waiting in the Mt. Sinai mortuary; members of the family would be at the chapel soonest possible to make the arrangements. Then, with Fred Bishop supplying the data on Mark's parentage and siblings, I wrote out the "beloved husband of," "devoted father of," "dear brother of" and "funeral arrangements will be announced" and telephoned the obituary notice to the *Times*. Jessie had said nothing, done nothing. She sat frozen, gnawing the index finger of her clenched right fist. Young Fred left us to go to his mother. I led Jessie to the elevator and hailed a taxicab to bring her home. In the cab I kept thinking, She ought to have some woman with her, I don't know where to reach her friends, I ought to call Celia whether Jessie wants me to or not. But, again, I remembered the unique, hateful German word. No, Jessie's instinct is true. Please, no schadenfreude tonight.

I asked for her key. She handed me her bag. I roweled till I found the bunch of keys and unlocked her door. Faintly, I heard music, which was odd. I switched on lights, led her to a sofa near the fireplace. It was choked with wood ashes. The antique clock was marking time.

"Lie down, rest."

"I have forever to rest."

"Let me have your coat."

"I'm cold, I'll keep it."

"I'll get you a drink. It'll warm you."

I was in the kitchen, searching for the liquor, when the phone rang. She didn't rise to answer. I went out, took the call at the telephone table in the apartment vestibule. It was the *Times*, calling back to verify the obit and request details of Mark's professional career. Dr. Bishop, it appeared, was sufficiently distinguished to rate a news story. I said I'd collect the data, phone them; yes, I understood about deadlines. Jessie must have overheard the conversation, for when I returned to the living room, her fist was stuffed into her mouth to stem the flow of tears. "Cry," I said. "For God sakes, weep. It's your privilege."

Her eyes rebuked me with an anger beyond grief. She rose, kicked a footstool across the room, stood on it, to open the glass case of the clock. She seized the brass pendulum, held it, twisted it savagely. The ticking stopped. She returned to the sofa to sit huddled in her coat. Again, I was aware of music.

The phone rang. I answered it. The voice of an exasperated woman said, "I've been trying to reach you, Doctor. Several urgent messages. Mrs. Harry Maxon, SC-four-nine-two—"

"Dr. Bishop is not available. He will not be," I said. "He passed away an hour ago."

I was afraid to look toward Jessie when I hurried past her to the kitchen. I found the brandy bottle, took a tumbler, poured an inch of brandy for her.

"I'll fix you a sandwich, coffee," I said.

"Why?" she answered.

"Keep up your strength; you'll need it."

"Why?" She took the brandy at a gulp.

"Isn't there a friend, a neighbor, I can call? Someone to stay with you?"

"You're here, aren't you?"

The phone rang again. It was Celia. Before she realized a man had answered, she shrilled, "Jessie, I've been trying all day—"

"Celia, this is Sam. It's all over. Eight o'clock this evening. . . ."

"Keep her away from me." Jessie's voice had carrying quality, always. Whether Celia heard or didn't, I'm not sure. All Celia's subdued voice said to me was, "When are the services?"

"Watch the *Times*," I said.

"I'm sorry," Celia said. "He was a nice man."

Jessie removed her coat. She poured herself a second brandy, double dose, gulped it. I went to the kitchen, found the lean end of a boiled tongue in the refrigerator, a rusty heart of lettuce, a tomato, some rye bread, not altogether stale. I stuck the bread into the toaster, filled and plugged in the percolator, set a tray with napkins, mustard, cream and sugar, two plates, two cups and saucers—I also had not eaten since early morning, several centuries ago. When I carried in the tray, Jessie was horizontal, eyes closed; she might have been asleep. The phone jangled again. She leaped up, screaming, "Take it off the hook!" I took it off to inform the chapel they would have to wait; Mrs. Bishop was presently in no condition to select a casket. I left it off the hook, returned to the kitchen to pour and bring in coffee. I lighted a cigarette, passed it from my lips to hers. She puffed once, dropped it into the saucer to lie drowning, browning, in the coffee lees. "Poor darling Mark," she whispered. It was the first time—and the last—she spoke his name to me. She relapsed into the staring numbness while I warmed her hands between mine, heard the eerie music out of nowhere, and dredged up platitudes.

"Jessie, this is the inevitable. We face death from the instant of our birth." I wasn't fooling around with Jehovah's will. The buck-passing had ended for me at Ilene's funeral.

"Jessie, the doctors tried their best. They were his friends."

344

"Jessie, you gave him a dozen happy years. That's a memory to cherish."

"Jessie, life has given you so much. Success, fame, true love. Be grateful."

"Jessie, you're a strong woman, you have guts, you had the courage to go after what you wanted. Most of us are cowards."

There was a flicker of anger in her eyes. I was ripping through the fog.

"Jessie, loving greatly is a danger always. There can't be a happy ending ever, since one must die before the other. There ought to be a bit of hate in every marriage, so there'd be a tempering of relief when one partner dies."

"How'd you get so smart so young?" she jeered. We were getting back to normal. "Pour me another brandy," Jessie said.

Around midnight, I said. "You ought to go to bed, try to sleep. Do you have some pills? . . . No, I guess you shouldn't take them; the brandy may do the trick. Lean on me, I'll help you."

The music grew louder as we approached the bedroom, something for violins by Brahms, I think. A radio had been pouring music into this room while Mark was uptown dying. And the lamps were on, the blinds drawn, the large room—the room that through an irrational sense of delicacy I had never seen—was in the disorder of the sudden heart attack, the beds unmade, both pillows head-hollowed, a black physician's bag open on the dresser, a morphine vial, a hypodermic, half a glass of water, Mark's wrist watch, wallet, change, car keys, crumpled handkerchief, on the night table between the beds, his shirt and trousers in a slipper chair, his shoes and socks neatly side by side below, a book splayed open atop the bedside radio. *The God That Failed*, one of them had been reading when the coronary struck. I clicked the radio off and closed the book. Jessie's fist stuffed her mouth. This time the plug didn't work. Her tears spurted, dripped. She trembled, head to foot, shook violently, couldn't stop shaking. I held her, thinking holding tight might stop that awesome shivering. "I'll get you a nurse," I said. "I'm going to phone a registry. Don't worry, I'll stay, too. But you ought to have a nurse who'll know how to look after you. Shock is illness, grief is illness. . . ."

"The doctor's not available." She drew away from me, to

crouch on the bed, a wounded little animal. I picked up the phone on the night table. The wire was dead. I remembered I'd left the receiver off the hook in the vestibule. I walked back to hang it up, look up the phone number of a nurses' registry, make the call, get the promise: yes, as soon as possible, we'll try our best; sorry, it will be at least an hour.

When I returned to the bedroom, she lay naked on the rumpled sheets, the deep navel, the whitened gall-bladder incision scar blatantly exposed. Shocked, I began to retreat. She gripped my wrists and pulled me down, her hands in determined frenzy, plucking at my clothes, pressing on my crotch. Then she lay motionless, expectant, not quite passive, since a quiver of urgency was in her thighs, waiting for me to quicken her, to supply the proof that she was alive. His death was in her, wrestling, warring with her unquenchable vitality, and I was here and she was bound, instinctively, to use me, the always faithful friend, for reassurance that she had not also died.

Afterwards, she stayed a moment, eyes and lips tightly shut, then slowly opened the gray eyes, awakening, bewildered, as if for the first time aware of me. "Lecher," she gasped. "Pervert," she screamed. "Lousy, filthy, fucking bastard!"

Her obscenities were ringing in my ears when I slammed the apartment door and ran toward Fourth Avenue. I must have kept running, for somewhere in the Thirties a policeman gripped my arm, asked me where in hell the fire was. He demanded identification and frisked me before he let me go, advising me a man my age ought to take it easy, I could get a heart attack.

In the morning, I found Jessie's keys in my pocket, stuck them in an envelope, called a messenger, paid him to take them to the Gramercy Park address, phoned Baumberg, told him I was sick, I'd not be in today, yes, it was serious, no, it wasn't serious, okay, my nerves were shot, be human, let me have one day of rest.

All day I lay alone in darkness, not touching food or drink, while accumulated names, of people dead and living, floated through my head, names recalling only bitterness, frustration and defeat, nowhere fragments of comforting harmony. One thing I knew for sure when that weird cacophany was ended was that

Sam the shnook was dead. Whatever years remained for me would be spent in selfishness.

Next day, I told Baumberg I'd had card-calling up to here; if he couldn't place me in the Geneva office, I'd cut out from the J.A.C., find a newspaper job somewhere. Since I'd mentioned the Geneva post before, it was not a bolt from the blue. He made a few phone calls, dispatched a couple of cables, suggested I ought to see a doctor, get a checkup, I looked like the wrath of God, and to my amazement added that he envied me; he wished to hell he could get away from this madhouse.

I renewed my passport, phoned my parents (another visit would have cracked me up), signed a will, providing for the old folks in case something happened so that I couldn't mail them monthly checks, and packed my few possessions. Mark Bishop was buried without my attendance. Who further consoled his widow I neither knew nor cared.

The boys at the office wanted to give me a farewell luncheon. I said no. Leo Wullstein and his wife drove me to the airport. "Why he's running to the Alps, I do not know," Leo said. "All of a sudden, and he does not even own a pair of skis. Anyway, Jewish people should not ski. They have enough troubles without breaking legs for sport."

Leo's wife kissed me and wished me luck in Switzerland.

Fourteen

Yuli had a small flat, spanking neat and sunny. She cooked a chicken paprikosch while I went out to purchase wine. That evening she transferred the gold and lapis ring from her right hand to her left. Two weeks later a rabbi said the words that made us man and wife. She was all I'd hoped and dreamed she'd be.

Middle-aged marriage is outwardly sedate, inwardly profound. You admire the Alps but you don't attempt to climb, since you're encumbered with the baggage of your years and you have a frame of reference; you know who you are. The past is always with you though it's seldom talked about.

Yuli had her job; I had mine. We had a home together where we loved, made love, exchanged today's experiences, made tomorrow's plans, had a colleague, a friend, in for dinner, or sat together reading or listening, via radio, to symphony and opera. Companionship and joy we had, plus gratitude for shelter in each other from the world's assorted cruelties.

For holidays we flew to London, Paris, Amsterdam, Copenhagen, the cities whose spirit was uncompromised. We strolled in their parks, enjoyed their orchestras and museums. In London I had a binge of playgoing. We prowled their shops, viewing, rarely purchasing, though we did acquire a few things for our flat: a Daumier lithograph in Paris, an antique pewter teapot in London, a porcelain swan in Copenhagen. I would have enjoyed a shopping spree, I had owned so little, but Yuli balked, and not from stinginess. Possessions, she explained in the warm darkness of our bed, were a trap that led to death. Fine furniture, a grand piano, a library of rare books, crystal, china, silver, Persian rugs had tied the Rakosch family to a flat in Budapest, from which they might have fled in time to save themselves. Our meals, however, were abundant. Food is survival, understand. I thought she cooked too much, but she hoarded the uneaten crumbs. Once, absent-mindedly, I scraped a crust into the garbage can. My wife became hysterical.

She dressed with taste, her blouses, dresses, usually with long sleeves, so that strangers might not be disconcerted by the numerals on her arm. To me, they had become invisible. To her, also, I believed. Occasionally, we entertained V.I.P.s from the States. They agreed I had a stunning wife. "What a figure!" "What eyes!" "What perfect, unblemished skin!"

Baumberg wrote the Sloans were coming through Geneva, en route to Israel to dedicate the Memorial House; lay down the red carpet. I cabled I'd be out of town, long-standing plans I couldn't change; I'd instruct my secretary to do the bowing from the waist. Under no circumstances did I propose to spend one hour entertaining either of the daughters of the late Herman Weiss.

And for five years, all I knew about Jessie was what I read in the Paris edition of the *Herald-Tribune*, a sentence that Jessica White, from whom Broadway had not heard in years, was at work on a play and, after an interval, a news story about her appearance before a Congressional committee to answer questions about the presumed left-wing affiliations of two Hollywood acquaintances, the woman I had known as Paula, the man I'd called Ernie. Jessie had been adamant as well as sassy. "I have never insulted a guest in my house, nor would I dream of doing it, by demanding either a Wassermann or a certificate of political purity." They quizzed her about *The Arsonists;* it followed the Party line, didn't it? anti-Fascist prematurely. "That play was about my own father," she told them. "He was a victim of Nazi sympathizers in an American small town. He carried the scars to his grave. Obviously, the play was anti-Nazi, anti-Fascist; I was anti-Nazi, anti-Fascist. Were you pro?" She hadn't taken the Fifth since it was not herself the investigators were after, though they threatened a citation for contempt. "Jail me, do, I'd welcome it. Free room and board. Research opportunities." Though her spunk was creditable, I wasn't yet prepared to give her G for Good in anything.

Late in the 1950s, Leo Wullstein, grown overweight and hoary in the Committee's service, stopped off in Geneva with his wife, en route to Israel. Baumberg had consented to let Leo see the country he'd been publicizing since 1948. Leo, believing his own propaganda about starving European Jews, brought me a ten-pound salami and a pound of Nova Scotia salmon. Also, taking for granted I still wished to know about the folk I knew, he brought me an earful. While his wife was off with Yuli, wrist-watch shopping, Leo sat in my office and we chewed the fat.

My old friend, Jessica White, he informed me gratuitously, had been having it rough. Her play had closed before it reached New York, the Philadelphia critics had panned hell out of it, a feeble echo of the 1930s, lifeless, pointless, no insights; evidently she'd written herself out with *The Arsonists*. Hence, as a playwright, she was strictly just a listing in the Public Library card catalogue, and from that you don't go laughing to the bank. But recently someone had called him—no, he was positive it was not Joe Sloan—Sloan had told everybody his wife had had a nervous breakdown when her sister was called before the House Committee and, anyway, Joe wasn't as active with our organization as he used to be. He'd done his part, he'd told a television interviewer, when the going was rough; not many men in his position were willing to stick out their necks in fighting Hitler and he had, in his small way, helped to rescue Jews and bring them to America; it was a real satisfaction to see how they made good. As for Israel, he'd been in on the ground floor so to speak and at personal sacrifice. But now, though he'd continue to contribute and to wish them well with all his heart, he had to admit art had become his passion. Paintings, he agreed with the interviewer, were an investor's best friend. "You name it, he has got it," Leo told me. "That country house of his is a museum, walls, drawers, closets packed with paintings." Baumberg was sucking around, hoping to get the collection willed to a museum in Israel. The Sloans, if I remembered, had lost their only child. So who remained to inherit? Baumberg, if he could help it, wasn't going to let the pictures, or the millions they might bring, slip away to a Goy university or a disease foundation. But who was it called up about Jessica?

"Uh huh, now it comes to me. Marcia. Marcia Mitlin, one of the office secretaries. You ought to remember her, mattress on her back, maybe you laid her yourself. Not so young any more, has to pay her way, if you know what I mean. Seems Marcia had a boy friend she was sleeping with and buying the groceries, a half-ass artist that has his studio on the top floor of that walkup where Jessica lives. The place is rent-controlled, I understand, a bargain for the tenants, a shlock for the landlord. Seems there was a peculiar accident and this little old lady. . . ."

My hackles rose. "Little old lady! She's younger than I am."

"And you are no spring chicken," Leo consoled me, "and please do not interrupt, because this is the craziest accident anybody ever heard about. It seems this little old lady lives on the second floor. It seems the landlord is a stingy bastard, never enough steam; Marcia's boy friend got used to painting in his G.I. longjohns. It seems she was freezing down there on the second floor, so she went in the kitchen, lighted all the gas stove burners, the oven, the four on top, turned them on full blast, closed the door, sat there trying to thaw out."

"She minded cold," I recalled. "That was one thing she complained about."

"You get old, blood thins, I don't need to tell you," Leo said. "Well, anyhoo, it seems the concentrated heat melted the lead seal on the automatic sprinkler on the kitchen ceiling, just like it's supposed to in a fire. And Niagara Falls began to gush. A flood. Her apartment and went through to the one downstairs. And she ran through the building, ringing doorbells, hollering, somebody quick come help, she was being drowned. It seems this artist—he's a lousy painter, by the by; Marcia tried to stick some of our lay leaders with his crap—he was the only other person in the building at the time; everybody goes to business, see, and no super on the premises; in cheap walkups landlords aren't so particular about the maintenance. He was working in his studio; he heard the hollering in the hall. He'd seen this dame, half-crocked, a couple of times, trying to negotiate the stairs. So he ran down to see what was what, help her out. Her place was a shambles, old newspapers, old magazines, junk, all kinds, swimming in that living room. A rat's nest she had there. Sure, he recognized her. Her picture, and not flattering I can tell you, was in the *Daily News* and *Mirror* during those hearings. Anyway, it didn't take a genius; two names were on the door: Jessica White and Mark Bishop. The doctor,

351

remember? She married him, didn't she? What became of him?"

"He died," I said.

My voice must have been peculiar. Leo shot a speculative glance at me. "Well, when Marcia came that night to cook the boy friend's supper, he told her about this dame on the second floor. And Marcia remembered how glamorous, how sensational she'd been at the Sloan dinner. And so they got the idea to go down and ask her if she'd come up to the studio and have spaghetti and meatballs. And by how she ate, they figured she'd been living on gin and Uneeda biscuits, from which you don't get fat. And from a few remarks she dropped—she was quite a conversationalist, Marcia said, a vocabulary like a longshoreman, fantastic, coming from a little old lady—"

"Knock off the little-old-lady bit, will you? She's at least five years younger than—"

"Who you kidding? Take a good look at yourself in a mirror. Time marches on. . . . Well, anyhoo, this one had a hacking cough; Marcia wondered if she'd caught cold in that flood. But smoking like a chimney. Marcia's butts."

"S.O.P.," I muttered and received another puzzled look. "Standard Operating Procedure," I explained.

"I lead a sheltered life," Leo said. "Never heard the expression; s.o.b. I know real good. Anyhoo, Marcia and the boy friend got a pretty good idea she was hard up for the rent. How are the mighty fallen, and where are those who licked her ass when she was riding high? The wheel turns: one day you're up, next day you're down, and who gives a good goddam? She was comical about it; keep your chin up, kid, there's humor in the situation, like old friends giving you the business, even ones you risked jail to protect. Don't call us, we'll call you, which is not only a brushoff but an insult to an intelligent person's intelligence. 'Dahling, how wonderful to hear from you! Where have you been hiding? Let me have your number, dahling. I'm just dashing out, meeting my agent at Sardi's. I'll ring you back tonight. We'll make a date.' The phone never rang. That night. No night. Sit by yourself. Cold. Hungry. Chew your fingernails."

"You break my heart," I said.

"What's got into you?" he wanted to know. "You used to have

352

human feelings. Sympathy, empathy. Damn good thing some of us still have, the world would go even more to pot. Thank God there's still people like Marcia. A good kid, even if she has round heels. (I tell my wife sex promiscuousness has nothing to do with good character, morality.) Marcia asked her had she ever given thought to going out to get a job. She asked who would be so crazy as to hire her. Marcia thought there might be a spot at the J.A.C., Speaker's Bureau or publicity. Even typing or filing, if she would consider it; anything is better than nothing. 'That's very funny, goddam funny,' she said, but she said she was in no position to say no to something that produced X dollars a week. When she was young, full of big ideas about herself, she said, she'd spit in the eye of anyone who suggested such a thing."

I had a remark ready. I kept it to myself.

"You get older, you are used to eating," Leo went on. "And a drink to pep you up. But you've lost your sex appeal. 'Where, oh, where, to find the man who'll plunk down ten bucks to lay a white-haired hag?' That's what she said; the woman doesn't kid herself about herself. Well, Marcia talked to me, I went in to talk to Baumberg, and let me tell you there is a good egg inside that icebox, you know that as well as me, though I got a mean ulcer till I learned. Baumberg put her on, Speaker's Bureau. She didn't last. Hangovers and plane schedules do not mix. And the communities didn't go for her. Would you believe it, the younger generation, the new lay leaders that are coming up, never even heard there was a Broadway show called *Arsonists*. Fascism-smashism, from aleph they don't know. How she's eating now, I can't tell you."

"I could not care less," I said. 'Taint so, McGee, I care and too damn much. A kick in the groin is painful when it is inflicted, the blow to your manhood lasts.

Leo tsked. "You've been away too long. We shouldn't grow indifferent to old friends; they're disappearing fast. And when *are* you coming home?"

"Haven't given it a thought," I said.

"You like it here? You like the Swiss?"

"Heaven help me, no. Cuckoo clocks are ridiculous and I have no use for neutrals: love me, love my enemy." Yes, I hate neutrals, I thought. Yes, I have learned to hate and I am not ashamed to hate. The dimensions of an adult should be big enough to include hate. Only the immature make nice-nice-nice to everyone and everything. I am past that stage.

"Nu?" Leo was asknig. "Why do you stay?"

"Personal reasons. Here one monkey's off my back."

"I don't read you," Leo said.

"Don't try. In a way, I'm like the Swiss. One toches on two sides of the fence. Yes, I want it; no, I don't. Leo, I despise the whole fund-raising shmear, the big-giver oligarchy our Committee has become, the gimmicks, the card-calling, status-seeking. Yet I hug it to my breast, a shelter, a refuge, a reason for existence. And I tell myself it's service to my people. So I settle for Geneva, half-way house." I was getting in deep, producing words for feelings that had just begun to surface. "This is one hell of a way to make a living, but how else—"

"So I have a joke for you," Leo interrupted. "About Chaim's grocery."

I gave a little start; a random shot had hit a nerve. Leo didn't notice. When he undertook to tell a joke, he concentrated totally. "It seems Chaim opened this little grocery, and a couple of weeks after he opened the store, his friend, Yankel, dropped in. 'Nu, Chaim, how's by you commencing the business?' 'Terrible, believe me, in the two weeks the store is open, I didn't sell for five cents black pepper.' 'So wait, be patient, Chaim. The neighborhood didn't find out yet the store is here. It will improve, you can take my word.' 'From your mouth to God's ears,' Chaim said. So a couple months later, Yankel is in the neighborhood again. He stops in. 'So tell me already, Chaim, the good news. Business is okay, no?' 'By the landlord, by the electric company, by the jobbers. By me is only bills. In a week, two dollars I don't see,' 'That's terrible, Chaim. Shabbos I'll go in shul, ask God he should take an interest in Chaim the grocer, help him out a little.' Well, after a year, Yankel turns up again. 'Hello, Chaim, I see you're still here in the place. So the business got better?' 'By the A. and P., not by me. Nothing, positivel nothing. A whole day I don't see one living person in mine store.' 'So, Chaim, why do you stay? Close up the store.' 'Dope! Idiot! How will I make a living?' "

He laughed at his joke. I didn't. Under my breath, I said, "Herman Weiss."

"Who's that?" Leo asked.

"The reason why," I said.

It was a letter from my father that eventually brought me—us—to the States. "Mama don't feel good," Papa had written. "She has pains in the stomach. The doctor said—we got it a new doctor, Sammy, Doctor Rabin, from New York he comes, a brother-in-law from Hymie Rogoff, he married Pearl, the sister, a nice girl, only not young, a long time a old maid, the father has to promise to fix up the office, costs a fortune the machinery for tests. He gave Mama tests, took pictures from the insides, says maybe is a little gallstones, she should take it easy on the chicken shmaltz, the fry cutlets, sour cream. She says what does he know, the young shneck, with the machines? She is sure and positive it is a little cancer. Lena Slomowitz, she should rest in peace, had such kind pains in the stomach. Half a doctor your mama always was. So she is sure and positive she is dying from the cancer and she is crying out the eyes. 'So long as mine eyes can see, my Semmele I want to see. And his wife. What good is to have a daughter-in-law if you don't see?' Takke, why are you hiding her? She is a humpback, maybe, or, God forbid, a schwartze? Mama says if the ticket you couldn't afford, she has a knippel. For what is she saving? The graves is paid. If you need, she'll send."

I could afford and I was proud of my wife. I would have been as proud had her spine been crooked and her skin dark as the Queen of Sheba's. To my surprise, Yuli was excited about going, being claimed by my parents. Hers had died while she was young; her husband's had been taken in the Holocaust. At every turn in our relationship, her reactions to much I took for granted brought me up sharply. Not having personally experienced it, I could not grasp the poignancy of total loss of kin, whole families, unto third and fourth cousins. "I wondered, I did not wish to ask for fear the situation might be delicate," Yuli said, "why you did not sooner wish to bring me to your parents."

"Because they're nudnicks, like their son," I said.

She laughed and went shopping for presents. Over my objections that their wants were modest she bought a pair of wrist watches and stuffed an airlines bag with chocolates. In the excitement of preparing she dropped years. When you go to parents you grow younger; you become a child.

We flew into Idlewild, left our heavier luggage in Manhattan, then headed for Grady's Mills. A feeder airline and an interstate bus connected the town in the mountains with New York, the rail tracks pulled up, sold to a latter-day Max Slomowitz. Yuli had opted for the bus; she wanted to see the countryside. It was June, green and blossoming, pretty when you got beyond the Jersey used-car lots.

The houses on the Hill looked ramshackle. A brick building stood where Herman's Grocery had been. Its downstairs was a saloon. Brown-skinned kids were playing in the road.

And all that ailed Mama, beyond aging, I discovered right away, was a bad case of curiosity about my wife. Her welcome was effusive. "My, my! So good-looking, so refine!" though I scented disappointment. When Yuli, at Papa's insistence, stepped out into the yard to admire his radishes and carrots, Mama managed to sink a barb. "A nice face, a shlank figure, only maybe, Semmy, she is old for you? She already had her changes? You couldn't have a kaddish?"

I said we hadn't thought of having children. I believed I, too, was overage to start raising youngsters. Moreover, Yuli had had two daughters, lost them, murdered by the Nazis. Mama's eyes bulged. "My, my! Who can have against children!" I added that Yuli's first husband had been murdered by the Nazis too. "What you tell me!" Mama cried. "That woman had to live through this! She must be from eisen!" Then an avaricious gleam came into her eyes. "The husband left a nice insurance, no?"

I asked whether she had noticed the numerals on Yuli's arm. "Sure, I notice, sure, I see. I thought it was some kind cockamamie, like when you was a small kid, you bought for a penny in the candy store a color picture and with spit you made come out a picture on the hand. I made you wash off quick; the paint could be poison. I saw on her arm. I think maybe cockamamies is stylish now for ladies in Europe."

"Mama, those are Nazi numbers, the way they branded Jews. Like animals. Yuli was in a camp, a concentration camp."

I saw stark bewilderment. Dear Mama, you read; Papa reads. You must have read what was done to six million other Jews. Didn't it register with you that these were people like ourselves? If not, why not? Were you so insulated in your kitchen that the massive horror never did get through to you?

The fault was mine. Mama sent me out into the world; I never brought it back to her. Come to visit, break bread in the kitchen—how are you Mama, Papa?—listen to their kvetches, quarrels, the petty details of their days, say, yes, I'm feeling fine, my bowels are regular, I get my eight hours' sleep. Then off again, impatient to wet-nurse the sorrows of the world.

Yuli came in from the garden, looking frazzled. Twenty minutes of Papa in the yard had been more wearying than eight hours of transatlantic flying, four hours on a bus. Yuli brought the presents out. Papa beamed, Mama frowned. "You spend too much. What for do I need? Where do I go? For who should I show off?" She let Yuli slip the watch over her wrist and stole a look at Yuli's arm while the bracelet was being adjusted. She reddened and grew flustered when Yuli kissed her withered cheek.

"Come, kinder, eat. Gets cold the supper."

The dining table was loaded. "A whole week Mama is baking, cooking," Papa told us proudly. "Like a slave, standing by the stove."

While we struggled through the meats (three kinds), the stuffed cabbage, sweet and sour, the tsimmis, the potato kugel, Mama kept up a nervous chatter. "So kinderlach, I am werry happy my son is got married and him and his wife can affoder to come on a airplane and bring expensive presents. I thank you werry much, Semmy and Yulia. A fine dodder-in-law I got, brings me a gold watch present. From my husband, he should live and be well, I never got; he could not affoder, he was a poor working man. By us was enough we have a clean house and what to eat. A pleasure to have a dodder-in-law. My whole life I was praying I should not die to leave my Semmy like a stone. So many fine chances he had, he passed by. He is werry smart, my Semmy, in Columbus College he went two years and by General Pershing, the big general—maybe you heard from him, Yulia?—he was working in the office. All the girls was after my Semmy. Mine old neighbor, Mrs. Ida

Weiss, she should rest in peace, an educated woman, werry smart —her husband, Mister Herman Weiss, a fine man, a zaddik, he should rest in peace, he lived here in mine house till he passed away—Ida Weiss she had a dodder, Celia, a girl with golden hands, an educated girl, she went like mine Semmy two years in the college, she could cook, sew hand embroidery, a balaboosta, first class, Ida and me, we talked many times, maybe our children will get merried. Only my Semmy is too slow. Daytime he is writing in the newspaper. Nighttime his head is in the liberry books. So she merries another feller from this town. He is a little prost, didn't gradjiated even from the high school. Only he was lucky, his papa had a good business, he made a lotsa money. She lives like a queen. And Sylvia Leeds—Sadie Finkel she was up here on the Hill, now she is Mrs. Walter Leeds in Brookfield Heights—she brought special a cousin to meet Semmy, a fine, educated girl with twenty thousand dollars. The best chances he missed. . . ."

Yuli's patient, sweet expression didn't change. Having endured much, my wife could bear even this. Besides, I'd warned her Mama was a nudnick.

Papa plunked down a bottle of rye. "Sammy needs a shnapps."

"Buttinsky!" Mama snapped.

"From simcha, Mama is a little nervous," Papa apologized.

"Who is nervous? Maybe Semmy, maybe Yulia. Like pigeons they eat from my supper I worked like a slave in the kitchen. Maybe they bring the big bag of chocolates they should have what to eat. For me, I don't need chocolates candy; the doctor don't let me eat rich stuff. Semmy, you will go see Dr. Rabin, have a shmoos with him, he will tell you I got cancer. Me he wouldn't tell. Only the bobbemeise, gallstones. . . ."

Sylvia Leeds rescued us. She rang up. Papa dashed to the hall to grab the phone; Mama shushed to listen. "Yeh, Sylvia, he is here. . . . Yeh, with the kalah. . . . Nu, what can I tell you? . . . Sure, Mama is happy. She is a mama, no? How is the little boychick? . . . A nice Bris? . . . Yeh, I understand. In a hospital is not allowed a big party. And how is the gramma? . . . Heh, heh, little Sadie Finkel a bobbe. . . . Yeh, I call Semmy to the phone."

Sylvia began with "Mazel Tov," as was proper, and went on to invite us to join her and Walter at the Fieldbrook Country Club at eight or thereabouts. "You'll want to see the gang, won't you? That's where they'll be. Thursday, maid's night out, we all have dinner at the club. Everybody's dying to meet your wife. We were taking bets you'd never let go mama's apron strings." She hung on while I consulted Yuli. My wife said yes, she'd like to go; she wanted to see as much of American life as possible. I decided Sylvia's gibble-gabble would be an improvement over Mama's revelations about my romantic past.

"A honor to be in company with a high-class crowd," Mama assured Yuli. "Yulia has a silk dress? She wouldn't shame you for the crowd?"

Yuli changed in my old bedroom into a cocktail dress she'd bought in Paris. It was deep-blue, like her eyes. I was sure she'd knock 'em dead. It had a matching long-sleeved little jacket that she wore on cool evenings. "You won't need that tonight," I said. "I might," she said. I phoned for a taxi to drive us to the Field-brook Country Club.

There was a full moon, straight overhead, pouring down its silvery opulence, drenching a sprawling white frame building (and its Greek-columned portico), blanching the golf course, dimming the spotlights along a driveway that was lined with cars, most of them convertibles. The club house windows were open. We heard music, saw slender girls in pastel summer dresses floating by in the arms of young men. "How beautiful!" Yuli cried. "Like a ballet!" I smelled the sweetness of syringa while we climbed the steps.

A white-coated Negro greeted us. "Mrs. Leeds's guests. Yes-suh!"

A tubby woman, hair mottled white and blonde, swooped from ambush in a doorway. She was tightly girdled under brown chiffon and hung with jangling golden ornaments. Her arms enveloped me, a bracelet scratched my ear. "It's Sylvia! You don't remember me!" I inhaled Arpege and Listerine.

"You haven't changed," I said.

"Liar and I love you for it." She landed a kiss near my mouth. "And this is the bride! Well!" She extended a hand. Yuli took it, smiling. Sylvia looked Yuli up and down. Yuli looked Sylvia up and down. "I like your dress," Sylvia said.

"Thank you," Yuli said. My wife had won the first round.

359

"Don't you want to check the jacket? It's quite warm inside."

"Thank you, I will keep it," Yuli said.

Sylvia linked her arm through mine. "Sammy, we were sure you'd never go and do it. Confirmed bachelor, mama's boy. I guess it took an older woman. . . ."

I rescued my arm. Yuli took out her handkerchief and wiped Sylvia's lipstick from my face. "Follow me," Sylvia said. "Walter's in the cocktail lounge."

The man who swerved from the bar was bald as an egg, tanned from chin to nape, corpulent and wearing bifocals.

"Don't you recognize Walter?" Sylvia cried.

"The dome's familiar," I said.

"*You* haven't changed," Walter said. "Same chinless wonder. So this is Mrs. Rosenbaum. What you saw in her I see, what she saw in you. . . ."

"These boys always were like that, tearing each another apart," Sylvia explained to my wife. "You'd never dream they were the very dearest friends, boon companions, I used to say."

"Get set at a table, Syl," my boon companion said. "I'll bring the drinks. What'll you folks have?"

Yuli said she'd like a cognac. I said Scotch and soda, light on the soda, please. Sylvia led us down a room, dim-lit, paneled in knotty pine, hung with hunting prints and sparsely occupied by people whom I didn't recognize. She kept glancing left and right, wig-wagging with her big black eyes, as if inviting one and all to notice: visitors in town. She led us to a table in the exact center of the room, pre-empted the chair between my wife and me. "Isn't this charming? Just like an English pub, everybody says. Sam, could you in your wildest dreams imagine this in Grady's Mills?"

Rhetorical question, not requiring answer, even had she given me the chance. She fluffed out her skirts, jingled her bracelets, and opened her big mouth. "Well, we owe you a Mazel Tov; you owe us one. Our Carol Frances had a boy, three weeks ago. Her third, the first two were girls, Sandra and Roni. And already Carol's inside dancing. Hear the music? That's a combo. Saturdays we have a full orchestra." She bent to Yuli, amplifying. "For we older folks. Fox trots, waltzes." She bent to me. "You remember Harold, our little boy? Little boy! You should see him, six foot two! He says I made him eat spinach, that's what did it. Heavens, all the vegetables my mama served was a sour pickle and a radish. Who knew from vitamins? Ceil Sloan and I used to talk, wouldn't it be lovely if my Harold and her Ilene—the way it turned out, Ilene so moody, it's just as well, isn't it? Harold lives in Philadelphia, he married a lovely girl, her father is in real estate, well fixed. He took Harold in the business. We wanted them to stay here, come in with Walter in the mill. She wouldn't give up Philadelphia. I can't see why. What does Philadelphia have we don't? They haven't any children yet. They're talking adoption. I say don't hurry, keep trying, adopt you always can, adoption is a cat in the bag, a pig in the poke, isn't it?"

The question apparently was intended for my wife. Yuli smiled noncommittally.

Walter arrived with our drinks and his and Sylvia's; they were having bourbon on the rocks. I said "L'chaim," he said "Skoal," Sylvia said, "Walter, honey, show our guests the pictures."

Walter opened a wallet that was fat with tinted photographs. Sylvia dealt them like bridge cards. "That's Sandra. She's the oldest. Seven. She looks like Walter's family, everybody says; I can't see it. She's very clever, already in the second grade. And goes to dancing school. That's her in the leotard, tummy sticking out. I just love to pat it. This is Roni. Roni's four. It doesn't do her justice; the sun was in her eyes. And she had a little cold that day. Carol sends her to pre-school. I think four's too early, don't you, Mrs. Rosenbaum?"

"My name is Julia," my wife said, looking tolerant and willing to be friendly.

"You speak good English, Mrs. Rosenbaum," Walter said.

"Thank you," Yuli said.

"Carol says Roni needs group adjustment, whatever that may be. Sibling rivalry, she says. An older sister, now a baby brother, that's hard on the middle one. Carol's very up on psychology. Now, here is Adam. The first man. Isn't he gorgeous! See his eyes, wide open, only nine days old. Too bad you haven't any children, Mrs. Rosenbaum, you really can't appreciate. . . ."

Yuli's fingers tightened on the stem of the brandy glass. She looked less tolerant.

361

Walter scooped the snapshots up and parked them in his wallet. "You will have to meet our precious dividends," Sylvia said. "I guarantee they'll be the high spot of your trip."

"When'd you get in town?" Walter asked.

"This afternoon," I said.

"And how do you like the United States, Mrs. Rosenbaum?" Sylvia inquired.

"I have seen it very little, just the airport, the skyline in New York, and through the windows of the bus."

"You came straight here! Well, Grady's Mills should feel honored, shouldn't it, Walter?"

"When you see Grady's Mills, you've seen America." Walter sounded disagreeable. I wondered whether overweight or thirty years with Sylvia had curdled him.

"Oh, honey, you're not being fair. You know this town is exceptional in so many ways, aside from its beautiful mountain setting. We used to own a cottage in the mountains, on the lake, sold it, didn't need it once we built this club. Right here, we have everything your heart desires, golf and tennis, a pool, a first-class chef. All our finest affairs are held here, Sam." She pinched my arm. "Remember when we used to think the Hiram Grady was the cat's meow? I was the first Jewish girl to have my wedding there. Now, our children get married in Temple and the reception's over here. Wait till you see our ballroom, Mrs. Rosenbaum!"

Yuli's smile was growing thin. It was a tossup between Mama and Sylvia for nudnick-of-the-month.

"We have two temples, Mrs. Rosenbaum. Conservative. Reform. We belong to Reform. That's the older temple. Walter was the founder and the president. They gave him a lovely testimonial banquet when he retired; you'll see the scroll over at our house. Walter felt he simply had to give up that responsibility. He's been carrying all the Jewish problems ever since I married him. Haven't you, honey?"

Walter growled "Urggh," meaning yes, no, or shut up.

"The Conservative Temple is more modern, the architecture, I mean. They spent a fortune on bronze doors alone. Some people say it gives the Jews prestige. I like ours better, it's more homey, more traditional, if you know what I mean. You be the judge.

362

I'll be glad to drive you around tomorrow, show you both, Mrs. Rosenbaum."

"Thank you," Yuli said.

Walter said, "Why don't you take off your jacket, Mrs. Rosenbaum. It's hot as hell in here." He mopped his dome with a cocktail napkin.

"Wait till next year, honey. We're air-conditioning the club. The boys didn't feel they could afford it up to now. I hope I'm not boring you, Mrs. Rosenbaum. Sam, I know, is interested. But, after all, you are a foreigner." She leaned in Yuli's direction. "Your outfit, Mrs. Rosenbaum. Is it an import?"

"I live in Europe," Yuli said. "Naturally, I buy my dresses there."

Sylvia faked a sigh. "I wish I could. The best I can do is the Bon Ton's Glamour Room. This is from there." She thrust her chiffon-covered bosom out. "They carry imports, too. Nina Katz goes abroad to buy. You'll meet her later; she and her husband are playing bridge." She touched Yuli's jacket sleeve. "Silk, isn't it? You can hardly tell what's real, what's synthetic, nowadays. Walter's mill used to use only wool; they've switched to synthetics. People don't want the real thing any more, do they?"

Walter inched his chair in my direction. "Been over to Israel lately?" His tone was small-talk-making. Nevertheless, it was the first genuine question he or Sylvia had addressed to me. I said I hadn't been, I was a forty-eighter, that could hold me for a while, but I went on to say that, however, through my job I was in touch with all that was going on, if there was anything he wished to hear about, before I realized he was staring vacantly across the room at one of the hunting prints. And it was here as it had been in New York when I returned in 1948: those I'd left behind were replete with themselves. I stopped talking. Half asleep, Walter sipped his melted ice. My shoulder blade was whacked. "Hey, schlemiel! I'd know you any place." I slued around and saw a big-nosed Indian. "You don't recognize me? Hymie, Hymie Rogoff."

Walter came alive. "How'd you come out, Hymie?"

"Hymie's been playing gin rummy with my brother, Myron," Sylvia explained to my wife. "Do you play cards, Mrs. Rosenbaum?"

"Myron is a momser," Hymie said. "He schneidered me."

Yuli looked bewildered.

"Hy, get yourself a chair. Let Walter get you a drink. Hymie's rye and soda, Walter. And Walter, honey, please freshen mine. Hymie, this is Sam's new wife."

Hymie leered across the table. "A shaine madel. You don't look Jewish, Mrs. Rosenbaum."

"Who does these days?" Sylvia tittered.

Yuli said nothing. Her unsmiling silence began to worry me.

"Hymie, I've been telling Mrs. Rosenbaum all about Grady's Mills. I've told her about this club and our temples. I was just about to tell her about our new Jewish Center. That's your baby. Suppose you. . . ." Her bracelets clanked as she waved, yielding to Rogoff momentarily.

Hymie scraped a chair to the table. "We have an Olympic swimming pool and two health clubs," he began.

I coughed to alert Yuli. Her face had become blank; possibly she was no longer listening.

"Let me tell her about the adult education program." Sylvia was bound she'd give no one else a chance. "In a way that program is my baby. Our rabbi sort of pushed me into it, you see. He mentioned he wanted to organize Bible Study and Jewish history classes at Temple for the young marrieds. A Sunday School we had, a very modern one, but he said—he's a very learned, very sincere type—he felt Jewishness had to be wall-to-wall, in the home as well as Temple, and how could parents pass on our traditions to their children if they themselves were ignorant? I said, 'Rabbi, you are absolutely right but let's not kid ourselves; the young crowd won't pay sitters so they can go to Bible class. And you have to consider what their interests are, furnishing the home, raising babies, stretching the budget so they can entertain.' He got a little huffy; he's a bit of a sourpuss. So Hymie and I put our heads together and we worked up a wonderful adult education program for the Center. We've had a man who's done some of the finest apartments in New York, discussing interior decoration—even I got some ideas from him. And a woman who's been on television twice, discussing marriage adjustment. And, then, I had the greatest luck. I happened to meet a woman who just moved into town, a very chic, attractive personality who'd done some little-theater work. And she agreed to do book reviews for us—a Books and Bagels Brunch, isn't that cute?—once a month. Books of Jewish content, you understand. And she does them so wonderfully you don't have to bother reading. . . . Oh, thank you, Walter, honey, my throat was getting dry. I guess I'm talking too much."

"Mahneshtana," Walter muttered.

"How about freshening my drink?" It gave me a small satisfaction to send Walter on the errand; he'd owed me a drink since Pesach, 1949.

Sylvia swigged her bourbon and picked up where the table service had interrupted her. "She did *Exodus* for us last week. I wish you could have heard her, Mrs. Rosenbaum, you'd have been thrilled. You've read it, haven't you?"

Yuli emerged from far away to shake her head no. I'd read it. If Sylvia had asked me, I'd have had to tell her I rated it with Jessie Weiss's *Arsonists*. We might have gotten into acrimony.

"*You haven't?* Oh, but you *must*. Irwin has it in the Bon Ton's book department, I'll ask him to give you a discount. It'll make you realize how those poor people suffered, all they went through, how wonderful they were."

Hymie chuckled. "That's what the man said." He pushed away his glass to make room for gestures. "Last Sunday I was out soliciting for the drive. I knock on a door, a new family in the Brookfield Heights Extension. The guy comes out in his Bermudas. I introduce myself, he introduces himself, he's pleased to meet a neighbor, we shmoos about his business and his kids and my kids. Then I tell him about the drive: I'm a volunteer out soliciting to help the people in Israel. He says that's a remarkable co-incidence, he's just been reading all about them in a book called *Exodus* and that book has made him proud he is a Jew, those brave, wonderful people. And I think, Great, five hundred at least from him. So I say, 'Okay, you know and you are proud. So out of your pride, how much are you going to pledge for those brave, wonderful people?' And he looks me straight in the eye and what do you think he said? 'Why, nothing,' he said. 'If we give them money, if we make them comfortable, they'll be just like us and then they won't be so wonderful.' And how do you like that!"

"The louse!" Sylvia cried. "We *are* wonderful. Just see how much we do for *them!*"

My spine was whacked again. I veered to gray hair, a grizzled Adam's apple, a seamed coppery face, bending over me. "Hey! It's Irwin Katz. Isie. You remember Nina? Nettie?" I tried to rise to greet the lady; it wasn't possible. We shook hands awkwardly over my shoulder.

"Pull up chairs," Sylvia said. "Give Walter your orders. This is our party."

"Scotch on the rocks for Nina, Coke for me." The table was getting crowded; a table leg was making inroads in my thigh. "The fair lady, I presume, is Mrs. Rosenbaum," Isie said.

Yuli managed a small smile. She looked drawn and weary.

"Enjoying your visit, Mrs. Rosenbaum?" Isie asked. "You play golf? The club has a good course."

Isie's wife wedged her chair in beside Yuli. Nettie Rogoff had been one of the nondescript girls in the old crowd. In maturity, she had become a carbon copy of all the stylish, brittle, successful businesswomen I'd met in my fund-raising travels. I watched her fingering the fabric of Yuli's jacket with professional interest before I tilted my chair to ask Isie, "How's your dad?"

"Not good. He retired. To Tucson, Arizona. Asthma."

I said too bad. I'd liked Sol, one of the best of his generation, hard-working, unassuming and with heart. Isie resembled him somewhat, being slight and deferential, except that in Isie there was a nebbish quality. Bossy wife, I decided. Like Walter's.

"Dad pledges here, of course," Isie told me. "Why should he help meet the Tucson quota?"

Sylvia, the nonstop yenta, said, "Walter wishes the young crowd would hurry up and make money. He's sick and tired of drive-drive-drive. He thinks it's time the younger generation took over its responsibilities."

"My rabbi—you have to meet him, Sam, while you're here in town, you'd like him, he's a very dynamic feller" (Hymie, I sensed, was pushing for the top position, Walter being tired of drive-drive-drive)—"he told those young shnecks when we were campaigning for our Temple building fund, You can afford wall-to-wall carpets, expensive draperies, custom-made furniture. How come you can't spare a few dollars to provide a house for God?"

"Hymie, that is so foolish!" Sylvia rattled her bracelets. "Carpets and draperies are *necessities.*"

I didn't dare to look at Yuli. It was just as well that Mrs. Katz was bending her ear about the Paris dress. "I haven't seen this model in any of the big houses. I go over to buy imports for our store, could you tell me where. . . ."

Walter brought the drinks. "Here's to Mr. and Mrs. R." Isie raised his Coke. "Health, wealth and happiness." He set down his glass. "Sam, I have a big surprise for you. My kid's in your old profession. My Barbara."

"Barbara Ann Kates, society editor of the *News-Record*," Sylvia chirped. "And how do you like them apples?"

Barbara Ann's mother looked up to mutter, "Better she should meet a nice Jewish boy, get married. . . . Mrs. Rosenbaum, would you mind taking off that jacket? I'd love to see the neckline. . . ."

Yuli acted as if she hadn't heard, which she might not have, since all at once the room had filled with high-pitched laughter. Sylvia clapped hands. "The younger generation! Now you'll see *something!*"

They advanced in a herd, tanned by tennis court and poolside, sleek and shining, strapping, supple.

"Carol!" Sylvia cried. "Rest already. Give Carol a chair."

I started to rise. Sylvia pushed me down. "Behave like a guest."

A young man, fair-haired, lively looking, said, "Hold everything, we'll pull another table over."

Hymie yanked my sleeve. "My Bobby. A Harvard graduate. Member of the bar."

Over the noise, Sylvia introduced Carol Frances and the dentist with the Groucho Marx mustache who was Carol's husband. "Hi!" Carol said. She reached across the table for the dregs of her mother's bourbon.

"Do you dance, Mrs. Rosenbaum?" the dentist asked. "You should. Exercise. You don't want to get fat, do you?"

The Harvard man straddled a chair behind me. "Dad says you people live in Switzerland. Wish I'd known. My wife and I—she's that redhead dragging chairs, I believe in women working—we did a little skiing there, we'd have looked you up. Went on to

Garmish, then flew over to Berlin. Say, have you been there lately? The way the Germans have built up their country. Remarkable. The recovery, the spirit, the hospitality. There's nothing they won't do to make you comfortable. . . ."

I saw Yuli's back stiffen. She covered her mouth with a handkerchief.

"Aren't you the kid who was almost brained by an anti-Semite's rock?" I asked.

Snapping fingers, he dismissed it. "Oh, that! Ancient history."

Yuli let her handkerchief down. "You may need to relive it," she said so softly I don't believe young Rogoff heard.

Hymie punched my spine. "Some kid, heh? Full of piss and vinegar. We're grooming him for co-chairman of the drive next year. He'll bring the young crowd in."

"Isn't some one going to introduce *me?*" a dark-haired girl squealed over skulls and shoulders. Her make-up was heavy, her dangling earrings might have been called exotic. "Come here, my darling, my sweetheart." Isie rose. "Folks, this is my Barbara."

My Barbara bowed, hand on diaphragm. "I'm working for your old employer, Mr. Rosenbaum. Flitting between here and Hilldale, covering social doings."

"Some changes in town," Sylvia crowed. "Bet you can't believe your ears, Sam."

"Take my chair, Barbara darling," Isie said. "You and Sam have notes to compare."

I couldn't imagine what notes I might trade with her except maybe to discuss what I'd read somewhere about the peril of eye infection from too much mascara. To be saying something, I asked, "How's Barry Neale?"

Her mouth corners drooped. "Paralyzed, poor thing. He's in a nursing home. His son, Barry Junior, has the city desk."

"I'm sure his father trained him well."

"Very well indeed." She extricated a jade holder from her handbag, forced a cigarette into it. I tipped my lighter to the cigarette. "Thank you, a courtesy, I can tell you, I do not get from my peers." Her head tilted, flirtatiously. "Do you know, you might have been my boss. Daddy told me all about it. How my grandfather, that sweet, sentimental fuddy-duddy, tried to get Mr.

Neale's job for you. But all of a sudden, you were off and gone from Grady's Mills." She brandished the cigarette and holder, whoosh, that was how Sam scooted off. "Mr. Rosenbaum, I am curious; why did you forsake us?"

I looked at Yuli. She was sitting rigidly upright, pale, with lips compressed. Her eyes were glittering with an anger I had never seen in them before. It occurred to me she had listened to too much; it was her turn to talk. And so I told My Barbara, "Ask my wife."

Yuli drew her jacket off. She pushed away the liquor glasses and thrust her arm into the circle of light beneath the table lamp. The numerals on her flesh were stark and terrible.

I heard gasps, nervous coughs, chair squeaks, scuffing shoes. Sylvia panted, "Oh, my God!" And then I heard Carol Frances saying, with loud self-confidence, "You should remove that thing. Pearl Rogoff's husband, he's a doctor here in town, he could recommend you to a plastic surgeon. While you're here you might consider. . . ."

"I have considered," Yuli answered, in a firm, quiet way. "The numbers would be gone; the scar would remain. And in any case, I do not wish to forget. It should be remembered." Bunching her jacket with her handbag, she turned an ashen face in my direction. "Please, Sam, I should like to leave."

There were no goodbyes; not another word was said.

Walter and Sylvia walked us out. "Where is the ladies' room?" Yuli asked. Sylvia pointed to the powder room. She didn't offer to escort.

"I'll phone for a cab for you," Walter said.

In the seconds when we were alone, Sylvia leaned to my ear. "Sam, did you have to go all out? Did you have to marry someone from a concentration camp?"

Walter joined us, saying the cab would be there in five minutes, asking how long did we plan to stay in town. I said I thought we'd probably leave tomorrow; my wife wanted to see New York.

"Think it over, hang around a couple of days. We could get up a little luncheon, big givers, introduce your wife, they'd see the—"

"Forget it," I said so sharply that he winced.

"I just thought it might be a gimmick," he stammered, "to help us get increases."

He saw us to the door. "Sam, what's doing with the Weiss girls?" he remembered to ask.

"I'm a stranger there as well," I said.

In the darkness of the taxi, I held Yuli tightly and she clung to me. "Mir darfen zach tulenin," I whispered. Though she knew no Yiddish, I believe she understood.

*   *   *

Mama was waiting for us on the stoop. "Nu?" she asked Yuli. "Did you think to find in a small place such a high-class, intelligent crowd?"

When Yuli didn't answer, Mama turned on me. "What'sa matter, Semmy, you came so early back? You didn't enjoy? So come in, tell me, I'll fix you a glass lemonade."

I said we'd rather not, my wife was very tired. Mama flashed an anxious glance at her. "So I go now, put clean sheets on the bed. Papa said give the young couple the big bed, he will sleep downstairs on the couch, there already he is snoring. I could use the small bed from your room where Mr. Weiss. . . ."

Her fluster helped me out. I said I knew she'd be disappointed, I didn't want to tell her sooner, but we'd been planning to leave in the morning anyway; I had appointments in New York, and since the early bus left from in front of the Hotel Grady, the best thing for us to do was take a room there for the night.

"You just come, you already going," Mama wailed, but I caught a note of respect. Important people, only important people, fly on planes to visit but depart quickly because they have important appointments. She'd seen Yuli, the high-class people had seen Yuli, her gossiping rights had been secured. "I wake Papa up to say goodbye," she said.

Papa, awakened, yawned, noted the hour on his new watch, said bravely, "You see, Mama, I told you it's not needed change the sheets."

Mama cried a little, as was seemly, yet I felt she was relieved, though this might be our final parting. It had been too much for her to welcome into her home a daughter-in-law who bore the

370

stigmata. "When you come again?" she twittered, not expecting me to name the day. Years ago, I had become a transient in her life, a stranger who bewildered her and troubled her.

The taxi rolled up. We embraced. Mama said to both of us, "Sleep good in the hotel."

I said, "Stay well, both of you. I'll write."

Papa said, "Please to meet you," to Yuli.

Yuli said—I think she said—"Thank you for Sammy."

A loud-speaker, radio or television, was blaring dance music in the saloon where Herman's Grocery used to be.

As the taxi moved away I looked through the rear window. I saw two old people standing at the curb, waving. The descending summer moon glinted on the crystals of watches out of Switzerland. The specks of light dwindled, diminished and were gone.

I didn't speak to Yuli in the cab, I was too ashamed. She didn't try to speak to me but sat taut, holding a handkerchief against her mouth. After we'd checked into the room, she said, "I am going to be sick." I heard her retching in the bathroom while I sat on a twin bed's edge, smoking butt after butt, knowing the visit had been catastrophic, hoping Yuli had not been hurt too much.

She emerged chalk-white.

"Shall I call a doctor? What can I do for you?"

"Nothing. Let us go to bed."

"Do you want to talk?"

"Not tonight. I cannot. Sleep."

"I cannot sleep."

We lay wakeful in our separate beds while the courthouse clock struck the hours to daybreak. At seven we dressed.

"You look like a ghost," I told her.

"I am," Yuli said.

I made her drink black coffee in the hotel coffee shop. We boarded the bus. Yuli watched the landscape. I tried to read a morning paper. After a while, keeping my head averted, too ashamed to look at her, I began to apologize for the ordeal I had put her through. My mother, I explained, was a simple woman; I hadn't realized she had progressed so little, knew so little of what had happened in the world; I was sure she hadn't grasped where I had been, what I had been doing all these years. Her kitchen

371

was like an island, within the island that was Grady's Mills. For my erstwhile friends, I wouldn't venture to apologize. They were inexcusable.

Yuli laid her strong hands over mine. "Sam, we live on an island, too, you and I. The island of our common knowledge and experience. We met on that island. We remain on it, forever separate from those who never knew the horror of the thing, only read about it in some book. To them, it is fiction, fantasy." She was talking easily and earnestly, as if it was she who needed to explain and, in her way, apologize to me. "Then comes a woman in a pretty dress who looks like any woman, smiles like any woman. How can they guess a ghost is at the table in the club? Don't shake your head, my dear, I am a ghost. I have lived in hell; I bear unholy memories. I have no right to be alive. Dear, think, if tomorrow I came back to Budapest and met people I once knew, would they welcome me? Surely, no, unless they, too, had known Auschwitz. They would be afraid of me."

I put my hand across her mouth. She lifted it off.

"I must talk, dear, I must explain to you. The world is cut in two. Two islands, *we* and *they*. And we cannot live together comfortably. Because, you see, in us, there is anger, in them, there is guilt." She paused. "I am not sorry I went to that place. It was painful for us both. But now I understand why it was permitted to happen to us." She managed a small smile. "We Europeans also are with guilt. We had those islands like your Grady's Mills. We had those ghettos of simple, otherworldly Jews, like your mother and father. The home, the synagogue, the small business that earned the daily bread was all the world they knew. And that is why so many died. They could not grasp the monstrous thing that threatened them, and no one made it clear. A Pharaoh, a Haman, these they knew. Those names had been repeated, drilled, over many centuries. But where was the name of Hitler written in the only book they read? And the other islands, like your country club"—she caught herself—"*that* country club"—exonerating me—"we had them, too. Not the same form, the same point of view. The comfortable people, the sophisticated people, the assimilated people, the self-satisfied people, who told themselves they could escape from Jewish history. Like the young man at the club who enjoyed Germany." Her shoulders drew together, shuddering. "For him I am afraid. For all who never learned and who forgive too easily." She looked away for a while, through the scummed bus window at the green fields, the new housing developments, the factories and crowded parking lots, turned back to me and put her cheek against mine. "Sam, in Vienna, many years ago, I asked why you came to us. I was too full of anger to believe what was so plain to see. You came because you were a man with heart." Then she asked, "Is all America like Grady's Mills?"

"Not New York," I said. "New York will be different."

It was. New York gave us the best it has to give, which is privacy.

We took a room at the Plaza; I wanted Yuli to enjoy a bit of luxury. We rested in excellent beds, took our meals in the room, phoned no one, read the *Times*, watched TV, and next morning, restored, we became tourists. We did the Empire State, the cruise around Manhattan Island, the Statue of Liberty, the Hayden Planetarium, the museums, all of which I, having been a resident, never had had time to see. We walked Broadway, gawking at the lights, and, paying scalpers' prices, got tickets for a hit musical. Yuli enjoyed every minute. I enjoyed it doubly seeing it through her sparkling eyes.

You can't escape forever, particularly when pocket money's running low. I needed to pick up a salary check. I took Yuli with me to the office. The cast of characters hadn't greatly changed since my time of servitude; each job had become a vested interest, a comfortable rut. Through Leo, the staff knew about Yuli, and survivors were no novelty. One time or another, one way or another, they had seen the brand. To them, Yuli was a well-stacked blonde and I a guy who didn't rate his luck. Baumberg, hair and mustache white, asked us into his sanctum, produced a bottle of Chivas Regal, said it was immoral to drink before lunch but he wished us long life and happiness. It was unexpected and extremely pleasant.

Leo took us to lunch at Lindy's. While we waited for cheesecake and coffee, he said with studied casualness, "By the by, Jessica White is on her way out." He lowered his voice. "Cancer. She's in her old apartment. Marcia sees her now and then." He didn't add, though his very telling it implied, "I think you also should."

"Who is Jessica White?" Yuli wanted to know.

"One of my oldest friends. The second daughter of Herman and Ida Weiss," I said. And the second pivot of my destiny, I thought. Through Celia, I had abandoned Grady's Mills, wandered off to Europe, met Yuli on a winter night. Because of Jessie, I had fled to Switzerland and claimed Yuli for my wife. The beginning and the end of the saga of my drift. And it was time, and overdue, for me to act like a mensch.

Fifteen

The taxi trip from the Plaza was the longest journey I have ever made. To be cheery with the dying is difficult enough. To return to a scene of humiliation takes gritted teeth and a tranquilizing pill. Yuli volunteered to come with me. I was glad but I was loath. Even at death's door, Jessie was unpredictable.

Yuli thought we should take flowers. She looked so troubled by my hesitation that, rather than explain, I said, "Choose what you think's appropriate." I waited on the sidewalk while she went into the florist's. She came out with a small cornucopia of white tissue paper. At any rate, she hadn't been extravagant.

My chest constricted when I pressed the downstairs bell. We had to wait, unduly long, it seemed to me, until the buzzer released the lock. The stairs were as steep as Matterhorn. My heart was pounding when I rang the apartment bell. The nurse who opened the door looked disapproving. "Mrs. Bishop is having no visitors."

I told her who I was, who Yuli was, how intimate a friend I'd been, from how far away we'd come. I thought if her patient was able to see anyone, she might wish to see me. She asked us to wait in the living room.

The room had been stripped, bookshelves emptied, fireplace swept, pictures taken down; weird patches on the grimy walls indicated where they'd hung. There was a peaked white oblong for the antique clock whose pendulum Jessie had stopped the night Mark Bishop died. Roped cartons filled the sagging sofas. Someone was impatient for this tenant to vacate.

Yuli admired the ornate ceiling and the fireplace mantel. There was nothing else to admire, except the vista of the fenced green park beyond the open, dusty casements. "Ah, but you should have known this room before it died," I said.

"You have been happy here?"

"More or less, now and then," I said.

The nurse returned. "Mrs. Bishop insists on seeing you. She regrets she doesn't look her best." She forced a thin-lipped smile. "Pub crawling last night. A terrible hangover." Bless Jessie, she was doing what she could to make this bearable.

The room at the end of the long hall had been converted to a sickroom, bleak and shadowy and smelling of the sickness, blinds drawn, an air conditioner humming in one window, a gooseneck metal lamp on a utility stand, bright bulb averted from the high single bed, a straight-backed chair beside the bed, a cot in a far corner where a nurse might nap, not a plant, a flower, a book, a picture, not even the little radio. I cannot tell you where or why the furnishings and ornaments were gone, whether sold to pay the rent or disintegrated in the flood Leo had told me about, nor can I tell you why my friend had chosen to await her death in this room of poignant memories rather than in the impersonal, antiseptic surroundings of a hospital, though I suspect that her imagination saw the gossamer of vanished happiness clinging to these walls.

She lay child-size, white-haired and waxen, a candle snuffed out, beneath a taut-drawn sheet, one hand exposed, all bones, the closed eyelids transparent. She might have been already dead. "Jessie." I spoke loudly to penetrate a morphine fog. "It's Sam. I've brought my wife."

The lids rose slowly, the gray eyes shifted just a little—eyes still remarkable. Yuli bent to touch the skeletal hand. I saw a tiny smile on the pale mouth, caught a hoarse whisper. "Lucky. Her." Yuli ripped the tissue paper. She laid a flower alongside Jessie's hand. My wife had bought a single dark red rose. Slowly, Jessie's head moved till the petals brushed her cheek. "Nicest thing . . . anybody's done . . . in years."

The nurse rustled behind us, warning that talking sapped her patient's waning strength. As if to refute, deny, that perverse creature on the bed summoned strength to croak, "Out, woman. Leave us be." Her lips parted in a grisly imitation of a grin.

"Mrs. Sloan provides. Wouldn't lend me one thin dime to live on. Spare nothing, doctors, nurses, for Jessie to die with." She had to halt to catch her breath. "Damn butts. Yours," she wheezed. Her hand inched toward her chest. "Hard to die. Takes guts." Her eyelids fluttered down.

I spoke the desperate lie. "You won't."

Barely audible. "Wanna bet?"

"Good luck," I said, and softly added, "dear."

My love is dying here, I thought, my once and lifelong love. I ought to kiss her brow. I ought to make a farewell speech: forgive me, Jessie, for what happened in this room, I should have had control, I thought I was giving you what you wanted, needed. The shock, the strain, betrayed us both. But I stood silent, motionless, beside my wife who in her years had looked on too much death, staring at the red rose and the waxen face until the nurse came in and touched my arm, saying we'd better leave.

Jessie roused herself a final time. Faint as breath, but unmistakable, two words drifted up. "Had enough." So low, so toneless, was the murmur, I couldn't know whether the inflection was for asking or informing until I heard the whisper following, "Vote Republican." It's hard to be certain, the eyelid's movement was so slight, but I do believe that Jessie winked.

We walked around the square. I needed to rest my eyes on something fresh, alive. We dropped into a cool, dim bar; I needed a stiff drink.

"A pity to meet her at such a time," Yuli said. "Was she a beautiful woman?"

"Not at all," I said.

"Was she brilliant?" Yuli asked.

"Clever, quick. Not brilliant," I said.

"You loved her?" Yuli asked.

"I'm not sure," I said.

"Those last words she spoke, I didn't understand. Was she political?"

"Not particularly. That was a slogan off the billboards of Eisenhower's first campaign. A gag, a joke, a mocking at her death. No other woman in the world would have thought up that curtain line." Then I said, "That's why I cherished Jessie Weiss."

She wasn't satisfied. "But what was she really, Sam?"

"A fresh kid. But fascinating," I said.

Jessie died within the week. Her write-up in the *New York Times* was half a column long, including a few quotes from her testimony before the House Committee. There also was a single-column cut of a photograph taken when she was riding high, the gamine with the impish grin and the lustrous eyes.

I told my wife I preferred to go to the services alone; she'd done as much as she could for Jessie, more, in fact, than she might have been expected to. I mentioned the red rose. "I never had the nerve to bring her one," I said. "She'd have laughed at me."

The *Times* obituary page is a prime advertising medium. Everybody reads it so as not to miss the passing of a friend, foe or celebrity, to be notified of when and where to grieve or gloat or gawk at notables. Whoever had arranged Jessie's funeral had underrated the pulling power of the press. A small chapel had been booked. By the time I arrived, there was standing room only. Jessie would have been pleased. I strained for familiar faces, the Westport crowd, Celia, Joe, Fred Bishop, Horace Simon. From where I stood, I saw no one I recognized.

The air conditioning was on. The chapel had a clammy chill. Up front stood a closed mahogany casket with a sheaf of purple asters on its lid. Purple's for old ladies, isn't it? Wasn't she? Menorahs at each side. Five, not seven-branched. Almighty God, are they even cheating You on candle power? Ah, but they have the little glass of wax, the memorial light. That makes her a proper Jew, doesn't it?

A few bars of organ music were piped into the chapel, to put us in the mood, thirty seconds of reverential silence, before a rabbi mounted a pulpit. He was young, athletic-looking, with slicked dark hair, rimless eyeglasses and a magisterial black robe. No tallith, no yarmulka, not even a white beard. Terrible casting, costuming. Jessie would have been furious. He spread a paper on the lectern, cleared his throat. "We have gathered here to bid farewell"—his voice was oil and honey—"to a great Jewess, a distinguished and devoted and dedicated daughter of the Jewish people, to a noble and great-hearted bearer of the Jewish heritage—"

That set me off. Garbage! Strictly garbage! All funerals should have fools like this—you could make a business out of renting them—fools to roil, to irritate, with fatuous untruths; otherwise these partings would be unbearable. Yet I'll bet my bottom dollar Jessie would have accepted this as a fair description of herself, even though, sprawled on her couch, she had airily dismissed her Jewishness.

What, tell me what, was Jewish about Jessie? Birth. Born to Ida who bragged of kinship with the Vilna Gaon, to Herman who twice every day and all day Saturday communed with the God of Israel. And how much of what they were did they pass on to her? A smattering of Yiddish, spice and salt for her vocabulary. Not another bit. Now, had she, in her adult years, set foot in a synagogue? Had she grieved for the Jewish tragedy? Had she rejoiced in the nationhood? Contrariwise, she'd sluffed it off, with a liberal's platitudes.

Ah, but you forget *The Arsonists*. Quite so. Better so. Coattail riding, exploitation of a bit of current history. Universal theme? Universal sympathies? This I doubt very much. Make a fast buck out of Jewish tsoris. Free-load on the legend of a people tortured but triumphant, indestructible. *You* went along for the ride, my Jessica.

Situation normal. Here I was at Jessie's funeral, quarreling with her. Now, I could. Boxed and sealed, she couldn't answer back and make a nothing out of me.

Distinguished and devoted and dedicated daughter of the Jewish people. Which Jewish people? Two. Ida Weiss and Herman. They gave her the genes. You cannot sluff genes off. Through fifty centuries they've been handed down, bearing strength with which to confound and outlive our enemies. Yet my wife, without the genes, had borne the awesome burden of the Jewish tragedy.

Distinguished daughter. The idiot in the robe never knew the dame. A lively babe and gallant. Her sole distinction lay in courage, the courage to be human, to be selfish, not pretending or prevaricating. Wanting love and giving it. Yes, after her fashion, even to Sam Rosenbaum. *Dedicated*. To what? To life. Isn't that sufficient? "Hard to die," she'd said, not "hard to live." And she'd greeted death with a wisecrack and a wink. That, Rabbi, is distinction.

Devoted daughter. She ran from her father's house, didn't she? Fled from the ghetto on the Hill, from the shul, the God, the peoplehood of Israel. But I fled also, didn't I? I took my tallith off the rack. I do not pray, I do not keep the Laws. Yet I've remained a Jew, haven't I? By profession? No, by instinct, choice and will. By what in me that says I am a Jew. For suffering or for triumph, I belong. You can't get rid of me. What really drove you into limbo, Jessie Weiss?

"It is a source of profound regret to me that I was not fortunate to be personally acquainted with the departed. I have, however, enjoyed the friendship of her devoted sister, Mrs. Celia Sloan, who with her husband, Joseph Sloan, have been bulwarks of our congregation. Their benefactions have provided inspiration to all who labor for the oppressed of our people and the preservation of the ideals of Judaism. These worthy daughters of a saintly father, Herman Weiss, each in her separate way, has enhanced a noble heritage. . . ."

Herman Weiss had two daughters. So far, true. He left a noble heritage. True. But to whom? To Celia, social climber, on the ladder of Hadassah and the Temple Sisterhood. "Thou shalt honor thy father and thy mother." With a plaque in Jerusalem and a maid's room on Park Avenue. To Jessie. She was the one with the brains. She insisted that she loved her father. Yet she couldn't stand her father's house. Why not? Because it wasn't his. It belonged to Ida, to the right-hand woman of the right-hand man of God. Ida. Jessie. Ida-Jessie. Jessie wasn't Herman's daughter, she was Ida's. She was exactly like Ida. Aggressive, know-it-all. Like Ida, too, fearing and adoring Herman.

Now, I have it. And it's a classic case for Dr. Freud. "I love my old man." But in a way not even you, smart Jessie Weiss, could admit to yourself. Ida was your rival, not Celia. And that was why you ran, not knowing why you did. But Celia was the one deprived, for Herman, in his way, admired, loved and wanted you. And Herman fled from Celia, who had only cash to give. He ran to you. I can see him on that porch in Westport, praying, and with such a contented look. Why didn't you keep him at your side? Inconvenience? Afraid you'd have to keep his rules? Or afraid of yourself? So you married Mark. A doctor. Father image. "Stay off that stuff, it's loaded." Quote, unquote, Rosenbaum.

How'd you get so smart so young? Not young. Only with the years does wisdom come. Too little and too late. And what difference does the knowing make?

I'll be damned, they've hired a chazan, too. He's chanting "El Mole Rachamim" for Jessie Weiss. Let her squirm inside that box; she's hooked, we've made her one of us again. Yet I'll bet she's pleased. Gathered up, gathered in, given the full treatment, reclaimed, redeemed. Just in case there is another world, she has one foot in.

I was soaked in sweat. I'd never quarreled so intensely with Jessie or myself.

Being near the door, I was one of the first out. In the lobby, where certain of the mourners were milling, waiting for the cemetery limousines, I noticed a veiled, slender, aristocratic woman with blue-gray hair and a stylish costume of the blackest black. She recognized me before I knew who she was. "Why, Samuel! I didn't know you were in New York. You didn't phone!" She threw back her veil. Never had I seen Celia look so well. "Wasn't that a lovely service? Such a tribute to our family! I kept thinking dear Papa would have been so proud of both his little girls. And I suppose you saw the write-up in the *Times*." She opened her handbag and took a clipping out. Her pink-tipped finger moved slowly down the strip of newsprint to its final line. "She is survived by her sister, Mrs. Celia Sloan of Greenwich, Connecticut."

"I'm saving it for my scrapbook. Samuel, you must come out and see my book. I have all the stories, all the items, yes, even those you wrote about our parties back in Grady's Mills. I've saved everything, my wedding write-up, the reviews of Jessie's plays, all pasted up, the story of the lives of the two Weiss girls. It's quite a story, isn't it? All we accomplished in the world, two little girls from the Hill."

Someone touched her elbow to lead her off. "Call me!" she commanded before she dropped her veil and snapped her handbag shut. I watched her stepping gracefully into a black Cadillac. Joe

I didn't see at all. Whether Jessie lived or died was, apparently, no skin off his nose.

Yes, Celia had come out on top. All Jessie had achieved in school, career and love would turn to ashes and yellowing newsprint. But Celia, ineffectual and unloved, was alive, and survival is what counts.